The Chronicles of Elantra
by
New York Times bestselling author

Michelle Sagara

CAST IN SHADOW
CAST IN COURTLIGHT
CAST IN SECRET
CAST IN FURY
CAST IN SILENCE
CAST IN CHAOS
CAST IN RUIN
CAST IN PERIL
CAST IN SORROW
CAST IN FLAME
CAST IN HONOR

And
"Cast in Moonlight"
found in
HARVEST MOON
an anthology with Mercedes Lackey and Cameron Haley

MICHELLE SAGARA

CAST IN FLIGHT

MIRA®

MIRA®

Recycling programs
for this product may
not exist in your area.

ISBN-13: 978-0-7783-1970-2

Cast in Flight

Printed in U.S.A.

First printing: November 2016
10 9 8 7 6 5 4 3 2 1

To the denizens of the War Room, without whom writing would be a much, much more isolated—and isolating—activity.

CAST IN FLIGHT

CHAPTER

1

Morning was not Kaylin's friend.

Helen's Avatar stood in front of the open bedroom door, her expression as pinched as it ever got. Sentient buildings were in most ways a living marvel, but they definitely had their drawbacks.

"I'm not hungry," Kaylin told Helen as she dragged herself out of bed. "I need sleep more than I need food." She could see only one of her shoes. "Is there *anything* you can do about Nightshade and Annarion? I never thought I'd say this, but Dragons roaring at each other at the top of their lungs was more peaceful."

"I'm sorry, dear. I've done what I can to isolate the noise in the house, but Annarion's voice travels through most of my barriers."

"It's not just Annarion. I can hear every word Nightshade is saying."

"That would be because you bear his mark, dear. He can't control you through it while he's under my roof, but the connection is still active."

Kaylin reached up to touch her cheek. Nightshade's mark looked like a tattoo of a small flower, and she'd had it for long enough she was barely aware of it, except in moments like these.

Helen looked down at her hands, which weren't really hands; Helen was a building. Her Avatar appeared to be human. It wasn't. Clearing her throat was also an affectation, and she did that, as well. "Regardless, breakfast is an important meal. You have work today. You need food." Helen's Avatar folded her arms. As far as Helen was concerned, this was a fight worth having, and as it happened, Helen won all these fights.

The winged lizard flapping around Kaylin's face in obvious annoyance made it hard to pull clothing over her head. Kaylin swatted halfheartedly at her familiar.

"That's what buttons are for, dear. If you unbuttoned—and folded—your clothing, getting dressed would be less chaotic."

Small and squawky settled on Kaylin's left shoulder with a little more claw than usual. "I used to daydream about having an older brother," she said as she spied the missing shoe under her bed. "If nothing else, this has cured me of that."

"I have a question."

Of course she did. "What?"

"Annarion is upset at his older brother."

"Clearly."

"He is not saying anything that you have not said, or thought, yourself. He dislikes the governance of the fief of Nightshade."

Dislike was *far* too mild a word.

"You hate it."

Kaylin exhaled. "I grew up there. Barely. I survived. But a lot of people—a lot of kids—didn't. When I see what Tiamaris has done with his own fief, it's very clear to me that life in Nightshade didn't have to be like that. Nightshade's the fieflord. He could have chosen to do what Tiamaris is doing. The fief is his. So yes, I agree with every single word Annarion's been saying. Or shouting. Or screaming."

"But you feel pain on Nightshade's behalf."

Kaylin grimaced. "Nightshade spent *centuries* trying to rescue Annarion. I think he might have killed his father because his father chose to sacrifice Annarion to the green. The only person on earth Nightshade cares about that way is his younger brother. In some ways, his choices revolved around Annarion. He's outcaste because of those choices.

"Getting Annarion back should have been a good thing. And I think it is. But…Annarion's so disappointed, so hurt, it's caused almost nothing but pain." And that pain? It was killing Kaylin's ability to sleep. No one who had half a heart could sleep through the ruckus. "To both of them."

"And you don't want Lord Nightshade to be in pain."

"I think he *deserves* it, to be honest. But…not from Annarion."

"People have always been complicated."

"Even the immortal ones?"

"Especially the immortal ones."

No one with any intelligence wanted to get between two brothers while they were fighting. No one with any sense of self-preservation got between two Barrani when they were fighting. Kaylin hoped fervently that Lord Nightshade had returned to his own castle this morning.

Kaylin chewed on her thoughts while her familiar chewed on her hair as she walked down the foyer stairs toward the dining room. The dining room's fancy doors were open, there was food on the table, and she was—as usual—late. Annarion was seated beside Mandoran. If Nightshade was Annarion's brother by blood and lineage, Mandoran was a sibling by shared experience. Seated across from Mandoran was Bellusdeo, her golden hair pulled back in a braid that was looped together on the back of her head. Given the slightly orange tinge to her eyes, it was clear she and Mandoran had already started their daily bickering.

Having a Dragon living in the same house as a Barrani who'd lost his family to the Draco-Barrani wars was never exactly peaceful.

Before she could enter the dining room, Annarion looked up from his untouched plate. "I want to know how you first met my brother."

No, mornings were definitely not her friend.

"I don't think," Helen said to Annarion as Kaylin made her way—silently—to her chair, "that Kaylin wishes to discuss your brother at breakfast."

Or ever.

"I told him you'd say that," Mandoran added, half-apologetically. Half was usually as much as he could muster.

"I'm surprised he didn't listen," Bellusdeo said, picking up a fork as if it were a fascinating, rarely seen utensil. "Usually you're the one who chooses to be selectively deaf." She smiled at Mandoran. "I've come to find it quaintly charming."

Mandoran's eyes shifted to a steady, deeper blue, the universal sign of Barrani fear or anger. And he certainly wasn't afraid. "As charming as a Dragon in mortal clothing?"

"Oh, infinitely more so. I assume once you've developed better command of your manners, I will be far less entertained. But I don't expect that to happen in the next decade. Or two."

Mandoran's natural dislike of Dragons as a race left Kaylin stranded with Annarion, who was still staring at her. No one could outstare Barrani.

"Why won't you speak about my brother?" he asked. The

question was softly spoken, but his tone made it more of a command than a request for information.

She considered and discarded a number of replies as she began to eat. She wasn't hungry, and even if she had been, Annarion's question would have killed her appetite. But she'd grown up on the edge of starvation, and she could always eat.

None of her possible replies were good. The truth was, she liked Annarion. He was—for a Barrani—honest, polite, self-contained.

"I don't suppose you could ask your brother."

Mandoran took a break from his barbed "conversation" with Bellusdeo. "He's asked."

"Nightshade didn't want to talk about it?"

"No, he talked about it."

"Then what's the problem?"

"He was lying."

Annarion glared at Mandoran, looking as if he wanted to argue. He turned back to Kaylin instead. "I want to know your side of the story." Meaning, of course, that he agreed with Mandoran's assessment.

"I've got the usual mortal memory," Kaylin replied evasively. "And I might lie, as well."

Mandoran snorted again. "Your attempts at lies are so pathetic you should probably use a different word to describe them."

Kaylin glared at Mandoran. Bellusdeo, however, said, "He has a point."

Kaylin wasn't certain how she would have answered. She was saved by the appearance of the last of her housemates. Moran—Sergeant Carafel in the office—entered the dining room. Moran was almost never late for anything, even breakfast.

Clearly, she had some reason for being late now, and it

wasn't a pleasant one. Her wings—or what remained of her wings—were stiff and as high as they could get with their protective bindings. Her eyes were blue. Aerian eyes and Barrani eyes overlapped in only one color. Moran was either angry, worried or both.

Kaylin had risen before she realized she'd left her chair, which did nothing to improve Moran's mood. Moran did not appreciate any worry that was aimed in her direction. Ever.

"As you were, Private." She sat on the stool provided for her; Aerian wings and normal chair backs didn't get along well. To Helen, she added, "The mirror connection was smooth and solid."

It certainly hadn't started out that way. Helen had a strong dislike of mirrors, or rather, of the mirror network that powered their communication. Regular silvered glass didn't bother her in the slightest. "I made a few adjustments, dear. I'm terribly sorry that the faulty connections to date have caused so much difficulty for you."

"They haven't," Moran replied, her voice gentling, her eyes darkening.

Helen's Avatar smiled. "They have."

"The people on the other end of the connection have caused—or are trying to cause—the difficulty. It has nothing at all to do with you. If the connection had been faultless and solid, it would have given them more time to make things even less pleasant. I'm grateful for the respite." Her eyes had shifted to a more neutral gray by the time she reached the end of her reassurance. She looked across the table at Bellusdeo.

"Was it the Caste Court?" Kaylin asked. Helen frowned at her but said nothing.

Moran glared Kaylin into the silence Helen would have preferred, but then relented slightly. "It was two castelords and one Hawklord. Before you ask, none of them were particularly happy. And it is *caste* business. Aerian business. Is that clear?"

"Yes, sir."

"Good." Moran then turned to Bellusdeo. "Are you accompanying us to the Halls today?"

Bellusdeo's eyes were golden. "Of course."

Moran then concentrated on breakfast. Annarion's attention had fallen on the Aerian, as had Mandoran's. Neither of the boys interacted much with her except at meals, and while Moran was polite, she wasn't highly talkative.

"Helen," Mandoran said, "what happened?"

"I don't think she wishes to discuss that, dear."

"That's why I'm asking you."

Even Annarion looked pained. "He's gotten worse since he arrived in this city. He used to be capable of actual manners," he said to the table at large.

"When they were necessary, yes. Here, no one needs them, and I hate to go through the effort when it won't be appreciated in the slightest."

Less than ten minutes later, Teela and Tain appeared in the dining room as if they'd been summoned. What was left of the breakfast conversation died as they were noticed.

"What, are we not welcome?" Teela asked as she sauntered in. She was wearing a sword. So was Tain.

"You are always welcome," Helen told her. "Any friend of—"

"Yes, yes. Thank you, Helen." Chairs appeared at the long dining table as if by magic. Well, actually, by magic. Teela turned one of the two so that its back almost touched the table's edge. She sat, folding her arms across the top rail and resting her chin on her forearms. To Moran, she said, "What kind of trouble are you expecting?"

Moran glared at Mandoran. She knew the boys could communicate with Teela the same way they communicated with each other. They knew each other's True Names. All of the children that had been taken, centuries ago, to the West March did. Kaylin thought it a bit unfair that Moran immediately blamed Mandoran.

Mandoran apparently didn't. "What?" he asked, spreading his hands. "You asked the Dragon if she was heading into the Halls today. You know it gives Kaylin's sergeant hives the minute she crosses the threshold. You've never asked before. Obviously you're concerned that something requiring brute strength—or magical competence—might happen."

Moran was silent.

"There are perfectly competent Barrani here. I'll be damned if I let you depend on a *Dragon* for heroics. And Teela has to go to the Halls anyway."

The Dragon in question said, "I'm still going. And in case it's escaped your notice, Barrani can't fly."

"Some can."

"Not naturally."

Mandoran shrugged. "If we're going to get technical, you can't *legally* fly, either. Not without Imperial permission."

The word *permission* touched off a distinct orange in Bellusdeo's eyes.

Teela glanced at Moran with some sympathy. "I hear," she said, her eyes almost green, the Barrani happy color, "that you have a lovely suite of personal rooms. I do hope they make up for the shared spaces."

Moran was silent for half a beat. "Yes," she finally said, "they do. They're very quiet and very peaceful." She surveyed the table with weary resignation. "I suppose I shouldn't have expected that the rest of the house would be the same— Kaylin lives here, after all."

★ ★ ★

Helen wouldn't tell Kaylin the content of Moran's mirror-based discussion. Normally, this wouldn't have bothered Kaylin; today, for reasons she felt were obvious, it did.

"They are not obvious to Moran, dear," Helen replied, although Kaylin hadn't spoken that part out loud. It didn't matter. Helen could read the thoughts of almost anyone who crossed her borders. This bothered some of the immortals; it didn't bother Kaylin. Helen was not judgmental about anything. "You understand that she is older, of a higher rank, and has handled far larger responsibilities than you currently officially have?"

"Yes."

"She did not come here to put you in danger."

"I know all that, Helen."

"She does not wish you to worry. And, Kaylin? While this *is* your home, Moran is a guest here. Her privacy and her concerns are important to me. Had she no privacy, this would not be a home to her; it would be a prison. An imposition. That is not what you wished for her when you invited her to stay."

"But Moran's worried about her physical safety!"

"Yes. But she is not in danger while she is here."

"She's not *staying* here, Helen. She's going to the Halls of Law."

"Yes. That is also her choice."

The small dragon squawked in Kaylin's ear. When she'd ignored enough of this, he started to chew on the stick that kept her hair out of her way. "Fine."

"Are you coming?" Mandoran shouted.

"Yes, yes, I'm coming." Kaylin was at the front door of the foyer before the implication of his question sank in. "Where do you think you're going?"

"Nightshade's supposed to visit today. I'm going to the Halls with the rest of you."

"Mandoran—"

"I don't have trouble masking my presence. Annarion still does. But he's going to spend another several hours shouting at his brother. Or being coldly disappointed in him. I'm not sure which one is worse. Being here while he's doing either, however, sucks." He grinned, his eyes almost green. "And it sounds like you're going to be having far more fun today than I would if I stayed here. I wouldn't miss it for the world."

Kaylin sent Teela a mute glance.

"Don't labor under the misapprehension that I can tell Mandoran what to do."

"She's already tried," Mandoran added cheerfully. "I've been using some of your favorite phrases in private."

Given what Kaylin's favorite phrases were, the private part was probably for the best. She offered Moran a very, very apologetic glance. "It's not always like this," she told the sergeant.

"No," Moran replied, her eyes a steady blue. "It's frequently worse."

Stepping outside the open gates that formed the demarcation of Helen's territory, she felt her skin begin to tingle. Kaylin had what she called an allergy to magic, at least when she was trying to be polite. It made her skin ache. The stronger the magic, the greater the ache; in the worst cases, she felt as if her skin had been sanded off the rest of her body.

She looked down at her arm; the marks that covered two-thirds of her body weren't glowing through the long sleeves she always wore. When they did, they took on a particular color—usually blue or gold, sometimes gray. It was never precisely a good sign.

Teela noticed her glance immediately, and her eyes lost their green, the Barrani happy shade.

Bellusdeo's eyes were orange. Mandoran had annoyed her enough—or had reminded her of how annoyed she should be. The Dragon glanced at Moran, who was silent, her eyes a blue that almost matched Teela's.

Mandoran's, on the other hand, remained green. "Once you get used to the smell," he said to no one in particular, "the city's not so bad." They had turned onto the more crowded streets; people multiplied, and carts, wagons and carriages began to demand room. Or at least their ill-tempered drivers did.

No one appeared to hear him.

"Kitling?" Teela said.

Kaylin nodded. "It's getting worse." And it was. Her arms now ached. Magic sensitivity wasn't exactly directional, but Kaylin looked up. The sky—absent a few patrolling Aerians—was crisp, clear and empty.

The small dragon jerked to a full sitting position. He opened his mouth on a very, very loud squawk.

Teela cursed, drawing her sword.

"Corporal?" Moran said quietly.

"We have visitors."

Kaylin reached out and grabbed Moran by the arm. In the Halls of Law, it would have been safer to cut off her own hand—and probably ultimately less painful. The marks on her arms flared; she could see the dim glow of their outlines through her sleeves. That cloth rubbing against her skin was hideously painful.

Moran didn't fight her. That's what she would remember

with wonder later. Moran let herself be drawn—instantly—into the tight circle of Kaylin's arms. Kaylin barely had time to close her eyes as the world directly in front of them exploded.

CHAPTER 2

Stone shattered as if it were brittle glass, fanning out from the spot where Moran had been standing. None of the resulting shards hit Kaylin or Moran; they were protected by a bubble of shimmering gold, courtesy of Kaylin's familiar. But Darrow Lane wasn't empty at this time of day; the shards hit pedestrians, wagons and fences. It was the pedestrians who screamed. Other voices picked up the sound as fear turned to panic and people began to flee, often into other people.

Kaylin looked up, scanning the windows of the buildings to either side of the road. Some were open. An old woman and a young child peered down at the street. While it was possible they were responsible for the magical attack, Kaylin doubted it.

"Private."

Kaylin immediately loosened her grip on Moran. She didn't completely release her. "Don't move from here," she told the sergeant. "We have no idea if that was the only attack."

Moran looked at the broken stone inches from her feet. "I need to clear the area."

"You don't need to clear the area. You're the target. If

you attempt crowd control here and they're not done yet, you'll just get people killed." It was a small miracle that no civilians had died, and Kaylin knew better than to bank on another one.

"You need the streets cleared?" Bellusdeo asked. She turned toward Kaylin. The front of her very practical clothing was smoldering. There were more holes in it than there was cloth. Bellusdeo had not been within the bubble's radius. The Dragon's eyes were very, very orange. If eyes were windows into the soul, Bellusdeo's was on fire.

Kaylin nodded.

"Good."

Bellusdeo roared.

In the middle of the crowded Darrow Lane road, this caused even more panic, which was probably why Dragons were technically forbidden to speak their mother tongue in public places. But the roar, unlike the explosion, continued for enough time that people could identify its source and get the hells away from it.

Kaylin then looked for the rest of her companions.

Mandoran was untouched; Tain wasn't in immediate sight. Teela was. In her left hand, she carried a naked, runed blade; it was glowing brightly. Something about the metal of that blade reminded Kaylin of Severn's weapon chain, which could combat magic if wielded properly.

"Mandoran," Bellusdeo said, "you've been picking up Elantran at an astonishing rate. You've perhaps heard some of their colloquial phrases?"

"Far, far too many. Why?"

"I'm wondering if you've encountered this one: 'it's better to beg forgiveness than ask permission.'"

Mandoran looked at Bellusdeo, his perfect brow rippling in minor confusion. "I don't think either of our peoples are much given to begging for anything. Why do you ask?"

Bellusdeo roared again. The first roar had pretty much cleared the street around them for a good ten yards, although it had also panicked horses. Her smile was almost feline. She didn't bother to shed her ruined clothing; there was no salvaging it. She dropped to her hands and knees and began to shed her human appearance, as well.

Kaylin found the transformation between two solid shapes disturbing; she always did. Flesh wasn't supposed to be liquid; it wasn't supposed to twist and expand, changing in both color and texture. Bellusdeo grew golden scales, the largest of which could have served as a very good shield had it been detached; she gained both height and length. And wings.

"Kitling?" Teela shouted, not bothering to glance back.

"We're good," Kaylin replied.

"Moran?"

"I'm fine. The road isn't," the sergeant added, looking down at the blistered, cracked and shattered stones at their feet. "If you let go of me, will I still be safe?"

"Depends."

"On?"

"On whether or not Teela's going to do something with that sword other than pose."

Mandoran laughed. He was the only one who did. "She's going to have to move fast," he said.

"Mandoran, don't—"

"I won't hurt your precious citizens. Well, not all of them, at any rate."

Bellusdeo spoke in a lower and fuller voice that was nevertheless distinctly her own. "I'll leave the corporals in charge of apprehending the would-be assassins. Sergeant?"

Moran looked at the golden Dragon. And she was a golden Dragon now—a very large, very imposing one with jaws that were the size of Kaylin.

"I assume you haven't ridden bareback Dragon before," Bellusdeo said to the sergeant.

"There's a first time for everything."

"A last time, too," Kaylin muttered. She was still holding on to Moran.

Bellusdeo's orange eyes paused over her worried expression—which was clearly reflected in them. "Magic?"

Kaylin nodded. "I don't think they've finished yet."

"Then get on—and *don't* let go of Moran until you're seated."

Mounting a Dragon wasn't exactly a no-handed operation, but Kaylin kept this to herself. She understood exactly why she was going to try her best to obey the command: if it weren't for Kaylin's alert and bristling familiar, Moran would be dead. Kaylin would probably be dead as well, if it had come to that.

"Has anyone ever tried to assassinate you before?" Bellusdeo asked the Aerian.

To Kaylin's surprise, Moran answered, "Yes."

"Often?"

"No. And before you continue the interrogation," she added, struggling her way into a seated position between spinal ridges along the Dragon's back, "never with magic."

"I thought the damn Caste Court wanted you *back*," Kaylin said, trying not to sound as outraged as she felt.

"Some of them do. Some, clearly, don't."

"And both factions are going to cause boatloads of trouble at the office."

"Yes. I did warn you."

Kaylin snorted. As Bellusdeo pushed off the ground and lifted her wings against the pull of gravity, Kaylin shouted, "You've got nothing on Bellusdeo!"

"Don't," the Dragon rumbled in response, "make me drop you. You might deserve it, but the sergeant doesn't."

The streets directly in front of the main entrance to the Halls of Law were crowded; they often were. Bellusdeo could have landed in them anyway—the approaching shadow of a very large Dragon was more efficient at clearing the streets than a full squad of mounted Swords. She chose instead to land in the stable yards, which had the advantage of fewer civilians. There were more horses, and the horses weren't thrilled, but that would quickly become someone else's problem.

Kaylin slid off Bellusdeo's back; Moran followed. She was a lot shakier on her legs than Kaylin, but then again, she'd never ridden on something the size of a Dragon before. Or possibly on anything else, either.

The small dragon, flopped across Kaylin's shoulder, lifted his head and squawked.

"We're good to go," Kaylin said.

Bellusdeo was reassuming her mortal shape. Given her lack of clothing, she instead donned Dragon armor, scales becoming plates that girded the whole of her body. Kaylin knew this included a helm, but Bellusdeo wasn't fond of helms. Her hair was a glorious spill down her back; it matched and softened the rest of the armor.

"The Emperor is going to kill me," Kaylin told the Dragon glumly.

"He wouldn't dare," Bellusdeo said with a quirky smile. "This one wasn't aimed at me."

Before Moran could speak, Kaylin turned to her and said, "Don't even think it."

"Think what?"

"Helen is the safest place for you to live in Elantra. You're not moving out. There's a reason the Emperor is willing to let Bellusdeo live with us."

"I hadn't even considered it," Moran replied. When she saw Kaylin's expression, she added, "It's the truth. I'm busy considering who might feel desperate enough to kill me today. And why."

"How many candidates are there?" Bellusdeo asked as they headed into the building.

"More than one." The sergeant's eyes were a steady, darkening blue. "I'd ask you not to mention this," she added, "but given our method of arrival—and escape—it's impossible to keep it secret."

"From who?" Kaylin demanded.

"Lord Grammayre." She closed her eyes. "And the rest of the Aerians."

"The rest of the Aerians are *Hawks*, Moran. There's only one way to take this."

Moran's expression made her look older and frailer. "The rest of the Aerians are people, kitling." She almost never used the Barrani-coined diminutive. "They have lives outside of the Halls of Law, and most of those lives take place in the Aerie. It's not as simple as you'd like it to be."

"No, of course not," Kaylin replied. "Nothing ever is."

The first argument occurred within the Halls, rather than outside the main doors. Kaylin didn't want to let Moran go to the infirmary on her own. Moran pointed out—correctly—that Kaylin's job depended on a *different* sergeant, and he was probably orange-eyed and long-clawed by this point.

"He needed a new desk anyway," Kaylin replied. "I don't expect mages to show up in the infirmary to kill you. But it doesn't take a mage."

"I can take care of myself."

"You could, before. But you can't even *use* one of your wings." Those wings were not just for flight; they could be used to devastating effect in close physical combat. Although Kaylin had never seen Moran fight that way, she *had* seen Clint at work. It wasn't pretty. "Let me heal it, Moran."

"No."

"Let me heal it, or I'm not going."

Bellusdeo silently lifted Kaylin off her feet. "If it's acceptable to you, Sergeant," the Dragon said, "I would like to remain in the infirmary with you. The private, of course, has other duties."

"The Emperor isn't going to like that," Moran said, but her lips were quirked in an odd smile as she met the Dragon's gaze.

"No, he isn't, is he?" Bellusdeo's eyes lost a lot of their orange then.

Moran's lost a lot of their blue.

Kaylin's gaze bounced between them while her feet dangled off the ground.

"Yes, it's acceptable to me. Please see Private Neya out."

"Don't even think it," Bellusdeo said as she deposited Kaylin on her feet. "I am tired of being treated with condescension."

"I don't—"

"I am a Dragon. You are a mortal. The sergeant is willing to have me play bodyguard in the infirmary. Push the issue, and she will have neither of us. Is that what you want?" Before Kaylin could reply, she added, "I am endeavoring not to feel insulted. Your hesitation implies that you think you would be more effective."

Insulting Dragons was the definition of career-limiting. And Bellusdeo was right. Mostly. "What if there's an Arcane bomb?"

"Fine. If it makes you feel better, you can leave your familiar here, as well."

The small dragon squawked.

Bellusdeo rolled her eyes. "Yes, I realize that. But they're not going to get an Arcane bomb through the front doors, the side doors or the back doors. And anything *else* is just going to annoy me, not kill me." She walked back into the infirmary and shut the door, loudly, in Kaylin's face. The familiar stayed where he was, but complained more.

Moran was right.

As Kaylin approached the office space designated for the Hawks and their much-hated paperwork, she could practically hear Leontine growling. Marcus was seated at what remained of his desk.

He did, however, have paperwork, and it seemed to be more or less in stable piles.

His eyes were orange, his bristling fur made his face look 50 percent larger, and his fangs were prominent. Clearly, he'd already gotten the news.

"Private!"

She scurried over to the safe side of his desk, which at this point meant the side that was farthest from his unsheathed claws.

"Where's the Dragon?"

"...In the infirmary." Marcus's eyes went from orange to near red. Bellusdeo was the only female Dragon in existence. Her survival and safety meant more than almost anything else to the Emperor; having her tangled up in magical assassination attempts—even if they weren't aimed at her—was going to cause what was politely referred to as "politics."

"Bellusdeo wasn't injured. At all. She's there to help Moran." This reassurance smoothed some of the Leontine's fur. Marcus's eyes remained orange, however.

"What happened?"

"I'm not entirely certain." This was apparently the wrong answer, but Marcus held on to patience. Barely. "Someone attempted to kill Sergeant Carafel. With magic. While we were on the way to the Halls."

"They failed."

Kaylin nodded.

"You entered the building through the stable yards."

Kaylin nodded again. When Marcus glared at her, she confessed that Bellusdeo had flown Moran to the Halls.

"Marcus, what's going on? Why is someone trying to kill Moran?"

"Did you see the assassin?"

"No, sir."

"Did you see anything?"

"No. I felt it before it hit. I would have stayed to investigate, but Teela wasn't certain they'd finished yet, and we wanted to get Moran to safety. If the assassin was actually an Aerian, we had Bellusdeo. In aerial combat against Dragons, the Aerians are kind of mortal."

"You are going to make me lose most of my fur," he growled. His eyes were probably as gold as they were going to get for the rest of the day. "Corporal Handred is waiting for you. Get to work." The mirror at his desk demanded attention. Loudly.

Kaylin almost escaped it, heading for Severn, who was leaning against the wall beside the duty roster's board. If she'd run, she might have.

"Private!"

Severn met her gaze, raising one brow in question.

She mouthed *the Hawklord*, her back turned to Marcus. There was no point in whispering; Leontine hearing would pick it all up anyway. She turned back to the sergeant.

"The Hawklord would like to see you. Now."

Severn accompanied Kaylin up the Tower stairs. While they walked, she told him about her morning. Unlike Marcus, he seemed to take the information in stride. No one had been injured, except for the would-be assassin. Teela and Tain hadn't arrived at the Halls yet, so it was possible they were still in pursuit.

"I asked Clint what was going on with the Aerians," Kaylin added. "He won't say a damn thing. But he definitely didn't want Moran to be living with me."

"Probably for your sake," Severn pointed out. "And given the start of your morning, he's not wrong to worry."

"I'm going to have to invite him for dinner one day. He'll change his mind."

Severn glanced at her and shrugged, which was his polite way of disagreeing.

"No assassin is going to get anywhere near her while she's with me."

"She doesn't spend every hour of her waking day in your house. She spends some on the way to the Halls, in the Halls, and on the way to your home."

Kaylin glared at him.

"I'm not disagreeing with your decision. I think Helen *is* the safest for Moran—and given the sergeant's general expression these days, Helen might be offering more than just safety. But Clint's right. You're in danger while you're with her. You accept that danger. Don't look at me like that—I accept it. I also acknowledge it."

"What do you think the Hawklord's going to say?"

"I don't know. Even odds he's going to tell you to ask Moran to move out."

"He can get stuffed."

"I didn't say he'd expect you to agree."

Kaylin hated politics. Hated them. She hated the stupid decisions, the game playing, the grandstanding. She hated political decisions made by people who never had to do any of the law's *actual* work. She hated the pervasive sense of superiority and smugness that underlay all of the rules.

She was going to try very, very hard not to hate the Hawklord. He wasn't the source of the bureaucratic rules that were often handed down; he was simply the mediator, and their only shield against the worst of them. She told herself that grimly as she faced his closed doors—and the door ward that girded them.

"Let me," Severn said quietly.

She shook her head. "I don't know if he knows you're here."

"He knows."

"Fine. I don't think he summoned you. He'll probably

tolerate your presence. You *are* my partner, after all." Gritting her teeth, she lifted her left hand and placed it against the ward. As usual, the magic required to open the door shot through her palm, numbing it instantly; all of her skin screeched in protest. The small dragon squawked.

She was tempted to let her familiar melt the damn door ward. She just didn't trust him to melt only that. And her meager pay wouldn't stretch to cover the cost of doors specifically prepared to carry magical wards.

The doors rolled open. The Hawklord was standing in the circle at the center of the Tower, his eyes a dismal shade of blue. Kaylin was heartily sick of blue eyes, and the working day had barely started. Unfortunately, she didn't expect to see many colors that weren't blue or orange today. Severn, being human, had eyes that didn't change, for which she was grateful.

"Private," the Hawklord said.

She executed a very precise salute. Severn, by her side, did the same, and did it better.

"Corporal." There was a question in the word; it bounced off Severn's completely shuttered expression. "Very well." The Hawklord gestured; the doors closed. Only when they were completely shut did he speak again. "Private, you've had a very eventful morning."

"Sir."

His brows rose very slightly. "Is that a 'yes, sir,' or a 'no, sir'?"

"It's a sir."

"I see. You are no doubt aware," he continued, turning away from Kaylin and toward the Tower's central mirror, "that my morning has become vastly more eventful as a result of yours?" He gestured the mirror to life, and its silver, reflective surface absorbed his reflection, scattering it to the edges of the frame. What remained was a kind of pale, ash-gray sheen. Or at least that's what Kaylin could see.

"How is Moran adjusting to life with you?"

It wasn't the question she'd been expecting, but it wasn't promising.

"Shouldn't you be asking Moran that?"

"She is not currently present. You are." His tone made clear that his tolerance for insubordination was quickly reaching an all-time low.

"She's doing well. She likes Helen."

"The...Avatar of your home?"

"Yes. Helen likes her. She has her own rooms in the house—everyone does." She hesitated; the Hawklord was expressionless. "Helen makes rooms for people who are going to be permanent guests. She made rooms suitable for an Aerian. She's got furniture suitable for an Aerian, and the ceilings are tall."

"Moran is not flying."

"No. She won't let me heal her."

"Yes. I forbade it."

Kaylin stared at him in outrage. She managed to shut her mouth before words fell out.

"I did not expect you would become involved with the sergeant. She is in the infirmary; you are a street Hawk. You have a sergeant, and if he growls incessantly about the difficulty of having you in his ranks, he is capable of containing any damage you cause." The Hawklord exhaled. "I did not expect that you would come to work with a Dragon in tow. I have been told very, very quietly that the Dragon is worth more to the Emperor than the rest of the Hawks combined—including myself."

"...By the Emperor?"

"Yes. Lord Bellusdeo has occupied much of my time. I would ask you to leave her at home, but it has *also* been made clear that the choice is to be Lord Bellusdeo's. I did not expect to add Moran dar Carafel to the list of things with which I must deal. What are you trying not to say?"

"...The Emperor is fine with Moran living with me."

The Hawklord closed his eyes briefly. "Is it too much to hope that you did not hear this directly from the Emperor himself?"

"Yes, sir."

"The Emperor may change his opinion soon. It is his pre-rogative."

Kaylin said a lot of nothing for a long time.

"I wish to know two things. First: tell me what happened this morning. Records, map." The mirror finally surrendered an image that Kaylin could see. She obligingly approached it, scanning the lines that were supposed to represent streets and buildings. She lifted a finger, and a point appeared—in bright, scarlet red—beneath it.

"Here." Kaylin then recounted the events of the morning, leaving out the general snark that passed for conversation between Bellusdeo and Mandoran. In fact, she tried to leave Mandoran out of the discussion altogether. The Hawklord wasn't buying it, and she surrendered and answered his pointed questions.

"Have you examined the site?"

"No—we came straight to the Halls. Moran was the target, and we couldn't see the assassins; we wanted to get her to safety. The Halls have some of the most impressive protections against illegal magic in the city. Only the palace has better. Are the Imperial mages at the site?"

"That would be one of the many, many difficulties this morning has caused."

"What difficulty?"

"The nature of the assassin is unknown, yes?"

Kaylin had just finished saying as much, and chose to wait.

"The Aerian Caste Court is, however, attempting to invoke the laws of exemption. They do not wish the incident to be investigated at all."

As a Hawk, Kaylin despised the laws of exemption. The laws were the laws. Crimes were crimes. But exemptions could legally be granted to the racial Caste Courts if both the criminals and the victims were all part of one happy race. She understood, as only someone born in the fiefs could, that money and power created their own special laws of exemption on *either* side of the Ablayne River—but damn it, she hated *official* sanction.

"On what grounds?" she demanded.

He was silent.

"First," she said, raising a finger, "the attack took place on *Darrow Lane*. It's one of the busier stretches of Elantran streetfront, and it is definitely *not* in the Southern Reach or the Aeries." The Hawklord nodded. "Second, we couldn't see the would-be assassin. We have no idea who, or what, he or she was. They could have been Barrani. They could have been mortal. In order for the laws of exemption to be invoked, the assassin would have to be an Aerian." She slowed down then.

"Is there a third point?"

"Third: there was visible property damage. The street was shattered. No argument can be made that the magic used didn't affect the rest of the non-Aerian population. People were probably injured by bits of flying debris. Um, can I go back to the second point now?"

"Yes."

"If the Caste Court is attempting to invoke exemption, they're pretty much declaring the assassin was Aerian. Which strongly implies that they know who the assassin is. Or was."

"Yes."

Kaylin swore. A lot. The Hawklord didn't even grimace.

"Lord Grammayre, who exactly *is* Moran?"

He exhaled and turned back to the mirror. "You said that Teela, Tain and Mandoran were in pursuit of the assassin."

Kaylin nodded. "Teela must have expected serious trouble. She brought her runed sword. If they catch the assassin, and the assassin isn't Aerian, the Caste Court can go—"

"Yes. The second matter I wished to discuss with you is Moran's rooms."

"Her rooms have nothing to do with the Halls," Kaylin replied.

The Hawklord waited.

"She's a guest. She's under Helen's protection. If Moran won't discuss the rooms with you, it's not right that I do."

"I have spoken, briefly, with Moran about her current living situation." He waved a hand across the mirror. "Records, personal."

Kaylin dared a glance at Severn; Severn was frowning. It was his concentration frown; he wasn't expecting danger. He watched the mirror's rippling surface while it stilled.

The Hawkord did the same.

The image that came into view made Kaylin wonder if the Hawklord had somehow already *seen* the inside of Moran's rooms. She understood that asking questions to which one

already knew the answer was an interrogation technique—
a way of gauging how much someone else knew, or how
much they were willing to admit to knowing. It was also a
way of determining how much truth you were likely to get.

"Do you recognize this?" the Hawklord asked.

The Records capture looked like Moran's rooms. The ones
he'd asked about. But as the mirror's view pulled back, she
realized that these weren't Moran's rooms. There was too
much sky and too much rock in the distance. Mostly rock.
She could see Aerians flying precise, tight circles to the right
and above. She thought she recognized the formation, but it
broke and regrouped.

"No," she said, to the Hawklord's question. "I don't. This
is in the Southern Reach?"

"In one of its outer recesses, yes. It is considered a
primitive—a very primitive—residence. They are not much
used in modern times."

This primitive residence, however, wasn't uninhabited.

All of Kaylin's experience of Aerians was in the Halls of
Law, or rather, with Hawks. There were no *old* Aerians in
service to the Imperial Law. This was Kaylin's first glimpse
of an elderly Aerian. Her hair was silver with age; hints of
iron added color to what otherwise would have been a uniform white. Her wings were frosted in the same way, but
they showed no other sign of age to Kaylin's admittedly unfamiliar eye. But they were rigid, held high.

"Who is she?" she heard herself ask the Hawklord.

"She was Gennet."

"Her flight?" No one used flight names in the office; the
Hawklord had gently forbidden it. But Kaylin knew—from
racial integration classes—that the Aerians were not distin-
guished by family name so much as flight name. She'd bad-

gered Clint for his, but he pointed out that he was working on roster time, which meant he wasn't obliged to answer. Was, in fact, obligated to do the opposite.

The Hawklord was silent for so long, Kaylin was certain he didn't intend to answer. "She had no flight," he finally said.

"How could she have no flight?"

"You think of flights as family," he replied. "They serve that function; they are almost analogous. But they are more—and less—than that. Gennet, at the time of this Records capture, had kin, but she had no flight."

"Did they kick her out?"

"No, Kaylin."

"Did she leave?"

"No. And it is not of the flights that I meant to speak." But he watched, and so did Kaylin, as a child came running out of what looked like the mouth of a cave. An Aerian child. She was young, perhaps six or seven, maybe older. Her hair was dark, long; it fell about her shoulders and down her back, swishing as she moved. She was looking up, and up again. Kaylin could see the shadows cross her upturned face.

"That girl," Kaylin began.

The Hawklord lifted his left wing in a snap of motion, as if he were shaking off liquid. The image shattered, scattering across a surface that quickly became simple and reflective. Kaylin faced herself and the Hawklord in the oval frame.

"That child was all that remained of Gennet's family."

"Gennet's dead," Kaylin said flatly, although she meant to ask instead of state.

"Yes."

"How do you have this in Records?"

"It is personal."

"These are official Records!"

"Yes. Yes, they are." He turned to study her. "Have you seen Moran's quarters?"

Kaylin nodded. When he failed to look away or respond, she said, "Yes." And then, taking a deeper breath, and remembering everything she owed this Aerian, she continued. "Yes. Her rooms look very, very much like this impoverished residence. I think—I think she was happy there. That *was* Moran, wasn't it?"

The Hawklord didn't answer.

CHAPTER 3

Teela and Tain had arrived at the office by the time Kaylin had finished her meeting with the Hawklord—or until the Hawklord had dismissed her, which was more accurate. She had gotten no further information from him, and she wasn't certain what to do with the information she *had* gotten. She couldn't figure out what the Hawklord wanted her to do.

But she was angry—and disturbed—by the Aerian application for exemption status. She wasn't certain what she hoped Teela and Tain had found. No, actually, that wasn't true. She *wanted* the assassin to be a Barrani Arcanist, because everyone with any capacity for thought considered them to be raging social evils.

She didn't want them to catch an Aerian.

She accepted, as she glumly made her way down the stairs, that she was being unfair. The only Aerians she'd met were all Hawks, and she desperately wanted the Aerians to be above something as grim and illegal as assassination. But of course Aerians were *people*. If the Hawks managed to be Hawks first, it didn't mean there was nothing left over.

Kaylin had always wanted family, ever since her mother died and maybe even before that. But she wondered if the lack of family was a possible advantage to her working life. She didn't have family responsibilities that tied or bound her; she didn't have to choose, consciously and continuously, between being a Hawk and being a human.

She hadn't expected Clint's reaction to Moran's injury. She hadn't expected to be told to butt out, to not care, to offer no help—except by Moran. She wanted to storm to the front doors and shout at Clint the way she'd been smart enough—barely—not to shout at the Hawklord.

She's a Hawk, damn it.

"I think everyone knows that, kitling," a familiar voice said. "Everyone knows you think that's the only thing that matters, as well." When Teela came into view at the arch that separated the Tower stairs from the office, she looked up. "I assume you didn't mean to say that out loud?"

"Does it matter?" Kaylin replied, flushing. "It's not like it's going to change anyone's attitude anyway."

The Barrani Hawk shrugged. "If you're going to think out loud, you might want to do it in a place with less acoustical emphasis."

Teela had not chosen to meet Kaylin at the foot of the Tower stairs for no reason. Although Tain was absent, Mandoran could be seen in the distance, sprawled across Teela's chair. The rest of the Barrani Hawks—there were only two in the office at the moment—viewed him with healthy suspicion. If he noticed, he didn't care.

"Did you catch him?"

"That's making an assumption."

"Fine. Did you catch her?"

"No."

"Did you at least *see* the assassin?"

"Not directly."

"Teela—"

"Kitling," Teela said gently, "we've been pulled off of the investigation. The Aerian Caste Court—"

"Can stuff itself!"

"Perhaps," was the neutral reply. "But until the Caste Court is told to, as you put it, stuff itself by the *Emperor*, that call's not ours to make. What did the Hawklord say?"

"He told me that the Caste Court had applied for pretty much instant exemption."

Teela nodded, as if she'd expected no less. It made Kaylin feel vaguely stupid or naive, neither of which she enjoyed. Her life in the fiefs—or her life since she'd been thirteen—should have destroyed that naïveté completely.

But they were *Aerians*.

"You need to stop idolizing the Aerians." As comforting statements went, this was about rock bottom—but it was pure Teela.

"I don't idolize them."

"You do. Kitling, they have wings, yes, but they're mortal. They're *people*. Wings don't give them any moral or ethical advantage over anyone else who lives in this city. I know there were no Aerians in the fiefs. But there were no Dragons, either, and you don't expect the Dragons to somehow be paragons of virtue. They're not a single thing. They're people, like the rest of us. And some of them are going to be unpleasant sons of bitches. It's just the law of averages."

"I don't expect them to be paragons," Kaylin replied.

"Good. That'll make things in the near future much less painful for you."

Kaylin did not immediately leave to go on patrol. She should have, but Marcus was busy growling at paperwork and his mirror. He was aware that she'd returned to the office, but he wasn't yet of a mind to object. Or dock her pay.

She tapped Mandoran on the shoulder. He looked up at her. "Are we leaving?" he asked, deserting the chair Teela was almost certain to kick him out of anyway.

"Yes. We're patrolling Elani. You always enjoy that."

"And the Dragon?"

"She's staying here."

"Good."

Kaylin exhaled heavily. She *liked* Mandoran, most of the time. It didn't stop her from wanting to smack the back of his head. "You know, I think you'd actually like her if you could treat her with a smidgen of respect."

"Not worth the effort," he said, straightening his clothing. His hair, being Barrani hair, was straight and perfectly untangled.

"I like Bellusdeo."

"Yes. And she likes you. Bellusdeo and I were born, raised, and trained in a world that doesn't exist anymore. I am never going to be happy about Dragons. And she is never going to be happy about Barrani."

"She seems to like Teela."

"Teela is hardly Barrani."

"I heard that," Teela said, a distinct edge in her voice. "And if it came from anyone else, they'd be picking up teeth. Or body parts." To Kaylin, she said, "*Try* to keep him out of trouble, hmm?"

Kaylin's beat was Elani Street, and she headed there with Severn and Mandoran in tow. Only years of long practice stopped her from patrolling in ground-eating, angry strides. She made clear what she thought of politics in several different languages, settling at last on Leontine as the most appropriate, because it implied the most violence.

Mandoran understood every word; he'd picked up most of the phrasing from Teela without the need to actually learn it himself. Kaylin's extremely foul temper seemed to be a balm to what had started out as a gloomy, bored mood.

"Did you see the assassin?" Kaylin demanded.

"Of course I did."

"Did Teela?"

Sensing her mood, he answered. "No. And before you ask, I don't know why I could see her and Teela couldn't. She could, however, take a look through my eyes."

"Male or female?"

"Is there a bet riding on the outcome?"

Kaylin rolled her eyes.

"What? If you could be careful enough to count every breath you take during an average day, you'd bet on that." It was more or less true, which was annoying. So far, the morning had been nothing but annoying.

"Let me guess. You didn't think to make a bet."

She hadn't. "It doesn't matter. Was the would-be assassin an Aerian?" It was the only question that actually mattered. She desperately wanted the answer to be no, because she desperately wanted to be able to thumb her nose at the Caste Court. And if she were being honest, that wasn't the whole of the reason.

She was upset because Teela was probably right. For some reason, Kaylin expected better from the Aerians.

"It depends."

Kaylin glared. "On what? Did they have wings?"

"Yes."

What was left of her hope curled up in a ball on the inside

of her chest. Mandoran, however, stopped walking, forcing her and Severn to stop. When she turned back, he said, "Am I Barrani?"

She didn't answer the question immediately, although anyone else looking at Mandoran would have. He looked like the Barrani. He didn't look young or old; his age was only obvious, according to Teela, because of his behavior. But he had the same skin tone, the same eyes, the same perfect hair and flawless skin, and even the same height.

But she knew that the answer was both yes and no. Mandoran was in Elantra for Annarion's sake, but he was trying to relearn the art of being Barrani, the race to which he'd been born, for his own.

"Does Teela know?"

"Of course she does. Teela couldn't see her," he added. "I imagine only your familiar and I could. She could see what I saw, when she chose to look."

"Her."

Mandoran grinned. Kaylin couldn't. "Teela's talking to your sergeant now. Oh, no, wait—she's heading up the Tower stairs to talk to the Hawklord." He frowned. "She's just shut me down, so I can't give you a report on what he has to say. This is bad information?"

"It means the Caste Court is likely to get its damn exemption, yes." She walked for two full blocks, Mandoran keeping easy pace with her stride. "She wasn't like you."

"No. But she wasn't entirely Aerian, to my eye. She had the form, the shape, the wings—and she also had an odd weapon, as well as a healthy command of magic. But Teela said her invisibility wasn't entirely due to a spell."

"What was it due to, in Teela's opinion? Don't give me

that look—if I ask Teela she'll just pat me on the head and tell me to mind my own business."

"Not entirely clear."

Kaylin hesitated. "Can we take a small detour?" she asked Severn.

He nodded. "Darrow Lane?"

"How did you guess?"

As it happened, they didn't make it to Darrow Lane—an area that would have taken "investigational difficulty" to new heights, given the midday traffic. Kaylin had been considering the logistics glumly while they walked very briskly to the site of the attack, but she stopped as a passing shadow grew larger and darker overhead. It was an Aerian shadow, and it wasn't doing a patrol flyby. She wasn't surprised to see Clint join his shadow as he landed.

She wasn't even surprised to see that his eyes were very blue. Disheartened, but not surprised.

"I've been sent to find you," he told her.

"You've been sent to chase me away from Darrow Lane."

"I've been sent to make certain that you observe the... etiquette of the laws of exemption, yes." His expression made clear that he didn't care for exemptions—but no one in the Halls did, unless the exemptions were for the Barrani. That was just practical. The Barrani were pretty much death for any Hawk who wasn't.

And, Kaylin thought silently, even the Barrani didn't care much if the Barrani were murdering each other.

"Clint—what's going on?"

"I'm not on the Caste Court," he replied. "And no matter how much I rise in rank, I'm never going to be on the Caste Court. I can't answer your question."

"Would you, if you knew?"

"Laws of exemption," he replied.

Her hands found her hips as she looked up at her favorite Aerian. "Laws of exemption apply to *legal* consequences. They don't govern answering bloody questions!"

"Kitling, the human Caste Court isn't the Aerian Caste Court. They exert different powers. The human Caste Court might as well call itself the 'Order of Merchants with Jumped-Up Titles and Pretensions' for all the difference it makes to anyone who isn't the Emperor. Do you know what happens to outcaste humans?"

Kaylin frowned. "What do you mean, what happens?"

"Are you, that you know of, outcaste?"

"No." She paused. "I don't think so."

"Exactly. The human Caste Court doesn't give a damn about you. As far as I can tell, they don't give a damn about humans in general, except the rich or powerful ones. You don't give a damn about them—you probably can't name the members that constitute the Caste Court."

"It's not relevant to my life or my work," she said, sounding defensive, hating it and unable to stop. She'd never liked being called stupid, even by implication, and while she'd made strides in her *response*, the feeling never completely vanished.

"No, it's not," Clint replied, his voice gentling. He'd known her for years. "You're a Hawk. You're a human. There's no point in learning all of this crap because it doesn't make a difference to either your life or your work. But, kitling, the Aerian Caste Court isn't the human one."

"You've never mentioned it before."

"It's never been relevant. If Moran weren't a Hawk, it

wouldn't *be* relevant. There's a reason she's in charge of the infirmary."

"Because she's terrifying?"

He winced, giving in for a moment to amusement. It died fairly quickly. "Other than that. Do you know what happens to outcaste Aerians?"

She didn't. She shook her head. "Was it covered in racial integration classes?"

"No. The human Caste Court adopted many of the practices of the Barrani Caste Court. They adopted many of the same attitudes and the same pretensions. If Barrani are made outcaste, and they are powerful, they are simply shunned.

"But the Aerian Caste Court adopted many of the practices of the Dragons. Do you know what happens to outcaste Dragons?"

"They die. Unless they fly into Ravellon."

"Yes. It is the duty of each and every Dragon to exterminate the outcaste."

"Well, yes—now. There's only one remaining flight, and its boss happens to be the Eternal Emperor."

"The Aerian Caste Court is far crueler, in my opinion, than the Dragon Court."

Kaylin almost gaped, and pressed her mouth into a tighter line to stop that. "What happens to outcaste Aerians?" She had never asked. It had never occurred to her that it would be relevant, and—damn Teela, anyway—she had never truly imagined that an Aerian *could* be outcaste.

"They cut off our wings and abandon us on the ground."

She stared at him. "Cut off your wings."

"Yes."

"Your *wings*."

"Yes." He looked down at her, some of the harshness leaving his expression.

"But Moran—"

"The sergeant will never be made outcaste."

"So…they'll just murder her instead."

"Yes."

"Clint, I don't understand what's going on."

"No. But, Kaylin—you have a knack for kicking the hornet's nest, even when you can't see it. Look, I've known you since you were a kid. I know that you'll only kick the nest when you're in a big hurry to help someone; you probably won't see it until there are swarms of angry insects buzzing around your face. I can *ask* you not to get involved." His acute stare made it clear that he already had. "What I need you to understand, in this, is that the hornets aren't going to sting *you*.

"If you kick *this* nest, they're going to sting Aerians. In the worst cases, we won't get welts. We'll lose our lives in every meaningful sense. And yes, before you ask, mutilation *is* covered by the racial laws of exemption as long as both the involved parties are Aerian. The only person—the *only* person—who can safely discuss this with you is Moran. Ask me, ask anyone else, and get any answer…" He trailed off, his meaning clear.

"I can't even look at the attack site?"

"No. The exemption has been granted."

There were no more detours on the way to Elani.

Mandoran's eyes were a restless green with hints of blue when he turned to Kaylin. "He's wrong about the Barrani Court. In theory, it *is* the duty of Barrani Lords to kill the outcaste."

"Nightshade," was her flat reply.

"We're a pragmatic people."

"You invented freaking *table manners*, I swear. How is that pragmatic? Using utensils I get, but why do we *need* five forks?" Kaylin had to force herself not to march.

"It's almost never five." More seriously, he continued, "We're pragmatic. Only when politics are heavily involved does it become trickier."

"Meaning?"

"If the High Lord wished to rid himself of a particularly fractious member of his Court, he would order that lord to destroy the outcaste in question—let's use Nightshade as our example. If the fractious lord doesn't wish to become outcaste on a flimsy technicality, he has only one choice. He must attempt to destroy Nightshade." Mandoran's tone made clear how unsuccessful this theoretical lord would be.

"So…don't tick off the High Lord."

"That's always good advice. Nightshade has survived all prior attempts on his life, and he is considered a favorite, in spite of his status, with the Lady. And now you've distracted me."

"You were doing most of the talking."

"True. What I meant was, if the High Lord were intent on the destruction of a Barrani Lord, that lord would die. Period."

"Clint's not wrong. That wasn't what he was saying."

"No? I admit Teela doesn't have all that much information about him, at least that she's willing to share."

"He's telling me that my interference could cost him his wings. His literal wings. Because the implication is the Caste Court takes its excommunication very, very seriously. And clearly, Moran is at the heart of it. He's also telling me that

Moran won't be stripped of her wings. The worst she can do is die.

"But he didn't make that claim for the Hawklord." Her shoulders were bunching themselves up near her neck, which annoyed the familiar, who squawked loudly. "And I owe Lord Grammayre my life. All of it." She glanced at Severn. "What do we do?"

"Our jobs," he replied. "And until we figure out where the hornet's nest is, only our jobs."

The Elani beat was relatively quiet. The Hawks broke up one fight, stopped someone from breaking a window, gave directions—and withheld advice, which was much, much harder—to new visitors to the quarter. Mandoran headed into Margot's house of fraud, leaving Kaylin and Severn to their actual work.

"If you're doing that just to annoy me, it's working," Kaylin told him.

Mandoran grinned. "Teela's advice. So you know who to blame."

It was, if one ignored the assassination attempt—and apparently, she'd been ordered to do just that—a very normal day. The type of day she yearned for every time she left her own front doors.

The unusual part of the Elani patrol—and really, on a street full of fortune-telling frauds and miracle-medicine sellers, angry ex-customers trying to cause damage *was* the usual—came at the end of the patrol. Mandoran had rejoined them, his lips a suspicious shade of red that didn't look entirely natural. He probably deserved to be clipped by a door that flew open without warning.

The door belonged to Evanton's shop. Grethan, Evanton's apprentice, stood in the open frame, looking vaguely anxious. The anxiety cleared as the small dragon launched itself off Kaylin's shoulders and onto the young apprentice's.

Kaylin and Severn, who had come to an instant halt, shared a glance before speaking. "Were you looking for us?" Kaylin asked.

Grethan nodded. "Evanton wants to speak to you. He's in the kitchen with tea. And, um. Tea."

"Um?"

"He has another guest. The lady's been in, on and off, for the past three weeks. She wants him to make something he's not certain he wants to make."

"And...he's asking *my* advice? Did he fall and hit his head?"

"No. If he fell, he'd probably manage to hit my head instead," was the morose reply. "I'm not sure why he wants to see you," he added.

"Does he want to see the rest of us?" Mandoran asked, remaining outside in the street. Given Mandoran's previous visits—which had involved a lot of water in the wrong places—this was a perfectly reasonable question.

"He didn't say," Grethan replied. "But I think it should be fine."

Mandoran looked dubious.

"I think he actually likes you and your brother. He just thinks you're walking disasters waiting to happen."

"They are," Kaylin said before Grethan could continue. "You coming in or waiting outside?"

The small dragon liked Grethan; he always had. Grethan therefore remained his perch of interest while the apprentice led them to Evanton and his mysterious guest. They were, in fact, in the kitchen, a functional room that had never been intended for guests. The table could comfortably fit four. Evanton's expression made clear that it was going to uncomfortably fit five, although he did take pity on Mandoran after everyone else was seated. "You can wander around the store, if you'd prefer. I would ask that you not touch anything without checking with Grethan first."

Mandoran looked to Kaylin, who nodded with some envy.

Kaylin tried to gauge the importance of this visitor. Evanton didn't let just anyone into his kitchen—probably some mix of pride and self-preservation—but guests of import or power were usually led through the rickety hall in the back to the Keeper's Garden.

Tea was poured, and Evanton had a cup situated somewhere in front of him, although he didn't generally like to drink it. He watched Kaylin for a long, silent breath.

"What did I do wrong this time?" It was a surrender on her part. Someone had to speak first, or they'd be here all afternoon.

"That really is the question, isn't it?" Evanton exhaled. He turned to his guest. "This is Private Kaylin Neya, and Corporal Severn Handred. They are, as you can see, Imperial Hawks, ground division."

"I'm not sure we call it a division," Kaylin said. "The rest is accurate."

She was an older woman. Not as old as Evanton, of course, but her hair was silver with shots of rooted black, and her square face was lined. Her eyes were a pale gray. She was what Kaylin thought of as handsome: there was nothing frail about her, but she had a compelling face. At one point in her life, she might have been considered beautiful. She apparently had no name she was willing to have divulged, because Kaylin and Severn were the only ones who were introduced.

Kaylin didn't much care about manners for their own sake, but she was as curious as the next person, and the lack of an introduction made her wonder who the woman was, what she was hiding and what laws she'd broken. Then again, Kaylin was a Hawk, and her mind often ran in that direction, full tilt.

"Grethan said you wanted to see us."

"Yes. I wish to ask your opinion."

Evanton's guest clearly didn't want him to do so. She drank her tea looking stiff and increasingly uncomfortable in every possible way.

"Ask, then—we're on the clock, and the sergeant is in a foul mood."

"I would imagine he is, given the assassination attempt."

Kaylin stiffened. Severn appeared to relax. Only one of these things was accurate. "You're not just bringing that up to make conversation."

"No. I try very hard not to waste my own time, given the number of people who seem willing to waste it for me."

"What do you know about it, and how much do you want me to pass on?"

"I know that the would-be assassin was an Aerian."

"How do you know that?" Severn asked, in the conversational tones people used to talk about either sports or weather.

Evanton ignored the question. "This is not a matter for the Hawks," he said. "I believe it will be classified under exemption status. The target was Aerian, the assassin was Aerian. And I do not believe the target will seek to have justice done in the Imperial Courts. I would even be willing to wager on it." Evanton was aware of the Hawks' propensity for betting, and he knew whom most of that habit had come from.

"With your own money?"

"Not with money."

"Odds?"

"Any odds."

"Fine." Kaylin folded. "What do you know about the attempt?"

"Very little. It was carried out by magic. The mage responsible will not be catalogued in the Imperial investigative archives, so there is no point at all in bringing in Imperial mages, even if the case were remanded to the regular system."

"Do you know *why*?"

Evanton looked to his guest, who stiffened, her hands tightening around the bowl of the teacup as if to draw strength from it. She looked across the table at Kaylin. "If Moran dar Carafel is dead, the wings will pass on."

"The wings?"

The woman's lips tightened; this was followed by a downward shift of shoulders as she bowed her head. She was silent for long enough that Kaylin thought she wasn't going to answer.

Evanton said nothing; he waited, as if he were patience personified. Given the way he generally treated both Grethan and Kaylin, this was unusual. "I was reluctant to involve you," he said—to Kaylin. "I am *still* reluctant. You have a way of causing snarls and snags in the cleanest and simplest of tasks—most of which are not predictable and therefore not controllable. But in this case, there is no other option. Lillias, if you will not speak, I must allow the Hawks to go back to their duties."

Lillias. It was not a familiar name. Kaylin waited while the woman struggled in the silence left by Evanton.

When she finally lifted her head, her eyes were a deep blue.

CHAPTER 4

Part of Kaylin was wondering if she'd seen the woman's eye color incorrectly the first time, because part of Kaylin wanted that to be the truth. But this blue was a color specific to Barrani and Aerians; she had never seen humans with eyes this particular shade.

And she had never seen Aerians without wings.

She wanted to ask the woman if her wings were somehow hidden, invisible, but she already knew the answer, and her mouth was suddenly too dry for questions. Every word Clint had said while he stood in Darrow Lane came back to bite her. She tried to keep the horror off her face, but had no idea whether or not she succeeded.

But she *would not* show pity to a stranger she knew almost nothing about, even if the thing she did know was larger than nightmare.

"Moran dar Carafel's wings are unique in the flights of the Southern Reach. They are not unique in the history of the flights. They do not exist in every generation. But if one is born with those wings, they are the only ones who can or will bear the markings. No others will be born while the bearer lives." She spoke slowly, as if weighing all of her words and picking out only the good ones.

"Are the marks determined by gender?"

"No."

"Are they significant in any other way?"

Silence. When it was broken, it wasn't broken with an answer. "Moran dar Carafel was injured in her duties here, duties which would be almost anathema to the leaders of the flights. She was not given permission to undertake them; she was not given permission to risk her life in combat. She could not, however, be made outcaste." The last word was said bitterly. So bitterly. "And now, she is crippled."

"The wings will heal," Kaylin said, with more force than the statement merited.

"Will they?"

One way or another, they would. She nodded grimly. "Aerians are trying to assassinate Moran because they want someone else to be born with those wings." It wasn't a question. It was a statement.

"Her birth was a grave disappointment," Lillias agreed, staring into her tea as if she were reading leaves and not much enjoying what she found there. "She was not, originally, Carafel. Her mother, and her mother's line, lived in the outer Aeries, beneath open sky. We have a saying in the Aerie—" She stopped. Shook her head. "Her mother was adopted into dar Carafel—and even that was bitterly divisive."

"Her father?"

Lillias grimaced. "The child was not legitimate. Were it not for the wings, nothing would be known of the father."

"And because of the wings?"

"It was proof that he was of the first families. No one came forward to claim either the mother or her daughter as their own, and the mother never revealed the father's identity. There is prestige, of course, in bearing such a child, or there should have been. The mothers of such children are accorded respect in great measure; there is no equivalent in human society. But the child was illegitimate. Either the father perished, or the father was mated, bonded—or both."

"Wouldn't this also elevate the father?"

"Yes. But not if the father was bonded—married?—to another."

Evanton nodded.

"If he was of the high clans, and he was married, it would be a disgrace. It is possible Moran's father is alive and well. It is possible he is dead. It is also possible that he would have been free to marry her when evidence of the child's importance was known."

"You don't believe that."

"No. Moran did not have a happy childhood. Her mother withered in the confines of the High Reach, treated with the contempt reserved for an unbonded mother in the upper reaches, and when she finally passed away, the child was returned—for a time—to her grandmother's care. It is there that she was happiest."

Kaylin nodded.

"She could fly," the woman's voice softened. "You have never seen her truly fly."

Kaylin could remember seeing Moran fly only once—but even so, it was a blur; Kaylin had been on the back of a Dragon at the time, and she'd been watching large chunks of the High Streets turn into molten rock. She'd been watching Aerians falling from the sky. Some would never rise again.

She shook herself. "No," she said. "I've never seen her fly." It wasn't even really a lie. She had never seen her happy, either—but she'd imagined that, as a sergeant, happiness had somehow magically been drained from her; Kaylin didn't know any happy sergeants.

This was different. The silence that fell after her comment was heavy, weighted; it destroyed all movement at the table, and all sound. Kaylin dragged her head around to meet Evanton's gaze, because it was Kaylin, not Lillias, that he was watching.

"Why did you want to see me?" she asked him.

"Because Lillias needed to speak with you."

"You said she asked you to make something?"

"No, Kaylin, I did not." His frown was pure Evanton— well, pure Evanton when he was displeased with poor Grethan. He exhaled. "Lillias?"

"She is not of the people," Lillias mumbled.

"No, she is not. But technically, neither are you."

Kaylin sucked in air. Sucked it in and had trouble expelling it again. Evanton's voice had been, was, gentle. But the words…

"Can I ask why you were made outcaste?" She cringed even as the words left her mouth. "No, I'm sorry, let me take that back? Can I ask if it had something to do with Moran?" The woman was older than Moran, even given the age that despair and desolation added to her features.

"Yes."

"Have you spoken to Moran since?"

Silence.

Mandoran had said that he had seen wings during the failed assassination. Lillias clearly didn't have any. Whoever the assassin had been, it wasn't her.

"How much danger is Moran in?"

Evanton clearly considered this a stupid question.

"More danger," Lillias replied, "than you can imagine.

The Keeper told me that you were responsible for her survival this morning."

"Not me," Kaylin said. "She survived because of my familiar and a Dragon."

Lillias frowned and turned to Evanton. In Aerian, she asked, "Is this true? Is there a Dragon involved?"

Kaylin answered before Evanton could. In Aerian. "Yes. It's true."

The woman's eyes were already as blue as they could get, so they didn't darken. Her skin did; it flushed. It occurred to Kaylin that the elderly seldom blushed.

"I'm a Hawk," Kaylin said gently, although she was wearing a tabard that clearly marked her as such. "We've got a lot of Aerians working in the Halls, and I joined the Halls when I was a child. My Aerian isn't great, but I can speak it. I'm sorry." Keeping her voice gentle, she asked, "What did you ask Evanton to make?"

The woman's hesitation was sharp, filled with questions or doubts or both. But she eventually bowed her head and said a word, in Aerian, that Kaylin had never heard before. *"Bletsian."*

"I'm sorry—I'm not familiar with that word."

"No, you wouldn't be," Evanton said. "Neither would the majority of the Aerian Hawks. It is an old word. The Dragons would be familiar with it." He frowned. "Or at least the Arkon would."

"It's magical?"

"Yes. Before you look askance, you have two enchanted daggers on your person. Not all magic is of the Arcanist variety, as you should well know."

Kaylin, still frowning, turned to Lillias. "Why would you come to Evanton for magic?"

"Why did you?" Evanton countered.

"Teela made me. I would never have known otherwise, given the location of your shop."

"Margot," Evanton said, pinpointing the chief source of Kaylin's dislike, "is not entirely a fraud."

"We're not talking about Margot."

"No. I merely point out that your dislike of her—while possibly deserved—does her an injustice. It is possible to be both genuine and distasteful."

"Most of what she does—"

"Is fraud, yes. But not all. And, Kaylin? Where else would she be safe to practice her gift? She is in the open here."

"Look—"

"She is not confined to the Oracular Halls. Or worse."

Kaylin closed her mouth. "We weren't talking about Margot."

"No. You were implying that nothing genuine is known to be found in Elani."

"Baldness cures? Come on, Evanton."

"Elani, very much like any other neighborhood, is not all one thing or the other. I, after all, am here. And it is to me Lillias came."

Lillias was listening to this conversation with obvious confusion. "Where else would I go?"

"Private Neya feels you should have approached either the Imperial Order or the Arcanum."

"Kaylin doesn't feel *anyone* should approach the Arcanum," Kaylin snapped.

"Ah."

"Lillias," Severn said, joining the conversation—as he so often did—late. "Forgive our ignorance. What is a *bletsian*?"

"It is a blessing," the old woman replied. "A blessing of wind, of air."

"It is a gift," Evanton told Kaylin, "that she wishes delivered to Moran dar Carafel."

"Moran's not big on gifts."

Evanton ignored this. "She cannot deliver it in person. You, however, can. If you are willing to do this, I will create what has been requested, and I will hand it directly to you. There will be no tampering and no interference."

"Lillias, what does this blessing do, exactly?"

"It confers," Evanton said, after it became clear that Lillias would not answer, "flight. Literal flight. It does not, and cannot, last, but some small part of the elemental air will carry the bearer as the bearer desires until the breath of wind is consumed."

Kaylin looked at this wingless, outcaste woman. "You're certain," she said to Evanton, although she didn't move her gaze, "whatever you give me will be safe for Moran?"

"Yes."

"Because the assassin used magic. And not a small amount of it," she almost growled. "And no, I don't—and won't—know who the assassin was, or what magic was used, or how powerful the spell was, because the entire thing is under exemption embargo."

"Kaylin," Evanton replied softly, "stay out of this."

"You're asking me to deliver a magical trinket to a sergeant in the Halls of Law, and I'm supposed to stay out of it? She's *living in my house*, Evanton."

"I am aware of that. I do not disapprove in any regard save one: you know too many Aerians, and you consider them family."

"I consider them Hawks!"

"They are. My point, however, stands. This is not your fight, Kaylin. Do not make it your fight." To Lillias, he said,

"You see how she is?" As if Kaylin had been a topic of discussion.

Lillias turned to Kaylin then, as if making a decision. Her expression was more open, more generous with pain and loss, than it had been when Kaylin had first entered the kitchen.

"Moran's mother did not immediately reveal the child. She was poor, even by the standards of the flights. She was considered fine-feathered, strong, healthy—but she was of no good flight. She bore a child, hidden, with only her own mother in attendance. But the child was *Illumen praevolo*."

Kaylin opened her mouth to ask the obvious question, but before the words could fall out, Evanton reached out and placed a hand over hers. He shook his head, his expression implying that an interruption wouldn't just break the flow of words—it would dam it entirely.

Lillias spoke the words as if they were almost a prayer. Given Lillias's constant hesitance, Kaylin filed the words *Illumen praevolo* away for later use.

"Had she gone to the Upper Reach immediately, it is likely the child would have been removed from her and passed off as the legitimate issue of a more suitable man—and that is why she did not do so. She kept the child hidden until the child could no longer be hidden.

"And so, the flights came, at the whispered rumor that a *praevolo* had been born. Before you make that face, understand that humans are not the only sellers of dreams and fraud. The rumor was not given credence until it grew; such rumors are always with us in the absence of a *praevolo*.

"She was underfed, undereducated, undertrained. Were it not for her markings, her wings—so unlike her mother's— she would have been considered mediocre at best. But she was, indeed, *praevolo*. They could not deny it and did not try. They offered the mother respect, praised her for keeping the child alive and hidden. They bade her to continue to do so, flew her to new quarters vastly larger and better appointed, and left to make their report.

"The castelord was enraged at what he considered the *waste* of it. A child who might have been a boon if born to the Upper Reaches was now a weakness. Had she been just another—what is your word? Bastard?"

At Kaylin's stiff nod, she continued, "She would have been insignificant. But the castelord felt that she had illegitimately taken hold of the equivalent of an artifact, something to which she should not have been born, and of which she could never be worthy. The Caste Court decided, at that time, that her death was regrettable, but necessary. If she perished, the wings would return again, and this time, they would be watching, they would be alert. They would not make the same mistake."

Kaylin hadn't touched her tea; if she were drinking it, she'd've choked.

"It was the Caste Court's decision to make."

Kaylin *hated* the laws of exemption with a blinding passion at this moment, because Lillias was talking about the *perfectly legal* murder of a child. She managed to contain every visceral Leontine phrase that tried to tear itself out of her mouth. "Moran's still alive," she said. "Did they decide to wait and see?"

"No. An attempt was made. Three attempts were made, actually. Two involved poison. Neither poison was successful. It was assumed that the poisoner was incompetent, or deliberately treacherous. As it happened, they were neither. They poisoned the food. The child ate the food. The poison failed to take effect, and the child did not die. Her mother, however, did.

"History was then studied, but our historical records are

not like your Records. The castelord could find histories of the deaths of the *praevolo*, but not one had fallen to disease or poison. Not one died in childhood of the things that might otherwise take the young.

"And so it was decided that she would have to die in a different fashion—history did record other deaths; the *praevolo* were not immortal or invulnerable. Moran's grandmother died in the third attempt. Moran had servants, of course, but they did not serve her, and they were ordered to other duties that day. The child was alone with her grandmother.

"Not all of the servants who absented themselves intended to turn a blind eye. One traveled some distance up, to find someone who would listen—and care. The orders were quiet but absolute—they were not meant to leak down to the people beneath the Upper Reach, as there was some concern that the decision would not be popular.

"Someone intervened. Not in time to save the grandmother, but in time to save Moran."

"But wouldn't they just try again?"

"They would, yes. They would have. But Moran's wings were then made public. She was flown—no, Kaylin, she *flew*—through the entirety of the Aeries; through every crag, every valley, to every peak of the Southern Reach. She wept and she raged and she soared until flight was the only thing she felt, the only thing that mattered. And we saw her. Upper Reaches to Outer, we *saw* her. We knew that she was *Illumen praevolo*. Every one of us.

"They could not kill her then."

"But they're trying to do it now?"

"She cannot fly," Lillias said, as if that explained everything.

"She can't fly *yet*." And this was going to get them both

nowhere. "What do the wings mean? What exactly *is* the *Illumen praevolo*?" Kaylin demanded.

"The wings mean nothing," Lillias replied, ignoring the second question. "Because Moran dar Carafel will allow them to mean nothing. In the past, that was acceptable, but only barely. But now, it is much less so. As I said, she cannot be made outcaste. She can be summoned to the Aerie, but because she is an Imperial Hawk, she can disobey. The laws of exemption require her permission to be invoked if she is at the center of the controversy."

For one moment, Kaylin saw the bright gleam of a way out. It guttered. If the laws had been invoked, if Clint believed they had been accepted, it meant Moran had accepted them, too.

Lillias shook her head. "She has not chosen to heed the summons."

"She probably can't, if she can't fly. Yet."

"She was capable of flight before. She has never heeded the summons. The castelord responsible for the death of her mother is dead. The Caste Court is comprised of different men, different women. Until she was injured, she lived in the Upper Reaches, but she spoke with no one. She has never forgiven the Aerie for her mother's death."

"Or her grandmother's?"

Lillias said nothing.

"Why do you want to help her?"

"Is that what you think I am doing?" the old woman replied. Before Kaylin could answer, the woman closed blue eyes. "Do you believe in her?" she asked softly.

It wasn't the question Kaylin had been expecting. Then again, she wasn't certain that she'd expected *any* of the conversation Evanton had forced on both of them.

"How can I not believe in her?" Kaylin replied, although

it took time. "I'm a Hawk. She's a Hawk. She got her injury fighting something that was powerful enough to take down Dragons. Plural. She got that injury doing her duty—doing what the Aerians *could* do that the rest of us, wingless, couldn't."

"And her duty to her own people?"

Kaylin struggled with this for longer. The Aerians had murdered her mother and her grandmother. She owed them nothing. There were racial tensions among Hawks. But there were personal tensions, as well. They were all people. And they were all people who'd decided, despite race or even because of it, to serve the Imperial Law that protected those who didn't *have* a lot of money or power. Were they perfect? Hells no. But they were *trying*. It was more than the fieflord of Nightshade had ever done. It was more than any fieflord, with the exception of Tiamaris, had ever been rumored to do.

Kaylin felt no particular attachment to her own race. She had daydreams of being born to a different one—Aerian, usually. She hadn't ever considered what she owed the human race. Then again, she hadn't really considered what she owed anyone who wasn't a Hawk.

She was Chosen. That was special. But Chosen, or rather, being Chosen, didn't depend on race. Kaylin wasn't certain what it did depend on. She wasn't even certain what it meant on most days.

Had it been dependent on being human, had humanity somehow *required* it, would she have changed her entire life to fulfill the debts and obligations she'd never asked for? Would she do it if that debt and obligation had indirectly killed her mother?

"I'm sorry, Lillias," she finally said. "I don't know. I admire her. She's always been slightly terrifying—especially if you're already injured and she decides you need to be strapped to a bed for a week—but she's a Hawk. I don't see her the way you see her."

"Do you even know how I see her?"

"No. You haven't said. I'm willing to listen, if you want to talk about it."

Lillias nodded. She turned to Evanton instead of speaking.

Evanton turned to Kaylin. "I will do as Lillias has asked. But, Kaylin—stay out of this. Everything you can safely do, you've done. And I do not think you are ready to pay the cost for more." He rose. "I will see you out." To Lillias, he added, "I will be but a moment."

Kaylin hit the street in an internal fog of confusion and anger. She had retrieved her familiar from Grethan's shoulders, and he had immediately wrapped himself around hers, squawking in soft complaint as he did. She barely noticed, he was so much a part of her life. "Did he do that on purpose?" she asked her partner. Mandoran, retrieved from the bowels of the oldest shelves in the building, glanced at both of them.

It was Mandoran who answered. "Of course he did."

"Do you even know what I'm talking about?"

"Introducing you to the Aerian woman. The wingless one." Mandoran stared at Kaylin, his eyes an odd shade: not green, but not blue, and not the usual blend of both, which was almost the Barrani resting state. "You like Aerians. You like Hawks. You like Aerian Hawks better than you like most of the rest of the Hawks, with some obvious exceptions. She lost her wings. She's outcaste.

"If you push this, some of your Hawks are likely to end up the way she did. He wants you to understand that as more than theory." Mandoran stopped in front of Margot's sandwich board. "Did you?"

"Did I what?" she asked, irritable and restless.

"Did you understand it? Could you imagine Clint without wings?" He froze for a moment, his eyes going flat. "Teela tells me I should apologize for that."

"Don't bother unless you mean it."

"That's what I told her."

The rest of the day was uneventful. The Hawklord did not demand to see her again, and Marcus, while growly, was content to snarl at everyone and not Kaylin in particular. Teela and Tain had not returned from their own beat when Kaylin checked out; Severn remained with her instead of heading to his place.

She stopped at the infirmary to pick up Bellusdeo and Moran and discovered that there had been trouble on the banks of the Ablayne—no surprise there. If there was trouble anywhere in the city, odds were it had occurred on or near the Ablayne's many bridges. The bridges that fed into the fiefs, with the growing exception of Tiamaris, were in low-rent areas.

But this trouble was only a mundane knife fight, and the Hawks had come out on top, although they'd pulled in a couple of Swords; it was the Swords who required medical attention, and they received it with their usual stiff upper lips. The Hawks, Kaylin reflected, cursed more. And in better languages.

They were late heading home, and by the time Moran was ready to leave, Teela and Tain had returned. They were waiting, lounging really, outside the infirmary doors. The infirmary was strictly for mortals, as far as the Barrani on the force were concerned. Moran contested this from time to time, but the Barrani, accustomed to kin who were just as likely to kill them as come to their aid, weren't bothered by the sergeant's demeanor.

Moran's lips tightened as she caught sight of the Barrani, but she said nothing. She locked the office with the touch of a palm and a three-word command, and headed out of the building.

The guards had changed shifts, and happened to be human, not Aerian, which made passage between them less awkward. And it was going to be awkward, because Mandoran's question still cut her when Kaylin returned to it.

She wanted to help Moran.

Was she willing to risk Clint losing his wings, if she made a mistake?

Was she willing to risk Lord Grammayre losing his?

Helen was waiting for them at the door, and as Kaylin stepped into the front foyer, she felt her jaw unclench. There had been no further problems on the way home. No invisible assassins, for one. Helen gently draped an arm around Kaylin's shoulder, taking care not to crush the familiar, who lifted a lazy eyelid to look at her before he shut it again.

"Why is he so exhausted?" Helen asked.

"Who knows? All he's done today is complain and sit on people's shoulders." Except for saving Moran's life. Kaylin glanced apologetically at the familiar, who failed to notice.

The small dragon squawked without opening his eyes.

"You visited the Keeper?" Helen asked Kaylin.

Moran stiffened. "I'm going to take a bath," she told Helen. "I'm not sure I'll be down for dinner."

"That's fine, dear. I'll have food sent up if you aren't." She watched Moran mount the large staircase, but waited until she had disappeared before speaking again. "She's worried about you," she told Kaylin.

"I'm beginning to understand why people hate worry so much," Kaylin replied. "You guys eating here?"

Teela glanced at Tain, who shrugged. "Looks like a yes. We're going out drinking after, if you want to come."

"Maybe."

The Barrani exchanged another glance.

"I'm going to get changed for dinner," Bellusdeo told them all. "I'd appreciate it if you didn't leave without me." Her eyes were close to gold as she met Teela's. Teela's were closer to blue.

Unable to ditch her Barrani guests, Kaylin looked to Severn, who raised a brow. But he did nod, and headed toward the dining room, which had become the equivalent of an informal parlor. There was a lot of room, it had chairs and it was always well lit. The Hawks used it the way they used the benches in the mess hall; the parlor was almost intimidating in its formality by comparison.

Kaylin hung back.

"She knows what you're doing," Mandoran said cheerfully.

"Great. Can you tell her that I enjoy being worried about as much as she does?"

"Yes," Teela said, before Mandoran could reply, "and when you've got centuries of experience under your belt, I'll stop."

Which, of course, meant never, because Kaylin wasn't immortal and was, in all likelihood, never going to see *one* century.

She kept seeing Clint without wings. It was his wings she had loved first. Everything else had followed, as wings—and what they meant to Kaylin—made way for the person to whom they were attached.

And yes, that probably meant Teela was *right*. The Aerians were people, just like any other people; the fact that they had one physical characteristic that was at the heart of Kaylin's many, many daydreams and longings was *Kaylin's* problem, not theirs. They didn't owe her her dreams. They didn't have to live up to them.

To Helen, she said, "Can I use the mirror?"

"Now, dear?"

Sarcasm came and went. Kaylin managed to keep it to herself, but Helen, who could read the thoughts of almost anyone who entered the house, heard it all. Helen, like Tara, didn't mind hearing it all.

"Why is now bad?"

"Lord Nightshade is still speaking with his brother."

"And?"

"I still don't trust him. It requires a diversion of attention in order to properly contain the intrusion of the mirror network."

"I honestly don't think he's going to do anything damaging or stupid—at least not to you."

"No. But Annarion is at his least stable when his brother is visiting, and it takes some effort to contain the possible danger of his instability, as well."

Kaylin exhaled, nodding glumly.

Moran did not come down to dinner. Bellusdeo and Maggaron did, the former dressed in something other than her armor. Kaylin was certain she'd be hearing about the armor sometime in the morning, and tried not to think about it too much.

The entire dining table fell silent when Annarion joined them, because Annarion brought his brother. Both he and Nightshade were blue-eyed, and it wasn't the resting state of caution and natural superstition; it was dark.

Annarion bowed very formally and very correctly; Mandoran snorted. Loudly. While both Teela and Tain had stiffened into the type of formality that signaled the possibility of upcoming death, Mandoran lounged. He nodded at Night-shade as if the fieflord were mortal.

Helen set a place for the unexpected guest without being asked. But Helen, like Teela and Tain, had an air that was distinctly more martial. The dining room became, with the insertion of Nightshade, a small battlefield. On the other hand, the cutlery didn't turn into daggers or swords.

Nightshade's seat was not beside Annarion; nor was it beside Kaylin. It was between Bellusdeo and Teela. A dark, perfect brow rose as he glanced at Helen; his lips folded into something too sardonic to be a smile. An acknowledgment, perhaps. Her suspicion did not offend him.

No, Kaylin thought with some surprise. The only thing in the room that appeared to do that was the younger brother he had come to visit.

CHAPTER 5

The table was silent for a good five minutes. This was almost miraculous for a house that contained Kaylin and Mandoran. Kaylin was willing to swallow words; she was too ill at ease to speak without thinking, and her thoughts were so tied up in the Aerian problem she didn't have any left over to waste on not offending Barrani.

You will not offend me. No one but Kaylin could hear Nightshade's voice, a reminder—probably deliberate—that they were bound by his True Name. She started, flushed and met his gaze. His eyes were much greener, but given his seating, not green.

You have this thing about dignity and proper respect. All of you do, except Mandoran, Kaylin replied.

I was long considered overly tolerant among my own kin.

How many of those that believed this are still alive?

His eyes widened. She'd surprised him. And amused him; the two expressions chased across his face, easing the lines of tension slightly. *A few. At least one of them is at this table now.*

He could only mean Teela. Kaylin's gaze swiveled toward her, and veered at the last minute. Too late. This amused

Nightshade, as well. It had never been Kaylin's life's ambition to amuse Lord Nightshade.

"I hear," he said gravely, "that you had an eventful morning."

She nodded, glaring at Mandoran. Mandoran shrugged his lazy, bored shrug. It was too long, too indolent, and too graceful to properly be the fief shrug that he was trying to copy. "Annarion was worried."

"Don't try to shift blame," Bellusdeo said. "You were bored."

"Well, I was until the street cracked," Mandoran replied with an unrepentant grin. "Pursuit was interesting, as well. Everything else has been a letdown."

Nightshade glanced at his brother, who was glaring at Mandoran silently, but not, Kaylin was certain, wordlessly.

"Annarion said only that there had been an attack, a possible assassination attempt. Did he not refer to Lord Bellusdeo?"

Mandoran snorted. "No. I'd understand it if someone tried to kill *her*."

Maggaron was destroying cutlery in the sudden tension of his grip. His very large grip. No one spoke.

Interesting. Who was *the target?* Nightshade asked Kaylin.

She really hated Mandoran at the moment.

And that is interesting. You lie even when no one else can hear you.

Someone can always hear me, she shot back.

I have been somewhat occupied of late. Your Helen does not trust me at all. She is willing to tolerate me, but only for Annarion's sake. She does, however, bear obvious fondness for him. I am therefore guarding myself on two fronts, and even this conversation is likely to annoy her immensely.

He was probably right.

I cannot hear your thoughts when you are in your home.

You can hear them now.

Yes, and that is unexpected. I am not certain why she allowed my words to reach you. Perhaps she hoped that it would make the rest of the discussion less awkward.

What discussion?

He chuckled, although his face was perfectly composed. *You did not answer my question.*

Not mine to answer. She thought of Moran—just a brief flicker of awareness of how little Moran wanted to be the subject of *any* discussion. And of course, that stray thought was enough.

But she hadn't expected the stillness that spread out from Lord Nightshade. She'd thought him still and composed when he sat; she'd thought him still and composed during the opening salvos of what promised to be a less-than-comfortable dinner. He was frozen now, for one long minute that threatened to spiral out of control, taking what little sound and light there was entirely out of the room.

"What," Nightshade said, "are you doing housing the *Illumen praevolo*? Have you lost your mind?"

Kaylin wondered, briefly, why he'd asked the question out loud.

"I thought it best," Helen replied. "I am somewhat occupied at the moment, and I did not feel that dinner conversation would become difficult. I apologize for my lapse in supervision."

Kaylin realized two things then. First: Nightshade would no longer be able to speak with her through the bond of True Name; Helen had killed that avenue of private discussion. Second, and more troubling, that Helen *had* allowed it to begin with. Kaylin didn't believe that the lapse, as she called it, was accidental. Nor did she think that Helen truly believed that the conversation would not be difficult, given the way she clearly felt about Nightshade.

Her house had *lied* to her. What she couldn't understand was *why*—and just in case Helen was listening in, she made it clear that she didn't need to understand why right this very second. Later would do, if they all survived the meal.

"What did you say?" she asked Nightshade.

"I asked if you had taken leave of your senses."

"Before that."

"Illumen praevolo?"

They were the exact words Lillias had spoken. Lillias had been fragile, nervous, afraid. Nightshade was none of those things. "Yes, that. What does it mean?"

"It means nothing to humans," he replied. His eyes were a glittering blue, hard as sapphires as they absorbed the room's light. "It means much to Aerians. Was it the *Illumen praevolo* who survived the assassination attempt?"

"Yes."

"They do not belong here."

"Thanks, but it's my house. My castle. I get to decide that."

"Did you know, before you offered shelter?"

Kaylin was irritated. "What do you think?"

"I think you were ignorant."

"Good. Now that we've got that out of the way, tell me why you think she doesn't belong here."

"She?"

Damn.

"How did you even come to meet her? I suppose I should

not be surprised; you are certainly acquainted with the Lady and with Lord Bellusdeo."

"She's not like the Lady," was Kaylin's flat and certain reply. "And she's not like Bellusdeo, either."

"No. She is not, but she occupies a central, singular place for the Aerians, as the Consort does for the Barrani, or Lord Bellusdeo for the Dragons. It should not surprise me," he said again, "but it does."

"Do you know what her role is?"

"We will trade information, perhaps. How did you encounter her?"

There was a beat of silence before Kaylin exhaled. "She works in the Halls of Law."

His eyes shifted from blue to a very surprised gold, a color she very seldom saw in Barrani. "You must be mistaken."

"I think I know the Halls of Law, and I think I know a sergeant when I see one. She works in the Halls."

"A...sergeant." He closed his eyes; when he opened them again, they had reclaimed the color blue. It was a lighter shade than Teela's. So was midnight sky. "No wonder they tried to kill her. This has happened before?"

"Not while she's been a sergeant." Kaylin set her cutlery down and folded her arms, tilting her chair back on two legs. She wasn't hungry, and while that didn't usually stop her from eating, she wanted to concentrate.

"Never?"

"Not that I know of, no. But I'd say 'never' covers it."

"Ah. And before that?"

"It's not in Records." She stonewalled. He couldn't read her mind now. He couldn't see her thoughts. "Why would you expect that this wouldn't be the first attempt?"

He smiled. "Because she is living here, Kaylin. Perhaps

you do not understand why this is a crime in the minds of the Aerians."

"Some of the Aerians."

"As you say. Why does she not dwell with her kin? Why does she choose menial employ? She is *Illumen praevolo.*"

"And I'm the Chosen," Kaylin shot back. "But I need to eat."

"The Chosen does not mean to humans what your Aerian will mean to the Aerians. Perhaps it should."

"It certainly should," Bellusdeo interrupted. "She is not treated with nearly the respect her burden is due."

Kaylin lifted a hand in Bellusdeo's direction, and the Dragon fell silent. She probably wasn't happy about it, but Kaylin didn't check; she was watching Nightshade as if he were the only person in the room.

"Do your Aerians not speak of it?" Nightshade asked her.

"No. And I can't ask them."

"And she does not explain?"

"No. She thinks it's not safe for me to know."

He smiled; it was winter, but beautiful. "And so you come to me."

"I didn't—" She exhaled and regrouped. "Yes. Yes, I'm asking you."

"Has it occurred to you that your companion may be correct? No, don't answer. You will say yes, but mean no. It is vexing. If you wish to know how I come by this information…" he began.

"I know how."

"Ah. I forget. Yes, you probably do. The *praevolo* is not a position like the Consort within the Barrani. To become Consort, there are tests. Tests of the Tower. Tests of the Lake. Failure does not always mean death, but the closer one comes to success, the higher the possibility of death becomes. We are not, like humans, a people to whom children come quickly or easily; the risk of death can be a strong deterrent.

"But it is the line's risk to take. Your friend did not have the distinction of determination or choice. She was born to it. It has been an essential part of her nature since that birth."

Kaylin nodded, trying not to be impatient. Or not to be obviously impatient, at any rate. "I understand that part. I don't understand why it's significant. I don't understand what it *means*."

"As I have said, to humans, it means nothing."

"She's not a human, and she's living here."

"How much do you feel you have a right to know?" he asked, almost gently. It was gentleness from Nightshade that she didn't trust. His violence, his arrogance, his intimidation were things that were obvious threats. "If she does not wish you to know, and it is her secret, her life, how much do those wishes count to you?"

There was a disgusted snort—a sergeant's sound—from the doorway; everyone looked up. Moran stood in the frame, arms folded, eyes a blue that almost matched Teela's in shade. "Lord Nightshade, I presume."

He raised dark brows.

"You were the Barrani who marked Private Neya?"

Kaylin almost stood; Annarion's expression had drifted from mild interest into disgust and anger and disappointment.

"It is not one of my many titles," came the cool reply. He was staring at her, at the rise of her wings, or her one wing, at the bindings that kept the other more or less safe and in place. "Is it you?"

"Don't ask questions when you already know the answer."

"Among my kin, it would be considered polite."

"We're not among your kin here." She glanced at Annarion. "We're in Kaylin's home. And Kaylin has never entirely grasped the intricacies of manners." She entered the dining room as a place—with a stool—magically appeared for her at the table. It was beside Kaylin, and required some minor shuffling.

"I asked you," Moran told the private, "to stay out of this." She didn't sound enraged. She sounded disappointed, which was worse.

"They tried to kill you."

"Believe that I'm aware of that."

"I'd like them to never try again."

"And I'd like to have normal, healthy wings and a living mother," Moran said with a shrug. "We don't always get what we want, especially when it comes to the big things." She glanced at Nightshade. "You were about to explain to the table what the *praevolo* is."

"But you are now here; your knowledge has precedence."

Moran shrugged again. The gaze she leveled at Nightshade was about as warm and friendly as Teela's. "My view is colored. If you've heard about the *Illumen praevolo*, you didn't hear about it from the Caste Court or the Upper Reaches; you heard about it from the rank and file. I'd like to know what they think."

"You've never asked?"

"No. It's not something that is ever discussed in the Halls. By any Aerian."

"Very well, if you have no objections."

"My objections have rarely counted for so little." She shot Kaylin a glance, and Kaylin flushed the color of guilt. There was so much awkward tension in the room, it might as well have been a fractious office meeting with the Lords.

"This is not the world to which the Aerians were born."

"No."

"It is the world they reached, in an era long past, through a stretch of endless sky, the *etande*, as it was called."

Moran was staring at the side of his face, her brows slightly furrowed.

"They had their reasons for leaving their home."

"The World Devourer?" Kaylin asked.

"No, nothing so immediately deadly. You are aware that the Aerians' flight is...improbable? They are, in build and general density, almost human. The activities that do not depend in any way on flight are not hampered by physical strength or build. Their wings, were they attached to the body of similarly weighted avian, could not achieve flight."

Kaylin frowned. No, she hadn't been aware of that, and she wasn't in a great hurry to claim her ignorance.

"They are not magical creatures. In an absence of any magic, they will not cease to exist. They will, however, cease to fly."

Moran was *really* staring at the side of his face now, but the midnight of her blue eyes had drifted into an early shade of clear night sky while she listened.

"So...their world ran out of magic?" Kaylin asked.

"Yes."

"And our world is more magic-rich?"

"Yes. Understand that in a world without magic, door wards and streetlights would not function. In order to utilize magical energies, there must be some sort of conduit—in most cases, training. But not in all."

"And the *Illumen*—"

"Yes, the importance of the *praevolo* in this escape was critical. It was the duty of the anointed to find a different world; the Aerian ancestors entered the *etande* without a compass.

"The *praevolo* is said to have preserved the power of flight for the people, and the *praevolo* followed a trail that only they could see; it led to this world. It is here they arrived—a world of Dragons, Barrani, humans, Leontines.

"And here, too, there was Shadow."

"Too?"

"I believe—although I am not certain, as the legends were somewhat garbled—"

"That it was Shadow that drove the Aerians from their first home," Moran said quietly. "At least that is most of our tale. The *Shadows* deprived our wings of flight."

"You are skeptical?" Nightshade asked her.

"Yes, actually. The Shadows seem a thing of magic, to me. But it's possible that, to destroy Shadow, the ancestors found some way to destroy magic. I don't think they understood what the cost would be, and I think that the Shadows *did* wane in that world. But the people could not survive—not as they had."

"Ah. And so, indirectly, the necessities of war with Shadow did cause the death of flight."

Moran nodded.

"So the *praevolo* was born during that time?" Kaylin asked.

"It's complicated," Moran finally replied. "Understand that we have legends and tales; we're not Dragons. We don't have ancient Records to which we can refer. I'm not sure that *born* is the right word." She hesitated. "It's the word that's been used. In theory, the *praevolo* is born to the Aerian people at a time of great need or great conflict. But I believe, even in the tales that are handed down, that the first *praevolo* was born then."

"You don't think *born* is the right word?"

"*I* was born. I wasn't created. There was no cabal of ancient, powerful mages standing beside my mother as she conceived me; there were none in the birthing rooms where I was born." Her smile was wan. "When I first encountered Records in the Halls, I searched them. And I went outside of the Halls, searching. I wanted information."

"Were you not told anything about your wings?"

"I was told a great deal," Moran replied. "I heard times beyond count that I was unworthy of the gift I had been given. I was told constantly about humility, chief among the characteristics I was to develop to *be* worthy."

"Yes, of course, dear," Helen said, although no one had spoken. She carried a drink—a hot drink, in a very mundane mug—to Moran, and set it in front of her, where lazy swirls of steam rose.

"I asked, in the beginning, what I was to be worthy of."

Kaylin leaned forward, hurting for the child that Moran had been, and hoping it didn't show. No one wanted pity, and Moran was not that child now.

"I was told that to prove my worth, I was to respect the authority of the Caste Court. They were wise and learned and of course, deserved their positions by consequence of birth. I was a bastard, illegitimate, and my father refused to step forward to claim kinship with me. I still don't know who he is," she added, staring at the rising steam as if reading some fortune in it. "I doubt I'll ever know."

"Would it make a difference?" Teela surprised Kaylin by asking. "Before you reply, I feel it necessary to point out that I killed mine—and I spent centuries building enough of a power base that I could survive doing so. He murdered my mother."

Moran took her time digesting this information; it wasn't information the Barrani who worked in the Halls would ever think to share. Her wry grin, and eyes that were now drifting into a more normal Aerian gray, cut years off her apparent age. The grin dimmed. "It's possible that my father murdered my mother. I don't know. He certainly did nothing to protect her, and he did nothing to protect me, either.

"But for all I know, my father might have been a younger son—no, less, a younger cousin, part of an Upper Reach flight in name only. He might have had no power."

"You don't believe it, though."

"...No." She shook herself. To Teela, she said, "Did killing him change anything?"

"Yes. I became the line."

"That would never happen—I *was* illegitimate."

"The Barrani do not fuss with legitimacy in that fashion," Teela reminded her.

"I confess I don't understand it; the Barrani inheritance wars are brutal enough when they start that legitimacy would seem to be of paramount import."

"To an outsider, yes. But primacy is decided by power. What I take, I must be able to hold against all. If I am foolish, stupid or incompetent, I will die. The line, however, requires someone who is none of those things. My death might be regrettable, but it would be seen as necessary. And our children are not so numerous that the parentage defines them. The only exception is the lineage of the High Lord— and even in that case, new reigns are ushered in by politics and death in almost all cases."

"Not the most recent one," Kaylin said quietly.

"No. And believe, kitling, that there are lords who have

been working constantly to ensure that the throne is in the hands of a ruthless, powerful man. A different man."

Kaylin frowned.

"Told you," Mandoran said as he turned to Kaylin. "He's been fighting a constant succession war since the death of his father. It shouldn't take more than another decade or two of your time before those challenges wither. Teela assumed you understood this."

"And that has nothing to do with our current predicament." Teela sent Mandoran a death glare; it didn't faze him at all. "You do not know your father. Of your wings, you know only that they are of great import to the Aerian people—but not how or why."

Moran nodded, shaking herself out of the web of memory that Teela's words had evoked. "What was I saying? The *praevolo*. I believe, although again, it's conjecture, that our ancestors did not suddenly find themselves in possession of a miracle baby. *Birth* is not quite the word used, but there's no analogy that I can easily think of in Elantran. Maybe blessing?"

Kaylin stiffened, but said nothing.

"And it's clear, given the stories, that the *praevolo* of that time could both fly—*soar* is the word that is used to refer to him—and fight. His prowess in both was considered proof of the benevolence and love of our gods."

"And their existence, no doubt."

Moran nodded. "I'm not terribly religious."

"You're a Hawk, which requires an entirely different kind of stupid," Mandoran said.

"Mandoran," Helen chided, as if she were his mother.

"Am I offending anyone?"

"In all probability, no," Helen replied. "But you are offending me."

Mandoran went still.

"Hazielle, my first tenant, was quietly and devoutly religious. Kaylin, my current tenant, is devoted to the Hawks. You are a guest here, and greater leeway is given to guests—but you will not insult them."

"I insult Kaylin all the time!"

"He does," Kaylin said, partly in his defense. Mandoran didn't appear to hear her. He was staring at Helen, and Helen—or Helen's Avatar—returned that stare with emphasis.

"Fine," Mandoran eventually said. His voice was all sulkiness, except for the bits that were humiliation. Kaylin wasn't certain this was smart, but even if it *was* her house, she wasn't Helen.

"No, dear," Helen said gently. "But that's why you can be my tenant. I could never live with another presence that was too similar to me."

Mandoran's snort was rude, but wordless. Teela pointedly turned her attention back to Moran. "You think that the *praevolo* was magically created?"

"I think the power of the *praevolo* must have been, yes. We know that a flight's worth of Aerians of both genders went into seclusion. They prayed," she added with a hint of self-consciousness. "Those that were unworthy faced the wrath of the gods."

"They died?"

Moran nodded. "They did not approach the gods with the proper humility and respect," she added. "Believe that I heard this particular story frequently. I couldn't make sense of it until I joined the Hawks. I had no idea how many gods crowded each other for space in Elantra until then." Her gaze darted to Bellusdeo and away. "I didn't entirely understand how dangerous the Shadows could be in a global sense until very recently, either.

"Be that as it may, I believe it was an investiture of power. And it worked."

"But the power isn't conferred that way now?" Kaylin asked.

Moran shook her head. "But it's only the flights of the Upper Reach—or the offspring of those flights—that are born with the wings. It's not a constant; there isn't always a *praevolo*. We went three generations without one. But the birth of one—of me, in this case—implies that their power will be needed."

"Has this proved historically true for the Aerians?" It was Bellusdeo who asked—of course it would be. If the genesis of Moran's damaged wings was related in any way to Shadow, it would suddenly become hugely relevant to the golden Dragon. She had lost a world to those Shadows, and she had the memory of immortals. She did not forget for one second.

"I am not permitted to speak of that."

"You aren't permitted to speak of this, either, if I had to guess."

Moran flashed a wry grin. "Technically, there is nothing in this discussion that circumvents the proscriptions. But… yes. Yes, they've been relevant. I'm aware that the relevance could be entirely in the hands of historians; historians weight everything with their own particular set of observations and meanings. And even if it was forbidden, and my discussion were to be discovered, the hands of the Caste Court are tied. I cannot be made outcaste."

Kaylin had assumed, until this moment, that this was because she was special, that her unique gift granted her immunity to the judgments of the Caste Court. But memories of Lillias, and of Clint's lecture, now blended together with Moran's information.

"They can't cut off your wings."

Moran stiffened. "My wings," she told Kaylin, "are not immune to damage, as you've seen for yourself. They could quite possibly cut off my wings, if they had enough power and the will to do so."

Kaylin felt cold in the brief silence that followed. "The Caste Court doesn't cut off wings."

"No."

"They remove them."

"Yes."

"Magically."

"Yes."

Kaylin's Leontine response was loud and heartfelt. And long.

She wanted to ask if the wings could be put back. If they'd been magically taken off, why couldn't they be magically returned? She wanted to ask *how* the wings were magically removed. How did that work? Could the Caste Court magically remove arms or legs, too? Or were wings like arms and legs? Once they were removed, did they rot?

Bellusdeo, however, had other ideas—and they weren't bad or wrong; they just weren't where Kaylin's head was mired. Kaylin therefore surrendered curiosity and pulled herself back into the discussion at hand.

"Were all such emergencies of, or related to, Shadow?" Bellusdeo asked.

"You mean the ones I'm not supposed to talk about?" Moran replied.

"Their relative secrecy is less of a concern, I admit."

The sergeant grinned. "I confess, Lord Bellusdeo, that you are not like any other Dragon I've ever met. I can't give you a definitive answer, and not because of secrecy. I honestly don't know."

"But they believe—or you believe—that it is involved now?"

"I am not, sadly, in the councils of the Caste Court. If I am not outcaste, I am—what is your word?"

"Pariah?" Mandoran helpfully supplied.

"Yes. I am a relative pariah. Speaking to me will not immediately target an Aerian for Court censure—but befriending me would draw much more attention than the rank and file really want. And don't make that face, Private."

"What face?"

"The one which implies you're about to storm off to the Halls and shout at the closest Aerians."

"I won't," Kaylin told her, thinking of Clint. And Lillias.

"They have families. They have flights. They have, in many cases, children. Their concerns are very correctly with the people for whom they're responsible. I am never going to be one of them." Her voice softening, she said, "And I'm happier that way. I don't want to be the reason their lives are destroyed. They don't owe me that."

"And you don't owe them anything?" It was Teela who asked.

Moran's smile was grimmer. "I'm a Hawk," she said. "There's that, if nothing else."

To Kaylin, being a Hawk was not supposed to be a—a consolation prize. It was more, it was much more, than that.

The tabard, the ranks, the laws, were supposed to be the thing that cut across the racial differences. No matter who, or how, they'd been born, Hawks had *chosen* to serve. To protect. And that service was offered independent of race, to anyone of any race.

"I'm proud to be a Hawk," Moran told Kaylin, as if Kaylin had been shouting out loud. "I wasn't very good at it, at first. As you might imagine, I didn't relish authority. I didn't trust people in power. I didn't trust the people of my own rank— and the Aerians were colder than even the Barrani. But I was determined to show them all. To prove to the doubters that I could, and would, do the work. The same work." She shook her head. "It's hard. The Hawks don't understand what my life has been like."

"Have you ever explained it?" Teela asked.

Moran look horrified at the idea. "And become an object of scorn or pity?"

"It would have the advantage of being based on facts. As far as I can tell, you were already an object of scorn."

"Perhaps. But not pity. Never pity. Do you know what would have happened to the Aerian Hawks if they knew the truth?"

Kaylin said, "Maybe you should let them decide whether or not it's worth the risk." But Clint—and she adored Clint— had made clear that to interfere in Moran's business courted a fate worse than death. And maybe the rest of the Aerians would feel, *did* feel, the same way.

If Kaylin were Moran, and in Moran's position, and that was what she could expect, Kaylin would be damned if she exposed herself to the hope of more. She understood why Moran had remained silent, then. If life was crap, you could accept it. There was no point having a temper tantrum, and in the wrong streets of the city, a tantrum would just hasten your death. You learned to accept what you couldn't change, and you accepted it quickly.

Justice, fairness, kindness—you could rail against the lack of those things in your life. Kaylin knew, because she'd done it. And then, she'd set about trying to survive that life, because justice, fairness and kindness were simply not on the menu anywhere she could afford to eat. Figuratively speaking.

She knew that hope was worse, somehow. If you had hope that things would change, you stood on the edge of a precipice. You stood on the edge of an abyssal chasm. And if hope was betrayed, you ended up worse off than when you'd started.

Yes, she understood.

But she also understood that without hope, without that taking of chances, nothing changed. Nothing could change. It was something she hadn't known when she'd first stepped foot across the Ablayne. It was something she had grown to understand with time.

"You're being arrogant again, kitling," Teela said.

Kaylin blinked. "Me? Arrogant?"

"Yes—in the most well-meaning way possible, but the end result is probably the same. You haven't lived Moran's life, she's not asking for your advice, and you're presuming that you can offer advice that would fundamentally improve her life." Teela's eyes were now blue green. "I personally prefer well-meaning, but would just as soon avoid condescension."

"I never give you advice."

"Exactly."

"It's just that I want—" *To help.* Kaylin bit back the rest of the words. Maybe Teela was right. But she didn't feel powerful enough, significant enough, to *be* arrogant. To be condescending. Awkward, flushing, Kaylin turned to face Moran. "I'm sorry," she said. "Teela thinks I have an obsession with Aerians." It took her another minute to fully meet Moran's gaze.

Moran, however, didn't look offended. Gently, she said, "I'm like the corporal in one regard. I prefer well-meaning. And, Kaylin? The Aerians have taken you under wing—and that phrase has a different meaning for my people. They've been kind to you. They've offered you acceptance, understanding and tolerance. You have no reason to resent them."

"I can't resent them on your behalf?"

"I don't resent them," Moran replied. "And I don't expect them to be perfect. You're already upset at them, and they've done nothing wrong."

"Shouldn't they have to do something *right*?"

"Not according to Imperial Law, no." When Kaylin failed to reply, she continued, "I don't know what your life in the fiefs was like. I've never asked. You don't know what my life in the Aerie was like. You've never asked. You assumed it was like the rest of the Aerian lives. The truth is harder, of course—but I often think we all have harsh, hidden truths. I would never have starved. I was not moved to theft or thuggery simply to keep myself fed or warm.

"I did whatever the Caste Court told me to do. I obeyed them. I tried—for years, I *tried*—to be what they wanted. There was only one thing left in my life that I loved, and I knew what would happen to it if I rebelled. And if I endured every insult, every beating, every ugly half-truth, in order to preserve the things I loved, how can I judge the rest of the Aerians for doing the same damn thing?

"How can I tell them what they *should* be doing instead?

How can I tell them to put their lives outside the Halls at risk when I didn't have the courage to do that myself?"

Kaylin was silent.

"You understand?"

And she did. It was why she still had trouble dealing harshly with beggars and street thieves. She'd been there, she'd done that, she'd been desperate. Were they breaking the law? Yes. On this side of the bridge they were.

She bowed her head a moment, found her voice and lifted it again. "Can we go back to the *praevolo*, or would you rather we not talk about it at all?"

"Let's compromise. Once we leave the dinner table, you never ask me about it again."

"Deal."

Moran then turned to Lord Nightshade. "I don't know how you came by your information, but I'd like to hear what your informant had to say. I consider my own sources to be highly dubious at this point."

"Some centuries ago, I met an Aerian," Nightshade began. "He was dar Carafel, a young man with magnificent wings and a strong dislike for politics. He had had some conflict with his flight, and when that conflict became dangerous, he fled. It was not possible to hide his wings—he was not a mage. Nor had he lived a life in which anonymity was essential. His father was a man of considerable power and considerable expectations.

"A child had recently been born to the flight, and that child possessed pale, flecked wings."

Moran was silent.

"It was, of course, a cause for celebration—but not for the young man. Not for his father. The balance of power had shifted with that single birth. The newborn infant's father gained instant respect and instant political support. The child was an infant, but the wings were significant, as I'm certain you are aware. The father of the Aerian with whom I spoke grew increasingly bitter as the *praevolo* aged. He grew to resent his son for the lack of those wings. I offered the Aerian shelter, and he chose, in the end, to remain within my castle." He glanced at Kaylin.

Kaylin said, "The statuary."

"Yes. What I know of the *Illumen praevolo*, I know from him. It is perhaps textured with his envy and his yearning; to him, the *praevolo* was both exalted and chosen. That child would have a life of luxury, a life of respect, a life of power."

Moran's face was about as expressive as stone, which, in a way, was expressive enough.

"The *praevolo* is born when there is a threat to the flights."

"Was there one?" Moran asked.

"I do not know. If there was, it was never large enough to be made public."

"What was his name?"

There was a long pause. "Karis."

Moran's eyes widened slightly.

"We spoke of the *praevolo*, and the significance of the *praevolo*. It was not theoretical, to him. He did not, however, understand all of the specifics. There were items that were associated with the *praevolo*; they had the weight of the Emperor's crown, to the Aerians."

Moran nodded slowly.

"You do not possess them?"

"I was a child. I was an illegitimate child. Nothing of the *praevolo*'s was given to me." She hesitated.

He marked it.

"Nothing of significance."

He nodded, then. "Your legitimacy has been questioned."

"Yes. Constantly."

"And you were not given the opportunity to prove your legitimacy."

"Oh, I was," was her bitter reply. "But never, ever publicly. The Caste Court did not know of my existence until I was almost seven. They were deeply suspicious of me, of my mother, when I finally came to their attention, and they tested me. Thoroughly." She looked down at her hands. "I wish I had had a chance to speak with your Aerian. I would have told him what life as *praevolo* was actually like."

Nightshade's smile was slender, but genuine. "He grew less unhappy with the passage of time." He rose; he hadn't eaten much. He bowed to the table, and to his brother. "It is late, and I am expected at the castle. It was an honor to meet you."

CHAPTER 6

Breakfast, the meal that Kaylin was never allowed to skip, was waiting. Moran had already come down from her room, and was speaking quietly to Annarion, of all people, when Kaylin entered the dining room.

"Where's Mandoran?"

"He should be here shortly." It was Helen's disembodied voice that answered. "There was a minor accident in the training room this morning; I have been making adjustments."

"Did it hurt him or you?"

"We are both quite fine," Helen replied, which wasn't much of an answer. But Kaylin had come to recognize that tone of voice. It was the only answer she was going to get.

Kaylin started to sit, but Helen interrupted her.

"Teela's coming to the door. Tain is with her. Shall I let them in?"

"Yes, please."

Helen appeared at the door to the dining room less than five minutes later, slightly in front of Teela and Tain. "Mandoran asks me to tell you that you will have to leave without him. He should be able to accompany you on the morrow."

"What, exactly, did he do?"

"He tried to walk through a wall," Annarion replied.

"Let me guess. He didn't bounce."

"No. He did some damage to the wall, and some to himself, but managed to separate the two before more serious injury could occur."

"Why in the hells was he trying to walk through a solid wall?"

"Curiosity. He's been playing with shape, form and solidity. We can't do it outside, at the moment."

She stared at Annarion. "Are you telling me you *can* do it inside?"

"I can't."

"But Mandoran can."

"Yes. But Helen says he's practically screaming *look at me* while he does it. But louder. He hasn't tried it outside of Helen's borders. And he won't," he added quickly. "But he wouldn't have had the mishap if he weren't trying to do it silently."

"Why can't you do it?" Kaylin asked him.

"I don't want to try, which is considered cowardly by half our cohort, and sensible by the other half."

"I consider it *extremely* sensible," Teela said. "And I'm sitting right in front of you."

Annarion grinned; Kaylin had no doubt he was passing information to the rest of the cohort, who were across the continent. The grin faded. "My brother will be here later this afternoon. Can I ask you a question?"

Kaylin nodded.

"If he were willing to remove the mark, would you be willing to have it removed?"

"It would make my life in the office a lot easier," she replied, then hesitated.

"But?"

"I think it's saved my life at least twice. Maybe more. I don't know why he marked me. I know it's the mark an *erenne* bears, but I'm still not sure what an *erenne* is. I can't get much of an explanation out of any of the Barrani I know—but I'm guessing it's bad, because they hate the mark. Mostly, they've gotten used to it, though," she added, trying to be fair.

"That's not an answer."

"I have his Name," she replied.

Annarion and Teela both rolled their eyes in an identical grimace.

"Would it be easier for you?" she asked him.

"It would be easier for me if he'd never marked you at all. It *is* comforting to know that it's only the mark, and not the rest of it; that you don't really understand what it means. But, Kaylin—he could have made you understand it. He could make you do it now."

"I have his Name," she repeated.

"One of the reasons Mandoran is willing—more than willing—to tell you *his* True Name is that you're not actually powerful enough to use it."

Kaylin reddened. "I don't think it's about power, per se. And I *have* used someone's Name against them, just...not your brother."

"They were probably trying to kill you."

"It makes a difference?"

"All the difference in the world, yes."

"What I was trying to say was that if he needs to find me, he can. We're connected that way, and as far as I can tell, there's no way to forget a True Name. I don't need the mark for that. Did he offer?"

"...No. I just wanted to know." Annarion rose. "Mandoran is cursing. I'll go and help Helen before he shrieks the walls down."

"Not that I want to defend Nightshade or anything," Kaylin said when Annarion had left the room, "but he had to survive centuries without his brother. He was outcaste. Is outcaste," she corrected herself. "It's not possible to be perfect for centuries. I can't even manage it for a day."

"An hour," Teela corrected her.

"You know what I mean."

Teela nodded, grinning; the grin faded as she considered Annarion. "It's not enough for Annarion that his brother hasn't harmed you. You hate the fief of Nightshade and what it meant to you. You particularly hate it now that Tiamaris has set up shop in the neighboring fief. You were afraid of the fieflord when you lived in his fief. You were terrified of the Barrani who served him. You had every reason to be both.

"Annarion is disillusioned. If you believe that that makes no difference to Lord Nightshade, you fail to understand the kinship they had in their youth. It's not your fight, Kaylin. It's not your responsibility. Nightshade *is* guilty of everything that has so disappointed his younger brother. Youngest brother, and only surviving one. So many of us," she added, voice softening as she fixed her gaze on the flame of a candle at the center of the table, "slip away from the ideals and the dreams of our youth.

"Many of my kin are raised without them. My mother—" She shook her head. "Those ideals, those beliefs—they're tested. They're broken. We accept their loss because we wish to survive. And perhaps we accept their loss because they're onerous, in the end. It is hard to live up to a dream, a day-dream. We surrender, then, the beliefs. We tell ourselves that those beliefs were proof of our naïveté, our foolishness. We deride our youthful selves, because we've faced the reality, the truth. We all do this. You did."

"I—"

"You thought that when you crossed the bridge, when you left the fiefs and the Ablayne behind, you would find paradise. A place where everyone was happy, where people were free, where starvation was impossible, where people would be kind and accepting."

Kaylin flushed and closed her mouth. All of this was true.

"Experience robbed you of that belief pretty quickly."

Kaylin nodded, squirming a bit in her chair.

"Not all of our early beliefs are simple naïveté, simple daydream. But it is sometimes hard to differentiate which are true, or possible. It is impossible for you to have the world-across-the-bridge that you daydreamed of with such visceral longing, because Elantra is occupied by actual people. People cannot be that perfect, even if every one of them had the same dream that you once had.

"We dream smaller dreams," Teela continued. "Nightshade is being reminded, in a way most of us will never be, of what he's lost. No; of what he surrendered. It is not comfortable. And Annarion is coming face-to-face with that loss, as well. The brother of his memories is not the Nightshade of today.

"But it's possible that enough of what Nightshade once was remains, somehow; Annarion believes that."

"You don't."

"No, kitling, I don't. My cohort accepts me because I was their equal, their companion. I was as helpless as they were, and was given as much choice as children generally are in my own future. They didn't dream of me."

"They did," was Kaylin's soft reply. "Terrano came for you. They were waiting."

Teela's smile was pained but genuine. "They didn't dream of me the way Annarion dreamed of his brother. The way any of us dreamed of our brothers," she added, remembering. "Annarion practically worshipped Nightshade in his youth. He knew that Nightshade would not abandon him; knew as well of the bitter, bitter fights between Nightshade and his father. Those fights were not enough to free Annarion, of course; Nightshade was much younger then, and much less powerful.

"Annarion isn't disappointed because Nightshade is outcaste. The Barrani are largely political when it comes to that designation, and some of our historical outcastes have been figures of great drama, great heroics. No, it's what he chose to make of his life, of the fief of Nightshade and even, in the end, of you. You're the harshest divide because Annarion actually knows you. He knows that you freed them—us, really—and that you risked your life, multiple times, to do so.

"He knows about your work with the foundlings. He knows about your work with the midwives. And he knows that being a Hawk isn't just a job for you; it's a vocation. He knows that you're Chosen," she added. "He looks at you, and sees someone who is mortal, but who is trying, constantly, to be more than the sum of her parts.

"And he knows that had his brother *asked* you, you would have done what you could to help."

"Asked me?"

"If Nightshade had told you about Annarion, if he had told you that he suspected Annarion was still alive, if he had told you that so much of his adult life involved attempts to reach him."

"I'm...not sure."

"Ah. A pity. Your opinion is noted."

"I mean it, Teela."

"I'm certain you do. In this, however, I concur with Annarion. Tain?"

Tain shrugged. "Not that I care one way or the other, but Teela's right."

"You have to say that—you're her partner."

Moran, minding her own business until now, jumped in. "I'm not her partner, and I agree with Teela's observations."

"Helping orphans and mothers is *not* the same as helping a *fieflord*."

Teela's eyes were green. She was both amused and relaxed. "Kitling," she said fondly, "there is a reason that people actually like you. To go back to my previous comments about daydreams and harsh reality, you *want* to be helpful. To be kind. You have learned from the things that have hurt you— but you haven't learned the same lessons that either Nightshade or I learned."

"When Nightshade was young, there was no Elantra."

"No."

"And mortals *were* pets. Or slaves." Or worse.

Teela nodded.

"Mandoran still talks about us as if we're trained rats."

"Mandoran enjoys baiting Dragons," Tain pointed out. "If you have to choose a Barrani example of wisdom, look anywhere else."

Bellusdeo snickered.

"My point is, Nightshade didn't make my choices. And Annarion wouldn't have made them either. Whatever he's done, it's what the Barrani of that time *would have* done."

"Yes. But Annarion doesn't see you as mortal, not really. He sees you as Chosen, but more. You held what remained of his Name. Of all of their Names. Only mine was absent. And you returned that knowledge without ever absorbing it first. You did what only the Consort could have done. It is difficult for the rest of them. They're not what they were, and they know it.

"But it's that flexibility that allows the difference in the way Mandoran views you and the way Annarion does."

"He's expecting too much from his brother."

"Of course. But, kitling, would you rather he expected too little?"

She had no answer to that. Breakfast finished; the Moran escort formed up: Bellusdeo, Teela, Tain, Kaylin. Severn didn't show up at the front door. The familiar lounged, as he usually did, across Kaylin's shoulders.

Only when they were at the halfway point between Helen and the Halls of Law did she answer Teela's question. "...I think so."

"You would rather he had lower expectations?"

She nodded, pensive. "It's the expectations that are killing him. Helen says he's very unhappy. I know Nightshade's unhappy as well, but in some ways I kind of feel like he's earned some of that. I *like* Annarion. I hate to see him so miserable."

The usual rejoinder failed to emerge, and Kaylin remembered that Mandoran was stuck in a wall in the basement somewhere.

Four city blocks from the Halls of Law, the familiar suddenly stiffened. He sat bolt upright, and this time, he spread a transparent wing across Kaylin's eyes.

"Moran!"

Moran moved instantly. She also tried to lift her wings, and failed with the injured one. It didn't matter. Kaylin threw her arms around the Aerian's waist.

Teela drew her sword, and Bellusdeo looked up. The

Dragon said, "I'm running out of inexpensive clothing, and I *don't* want to work at the Halls in full court regalia."

"Can you see them?"

The Dragon shook her head. "How many?"

"Three, I think. They're all Aerians, but…but they look funny."

"Funny how?"

Kaylin cursed in Leontine. The three looked down on the city streets, and their formation—and they had been flying in formation—changed. "You know those nets you dropped?" she asked Moran.

"Yes. I need to breathe," she added.

"They're flying with something that looks like those nets. You can't see them?"

Bellusdeo growled. In Leontine. She said something sharp, harsh and syllabic without speaking actual language. The hair on Kaylin's arms and neck stood on end. Magic.

"They're *not* those nets," Bellusdeo said. "We've got to *run*."

"What are they?"

"Shadow," the Dragon said.

It was impossible to run while looking up. It was impossible to run while holding on to someone's waist, if that someone wasn't under the age of two. Kaylin shifted her grip on Moran, holding her hand rather than her torso. She made it a block before she realized that the net itself had elongated as the Aerians had moved. That kind of precision flight-in-place was difficult. Whoever the three were, they were damn good.

She could see that Clint was on the door with Tanner; she could see that the doors were open.

And she could see that the net itself was going to fall regardless. Bellusdeo had said it was Shadow, somehow. It didn't seem to be sentient, or at least it didn't seem to be the type of Shadow that would consume the Aerians holding it.

But those Aerians, she saw now, were wearing some of that Shadow across their arms and chests, as if it were armor.

"Bellusdeo, fly?" she asked of the golden Dragon.

"Run."

The small dragon pushed off Kaylin's shoulders; the minute he did so, she lost all visual impressions of the Aerians and their dark, dark net, as he hadn't left his wing behind. She could, however, see him. He squawked.

Kaylin let go of Moran's hand. Without the small dragon, she had no protection against magic to offer, and Moran, wingless, could still run.

"What is he going to do?" Moran shouted as she sprinted toward the doors of the Halls, and the theoretical safety they provided.

"Hells if I know!" Kaylin shouted back. Teela could outpace her, as could Tain. Bellusdeo deliberately pulled up the rear, and Kaylin let her. She was displaced, yes—but she was a Dragon. A single Dragon was more than a match for anything the Barrani could do; Kaylin suspected she was more than a match for anything Shadow-enhanced invisible Aerians could do, as well.

She hoped.

Clint and Tanner let them in; Tanner headed in after them. "What's going on?" he demanded—of Kaylin, of course.

"We've got invisible assassins," Kaylin replied. "Aerians. Three, in the air." She started to add more, but was cut off by the very audible sound of screaming. This was fine, because the very audible screaming caught Tanner's attention in a stranglehold, and he headed back out.

Clint was cursing in Aerian. "Sergeant!"

To Kaylin's surprise, Moran turned immediately.

"We've got Aerians in trouble." He pointed.

Two of the three Aerians were visible. And they appeared to be injured enough that flight was causing them difficulty. The third, however, was nowhere in sight.

Moran, tight-lipped and incredibly grim, watched them falter. "It's Caste Court business," she said, voice flat and hard.

Clint opened his mouth. Closed it.

"I mean it, Clint. You call out the Hawks to aid in any way, and you're interfering in Caste Court politics—which is far, far above your pay grade." She looked out the open doors, and added softly, "And if you bring them in here, you'll probably be causing a breach of integrity in our security that will bust you down to an even lower pay grade."

Tanner, however, had done whatever it was that the guards on door did when they needed backup *right now*. Aerians filled the sky directly in front of the Halls; they saw immediately what Clint had seen.

Moran bowed her head in resignation. "Private. Lord Bellusdeo."

"Infirmary?" the Dragon asked.

"Yes. I'm sorry."

"I'm not," the Dragon replied. "There are two possibilities here. One: they did not consent to the use to which they were put. Two: they did. I'll agree with you on one thing, though: I wouldn't have them brought into the Halls. You might want to speak to whoever's in charge. Now."

Moran went to the infirmary. What she'd said to Clint was true, and it was all steel, all iron will. There had been anger in it. But the Hawks had flown to the aid of the Aerians, and the Aerians had been injured; they would bring them—bar interference—to Moran.

And Moran, Kaylin understood, would hold her nose and help. It wasn't her job. The infirmary was for Hawks, not random civilians of any particular race or political stripe.

"I don't see why we have to help them when they were trying to kill you."

"We don't know that," Moran said, voice stiff. "The rest of the Hawks didn't see what you saw. Hells, *I* didn't see it, either. They saw injured Aerians—"

"Who appeared out of nowhere?"

"Carrying Shadow nets as an act of benevolence and aid," Teela added, with just as much sarcasm as Kaylin felt.

"I'm not sure the nets were meant for me." Moran cast a guilty glance at Bellusdeo. It bounced off.

"I'll be back," Kaylin told them.

"Where are you going?"

"Hawklord."

The Tower doors were open by the time Kaylin had run up the stairs, which was unusual but appreciated. The Hawklord was standing in the Tower; the Tower's aperture opened to morning sky. Even from the door, Kaylin could see Aerians flying in numbers too great to be simple patrols.

She saluted as she entered and came to stiff, almost vibrating, attention.

"What," he asked, hierarchical preamble forgotten, "has happened?" He didn't say *what did you do this time*, but his tone—and his glare—implied it. He didn't give her permission to relax her stance, and she considered remaining at attention, but he sounded annoyed and very tired.

She told him as concisely as she could, staring at a spot just past his left shoulder.

"…I see. I believe you have a visitor," he added.

The familiar came fluttering down through the open aperture to land more or less on her shoulder.

"Did you have something to do with the current emergency?" the Hawklord asked the small dragon. The small dragon huffed, squawked and settled.

"That's a yes," Kaylin translated.

"Did you ask him to intervene?"

"No, sir."

"He did it on his own?"

"Yes, sir."

"Invisible Aerians. Shadow nets."

"Moran said—" She reddened, and corrected herself. "Sergeant Carafel said that we've got no proof they meant to kill her." She hesitated, and then added, "It's possible the net was meant to slow the Dragon down. Last time—"

"I am aware of what occurred." He pinched the bridge of his nose. "Very well. Have the Barrani thoroughly inspect the injured before they are relayed."

"Why don't we just send them to the cells? We can offer medical help there if it's required."

"What a clever, intelligent idea. I'm certain it's one that would never have occurred to any of your commanding officers on their own."

Kaylin kissed corporal goodbye for another promotion cycle.

"Join the Barrani in their inspection," he continued. "If you notice anything out of the ordinary, report it immediately. To me," he added.

Marcus was not going to like that.

Severn met her in the office as she headed to the front doors, and fell in beside her. She filled him in as she jogged. He stopped to unwind his weapon chain. When spinning, it was proof against a lot of magic. Among other things. He caught up as she hit the streets. The Barrani had clearly been alerted by mirror before she'd made it down the Tower stairs. Teela was there, as was another of the human women—Rakkia. Tain and Rakkia's partner stood back, armed and silent.

Teela met Kaylin's eyes, shook her head slightly. Rakkia said, more pragmatically, "I see nothing." She stepped out of the way as Kaylin approached the Aerians and stopped.

"What—what did you *do*?" she whispered at her familiar. She might have shouted, but for the moment, shock had robbed her voice of strength.

The familiar crooned. He set a wing, gentle this time, against her eyes.

She saw nothing at all out of the ordinary. No Shadow. No weird nets. No strange armor. But she saw normal wings. The familiar lowered his wing, and she saw very damaged wings. She'd seen Aerian wings take injury before. This was nothing like that.

"Kitling."

Ignoring this, she poked the familiar, who lifted his wing again, sighing loudly enough to tickle her ear. The familiar then lowered his wing as she approached the Aerians. They were male, and given their build, younger than most of the Aerian Hawks; they hadn't developed the training muscles the Hawks had. They were shades of brown, paler than Clint, and their eyes were decidedly blue, but no surprise there.

They were conscious, but mostly silent, except for weeping. The weeping made them seem younger than they probably were; they huddled together in pain. Or in terror. She wanted them to *be* terrified for one long minute. She was certain that the net they'd carried would have done Bellusdeo or Moran no good whatsoever.

But she'd always had a problem with tears.

"They've spoken some Aerian."

"Anything intelligible?"

"Yes and no." She glanced at the Aerians who were almost literally hovering on the periphery of a wide circle. "They're terrified. They're begging us not to take their wings. More or less. I didn't understand the last phrase. Clint translated."

Kaylin cringed.

"Half the Hawks are disgusted." By which she meant the Aerian Hawks, because the Barrani Hawks were clearly *all* disgusted. "Are they clean?"

Kaylin hesitated.

"You'd better be certain they've got no magic on them," Teela said. "And soon. The Hawklord is probably going to descend any minute now, and he's not in the mood to have to wait for answers."

"He told me to report to him directly if there was a problem."

"Yes. Directly will be to his face in probably three minutes or less."

Kaylin took advantage of the three minutes, focusing on her work. She did find time to utter a loud Leontine phrase, but that was as natural as breathing. The familiar squawked at her, and she sighed. "Yes, please."

He obligingly lifted one wing in what was almost a caress. Or a sympathetic pat on the head. He covered only one eye. She looked through both, closing one or the other as it became necessary.

In winged view, the Aerians looked normal. They were obviously in some pain, but given what they had probably been attempting, she considered that deserved. It was the unwinged view that was disturbing. They were *missing* feathers. They were missing some essential parts of their winged anatomy. She didn't know very much about the anatomy of wings, but these ones didn't appear to be recently injured. There's no way they could have flown with them. "Clint."

He came to her, wary now. She hated it. She understood it—he'd made it perfectly clear—but she hated it. It made her aware of the vast gulf that separated them; the Hawk they wore wasn't enough to bridge it. Not today.

"Can they fly?"

He looked at the ruins of their wings. "In an emergency, they could land," he finally said. "They cannot fly." But his expression was shuttered; it was wrong. There was pity, yes, but something else, as well.

She studied their wings through the wing of the familiar. She looked at the feathers, the ridges of their wings, the things that were missing in this world. She turned to look back at Clint; he looked the same when viewed through either eye.

Frowning, she asked, "Clint—could they *ever* fly?"

"...I'm not a doctor. But no. No, I don't think so."

Kaylin glanced up at Teela. "I wish Mandoran were here."

"You've lost your mind," Tain snapped. He might have said more, but Teela turned to look at him, and he fell silent. If it was a grudging silence, it didn't matter.

"I believe he sees what you see. It's not, however, standard magic."

Bellusdeo, silent until then, said, "It is Shadow magic."

Teela was right. The Hawklord landed five seconds later. He barely glanced at Teela, but did demand a report. The Barrani Hawk's voice was toneless as she described the events she'd personally seen. Since she'd more or less seen nothing until the familiar had taken to the sky, her part was

pretty simple. But the Aerians had appeared shortly there-
after, struggling to stay aloft, all thoughts of possible assassination or capture forgotten in their desperation to touch
down the right way.

The Hawklord approached them.

The two huddled together like frightened children.
"How," he demanded, "were you able to fly?" He spoke in
Aerian, his voice a crack of brief thunder. His eyes were blue;
they matched the eyes of his prisoners.

The prisoners remained silent, their wings—what remained of them—drawn tightly to their backs in either fear
or deference. Or both, since one was often a product of the
other. It was clear that they had no intention of answering.

"What is your flight?"

Silence again. Other Aerians had joined the Hawks on
the ground, and one or two were looking at the prisoners
the way Clint had—but not all of them. Interesting. Clint
knew, or thought he knew. But so did the Hawklord. She
wondered how political this was all going to get.

"Are they a threat in their present condition?" the Hawklord demanded. The general consensus among those who
could detect telltale traces of magic was no. The Hawklord
therefore turned to Kaylin, blue-eyed, almost quivering with
what Kaylin assumed was rage. She had never seen his wings
so combat ready, so rigid, as they were now. No wonder the
two men were terrified.

Kaylin said, "I think they're safe."

The familiar whiffled.

"Is that a yes or a no?" she asked him as quietly as she
could, and with no hope at all that it would go unnoticed.

"You are hesitating."

"Yes, sir."

"Why?"

The familiar lowered his wing and hissed. He was laughing.

"I don't understand what I'm seeing," Kaylin began. "But...you know how the familiar's wing works, right? Well, according to what I'm seeing through his wing...there's nothing wrong with the wings of these Aerians."

"And as a healer?"

CHAPTER 7

Kaylin blinked. This was not a subject that came up often, and never in full view of the rank and file, unless the only rank and file present was Kaylin herself. She swallowed. She looked at the terrified Aerians and had no desire at all to touch them.

"Can you ascertain whether or not what you see is relevant to us?"

She swallowed.

"Private."

Rolling up her sleeve, she exposed the ancient bracer that had been a gift—a dire, mandatory gift—from the Imperial Court years ago. She wasn't, in theory, allowed to take it off. In practice, it inhibited the use of the magic that had become hers when the marks that covered so much of her skin had first appeared.

The Emperor who had issued the orders was in the Imperial Palace. The man who was responsible for her livelihood was standing a couple of feet away, wings spread and eyes a study in fury. She took the bracer off. Severn took it before she could toss it over her shoulder.

The captive Aerians regarded her with both hostility and

fear. At the moment, she deserved it. She wondered if this was how the Tha'alani felt. Healing was not supposed to be invasive or unwanted.

Clint came with her, as did Severn; weapons were leveled at the Aerian prisoners, the warning in their presence clear, but unspoken.

She reached out and very gently placed a hand on the forehead of the slightly older man. His wings were as they appeared through normal vision. They weren't the result of an old injury. They were his body's actual shape.

Kaylin couldn't give sight to the blind or hearing to the deaf, unless either condition was caused by an injury that had occurred fairly recently. She withdrew her hand and touched the second man, who was staring up at her in misery. Like the first man's, his wings were complete in their damaged form.

These two hadn't flown in a long time, if ever. Until today.

"They're clean." She turned to the Dragon. "Whatever you sense, I don't. Shadow?"

"Not now, no. But it was faintly tangible when they were invisible." Her eyes were a very vivid orange; they hadn't yet descended into red, but it was a close thing. Bellusdeo's experience with Gilbert had softened some of the edge of her hatred of Shadow—but it was a pretty hard edge, and the blunting wasn't terribly obvious at the moment.

"Is it possible that the Shadow formed wings?"

"Clearly. You think the wings are still present."

"Yes, but I don't understand how. Maybe it's an afterimage, an aftereffect."

"Lord Bellusdeo." The Hawklord's terse voice interrupted what might have become a rather long-winded theoretical magic discussion. "Do you feel that the threat of Shadow incursion is present? The Halls are very heavily protected against magic we understand, but they are not a Tower otherwise."

"I wouldn't take the risk," Bellusdeo replied in Elantran. "Would you have any objections if I roasted them for the sake of certainty?"

"Yes. You consider it an actual risk?"

"I consider it a theoretical risk. Shadow magic is chaotic and unpredictable; we could defend against much of it, but it's always more inventive when it pairs itself with the living." She looked vaguely disgusted. She didn't, however, breathe fire.

The Hawklord appeared to be considering a matrix of unpleasant possibilities. "Very well. Take them to the holding cells."

"Weren't you supposed to be in the infirmary?" Teela asked the gold Dragon once the Hawklord was safely out of hearing range.

"I considered this to be the greater danger to Moran," Bellusdeo replied. "Also, I'm not on the payroll."

"Fair enough."

Kaylin glanced at Clint. Some of the other Aerians' eyes had shaded into a more natural gray. Not Clint. His eyes were still blue. He wasn't as angry—or as combat-ready—as the Hawklord had been, but he was close. Kaylin wondered if anyone was going to use the front doors today if they had any other choice. She certainly wouldn't.

Kaylin, Bellusdeo and Severn made their way to the infirmary and found Moran behind a locked door. The door was unlocked after some muffled conversation, which, on Moran's part, included a few choice Leontine phrases.

Kaylin forgot what she'd been about to say when she saw Moran's eyes. They were a pale shade of blue, too dark to be gray in any light. It was a color she hadn't seen all that much of until after the attack on the High Halls; she knew it now as sorrow, the natural response when people you respected and fought beside had perished.

Moran said quietly, "I've applied for a leave of absence."

It almost broke Kaylin's heart. Her mind, however, was still intact. "Did you recognize them?" she asked.

Moran said nothing.

"Kaylin," the Dragon said, putting an arm around the Hawk's shoulder. "Perhaps now is not the time."

But the answer was clearly yes. "They're in the holding cells," she told Moran. "Unless the Caste Court demands their release, that's where they're probably going to be staying. Moran—who are they?"

"I don't know them personally," she replied, ill at ease. "And it's going to be complicated for the Caste Court now. If the existence of Shadow spell or augmentation is proven, the Emperor will…not be pleased."

"The Emperor."

"The Emperor who created the laws of exemption, yes. There are strict limits to those laws, and for reasons that are obvious, they don't apply to the use of, or the contamination of, Shadow."

Bellusdeo said a single word—in native Dragon. It was only one, but Kaylin's ears were ringing, and the rest of her body was shaking. Dragon was simply not useful for communicating with people who didn't have ears of stone or steel.

The familiar squawked at the Dragon in mild annoyance. Kaylin lifted a hand—quickly—to cover the familiar's mouth. "No more native Dragon," she told Bellusdeo. "I actually need my ears." To Moran, she said, "The Emperor is coming to dinner tomorrow."

The blue of sorrow gave way to the purple of surprise,

which then gave way to a bluish gray that was probably as calm as her eyes were going to get this morning.

"If you take a leave of absence, will you stay with Helen?"

Silence.

"Because if you think you're going back to the Southern Reach, you can forget it."

"Kaylin," Bellusdeo said in warning.

Kaylin folded her arms. "If there's Shadow in the Aerie, and the people *using it* are trying to kill you, the Aerie isn't safe for you. And that would be fine—it's your life."

"Thank you," was Moran's somewhat sarcastic reply.

"But Shadow doesn't generally pick and choose. These Aerians—the ones in the holding cells—are involved. Do you honestly think that other Aerians won't be? If you're with Helen, nothing can hurt you—but all the attempts will be concentrated on *Helen*. No one within her walls is going to fall to Shadow. No one is going to become collateral damage. If you're in the Aerie—"

Moran lifted a hand. "Those Aerians are already collateral damage."

"I think they had some choice in the matter."

"Do you?"

Kaylin started to speak. Stopped.

"Did you have a choice when you were thirteen?" Moran continued.

Silence. Kaylin hated the reminder of the life she'd left behind. She hated the reminder of the harm she'd done in both desperation and fear. The only thing she'd seen was the need to survive, and survival had been brutal and ugly. Only when she'd given up entirely on survival—when life itself had become so crushingly ugly she believed she was better off dead—had she changed.

It hadn't been an act of courage.

It had been the ultimate act of despair. And even then she hadn't had the determination to end her own life. She had come here, to the Halls of Law, with every expectation that her life would be ended for her.

"…No," Kaylin finally said. "Not if I wanted to survive." She wanted to turn and leave—it's what she would have done a handful of years ago. She was awash in that particular form of self-loathing that was guilt. But she shouldered the weight; she'd started this, even asked for it in some fashion. "I expected better of the Aeries than the fiefs."

At that, Moran sucked in air, and Kaylin winced; she'd spoken the truth, but not with any particular care. "Frightened people," the older Aerian eventually said, "are the same everywhere. It looks different, but it's not." She turned away. Turned back. "But your point is taken. If my leave of absence is granted, I'll remain with Helen." She then looked past Kaylin to Severn. "Are my services going to be required?"

"The assailants don't appear to be injured. According to Private Neya, there were three; only two are currently in captivity."

"The third?"

"He must have escaped. I don't know what happened—small and squawky flew up, and two of them fell down. The third, he might have missed."

"What did he *do*?"

"…I don't know."

"The Hawklord's going to demand an answer. How does 'I don't know' generally work out for you?"

Not particularly well. "It's the truth. It's going to have to do. I don't know. I didn't see what happened. If I had to guess, I'd say that two of the Aerians are naturally close to flightless. Magical alterations were made—somehow—that allowed them to fly. The familiar did something to dispel that magic."

Squawk. The familiar was bouncing on her shoulder, having abandoned the lazy sprawl.

"If that's the case, it implies that Aerian number three didn't require alteration in order to fly. He or she merely required it to be invisible."

Squawk squawk squawk.

"Your familiar agrees," Bellusdeo said quietly. "You're making your thinking face."

"It's just..."

"Yes?"

"If I'm looking at them through his wing, the wings look whole. They look healthy. They *don't* look like little extensions of Shadow or whatever it is. The net they were holding? That screamed Shadow. But the wings don't. I think that the physical container for the power of flight was created, but it doesn't depend on Shadow to work."

"Meaning?"

"I think they could fly again. But I don't understand how. The lack of relevant parts in their natural, normal wings is real, it's physical. This is like—it's like someone found the phantom arm that people who've lost an arm feel, and they figured out how to make it temporarily solid."

Moran said a lot of nothing.

Kaylin wasn't certain what she would have said if given enough time, because the mirror went off. The infirmary had a rather large one. It was *not* quiet.

"Sergeant!" An Aerian appeared in the mirror, in a poorly lit room. Light was incoming, and behind him, Kaylin could see the dark red of blood.

Moran's eyes shifted to blue. Not purple. She wasn't surprised at all. But she was bitterly, bitterly unhappy. Kaylin, who had just felt the uncomfortable, ugly rush of guilt, recognized it when she saw it on another face.

All the things that she could tell herself but couldn't quite believe rushed up, because if she said them to Moran, they would be *true*. Nothing in Moran's expression allowed for any attempt at comfort. Kaylin's jaw snapped shut.

Moran's assistant entered the infirmary in his on-duty clothing. Kaylin wondered briefly where he'd been. She didn't like any answer she could come up with, and didn't ask. Moran waited for the assistant—a lowly private, just as Kaylin herself was—to pick up a large, heavy bag.

She looked far more like Red going out on a premorgue assignment than she did a doctor. Red, on the other hand, carried his own bag; he considered privates in general too careless.

The holding cells were crowded. The Hawklord had either not returned to his Tower, or had descended from it again. Barrani Hawks—Teela and Tain among them—were on *guard duty*. The only Aerians present were the Hawklord and Moran.

And the bleeding Aerians who had been deposited here.

Moran's Leontine was impressive, but she didn't slow down for it; she sped up. Her private, understanding instantly, sped up as well; Kaylin and Severn stepped out of the way to let them pass.

Kaylin almost couldn't understand what she was seeing. Almost.

But when she'd been fourteen—or fifteen, the years blurred a bit—and a mascot, not an actual full-fledged private, the Hawks and the Swords had, between them, managed to capture a Barrani criminal. He was wanted for a number of petty crimes, mostly involving drugs and prostitution. He had been taken to the holding cells, and he had been restrained; Barrani had been sent to guard him because mortal guards wouldn't cut it.

He had died.

Restrained as he was, he could have put up a struggle against mortal guards, excepting only Leontines, and since there was only one of those and he was a sergeant, he was definitely not on guard duty. He'd had no chance at all against Barrani.

It had caused the ugliest rift in the Hawks Kaylin had, until that point, seen. She'd seen impressive rivalries for things ranging from chairs, desks and pencil acquisition—but those rivalries had been, at base, friendly. The death of the Barrani prisoner—the helpless Barrani prisoner—had changed that. It had driven a wedge of fury, contempt, and not a little fear, between the Barrani Hawks and their mortal counterparts; it had made race an issue even if, in theory, they were all equal when serving the Imperial Law.

Not everyone was upset about the death—but enough were. Enough had been.

Petty Barrani criminals weren't Aerians. Kaylin held her breath, reaching for her wrist. She'd already removed the bracer. She didn't look to the Hawklord for orders. She didn't look to Moran. She particularly avoided looking at Teela and Tain. She was *certain* they hadn't killed the Aerians. And she was certain the Hawklord already knew who had. After the death of the Barrani, Records captures became mandatory for each of the holding cells that were in use.

"Private," the Hawklord said.

Kaylin ignored him. She knelt across from Moran and her infirmary assistant. One Aerian was dead. Just...dead. His throat had been cut, and he'd been stabbed in the chest, close to, if not through, his Aerian heart.

She placed her hands on the forehead of the second Aerian. He was—barely—alive. Everything was on Records. Everything. And that didn't matter. It wasn't as if the Hawks didn't know she could heal. It wasn't as if the Hawklord didn't. The Emperor was aware of her abilities. Were they legal? No. But she could figure that out later.

She sent the healing power of the marks on her skin out, into the wound. Someone had slashed his throat as well, but not deeply enough. They hadn't taken the time to stab him through the heart, possibly because they didn't have that time. It was the only thing she was grateful for. She heard Moran barking orders and felt a twinge of sympathy for the private on the receiving end. Belatedly, she hoped that private wasn't actually her.

The familiar was crooning, a wordless sound that almost managed to be musical, if music was slightly flat and occasionally squawky. She listened as she felt the wound begin to close.

"Enough, Kaylin," Moran said quietly.

"He's lost a lot of blood," she answered, without opening her eyes.

"We're aware of that. He'll survive on his own now."

"I can—"

"You'll be flat on your back for at least three days, according to Teela. You've done enough."

"But—"

"Hawklord's orders," Moran added.

Kaylin was grateful that she was only a private by the end of that grueling day. The office was in an uproar—but Hawks in uproar generally gave very strong meaning to the words *deafening silence*. There were always exceptions, but for the most part, Marcus was in low-growl mode all day. It wasn't considered wise to interrupt that or, more precisely, to draw his attention when he was in that mood.

Because she was only a private, she had no idea who had murdered one of the two prisoners and almost killed the other. The Records of cell captures weren't considered of relevance to privates. Or corporals. Or possibly even sergeants. They were above Kaylin's pay grade, and for the long, long hours of that day, she wanted them to stay that way enough that she could ignore the insistent *who would do this* that rattled around her head. Someone had just thrown away his career, and quite possibly his freedom, in order to ensure that the assassins never had the opportunity to talk.

Bellusdeo remained in the infirmary—on the inside, near Moran. Teela and Tain took up positions on the outside of the infirmary door, by command of their very growly sergeant. The surviving prisoner had not regained consciousness by the end of the day.

Kaylin and Severn weren't in the office for most of that day, though. They were out patrolling Elani Street. It was the first time in a long time that Kaylin appreciated petty fraud. She didn't even grimace when she caught sight of Margot on the way to Evanton's storefront.

"I don't mean to be offensive," Grethan said a moment after he opened the door, "but you look awful."

"It's been that kind of day. Is Evanton in?"

"He is. I don't think he was expecting you, if that's any comfort."

"Some," Kaylin admitted. She frowned. "*I* look awful, or *we* look awful?"

"Severn kind of looks the same as he always does. You look—"

"Awful. Just me."

Severn shrugged, fief shrug. "I didn't say it," he pointed out when she glared at him. "I haven't been a Hawk for nearly as long as you have. Before I joined the Hawks, I was a Wolf. We don't have an office the way the Hawks or the Swords do. We don't serve the same function. A death in the holding cells might *be* one of our assignments."

"It would never be a Wolf assignment."

"No?"

"They don't call in the Wolves if they can actually *put* the criminal in question *in* holding cells." She exhaled. "Sorry. You're right. But—it brings up all the old stuff. It reminds people of the last time. It's just—" She shook her head. "I don't want it to be an Aerian. I don't want it to be anyone in the Halls."

He was kind enough not to point out that the Hawklord probably already knew who the killer had been. Her ignorance at this point was irrelevant; it was pointless to cling to it. She knew it, and hated the whine that underlay her thoughts. But the hells with it. She'd let her ignorance go when she was good and ready. Or, more likely, when the Hawklord was.

She headed toward the kitchen, in serious need of cookies. Severn followed. Evanton was seated at the table, his apron a bit grimy, his expression a match for Kaylin's. They eyed each other warily. Since it was Evanton's shop, his bad moods took precedence over hers when all things were equal. Other than that, they shared.

"I have had two visitors today," Evanton said, going first. "Both Aerian, oddly enough."

"We had three, but they came together in a single group," she countered.

Evanton pushed the cookie tin in her general direction. "Both of the Aerians were from the Upper Reaches; they were representatives of castelords, or the Aerian equivalent. They felt it necessary to actually threaten me."

Kaylin winced. "So…not very bright representatives."

Evanton's smile was humorless and thin. "No. They were dissuaded from that avenue of communication quite quickly."

"Our visitors didn't bother with the threats or the negotiations. They were invisible, they had a net that appeared— from the ground—to be made of Shadow, and we *think* they were there to assassinate Sergeant dar Carafel."

Evanton winced.

"We managed to bring two of them down. One of them died in the holding cells, and not by his own hand."

"I'm not certain you're allowed to say that," Evanton said. "It's probably a breach of some sort of security or other."

"Probably."

"Do you think these two incidents are related?"

"The assassination and the deaths in the cell?" Kaylin asked in a very *Why are you asking if water is wet?* tone.

"No. The visit to my humble shop and the assassination attempt."

"Oh." She took a cookie. Or two. "Maybe. I was coming to ask you about that."

"Ah."

"This blessing thing that you were asked to craft—does it actually give the flightless flight?"

"Why do you ask?"

"Because two of the Aerians—the ones we caught— couldn't, in theory, fly on their own. Their wings aren't properly formed."

"You think they were deliberately crippled?"

"No. It's not like being outcaste. They *have* wings—but the wings wouldn't support their full weight. They could manage to hit the literal street without going splat. But they couldn't manage to lift off that same street."

"You're certain."

"Yes. Evanton?"

"Yes, Kaylin. That is exactly what the blessing of air does." He rose. "Do you think that the client you met is involved?"

"I wish I could say that hadn't occurred to me," was her stony reply. "But, in fairness, she wanted the *bletsian* for Moran. Who can't fly. I didn't press her for more information; I trusted *you* not to create something that would harm Moran. Now I have to ask—as a Hawk—how many *other* clients you've created these *bletsian* things for. And when."

"I am not the only person who can craft them," he replied, which wasn't much of an answer. "Grethan, tea."

Tea came twenty minutes later. Evanton frowned as Kaylin, in his words, entirely spoiled any appetite for lunch by eating her way through half of the cookie tin. She did, in her own defense, offer cookies to Severn, who took one.

"Aerian mages do not join the Imperial Order. I believe, in the history of the Southern Reach, there was exactly one. It is not," he added, "recent history. The Tha'alani have an affinity for the element of water. It will not surprise you to know that the Aerians have a similar affinity."

"Air?"

He nodded. "Air and fire. The abilities of the Aerians are similar to those of the Imperial mages."

"Have any Aerians ever been Arcanists?"

"Funny that you should ask that question now."

There were whole days when Kaylin regretted getting out of bed. She was torn, though. It was natural to hate and despise Arcanists; you practically lost your badge if you didn't.

She wanted to hate and despise something that wasn't...her own people.

And that was one step too far. She struggled with it, and won, but only barely. On the other hand, barely still passed muster. "Sorry," she told the older man. "I'm right out of humor for funny at the moment."

"I can see that. There have historically been more Aerian Arcanists than there have been Imperial mages."

"Why?"

"Because the Imperium, such as it is, is a largely human endeavor. The Aerians are not at home in halls that were not designed with wings in mind. They can—and do—work within them, but being a mage is not just, or even, office work. They dislike the cramped confines of both space and attitude.

"Arcanists are more racially diverse."

"Most of them are Barrani!"

"Yes. Barrani have a general contempt for anyone who happens to be mortal. They are not Aerians; they are mortals, as far as the Barrani are concerned. But as is the case with the Barrani in other avenues of interaction, power—and money—speak. It is easier to feel at home in the Arcanum than in the Imperium. The Arcanum does not revere Imperial Law."

"No kidding." She exhaled. "Is there an Aerian Arcanist now?"

"What do you think?"

Kaylin's Leontine, mixed liberally with borrowed words from two other languages, filled the small kitchen space.

"You are certain you saw whole wings?" Evanton asked when Kaylin at last stopped swearing and told him, in less colorful language, about the events of the day.

"Yes."

"But only with the aid of your familiar?"

She nodded again. The familiar had taken off, landing, as he often did, on Grethan's shoulders. Grethan had gone in search of food more suited to the small lizard than Kaylin's cookies, or rather, what she thought of as her cookies. "I wonder why he likes Grethan so much?"

"Given your current mood, it emphasizes his intelligence," Evanton replied.

"I thought maybe the wings were Shadow wings, somehow—but that doesn't seem to be the case. The net, though—I'd bet all of last year's pay that it was Shadow."

Evanton was thinking. Loudly. "Might I ask you to do one thing the next time you're with Sergeant Carafel?"

"You want me to look at her wings with the help of the familiar."

"Yes. I think it might be instructive."

Kaylin nodded glumly.

"If the wings somehow represent potential flight, it's possible that Shadow is responsible for the actual flight."

"But—how?"

"It is power, Kaylin."

"It's *Shadow*. Look, fire is powerful, but you can't pour fire into wings and expect to take flight. You can probably expect to be cooked if you're not careful, but that's about it."

"Shadow has always been the most flexible of the potential powers," the Keeper replied, unruffled. "There is a reason that it has been studied; a reason that it has appeal. Shadow is, at base, transformative."

"Yes—but I'm not sure you can *control* the transformation, and for the most part the transformation, all differences aside, is from alive to dead."

"For mortals, yes."

Evanton was mortal. In theory. Or he'd been born mortal. But he'd lived a long damn time, and if he looked ancient to Kaylin, he hadn't aged at all in the years—admittedly few—she'd known him. "How do you know what Shadow does?"

His brows gathered in the *what a stupid question* look he usually threw at poor Grethan. "I've been through several iterations of men—and women—who seek power. Any power. Most of those attempts don't directly affect me, as Keeper. But some—as recent history has proven—have come close to destroying everything. I will allow that if the weapons the Aerians were utilizing were of Shadow, it is highly likely that Shadow was the ostensible *bletsian* granted those who could not naturally fly." He rose. "It so happens I have something for you."

"Lillias's *bletsian*?"

Evanton nodded. "I ask you to wait here while I retrieve it from the garden."

Kaylin nodded. And had another cookie.

CHAPTER 8

When Evanton left, she turned to her partner. "An Aerian Arcanist. Any bets?"

"What are we betting on?"

"Which flight the Arcanist belongs to."

"As long as you're betting against dar Carafel, yes."

Kaylin shrugged. "Shadow as simple power?"

"It's Elani," Severn replied.

"Meaning it's a bill of goods we're being sold?"

"We're being asked to buy. But he's probably not entirely wrong. I don't understand how—or why—the Aerians had Shadow nets. The study of magic related to Shadow is illegal, even in the Arcanum."

"The Arcanists don't follow their own bloody rules. They're certainly not going to follow the Emperor's when they can avoid it."

Severn, however, continued to stare at his hands, as if they vaguely displeased him. She could take a guess at why, but didn't have to waste the mental energy. "Gilbert."

Since this was more or less some part of what Kaylin had been thinking, she nodded, pensive now. "Gilbert's the only Shadow I've ever met who wasn't…"

He nodded, freeing her from the search for descriptive words. "Evanton's not wrong. The first time you really spent time in the garden, it's because an Arcanist—with an Imperial death sentence hanging over his head—tried to co-opt the Keeper's powers in order to change the world."

"To rule it."

"To rule it by changing it. The heart of the elements weren't the Arcanist's concern. The power was. We have evidence—in the form of Leontines—that the powers of creation or transformation used there were, at the very least, susceptible to Shadow."

"You think it's more than just susceptible."

"I think there's a chance that the heart of the power is similar. The Towers were created to stand against Shadow— but the Shadows that have managed to breach a Tower knew what to look for, where to find it, what to do with it. They were trying to transform the Tower by rewriting the words at its core." He was talking about Tara and Tiamaris indirectly.

Kaylin nodded slowly. "But what if the Shadows knew what to do because they've been at war with the Towers for so long? Bellusdeo understands Shadow better than any of us because she lost a world to it."

Severn nodded, allowing the point. The problem was that Kaylin wasn't certain she believed it. Because Shadows—or at least Gilbert—had *words* at their core. Whatever and wherever that core was.

"You remember the Fishmonger?" Severn asked quietly.

Kaylin flinched. There wasn't a Hawk on the force who didn't remember that case, and no Hawk who'd joined the force after the Fishmonger was caught who hadn't been informed. The whole city knew about the Fishmonger. The Swords had been on full alert for almost a month by the time he was run to ground.

As a name for a man who had killed dozens in gruesome, horrible ways, it was stupid. But he'd earned the moniker because of where he'd found his victims, and how. He'd sold fish. He'd sold fish predominantly to the poorer citizens of Elantra, and on occasion, those citizens had vanished.

Parts of their bodies had been discovered *in* the fish, later. The Fishmonger had probably known more ways to kill a man than Red, the coroner, did.

There were still a few cookies left in the tin, but Kaylin put the lid firmly back in place, appetite completely absent. "Why are you bringing him up now?"

"Because he was human. We're human. We're not the Fishmonger. He didn't require magic. He didn't require power—elemental or Shadow or other. He did what he did with what he was born to. The Wolves were hunting him," Severn added quietly. "We had a different view, but we were looking at the same thing: the damage done, the victims.

"Gilbert is, in theory, of Shadow. You felt it the first time you met him. You *knew* it. But he's Shadow the way you and I are human. The Fishmonger was Shadow the way the creatures that come out of Ravellon are."

Kaylin nodded, frowning. "Do you think that Ravellon was like one big holding cell for the criminally insane? I mean, the Shadows? I hadn't really thought of it before now, but maybe it makes sense. Gilbert wasn't what any of us were expecting. I think that hit Bellusdeo hardest. But is it really smart to look at Shadow as if it were fire or water, elementally speaking?"

Severn hesitated. "When elementals are summoned—"

"They're sentient, if they're of any size." Kaylin struggled to catch the rest of the thought. "Shadow might be sentient the same way. But—fire wants to burn things. At any size.

The trick to the summoning is controlling or denying that impulse."

"Water wants to drown or crush things, Air wants to throw things into other things. Earth wants to crush or smother things."

"And you think Shadow is somehow like the elements?" Kaylin asked Severn. Her first instinct was to deny it. So was her second. "Life needs the four elements. If the elements desire destruction when they're summoned, that's sort of understandable. No one likes to be practically enslaved. But what do we need Shadow for?"

"Your guess is probably as good as mine. Maybe we don't need it—but it's possible that the Shadows we've seen are like uncontrolled elements."

"And Gilbert?"

"Doesn't require the control."

She shook her head again. The idea—to Kaylin—was preposterous. If Shadow was like the elements, there should be a single whole Shadow that existed, as the elements did, in the Keeper's garden. Kaylin had spent enough time in that garden to be certain there wasn't.

Evanton cleared his throat. He was standing in the doorway, waiting for a break in conversation. Evanton demanded a lot of patience—it was, he said, simple manners and common sense when dealing with the elderly—but was terrible at actually giving any of it.

Kaylin rose. "Sorry, we were just talking."

"Yes, I noticed. And unlike many of the conversations you have with your fellow Hawks while waiting, this seems to be of actual relevance. I am loath to interrupt you." Which meant, of course, he would. He lifted a hand; draped around his left palm was a slender chain that looked to be made of silver. "This is Lillias's gift to Moran."

"Is Moran going to be angry if I give it to her?"

"That is not my concern. The sergeant is not my customer."

"It's *my* concern," Kaylin said, staring pointedly at the pendant that dangled from the chain. It, like the chain that held it, appeared to be silver; it was, to no one's surprise, a small, stylized depiction of a feather.

"Yes," Evanton agreed. He handed her the item he'd made. "It is. Your problem, that is. If you will excuse me, I have work to do."

The rest of Elani was its usual fraudulent self. The merchants and street hawkers weren't happy to see Kaylin and Severn, but they never were unless discovery of their fraud prompted former customers to get a bit of their own back from the fraud's hide. Kaylin considered this attempt justified, and had pointed out to many that it was a consequence of lying and preying on the foolish dreams of the desperate. The criminals, though, pointed out that this was assault, possibly heading toward murder.

Today, however, no street brawls came to interrupt them. No commotion outside of Margot's. The only people who seemed to want the attention of the patrolling Hawks were people who hadn't seen—or hadn't yet paid attention to—the familiar draped across Kaylin's shoulders. To be fair, when he was like this, he didn't seem to be particularly real. He might have been a very unusual shoulder adornment; gods knew the merchants here sold some very strange ones.

"Where did you buy that?"

Since the answer was complicated, Kaylin didn't bother. "He found me," she said. "And stuck around."

A predictable offer of money in exchange for the small dragon followed, the amount escalating with each refusal.

On Elani Street it was practically criminal to refuse to sell something for the right price. The right price, however, was elusive.

"Please don't tell me that Margot is trying to get our attention."

"I don't think she's trying to get mine, if that'll do."

Kaylin muttered a short Leontine curse. Leontine wasn't really a good language for quiet cursing when on duty. "Can we ignore her? I've had a bad week and I don't want to add to it."

"She probably can't make it any worse."

"She's inventive. She probably can." Kaylin grimaced and gave in to the inevitable. She waited by the sandwich board in front of Margot's window until Margot came out to speak with them.

"I know you're not happy to see me," the redhead said.

Since this was more or less true, Kaylin shrugged.

"I'm not particularly happy to see you, either," Margot continued. "And I seriously considered ignoring your presence—but you didn't trip over my board today."

This made Kaylin flush. "I usually pick it up."

"Your partner usually picks it up," Margot corrected her. She was a very, very attractive woman. Her hair was a bright red, her skin was the type of pale that redheads of that variety usually sported, her eyes—today—were green. They changed color, not with mood, but with money and magical enhancements. Kaylin had no idea what their natural color was.

"I had a new client today."

Kaylin said, "Was he Aerian?"

"Funny you should ask that. No, he wasn't."

"Why is it funny I should ask that?"

"His questions seemed to revolve around Aerians. He was not young," she added, "and he was very, very well dressed. Almost too well."

"Is that even possible?"

"I'm thinking out loud. He was extremely expensively dressed. And I didn't recognize either him or the name he left. He was human," she added, as if this were necessary. It wasn't, really—most of the dupes that came willingly to Elani to empty their pockets were. But Margot's clientele spanned the gamut. One of her clients had once caused Kaylin extreme difficulty, being related to a castelord.

"I'm listening," Kaylin said when Margot paused. Margot didn't usually offer anything like help to the Hawks.

"You're wondering why I've approached you."

"Kind of, yeah. Can we go inside?"

Margot nodded, turned, and led the way in.

"I don't have much time," Margot told them. "I have an appointment later this afternoon."

"With the same guy?"

She shook her head. "With a *very important* client."

"And the rich man wasn't?"

She shook her head again, her gaze falling to the floor. "I'm not sure I'll see him again." She lifted her head and met Kaylin's eyes. "I know you think I'm a fraud. I'm not. Not entirely."

Kaylin nodded.

"Ever since the incident on Elani, I'm less of a fraud." She looked pretty bitter about it, too.

"Let me guess. Most of the people who pay you money don't actually want the truth."

"Got it in one. Look, we all need to eat, right?"

Kaylin said nothing.

"I don't have many other skills. The offers of employ I received when younger would probably curl your toes."

Kaylin said, "I grew up in the fiefs."

"…Or not. Look, I know you don't like what I do. I don't particularly care for what you do while you're here, either. But there are times I'm grateful for the Halls—mostly the Swords—and you could be a lot worse. I've had beat Hawks proposition me—"

Kaylin held up one hand. "I just ate," she lied. She didn't want to believe Margot, and she wanted to have *less* to disbelieve. But the implication that she'd lost her appetite was true.

"Right. The man wasn't asking about Aerians, not specifically. But the answers I received were about Aerians. And Hawks."

"Hawks?"

"Yes. Neither of these are guesses," she added. "I've seen that tabard for all of my tenure on Elani. I know it when I see it."

"And the Aerians?"

She hesitated. "I don't do much business with Aerians, so I don't know a lot about them. I know that they're generally normal people, but with wings attached. The wings differ in color. But I haven't seen wings like the ones I saw in my vision before."

"Go on," Kaylin said, her jaw tensing.

"They were pale, but speckled gold."

The speckles were brown. Kaylin did not correct the description. No one expected information gained in Oracles or visions to be accurate.

"You don't look surprised."

"No comment."

"You do look pissed off." She hesitated. "You want to know why I'm talking to you about this."

"You said that already."

"Yes." Margot exhaled. "I've spent a lot of time to get where I am. I've made my own decisions, my own choices; I have my own money now. I'm not beholden to—to anyone. Got that?"

Kaylin nodded.

"I'm telling you this because of the client. He did—or said—something just as I sat down."

"Show me the room you sat in—if you don't mind. Also, keep talking."

Margot said, "I don't want you to touch anything without my permission. Everything in the room I used is expensive. Everything."

"It's meant to impress the wealthy?"

"Yes. I have another two rooms, both of which see more frequent use. This room is meant to impress." She pointed to a curtain composed of long strands of beads. Or of what appeared, at a distance, to be beads. Margot clearly meant the "don't touch" part; she pulled the beads back to either side of the open arch herself, hooking them carefully in place before she entered the room.

Kaylin slid her hands behind her back and clasped them loosely as she followed.

Kaylin expected the room to be a gaudy, bright den of things—sort of an upscale version of the dust-covered, cobweb-anchored shelves in Evanton's store, but more practical. It wasn't. It was almost austere in its simplicity. There was, of course, a table, and on it a crystal ball, which was a prop for fraud as far as the Hawks were concerned.

Kaylin had visited the Oracular Halls a number of times, all on duty—she knew that Oracles and their prophecies didn't require something as fixed as a large glass ball. Vision was not confined, in Kaylin's experience, to fixed locations. She glanced at the rug, the wall hanging, the painting; she saw a vase, flowers and four chairs, all of which were empty.

The chairs, however, would have been at home in the palace. They were upholstered and very heavy. Margot indicated that the Hawks could sit, but her expression made clear that the chairs were far more valuable than her current visitors. Kaylin declined. It wasn't like she was ever going to be comfortable in Margot's company, anyway.

"First, I want it to be clear that I never talked to you."

"Well, at least it's believable," Kaylin replied. "What made you overcome your normal reluctance?"

Margot's smile was leaden. "I know you believe me monstrous," she said, "and in general I don't care. But the man who came to visit me today was unusual."

"Go on."

Margot turned to the painting on the wall. "Records." It was a good thing Margot's back was turned, because she missed seeing Kaylin's jaw fall open. By the time she turned again, Kaylin was back in control of her face.

What Kaylin had assumed was a painting was, in fact, a mirror. The colors of mountain and city and sky broke into tiny pieces, recombining into an image of this room, and one of the occupied chairs. "This is the visitor."

"Anything unusual about him?"

"Yes—but not visually."

Visually, however, he was impressive. Not a single hair was out of place. If he hadn't so obviously been human, he might have been Barrani. His eyes were a gray blue, which accentuated the subtle ice of his expression. He didn't look familiar to Kaylin, but she understood why Margot had pegged him as a wealthy mark. It wasn't his clothing—although that, to Kaylin's eye, was costly—but his carriage, his demeanor.

He was clearly used to both having power and wielding it to gain obedience.

She didn't like him. Then again, neither did Margot.

Severn was staring at the man.

"Another one of your former clients?" Kaylin asked, half joking.

"I'm not completely certain," was the serious reply.

Margot frowned, but said nothing. Kaylin, however, flinched. "What name did he give?"

"He didn't."

"You didn't ask?"

"Many of my wealthy clients come to me on the condition of secrecy. As long as their gold is good, I don't care what they call themselves, even if it's nothing. I usually recognize them regardless."

"Not this guy."

"No."

"You think he'll be coming back?"

"Not if I have anything to say about it. He came because he wanted the usual glimpse into the future."

"Fine. You intended to peddle something relatively harmless?"

"In legal terms, yes."

"What did you give him instead?"

Margot looked extremely uncomfortable, which didn't suit her. "I sat down at the table," she said, by way of answer. She suited action to words, and sat, her hands in her lap. Closing her eyes, she straightened her shoulders and neck, lifting her hands so they rested palms down on the tabletop. She then lifted her hands, turning the palms in, toward the crystal ball.

Kaylin felt her skin begin to tingle. Magic. It wasn't a strong magic; it was a normal one. The ball itself was likely enchanted. Then again, so were all the streetlamps. Magic was not illegal, Kaylin's frequent, fervent wishes aside. The ball began to glow. It wasn't with the radiance of streetlamps, though. "Is the room usually dark?"

"It's *ambient*," Margot replied.

"So...darker than this."

"Yes." Her grimace ruined the otherwise perfect picture she presented.

"So you set the ball glowing, and...?"

"I could not release it. I couldn't move my hands away from its surface." She did move her hands now, as if testing the ball for defects. "I couldn't stand. I couldn't look away from the ball itself. I think I managed to blink."

Kaylin was now looking carefully at the ball, which appeared slightly magical but otherwise normal. Magic left visible sigils to Kaylin's eye—but only strong magic. This was not strong. "Can I ask you to stand now, please?"

Margot seemed quite happy to be free of the chair, as if describing what had happened was like reliving the experience.

"Anything?" Severn asked.

Kaylin frowned and shook her head. "Nothing that I can see. If there was magic practiced, it didn't require a lot of power. Sorry, Margot. You can sit again if you want."

"I'd rather not, if it's all the same to you."

Kaylin nodded. "So, you looked into the ball as part of your regular routine."

Margot nodded. "I also burn incense during these readings."

"Anything special about the incense?"

"...No." Which meant yes, but Margot was breathing it in as well, so it couldn't be deadly. She didn't like Margot, it was true. She also hated paperwork, and wasn't willing to do it if it weren't for something she considered practical.

"I'm not sure how this normally works," Kaylin continued, because she wasn't. She was often ignorant—which she hated—but didn't consider herself stupid. Spending money in Margot's parlor was stupid. "Did he ask questions?"

"Yes. In general, there's discussion, a building of rapport."

The image of the man—still captured in Margot's personal Records—didn't imply rapport would be particularly welcome, at least not on his part. "Records, reenact," Margot said.

The man in the image began to move. "My apologies, Madame Margot," he said, his voice the type of hard-soft that set Kaylin's teeth on edge. "I have done some research on the various fortune-tellers in Elani—and elsewhere in Elantra. I would not have taken the time to visit you had it not been for one infamous difficulty in the past year."

Whatever Margot had said in response, the mirror that looked like a painting hadn't captured.

"The current custodian of the Oracular Halls, however, is not at all flexible, and any visit to the Oracles requires official Imperial permission. You, on the other hand, are rumored to be discreet. Discretion is a useful trait. I suggest you remember it."

"Is the part where you punch him in the mouth and boot him out of your store coming up anytime soon?" Kaylin asked. The urge to punch his image in the mouth had caused her hands to curl in fists.

"No, sadly. I did say I couldn't move, didn't I?" For the first time, however, she smiled, and Kaylin smiled back.

"I have a few questions that associates of mine need answered. They are currently extremely busy men. I wish you to look at these items, and I wish you to look into your crystal ball. Ah, forgive me," he added. He stood and walked around the table; Records capture was centered on him.

Margot entered the frame as he approached her. She looked

poised, elegant, cool—and annoyed. Kaylin doubted very much that she would have looked half as calm had she been in Margot's position, and a certain admiration tugged at her.

"First." The man lifted a feather.

"Records," Kaylin said. When the man continued to speak, Margot repeated the word, and then returned the capture to the feather. "Enlarge."

Kaylin glanced at Severn. "Did he leave the feather here?"

"No. If you're wondering if it's an Aerian feather, it almost certainly was, given what followed."

"We may have lost a very fine hunting bird," the man continued, when Records capture resumed its play. "We wish to locate it. However, it may prove difficult without more information. This," he said, fishing another item out of an interior pocket, "was the bird's favorite toy. It has been handed down through generations of those who are tasked with the welfare of the breed."

Kaylin *really* did not like this man.

"You'll break teeth if you keep grinding them like that," Margot told her. She ordered another freeze and enlarge, but this time, the object was a bracelet or an armband. It was either meant for large hands or slender arms; Kaylin couldn't be certain. Circular, it appeared to be made of silver or platinum. It contained evenly spaced gemstones of a pale blue color.

"And last." He held up a collar. "Now, I have a few questions I wish you to answer."

"Are *all* your wealthy clients this odious?"

"A handful would probably pass your judgmental muster," Margot replied. "This one, however, was in a class of his own."

"And if word gets out that you turned him in?"

"I'll deny it, of course. The Hawks and I have a known adversarial relationship. Those who matter would believe me."

Fair enough. "I don't suppose you know where he got any of these items."

Margot shook her head, impatient now. Kaylin stared at her, frowning. She glanced at Severn; Severn was paying careful attention to Margot—but almost all men did that. "Records," Margot said.

"I don't suppose you could grant me temporary permission to give commands?"

"What do you think?"

Kaylin poked the familiar. He sat up, growled in her ear—which was practically a new sound—and then looked balefully at the crystal. He ignored the mirror. He ignored Margot. Kaylin paid attention to what Margot was saying in the Records capture playback, but what she now wanted to see was the end of this session, not its beginning.

"It's dark," Margot in the past said. "It's dark, but the sky is clear. Over Elantra, it's blue." This made as much sense as most of what fell out of Margot's mouth. "There are Aerians in the darkness."

"Can you see their wings?"

"I can see that they have them," was Margot's curt reply. Her voice held an edge of something that sounded suspiciously like fear.

Kaylin lifted a hand, and Margot paused playback. "You weren't making that up."

"Good of you to notice."

"You're saying that this visitor somehow compelled you to have a—a vision?" She poked the familiar. The familiar sighed, bit her finger just hard enough to make a point, and launched himself off her shoulder.

Past Margot said, "No."

"How many do you see?"

"Enough that it's difficult to count."

"I will warn you," the stranger said in his velvet voice, "not to lie to me." He walked away from Margot and resumed his seat. Past Margot's voice was clear, but she was no longer visible.

"Dozens," she finally said. "They're not hovering, and they're not flying in the patrol formation. There's also a Dragon."

The man's face became instantly stone-like. After a pause to digest this obviously unwelcome information, he asked, "What color is the Dragon?"

"I'm not certain. I did mention it's dark."

"Is the Dragon gold?"

"No. Gold, I think I could differentiate."

"Take a closer look."

Kaylin in the present said, "Is he an idiot?"

"He doesn't seem to understand how visions actually work, no."

Kaylin would have bet a lot of money that Margot didn't, either, and clearly, she would have lost it.

Past Margot said, "That is not the way visions work. If it was a precise science, the existence of Oracles would have started seven different wars by now."

"Why did he want an Oracle?" Kaylin asked.

"Maybe he wanted to avoid angry Dragons," Margot replied. "I don't know." Margot's response was dismissive, which was typical for her. But the line of her shoulders was a little too high, and her eyes were narrowed in something that wasn't quite anger or hostility, both of which Kaylin knew quite well.

Something was wrong. Kaylin frowned and glanced at Severn. It was brief, but pointed.

Severn walked across the rug, bent, and examined something. The rug itself was a complicated weave of color and pattern. He rose and lifted an arm; the familiar came to land on it, as if he were a kestrel. He then carried the familiar back to Kaylin.

The familiar crooned.

Yes, Severn said, speaking privately, as he so seldom did. Kaylin was mortal. Kaylin had taken a Name—for herself, instinctively—from the Barrani Lake of Life. The only living person who knew it was her partner. The Name was a bridge he seldom crossed. *I think you're right. I think Margot's visitor never left. I'm certain the playback is genuine. I'm certain the visitor did somehow cajole an actual vision out of her. But I think something in that vision involved you.*

Is she likely to survive if we leave? Kaylin glanced, briefly, at Margot.

Would you care? Severn unsheathed his blades. Although the room was large, it wasn't large enough that he could wield the full length of his weapon's chain without lopping off someone's arm or leg.

Yes. If I've managed not to kill her all these years, I resent some stranger strolling in to do it first.

Grab Margot.

You think he'll use magic here?

Probably.

Past Margot inhaled sharply, and both Hawks stopped their discussion as the Records playback demanded their attention.

"What is it? What did you see? What changed?" the man demanded; he'd risen from his chair to lean over the table, staring into the crystal ball as if it could provide answers. As if.

Kaylin headed across the room to the mirror, and stopped at the midpoint between the table and the wall, which happened to be Margot. To Severn, she said, *Break the ball.* To present Margot, she said, "Can you speed this up a bit?"

Margot turned a familiar glare in Kaylin's direction, and the Hawk draped an arm tightly around the redhead's shoulders as Severn brought both of his blades crashing down on the glass orb.

CHAPTER 9

The glass shattered.

As it did, Kaylin felt the uncomfortable tickling across her skin become painful. She didn't otherwise notice. Shards of glass flew outward. By some small miracle—and by small, she meant dragon—none of them hit either Kaylin or Margot.

She felt acutely embarrassed. She'd assumed the crystal ball was a kind of second-rate magic that Margot used to fleece people—and she'd been right, of course. But the ball Severn had just shattered wasn't the one that had originally been sitting on the table. Kaylin was surprised she hadn't seen the difference immediately.

She was also chagrined. Destroying it had been a hunch. Destroying it *intelligently* would have been the brighter move. Severn had one cut across his cheek, but it wasn't deep. And he wasn't bothered by it. He didn't even look. He turned instantly toward the room's fourth occupant.

The man whose visit had been captured in the Records mirror was looking slightly surprised. He was standing in the corner farthest from the door, where no one was likely to accidentally run into him. He wasn't prepared for combat. He wasn't prepared for discovery at all.

Kaylin watched his eyes widen, saw his mouth open, saw his gaze rake Margot's face with slow blossoming fury.

"I didn't tell them," Margot told him, voice cold. "If you recall, I advised you against this course of action. The Hawks are a constant irritant, but they're not reliably stupid." To Kaylin, she said, "I would appreciate it if you escorted this man off the premises."

"How far off?"

"He threatened to kill me. He held me prisoner. He forced me to lure you into my shop."

"Did he?" Kaylin smiled. "He also used magic to control you, from the looks of it."

"That, too."

Kaylin turned to the man in question. Her skin wasn't crawling or screaming in protest, which she would have expected had he been using magic. But her marks were glowing. "Severn."

The man drew a weapon. It was longer than Severn's two blades, double-edged but also faintly curved. Kaylin definitively disliked the look of that blade. "You are very clever," he told Kaylin—but not Severn, who happened to be armed and closer. "But you are meddling in matters you do not understand. Stay on the ground with the rest of the worms; leave the skies to their kin. I will leave now. I will not cause you any trouble—but I suggest, strongly, that you don't attempt to detain me."

"Or?"

"Or you will die."

Kaylin's grin widened. Eyes on the man, she said to Margot, "I'm not sure I think threatening you is a jail-worthy crime. It's got to happen every day. But threatening officers of the law? That's bad." The marks on her arms had passed from a deep gold to the color of aged silver; she could see them through the dark fabric of her shirt. "Hey," she said to the familiar.

He obligingly lifted a wing, and this time didn't smack her face with it before he let it settle across her eyes. She looked through the wing and sucked in air in a way that drew all eyes in the room except Severn's, who was facing the armed man.

She cursed. Loudly. "Don't touch him!" She could see lines of Shadow, like very fine mesh, drawn across every exposed inch of the man's skin. It was probably crawling over the unexposed skin, as well. She glanced at Margot, and saw that Margot wasn't free of that oddly spidery effect, either, although it was much, much sparser.

With the familiar's wing as guide, Kaylin lifted a hand. It hovered over Margot's face, and froze an inch from her skin. She didn't want to touch either Margot or this Shadow.

The small dragon squawked.

"Once for yes, twice for no," Kaylin told him.

He sighed.

"Is the Shadow dangerous?"

Squawk squawk.

"I can touch it safely?"

"What are you talking about?" Margot demanded.

Squawk.

"I think I can see how he controlled your movements," Kaylin told Margot. "I'd like to break that spell, unless you want to be returned to his control in the near future."

With obvious derision, Margot said, "You can break it?"

"I think so."

"I'd rather not be subject to your magical uncertainty. No offense meant."

"None taken. You can visit an extremely expensive mage of your own choosing. I'm not sure he'll be able to help you, but frankly, I can't force you to allow anything, and I don't actually give a rat's ass if you get devoured by Shadow."

"Not likely," Severn said. "It's more likely that she'll walk into a busy street and stand still while she gets hit by a wagon or carriage."

Margot stiffened.

"They don't want you to talk. I'm assuming they wanted something from Kaylin, and I can guess what."

"Fine. *Fine.* But if you screw up, I'll take my complaint all the way up the hierarchy."

"You're welcome," Kaylin said sweetly. She felt herself relax. *This* Margot, she understood. Margot wanting to share information was so foreign it was unbelievable—and actually, it was unbelievable for a reason. Margot did things to protect Margot. Margot did things that were advantageous for Margot.

Margot wasn't particularly grateful that the Hawks had, in all probability, saved her life. Kaylin wasn't entirely certain she was grateful for it, either. But she'd probably hate herself if Margot died. That was the thing about being a Hawk. You couldn't choose. It was probably the reason for the laws as well—the laws defined what was acceptable or necessary. The individual Hawks didn't.

There were no laws about tripping over sandwich boards, though. Probably for the best.

The man snarled. "What are you talking about?" he demanded.

"You're wearing Shadow," Kaylin replied, although she didn't look at him. "You're covered in it. I don't know how you can do it safely—and at this point, I don't care. If you don't lower the weapon and come with us to the Halls of Law—"

"What do you mean, *Shadow?*" His voice had risen in tone.

Kaylin reached up, her eyes still cloaked in familiar's wing, and brushed fingers across the subtle strands of darkness that had settled around Margot's face. She felt no sentience there, although the strands weren't like spiderwebs; they didn't cling to her hand, and they didn't instantly break. They stretched.

Kaylin frowned, and pulled harder. They stretched until they were almost invisible.

"Well?" Margot snapped, sounding actively waspish.

"This may come as a surprise to you, but I don't actually see magic of this type every day."

"Great. You realize I pay taxes?"

"Yes. About half of what you probably owe." At Margot's expression, Kaylin grinned. It was like a smile. Almost. "I checked."

"My taxes are none of your business!"

"Technically, evasion *is* our business, as you put it. And I'm not the one who brought the subject up." She caught the strand, wrapped her hand in it, and pulled hard. This time, it snapped. She was left with a slightly flailing black strand. Margot was left with less Shadow, but pulling one thread hadn't unraveled the whole. Kaylin grimaced, glared Margot into silence, and worked on the rest.

"We'll want the Records capture of the meeting," she told Margot cheerfully.

"And I want to be the Empress," Margot snapped. "These are confidential Records."

"I'm certain you think they are. But we'll have the Records, or we'll have a long, long interview with you in which we try to reconstruct what actually happened." She turned to the man.

He had lowered his weapon and was staring at Kaylin. She asked the familiar to lower his wing, and he did; without the translucent mask, she could see the man's expression. He was pale, a color somewhere between gray and green. His eyes were a bit too wide, and he appeared to be sweating, something she hadn't expected.

"What do you mean, Shadow?"

Shadow meant many things in Elantra. Not a single one of them was good. There were stories about Shadow, and death by same, and in this case, the outrageous stories had something most rumors lacked: they were true. Or rather, they were all possible. And clearly, whatever he'd been told about the power he was exerting, none of it had involved Shadow.

He lowered the blade, kneeling to set it on the floor in front of Severn's feet before he rose again, lifting his hands, palm out, to show that he was unarmed. Technically, this was true. She tapped the familiar's leg, and he raised his wing again, sighing—loudly—in her ear.

"Is it the same?" she asked him.

He squawked—twice.

"Is it dangerous to me?"

Squawk.

She cursed. "Is it likely to kill him?"

Squawk.

She cursed in Leontine. "Fine. Is he actually human?"

Squawk.

"We do not get paid nearly enough for this," she told Severn.

"What are you doing?" he demanded.

"Trying to pull the Shadow off him."

"Your familiar just said—"

"If we're going to take him in—"

"I'll go with you," the man said. "I'll cooperate." She couldn't see his face clearly. Only his eyes were visible when the familiar's wings were high—and they were too white in the ink of his skin. "I was hired—" He stopped speaking. He started to choke.

Kaylin leapt forward, but she was too slow; the familiar pushed off her shoulder. Before she could catch him or stop him, he exhaled. Silver, sparkling steam escaped his open mouth in a familiar, multi-colored cloud. "No!" she shouted.

He squawked.

The man drew breath to scream—and scream he did. She couldn't see what was hurting him. She couldn't see anything out of the ordinary at all with her own eyes. She reached down, opened the collar of his shirt, popping buttons in her haste to give him room to breathe, although she wasn't certain it mattered.

But he *did* breathe. His glassy, wide eyes slowly narrowed. They remained open, but moving. His arms and his legs shuddered, his chest rose. He started to speak, stopped and began to choke again.

Kaylin pulled him up, grabbing his jacket to do so. The familiar circled him, hovering for a moment before he nodded and returned to Kaylin's shoulders. They watched as the man continued to choke; Severn got behind him and aimed several blows at his back, between his shoulder blades. The man began to cough, and Kaylin instinctively moved out of the way as he spit out something dark and wet.

Something visible and familiar.

Margot hissed an exclamation.

The man was too busy regaining breath to do the same, but his eyes once again widened as a small, dark, opalescent pool began to eat its way through Margot's most expensive rug. This Shadow was clearly visible to everyone who didn't have a familiar.

Severn yanked the man to his feet.

★ ★ ★

Margot was incensed by the time she saw the Hawks to the door. "You couldn't have done that at the Halls?" she demanded.

"He wouldn't have survived the trip there," Kaylin countered.

"And that's my problem how? Do you know how much that rug *cost*?"

It hadn't started out as a promising day. It wasn't promising now—in many ways it had become infinitely more complicated. But Margot was furious, and that had to count for something; it was the bright silver lining on a very dark cloud.

Kaylin had done nothing wrong. Nothing petty. There was no guilt associated with this; there'd been no passive aggression at all. She took a moment to enjoy the feeling, because the rest of the day was going to be a nightmare.

"We'll want a Records capture of that, as well," she told the seer. She said it very quietly, on the other hand.

Margot, once she had stepped into the street—and was therefore in public—was far more composed than she had been one invective-filled sentence ago. "I am always happy," she said with a smile that dripped venom, "to offer aid, where appropriate, to the Halls of Law. Give my regards to the Hawklord."

Kaylin nodded. The only thing she had done before forcing the stranger to stand was rifle his pockets. She now carried the feather, the bracelet and the collar. Given their significance, she wanted them somewhere where magic couldn't instantly incinerate them or destroy them—and at the moment, she was it. The familiar could protect them if they were on her person.

Severn said nothing; he secured the prisoner, who was

ashen and shaking, all former poise and confidence gone with the ball of Shadow he'd thrown up.

Word had clearly arrived at the Halls by the time Kaylin reached them. Clint and Tanner were on the door, but they weren't the only ones; there were four Swords, four *Barrani* Hawks, and a small handful of Aerians who were patrolling so tightly above the front doors it was difficult for them not to hit each other.

This did not make their newest prisoner much happier. He looked miserable enough that Kaylin quietly explained the Halls procedures where Shadow might be involved. Which did not make him any less terrified.

Teela and Tain were there. "Honestly, kitling," Teela said. "Can you not leave the Halls on a regular patrol without tripping over something deadly?"

Since it was a rhetorical question, Kaylin didn't answer.

"Mandoran is highly displeased," the Barrani Hawk added.

Of course he was. "Tell him to get stuffed."

Tain smiled. It didn't change the very blue shade of his eyes. "We're here to take your prisoner off your hands."

Kaylin nodded. She was fairly certain that the man—whoever he was—was no longer contaminated. If something killed him here, it wouldn't be Shadow. Given the death of the Aerian would-be assassin in the holding cells, she wasn't certain it mattered.

The Barrani knew. It was to the Barrani that the man was turned over. He had not regained either color or bravado since they'd left Elani, and it was very, very hard not to feel sorry for him. She thought of Moran, which dimmed the pity to manageable levels. There was no way his visit to Margot wasn't related to Moran. But he was human. Mortal. He could be prosecuted in the normal courts. Whoever was pulling rank in the Aerian Caste Court, his wings would be clipped now.

She was looking forward to that until she glanced at Clint. Anticipation went the way of ash in a strong wind.

Margot *did* transmit the Records capture to the Halls of Law. Kaylin was surprised; she'd expected more of a political tussle. Actually, she'd expected Margot to erase those Records and apologize when the official command made its way by courier to her shop. But if Margot was a fraud, she was a fraud on the right side of the law, by a tiny fraction; she probably couldn't plausibly deny obstruction.

Kaylin was still surprised she hadn't tried.

Margot didn't deserve to die. She told herself that as she entered the building. Margot might deserve to have her nose or her jaw broken by a particularly fortuitous punch—but she didn't deserve death.

Marcus was not in a good mood. His new desk had been delivered, and some of the sediment on the surface of the previous desk had been moved to the surface of the current one, but the move had not yet been completed. Marcus was not, therefore, sitting behind his desk—and the piles of paperwork that had grown so much in the past few months they could kill someone simply by falling on them.

Kaylin wondered if sergeants were *ever* in good moods. They probably took humor or joy as a sign of personal weakness and stamped both out without mercy.

"The Hawklord," the sergeant said, "wishes to speak to you."

"When?"

"Fifteen minutes ago."

"Marcus—"

The Leontine growled. "You've brought a man who was, in theory, in the thrall of Shadow into my office." Technically this was inaccurate, but now was not the time to argue technicalities. "On a *routine* patrol. I have a would-be assassin in the infirmary. I have—" he glanced at a pile of new-looking papers on his desk "—no less than four missives from a Caste Court demanding immediate inaction. I would appreciate it if you could find less trouble for the foreseeable future. Go talk to the Hawklord."

The Hawklord was, as Marcus had stressed, waiting. The doors weren't open, which meant Kaylin entered the meeting with a numb hand, courtesy of the door ward.

As was customary, he was standing when the doors opened. He wasn't in the center of the room, though. He was in front of his mirror. The mirror wasn't reflective— it was active. "Have you watched this?" he asked, without looking at her.

"If you mean Margot's transmission, no. I saw part of it while I was in her shop. I didn't see the rest. I'm still surprised she sent the damn thing." She was very, very aware of the items she now carried on her person, but failed to mention them.

She wanted Moran to see them first.

"I do. Were you aware that Oracles could be forced?"

"No. Have you asked the Oracular Halls?"

"An inquiry has been sent. Sergeant Kassan is not best pleased with your ability to find trouble," he added. "He is, however, impressed."

And not in a good way. Kaylin said nothing for a long moment. "Is the Aerian Caste Court attempting to somehow claim this is part of the embargo?"

"They would have a very difficult time, given the race of the man in question."

Which wasn't a no. Kaylin stifled a yawn. "I think it's highly likely that the Emperor will laugh in their faces if they make that attempt."

"I am pleased to see that you now know the Emperor so well you can predict his reaction." The Hawklord's gaze made winter seem balmy.

Kaylin gave up. "The sergeant said you wanted to see me."

"Yes. You will no doubt be happy to hear that there is a small possibility the entire case will no longer be remanded to the Caste Courts."

She was. She was very surprised, but she was pleased. Small possibilities had defined her life. "What's the catch?" she asked, as reality caught up with the brief moment of triumph.

"The acceptance—or rejection—of exemption status depends almost entirely on you. As of your arrival this morning, it was solely dependent on you, but your claims—of Shadow nets—could not be corroborated. There are two messages that relate to that. The death of the Aerian in the holding cell was caused by an Aerian who is no longer with the Halls of Law. He has been remanded to the Aerian Caste Court."

"Where he'll no doubt be celebrated and rewarded for murder." She would have clawed the words back if that had been possible. If the Hawklord's expression hadn't been so forbidding, Kaylin would have asked him which Aerian.

"Where he will no doubt fall ill of an unspecified sickness and expire," the Hawklord corrected, eyes narrowed.

"But that's—"

"Yes. It is a rough application of justice."

"Why would they want to kill someone who followed their orders?"

"Because the order was, technically, illegal."

"Not if they're exempt it wasn't."

"Private, the Caste Courts may well be the cesspit of power and politicking you believe them to be—but the Aerians *have* laws. They are not Imperial Laws, but there *is* a reasonable overlap. If I ordered you to go to the holding cells and kill our newest prisoner, what am I guilty of?"

"Conspiring to commit murder."

"And if you obeyed, what would you be guilty of?"

"Murder."

"Why, exactly, do you expect the Aerian Caste Court to be different?"

"Because they're trying to assassinate Moran. Which is illegal."

"Do not allow sentiment to cloud your vision. You're a Hawk."

Kaylin exhaled. The small dragon began nibbling at loose strands of her hair while she thought. "They'll kill him because he knows he was commanded to commit murder."

"Indeed. If they are otherwise principled, his family will not suffer." He lifted a hand. "Were he to stand trial in the Aerian Caste Court, they would. If he perishes of 'illness,' they will not. And you have diverted me. This morning's assassination attempt," he continued, as if he expected these attempts to become part of the Halls' daily activities, "relied upon you as eyewitness. There was no Records capture. There was no proof. The Caste Court could deride your report. They have already begun to do so."

"What did Margot actually send to the Halls?"

"Proof," he replied, "that Shadow is involved. The Records capture does include your response to what you perceived when you looked through your familiar's wing—but that is entirely dependent on your reliability. What you did toward the end, however, *was* included in Records. The prisoner clearly ejected a small patch of Shadow. Margot was kind enough to offer to send the rug on which that small patch landed. I have already arranged to have it retrieved; it should be in the Halls momentarily."

He turned. His eyes were a pale blue. "I will ask that you avoid all of the Aerians currently sworn to the Hawks until the situation is resolved."

Kaylin blinked. "You can't think they'd hurt me."

"I cannot command it," he continued. "You will continue to see and interact with Sergeant Carafel. I cannot prevent that, but I trust the sergeant. If you die in her presence, it will be because she has died."

"But if there's *proof*—"

"Yes. You are not Aerian. You are, essentially, proof. If you are dead—" the familiar squawked loudly at this "—we will not be able to fight to have this remanded to the Halls of Law. Shadow is, in the Imperial view, enough of a threat that it supersedes all other claims. But this one Records capture serves to underline your claims. Not one of us could see what you saw this morning."

"I think Mandoran could."

The Hawklord frowned. "Mandoran? One of Teela's cousins?"

"In a manner of speaking."

"Is the corporal aware of this ability?"

"Yes. I'm not sure he'd make a good Hawk," Kaylin added. "And I'm not sure he'd make a great witness." There was a difference between ability and presentation. She had no doubt that Mandoran would—without the familiar nagging him—see something out of the ordinary. She was also certain that his ability to convey this information without impatience or cheek was very, very shaky.

"I do not believe Mandoran would be considered an entirely reliable witness."

Kaylin nodded, slightly relieved. But the weight of the earlier request bore down on her, adding a gloom that the Halls weren't supposed to have. "You can't," she said, "believe that the Hawks would hurt me. Maybe other Aerians—but I've known the Aerian Hawks for almost half my life."

"It only takes one," the Hawklord replied. "Do I think it would be done easily? No. Without personal cost? No. But the Hawks who work here have families. They have children in the Southern Reach. They have flights there. None but Moran are dar Carafel, but dar Carafel rules the Caste Court. Dar Carafel rules the Southern Reach.

"It may be that the Hawks will defy dar Carafel. But even that will cost them, Kaylin. I would just as soon not put the pressure of temptation in their way. At the moment, two members of the Caste Court—neither dar Carafel—have heard of the Records capture."

"That was fast."

"Indeed. They are now claiming that Margot is using deliberate deception—at your urging. They are claiming that the Records capture is fraudulent."

"Wouldn't be the first time Margot's been accused of fraud. It's impossible to make it stick."

"The Halls are not inclined to throw their resources into making that charge stick. The Aerian Caste Court will certainly bring more of their resources to bear in this particular instance. I have discussed the situation with Moran—or rather, I've discussed this morning's attempt with her. I believe she will soon be taking a leave of absence."

"But she—"

"Not for her own good, no. For the Hawks. If it is known that she is taking a leave of absence, there will be other demands made of her. But the Aerians who are under pressure will find some of that pressure relieved."

"So...they'll just try to assassinate me."

"I believe that is what I was implying, yes."

Sergeant Kassan was having a bad hair day.

In Leontines, this was significant. His eyes were a steady orange, his face was an inch or two larger because his fur was standing on end, his claws had already started work on the new desk, and his fangs were prominent. He looked up as Kaylin entered the office from the Tower side, and nodded. She could practically hear the growl in the back of his throat from the stairs. It wasn't a loud sound, in the volume sense, but it killed all petty office conversation dead.

She made her way, Severn by her side, to the sergeant's desk. She didn't bother to stand at attention; his clipped nod made it clear that he considered it irrelevant *right now*. That was the problem with Leontines. They lacked consistency, and it didn't matter. If Kaylin lacked consistency in the same way, it was Kaylin who was likely to suffer.

"What did he want?"

You don't know? She managed not to ask this question out loud, but it took effort. "He's going to deny the remand."

The growl that had killed small talk in an office-sized circle around the Leontine desk returned.

"Did you see Margot's transmission?"

"I'm asking the questions, Private."

"Yes, sir."

"You heard Moran's taking a leave of absence?"

Kaylin exhaled. "I've heard it's been requested."

"Consider doing the same."

"My leave of absence is usually unpaid, sir."

"Are you doing anything useful to me while you're on leave?"

"…Sir. I'd rather not. Take the leave, I mean."

"Go pick up the sergeant. You're finished patrol for the day, and rumor has it you've got an important visitor for dinner tonight."

"Tomorrow night."

Marcus scratched the desktop. "Do you have any idea what the Aerians are up to?"

"They want Moran dead. They're probably going to want me dead, to make certain this remains in the Caste Courts."

"Why do they want Moran dead?"

"Don't know, sir."

"When you find out, tell no one but me."

"Or you could just ask the Hawklord." Her brain caught up with her mouth, and she reddened. Leontines were pretty frontal when they chose to attack. He'd probably already asked the Hawklord. Moran, however, was not under his command in any way, shape or form; the Hawklord could refuse to answer the question. And probably had. "What makes you think I'm going to find out?"

"You can't keep your nose out of anything—and in this case, it's your life on the line, as well."

"Sir."

"Now go get your sergeant and get out of here."

Moran had clearly heard of—or perhaps even seen—Margot's transmission. Kaylin had taken a detour on the way to the infirmary, stopping at her own small desk and office mirror, and had been denied permission to view the Records capture.

Given that she was responsible for its arrival, she thought this a tad unfair, and did her level best not to whine about it in the office. Marcus's hearing was Leontine hearing, and he was not in the mood for whining. Not that he ever was, but on normal days he could at least muster a sense of resigned, growly humor. She had intended to ask Moran about it, but Moran's eyes were the Aerian equivalent of Leontine orange. Her wings were rigid, and her lips were a tight line. Aerians, like the rest of humanity, didn't possess canines that overhung lip real estate.

"Marcus kicked me out of the office," Kaylin said. "I'm off duty."

"What did you do this time?" Bellusdeo asked, from the chair nearest Moran's very pristine desk.

"Nothing yet."

"What does he expect you will be doing?"

"Almost, but not quite, dying."

Bellusdeo rose. Her eyes were gold. The events of the day didn't particularly trouble her. "Did he happen to say how?"

"Later."

Small and squawky was draped across Kaylin's shoulders. He lifted his head, tilted it at right angles to his neck and stared at Moran. He then lifted his wing and covered Kaylin's eyes with it. She suddenly remembered that she had intended to look at Moran's wings through the familiar's. She wasn't surprised to see wings—whole wings—rising in perfect formation. The Aerian assassins had had whole wings when viewed this way. She wasn't surprised to see that Moran's wings were pale and freckled—well, speckled—because Moran's wings had always been like that.

She was very surprised to see that Moran didn't have the usual two wings that characterized her race. She had four. Only three of them were functional; the fourth was bandaged and wrapped for support. But it was visible, in the winged view. Kaylin frowned.

"What are you looking for?" Bellusdeo asked, her tone flat and almost impenetrable.

"I wanted to see what her wings looked like through the familiar's wing."

"And?"

"The prisoners had whole wings. Like ideal wings, even if their own weren't."

"That's not what I have?" Moran asked.

"Not exactly. You have whole wings, but you also have your regular ones. At the same time."

"Why?"

Kaylin had hoped that Moran could answer that question rather than asking it.

"Hells if I know." Kaylin decided that the entire conversation that was likely to happen when she presented Moran with both the gift and the question would best be had at home.

"You look awful," Moran told her.

"Clearly you've been avoiding mirrors yourself," Bellusdeo told Moran.

"I spent an hour with Margot," Kaylin said, by way of explanation.

Moran grimaced. "I'm surprised you both survived it. You did both survive it, right?"

"Let's head home."

Helen was waiting for them at the door. Teela and Tain were pulling an extra duty shift guarding the holding cell, but Severn chose to join her for dinner. They had been more or less gloomily silent as they walked through the city streets.

Helen stood aside to let everyone enter. "There's a message for you," she told Kaylin.

"A message?"

"I'm not sure what you call information delivered by mirror network."

"Who sent it?"

"Not the Foundling Halls and not the midwives," Helen assured her. "The message is currently in containment."

"Containment."

"I told you, dear. The mirror network is not secure. I am not about to add information to my personal Records without first ascertaining the contents are not malicious or harmful."

"Who does it *say* it's from?"

"Pardon?"

"You let the messages from the Foundling Halls and the midwives' guild through now."

Helen nodded.

"You let Marcus through to shout at me."

"He wasn't shouting, dear. That's the normal volume of a Leontine voice."

"And you always let Teela through."

"Ah. I see what you are trying to say. I cannot tell you who the message is from because I do not know the sender. I believe you do."

Kaylin exhaled. "Margot?"

CHAPTER 10

"Margot. You don't trust her. You don't like her. You certainly disapprove of her choice of career."

Since all of this was true, Kaylin held her peace. Defending Margot's intentions while in her own home was not high on her list of life goals. Margot was a petty thief and a self-important annoyance, but there were things Margot wouldn't do for money, one of which involved murder.

And Margot donated money to the Foundling Hall, and didn't make a big, public deal out of it, the way she did with almost everything else. One of these days, Kaylin was going to have to admit that she was not an evil villain.

"Did you examine the message?"

"Of course."

"So you know what it contains?"

"It appears to contain a conversation. Or several."

"In an expensive room? I mean, a room with expensive things in it?"

This question caused Helen to fall silent, and Kaylin surrendered. "Let me see it."

"Coming with you," Bellusdeo said immediately.

"I don't think that's wise, dear," Helen told the gold

Dragon. "Kaylin will have to view it in the least secure area in the house—it's the only area in which I am willing to be less self-contained, and it is therefore not completely defensible."

"I spent all day in the Halls of Law, in the infirmary. I think your version of 'not completely' is worlds better than the Halls' version of 'completely.'"

Helen admitted that she had a point.

As it happened, Helen's not-secure-enough-room was a very crowded room by the time she had cleared Margot's message for viewing. Bellusdeo, of course, was present—but it wasn't just the Dragon. Severn tagged along, and Mandoran and Annarion came up from the bowels of the training room, as well. Moran said, "I've seen it. I don't need to see it again." She was the only person who headed immediately to either the dining hall or her room.

"Don't give us that look," Mandoran said, clearly still unhappy about being merged with a random wall earlier in the day. "Teela made us come up. She wants to see it." He winced. "And now she's pissed off, too. You guys seriously have the worst jobs ever." All of this was spoken in Elantran, which Mandoran now used more frequently than his mother tongue.

"The best jobs ever, you mean?"

"The worst. Back in the day, we wouldn't have been tasked with keeping mortals alive. We'd let them squabble among themselves until things were sorted." Catching Kaylin's glare, he shrugged. "Mortals are easy to kill. You can practically do it by accident. Keeping them alive is a *lot* trickier than killing them."

"Thanks."

"You asked."

"I didn't, actually. I corrected you."

Helen generally waited until there was a break in conversation. This time, she gestured, and the mirror on the wall immediately lost its reflective surface.

Because they now had people who hadn't seen the earliest part of the transmission, Kaylin and Severn were forced to sit through—or, rather, stand through—a repeat. Mandoran asked questions. He clearly recognized Margot, and equally clearly still considered her striking or attractive, which did nothing to improve Kaylin's mood. She personally found Bellusdeo vastly more attractive than Margot—but Bellusdeo was a Dragon, not a mortal, and Mandoran's early life had been lived during the Draco-Barrani wars.

And to be fair to Mandoran—not that that held a lot of appeal at this very second—he wasn't asking more questions than Kaylin had asked when Margot had started the Records playback the first time.

When Margot started to speak of the Dragon, Bellusdeo tensed. She was unsatisfied with the answers Margot gave in regards to the Dragon's color.

"There's a lone Aerian," Margot was saying, lips thin. She looked as if she was struggling against the compulsion that had taken hold of her sight, and failing badly to gain any ground.

The man who was now gracing a holding cell leaned forward. "Describe the Aerian."

"They're too far away. Could be male, could be female. The only thing that's clear from this distance are the wings."

"What about the wings?" Sharper question.

"They're white, or maybe pale gray. They're spread for gliding, and they appear to be glowing." Margot frowned.

"Parts of the wings are glowing." Her forehead creased. "I think there might be something written on the wings themselves, but I can't read it. They're too far away."

"Look more closely," the man demanded.

Margot said, in a distinct and chilly voice, "That is not the way visions work."

"Visions can be invoked."

"Clearly. But they can't be controlled. The vision itself is given without comment. It's not like a Records capture. I can't enlarge what's there. I can watch it. I can try to remember it. I can't magically tell it to become clearer or easier to understand."

The man was clearly annoyed. He wasn't certain if he believed Margot, and that showed.

Margot was insulted. That was definitely genuine. "Are we finished?"

"No. What is the lone Aerian doing? Are they even in the same sky as the others you first saw?"

"I'm not certain." Margot closed her eyes.

"What are you doing?" her customer asked, ice and outrage weighting the words.

"I don't need the ball," was her curt response. "The ball is a toy. It doesn't have a use, except as a focus. It's an aid. A crutch." She didn't open her eyes. "If you'd rather do this yourself, please feel free. You can stare at the crystal ball.

"The Aerians in the sky are growing in number. Some of them are armed. I don't recognize what they're carrying. The Dragon is definitely with them. I think he's in command."

"Impossible."

"It might have escaped your notice, but the Eternal Emperor to whom we *all* owe loyalty is a Dragon."

"Is the Dragon the Emperor?"

"He's not wearing a crown. How should I know which Dragon he is?"

"Is. His. Color. Any. Clearer?"

Margot frowned, her eyelids flickering although they remained mostly closed. "Indigo or possibly black. It hasn't changed. His wing span is huge." Her jaw dropped then.

"What?" the man demanded.

"I think he just ate two of the Aerians. The others don't seem to be worried about it, either. Wait, they're carrying... nets. Nets, and maybe spears." She stiffened. "The skies—they're in the skies over Ravellon, and they're coming here."

Bellusdeo was red-eyed and frozen when Kaylin spared her a glance.

"There are people in the streets. Hawks in the sky."

"Hawks?"

"Aerian Hawks."

"Where?"

"Over the city streets. Not Elani. Closer to the fiefs—I think I can see the Ablayne. Swords are out, some on horseback. People are panicking. I think—I think the Dragon has just destroyed a bridge."

"Bridge?"

"It's not a familiar bridge. It's a *vision*."

"Where in the city is this unfamiliar bridge?"

Margot was frowning. "Not over the Ablayne. Actually, it's a bridge that makes no sense. It's not connecting anything I can see. Someone was standing on it."

"Who?"

"A Hawk."

"*Which* Hawk?"

Margot said, focused now, "Private Kaylin Neya."

Kaylin said something rude. In two languages.

"You are certain?"

"She knocks my sign down every other day. She harasses me whenever she gets the opportunity. She thinks my clients are either pitiable or deluded."

"They are," the man said, shrugging.

"She makes herself as unpleasant as possible, proving that the law doesn't have to be reasonable to still be lawful. Yes, I'm certain. You know her?"

"We know of her, yes."

"She's getting in your way?"

"Yes. I do not believe that will be the case for much longer." And that, Kaylin thought, was the reason for her "leave of absence." Marcus and the Hawklord actually believed Kaylin would be safe if she remained within her home.

"They are correct," Helen said. "While you are here, you are safe. So is the sergeant."

"Yes, but we can't *do* anything from here."

"You can survive. For your sergeant, I believe that is of considerable import."

"We don't kill Hawks around these parts," Margot was saying. "It's not considered smart."

"We are not, of course, bound by the same laws you are, and we are not nearly so powerless." And that, Kaylin thought, was the reason for Margot's cooperation. There was no way Margot had expected this man to walk away without leaving one dead redhead in his wake.

"If you agree to let me go, I'll help you with the Hawk."

"Pardon?"

"She patrols Elani. This is her current beat. If you want a clean shot at her, this is your best chance."

"She patrols here." The man's smile was slow, his eyes bright. "You've implied she is not your friend."

"I can get her in here." Her tone made it very clear that she was certain, and that she was the only certainty he had.

"Very well."

"I suppose a small and accidental fire is out of the question?" Bellusdeo asked Kaylin.

"Small and accidental by angry Dragon standards?"

"By annoyed Dragon standards, yes."

"The Emperor *might* forgive you. I wouldn't bet on it, though. Look—I'm not annoyed by it. What she did made sense."

"She offered to help him kill you."

"She had just about outlived any usefulness she had. He was going to kill her. She was just trying to extend her life."

"By helping him kill you."

"She's not as stupid as she looks. Her best chance of surviving this involved us. We don't patrol as singletons. If I did die, she'd follow. I expect she hoped to run for it the minute the actual fighting started. He'd asked too many questions, and spoken too freely, for her life to be worth much."

"You're certain she knew this."

"Yes."

"Why?"

Kaylin exhaled. "Because seven years ago, I would have done the same damn thing. Margot owes me nothing. In theory, it's my job to protect her from people like her customer. Law's great on theory, but it's not perfect in practice. We do our best. She could justify what she was doing until the cows came home."

"I don't understand why you use that phrase," Mandoran said—in Elantran. "I mean, have you ever owned a cow?"

"A cow wouldn't have survived half a day in the fiefs."

"And has anyone you've ever met owned cows?"

"No."

"So why 'cows come home'?"

"Can you ask Teela that? I mean, privately?"

"I did. She doesn't know, either."

"Now is not the time," Kaylin began. Margot's voice started up again, demanding silence from her audience. Figured. Margot's interruption couldn't have cut off Mandoran instead. Of course not.

"I didn't tell him everything I saw. You've clearly had some experience with Oracles. You know that nothing I saw was literal. Most of it won't make any sense without enough context—and I don't have the context. You do." She cleared her throat, looking—to Kaylin's surprise—nervous.

"So I'll tell you what I managed not to tell him. When I said I saw you in the city streets, I lied. I saw you in the air."

Kaylin started to ask a question and stopped. This wasn't a live communication. Margot had recorded it and sent it on to Helen.

"You had wings. You were flying. If I weren't so familiar with you, I would have assumed you were one of the Aerians. You're not. So it's possible none of the Aerians in the vision were actual Aerians, either. Or the Dragon. Whatever I said had some meaning to my visitor.

"I'm not about to chase down context for you. But I owe you for saving my life—and my life's worth a lot to me. I'm not about to give up my livelihood because you don't like it. I'm not about to give up my ability to live as I choose. But I owe you." She smiled. It was feline. "Tell you what. If you ever feel the need to have your fortune told, I'll do it for free.

"And before you ask: your wings were pale and speckled, too."

Dinner was not quiet, but the topic of conversation was not Moran, Margot, or the leave of absence Kaylin had been requested to take. Although these were foremost in Kaylin's mind, they carried little weight when compared to dinner guests. Or rather, to a particular dinner guest.

Tomorrow night, the Emperor was coming for dinner. As long as there were no unexpected emergencies—and given the nature of emergencies, they were very seldom expected—they were about to play host to the Eternal Emperor, in his civilian disguise.

As disguises went, it was pretty crappy. He exuded arrogance and power. But he divested himself of the Palace Guard, which Kaylin appreciated. They set her teeth on edge.

"You aren't planning on dressing like *that* tomorrow night, are you?" Mandoran demanded, when he realized Kaylin wasn't clear on the gravity of the situation. Kaylin exhaled. Absent assassination attempts and Shadow magic, the Emperor *was* the current emergency in the eyes of her household.

"Not exactly like this, no. But it's supposed to be informal. It's not like he hasn't seen me in my normal clothing before."

"If you're talking about the night of fire and death, that doesn't count. You were on duty."

"I wasn't, but I happen to think the clothing we all wore on the night of 'fire and death,' as you call it, is worth more respect."

Annarion cleared his throat. Loudly. When Kaylin glanced at him, he said, "We're trying to get him to shut up. It's working about as well as it usually does. He doesn't speak for the rest of us. The Emperor is intelligent. He knows what you're like. I don't think inappropriate clothing—your version—is going to be an issue. Mandoran and I will remain in the training room for the duration of the meal. Teela promises to avoid the dinner if at all possible, as well."

Helen appeared to be taking notes.

"What are you going to wear?" Kaylin asked Bellusdeo.

"Clothing."

The familiar squawked.

"I intend to be perfectly civil," the gold Dragon snapped at the small translucent one.

Kaylin thought about the prior interactions between Bellusdeo and the Emperor and winced. "Keep in mind that the rest of us need our hearing."

"Oh?"

"Don't converse in your native tongue while he's here. The rest of us don't understand Dragon, and don't have the vocal cords for it."

"And if he starts?"

"Are you a hatchling?" Mandoran cut in, with some scorn.

Bellusdeo flushed. Fair enough. *He started it* didn't work so well for the young foundlings who tried it, either.

"Pretend he's the monarch of a neighboring country. You were, I hear, queen of your own country for more than a few years. I don't imagine your diplomacy involved shouting and swearing."

"It involved armies and death."

Mandoran shrugged. "Fine. But the armies and death weren't the first line of action. Just...pretend this is the first meeting."

Bellusdeo snorted smoke. Nothing on the table, however, burned. "You're certain you want to stay in the training room?"

"I don't," Mandoran replied. "But I'm being overruled and outvoted at the moment. My head's a very noisy place."

"Ah. And I thought it was mostly an empty one."

Mandoran grinned, acknowledging a scored point. Kaylin wondered what the current tally on either side stood at, because she was certain the Barrani was keeping score. Then again, the Dragon probably was, as well. Ancient wars that had had a profound direct effect on the two people involved tended to bring an edge to every single interaction.

On the other hand, that didn't seem to be as much of a problem for Annarion.

"They can read each other's thoughts," Helen said, having obviously read Kaylin's. "This does not make them the same person."

"You can say that again."

Only when dinner was finished did Kaylin directly approach Moran. Moran had, as she usually did, absented herself from the Draco-Barrani hostilities. She had absented herself from the discussion of the Emperor as a dinner guest—although it was clearer, in that case, that she had thoughts. She didn't volunteer to avoid their guest, though.

Kaylin wanted to, but Helen forbade it. It was, after all, Kaylin's home, and she had responsibilities as hostess to her invited guests. Given the way the various Hawks had walked through her life—and her apartment—with little notice and frequently no invitation, Kaylin didn't really understand the fuss of hospitality. She figured anyone who had a key was allowed to drop by when they felt like it.

Clearly, this wasn't the Helen-accepted version of good manners.

"I'm tired," Moran said, pulling Kaylin out of her petty confusion. "Can this wait until tomorrow?"

"I'm not sure."

"Fine. But come back to my room. I find the ceilings here oppressive."

"I could make them taller," Helen's disembodied voice offered.

"Much taller, and Kaylin would find them oppressive," Moran answered, slightly amused. "And it's Kaylin's home."

★ ★ ★

When the sergeant was ensconced in the heated pool of water Moran called a bath, Kaylin pulled off her shoes, rolled up her pant legs, and dipped her toes in. The water wasn't steaming; it was warm. "I have a couple of things I wanted to ask you about." She opened the flap of the small pouch she wore belted to her waist. It was vastly more practical than an over-the-shoulder bag, especially when it came to running.

Moran stiffened, but she couldn't hold on to physical tension as efficiently when she was soaking in very warm water. "Please don't tell me, Private, that you're in possession of evidence."

"Technically, no. Did you recognize the items he passed under Margot's face?"

Moran was silent. It didn't last. "Don't give me cause to regret accepting your hospitality."

"I'm trying not to. But someone is trying to kill you. And frankly, someone's trying to kill me."

"Because I accepted the hospitality."

"Doesn't matter why. I don't want you dead. I didn't realize just how important Helen was in that regard. She'll let you leave if you want to leave; this isn't a prison, and she doesn't treat guests like prisoners."

"But she has a prison for intruders?"

Kaylin shrugged. "If she doesn't have holding cells, she can make them up as needed. You're not an intruder, and you're not a prisoner. She'll let you leave if you want. *I* might cling to your legs, begging, pleading and whining."

Moran chuckled. "I love these rooms," she said, half-wistful. "And I am more comfortable with Helen than I have been with anyone for a very long time."

"Helen doesn't want you to leave if you don't want to go. She's not angry with you. She doesn't blame you for anything that anyone's trying to do to me. Are you coming to dinner tomorrow night?"

Moran blinked. "Are you changing the subject?"

"Not really. If it weren't my house, I wouldn't be there for dinner, either. I suggested it, but Helen flat-out refused."

"It's not very hospitable, dear," Helen's disembodied voice said. "But Kaylin is right. You are not to blame for the actions of others. And I think you need the type of peace that I can offer. I'm not a Hawk. I'm not a ruler. I can't control the events that occur beyond my grounds. But I take some small pride in creating a space in which you can feel at home."

"Do you think I should discuss things with Kaylin?"

"You discuss things with her all the time."

Kaylin stifled a grin. Moran was still not quite accustomed to how literal Helen could be.

"I remember when you first walked into the infirmary. You looked at it as if it were a torture chamber, with better beds."

Kaylin reddened, but laughed. "I thought it was."

"I know. I tried not to take offense, as I recall."

"You didn't try very hard."

Moran grinned. "Prickly, defensive teens are difficult at the best of times."

Kaylin snorted. "You were just mad because I didn't acknowledge the infirmary as yours."

"And you learned better."

"I really did." She rose. "I liked the infirmary better than the morgue, if that's any help. I didn't really understand the purpose of the morgue."

"I didn't, either. But we don't bury our dead."

"No?"

"No. Our traditional burial customs would probably not meet with your approval—but being bound to earth is one of our worst fears. No one wants to be interred beneath it." She leaned her head back against solid, wet rock, exposing her throat. "Yes, I recognized the items. Or I recognized two of them."

"Which ones?"

"The flight feather, in a general sense. It's Aerian."

"And specifically?"

"The bracelet."

"What do you think the collar was about?"

"I dread the possible answer to that question. If you mean was it something I wore or would be forced to wear? I don't think so. At this point, though, I wouldn't put anything past dar Carafel."

"Whoever sent that guy to Margot clearly felt the collar was significant."

"Does he know why?"

"I doubt it. I can't imagine he doesn't know who hired him, though." She hesitated. "I think they'll bring in the Tha'alani."

Moran was as grim as Kaylin. The Tha'alani could, if they made physical contact with a person's skin using the stalks on their forehead, read thoughts. They could rifle through them as if they were drawers. There wasn't a secret you could keep if they came calling.

But they *hated* to do it.

Most crimes could and would be easily solved with consistent use of the Tha'alani. And most of the Tha'alani would be slightly insane if they were used that way. The Emperor did occasionally demand their services—he was the boss, after all. The Tha'alani had agreed because he was also a Dragon, and he could breathe them out of house and home if he felt like it. But if he considered their obedience necessary—and

Kaylin privately hated him for it—he also knew it was costly, not only for the Tha'alani in question, but for the entire race.

They didn't naturally keep secrets from each other. Only a few of them *could*.

"It's a good thing he was human, then."

"I'd be more interested in knowing what this morning's assassins knew. You know that Grammayre is going to fight the remand, right?"

Moran sagged. Kaylin almost kicked herself. She didn't understand Moran, and probably never would—but she respected her. "This case should be ours," she added, trying to keep defensiveness out of her voice. "You're ours." She shook herself. "The bracelet?"

"It's largely ceremonial. It has a place of honor among the artifacts of the pilgrims, as they're sometimes called."

"The ones who first arrived here?"

Moran nodded. "It was apparently worn by the *praevolo*. The first one. It's worn by the *praevolo* when they come of age."

"…But that would be you."

Moran nodded.

"Was it offered to you?"

Moran lifted her head. Her eyes were a very dark blue. "Yes. The first time, it was offered as a bribe. I was forcibly adopted into the dar Carafel line at that time. I was a child. I donned it before the Caste Court. But then it was refused on my behalf—by my mother. So it was returned to their keeping."

"And the second?"

"After my grandmother's death. I would not wear it. I was told that if I had been wearing it, my grandmother would have lived—and I hated them for saying it. Hated myself for the guilt I felt anyway. If it weren't for *me*, my grandmother would be alive. She'd be living in the Outer Reaches, but she was happy there. She died because someone wanted *me* dead." She closed her eyes.

Kaylin was surprised when the Aerian woman continued. "It does funny things to you, to know that the cost of being loved is death. I hated the Upper Reaches. I hated everyone who lived in them."

"What does the bracelet do?"

"I don't know. I only know that it belonged to the first person to bear these wings. In theory, it's a mark of honor."

"You don't believe that."

"Oh, I believe it's considered a mark of honor—but I think it does more than that, and I'm not sure what that is. I wouldn't trust the dar Carafel, though."

"Meaning?"

"They could have had a replica made, with their own specific magical spin. I keep thinking of Margot; she was being physically controlled by her visitor. What if they had altered the bracelet, or enchanted it, to do the same thing?"

"Why are you so certain it's the Aerians who were responsible for what happened to Margot?"

"You trust my people," Moran said, voice softening. "But you trust them because you've only seen those who became Hawks. I love my job, and I'm good at it. It took me years to win a place for myself among the Aerian Hawks, but the rest of you accepted me, wings and all, without complaint.

"Now I've lost the Aerians. Again. I don't know if I'll ever get them back."

Kaylin clamped her jaw shut to stop words from escaping. The small dragon warbled what she assumed was approval. Sighing, she reached into her pouch and pulled out the bracelet.

Moran's jaw would have hit the water—and sunk—if it

hadn't been attached. Her eyes shaded into purple, which was Aerian surprise, before returning to a familiar blue.

Kaylin looked guilty because she was.

"What are you doing with that?" The words were uttered in outraged sergeant, which was actually a very soft, very quiet, very well-enunciated voice.

"I thought it might be important."

"It's *evidence*," the sergeant snapped. "You are never going to make corporal at this rate. Never. The only possible way you could do it is if Sergeant Kassan is angry enough that he wants to promote you so he has a rank he can bust you back down to."

This was harsh, but probably true.

"No one asked." Kaylin flushed. How long had it been since she'd even tried to make that excuse fly? "Look—I thought it was possibly important to the Aerians. Whoever sent the man to Margot clearly thought these three items— feather, collar, bracelet—were relevant to *you*. They wanted information about you. And the stupid Caste Court exemption would mean that—" She struggled for a moment, then said, "I thought they were *yours*.

"And if I took them in as evidence, they'd be in lock-up for all of five minutes. Then the Caste Court would drop a collective screeching flock on the Hawklord's head, and he'd be forced to hand them over. Either that, or one of the Aerian Hawks—a different one—would lose his job."

Margot exhaled, and her eyes lost a bit of blue, as if she was remembering that she was off-duty here. "You're right about the latter."

"If you don't want any of them, I'll turn them in." She hesitated.

Moran stared at the bracelet—only the bracelet. "It's not mine," she finally said. "The *praevolo* wears it—but when the *praevolo* dies, it comes back to the flights. It's preserved. If there were some way to choose the *praevolo*, it might be different. But there isn't. Or there hasn't been."

Kaylin held the bracelet out. The familiar inched down her arm and sniffed it as if it were food. She wasn't expecting him to bite it.

He did.

CHAPTER 11

Moran, clearly unfamiliar with the small dragon, raised a brow but said nothing. Kaylin, however, shrieked.

"What are you *doing*?" She grabbed the familiar; his little jaws were a lot stronger than they appeared. He was attached to the bracelet, and he had no intention—at this specific moment—of letting go of it. He did squawk; the sound was even less impressive than it usually was, because his mouth was otherwise full.

Moran's eyes, which had been a kind of Barrani blue, narrowed in mild confusion. "You think he's going to harm it?"

"I'm sure that's not what he means to do," she said.

"Which means yes."

"Which means his idea of harmful and our idea of harmful probably don't really overlap much, yes." To the familiar, she said, "Do not do anything to destroy this bracelet."

Moran, however, seemed much more accepting of the general idea. "I didn't take the bracelet. In theory, the dar Carafel still have it. If something happens to it—on their watch—it's not going to reflect badly on me." And she smiled. The smile had Leontine in it, absent the teeth.

"He's not trying to destroy it, dear," Helen's disembodied voice added.

Moran didn't even tense. She'd become accustomed to Helen—and Helen's various intrusions—so quickly, it seemed natural. Or maybe it was just because she was mortal. Teela still found Helen uncomfortable. "Do you know what he's trying to do?" the sergeant asked the empty air.

"I believe he's examining it," Helen replied.

"He can do that with his eyes."

"Yes, in theory."

"And in practice?"

"In practice, there's something in the bracelet he's not sure he likes."

"Can you see it?"

"Not the same way, no."

"Do you think it would be harmful to Moran to keep it?" Kaylin interjected.

"To keep it? No. To wear it? I'm less certain."

"It doesn't feel magical to me. I mean—I'm not breaking out in a rash. Or worse."

"It is not, perhaps, magic of the kind that disturbs you. It is definitely magical in nature."

"How?"

"It occupies more space than its physical dimensions suggest, for one."

It didn't feel particularly heavy. Or rather, it didn't feel heavier than a bracelet of its size normally would. "Can you understand what he's saying?"

"It's a bit hard—his mouth is full."

Moran was watching both Kaylin and her familiar, and listening to Helen's careful, diplomatic concern. She smiled. The blue of her eyes faded to a normal Aerian gray.

"You didn't want to wear the bracelet," Helen said softly, "because you didn't want to be *praevolo*."

Moran exhaled heavily. After a long pause, in which water rippled only because Kaylin was moving her feet, she said, "I didn't want to be their *praevolo*. I didn't want to support the people who were responsible for the death of my family. I wasn't willing to die for them, and I wasn't strong enough to kill them. If I had worn the bracelet, I would be accepting them. I would be doing what they wanted." She tilted her head back, closing her eyes. "I intend to live for as long as I possibly can. I don't always enjoy my life—but the longer I live, the less likely it will be that an actual dar Carafel is born with the *praevolo's* wings. I won't be what they want. But I won't help them get what they want by dying, either."

"The *praevolo* does not, if I understand things correctly, exist strictly for the Caste Court. They exist for the entire race."

"Helen, I'm not sure this is the right time," Kaylin said.

Helen, however, did not agree. "Your mother and your grandmother did not abandon you intentionally."

"Of course not." Moran stiffened, and Kaylin surrendered. She lifted her feet out of the water, grabbed a nearby towel, glared at the familiar—who was still chewing what looked like gemmed metal—and dried herself off. This wasn't a conversation she was supposed to be part of.

"They were murdered. They were murdered by Aerians."

Socks. Shoes.

"But you are a Hawk, Moran. You've seen human murderers. You've seen executions. You've never decided that the human race—as a whole—is murderous and worthless because of them."

"Helen, I really think this is not a conversation Moran wants to have right now."

The familiar squawked.

"I've never said Aerians were worthless," Moran countered. "I've never said the entire race is murderous."

"No, you haven't. But, dear—you've isolated yourself as if they were."

To the familiar, Kaylin whispered, "Make her stop."

"I have not—"

"Moran, you have. You tell yourself it is for *their* good. Their own good, I believe. You stay separate because you do not want them to become victims of political pressure, power. And perhaps that is even true now. But in the past? You've been a Hawk for longer than Kaylin has, and you have formed no friendships among your own kin.

"Perhaps it *is* safer for them. Unless Kaylin invites them to visit, I cannot say that with any certainty. But I think I can say that you believe it is safer for *you*. We make different choices for reasons of safety. But I will say this—because I do not believe you are aware of it, as Kaylin is. I chose to destroy large parts of myself in order to remain free to choose.

"I do not regret that decision. But I do not deceive myself. Those parts are gone. Lost. They are destroyed. And there are times, even now, when I feel that loss keenly. Perhaps you are more like me than Kaylin is. Perhaps you do not regret the things you have destroyed as an act of self-preservation. But mortals are *not* buildings."

Moran was silent. Her eyes were blue, very blue. Any comfort she'd gained from the bath had been obliterated.

"No, dear," Helen continued. "I understand exactly why you made the choices you did. They were, and are, your choices to make."

"For now," Moran replied. She looked across the room at Kaylin, who was very, very sorry that she hadn't managed to leave Moran to her very private conversation with a building that really didn't understand the concept of privacy at a visceral level. To the familiar, Moran said, "Give me the bracelet." Her voice was like steel. Sharpened steel.

The familiar looked up at Kaylin.

Kaylin wanted to ask him if it was safe, but didn't. She reminded herself that safety was the illusion and the dream. Instead, she said, "Give me your wing for a sec."

The familiar lifted his wing—without smacking her face with it. To her eyes, the bracelet looked the same through the wing. She saw no trace of Shadow in or around it. She had no idea what the familiar had been trying to eat or chew at, but it didn't matter anyway. Moran had spoken in her sergeant voice.

She handed Moran the bracelet.

Moran put it on.

Kaylin could hear it snap shut; the sound echoed off the stones of the open-air spring. But her skin didn't ache. The marks didn't begin to glow. Moran didn't transform. She was a naked Aerian woman, partially submerged in hot water, the edges of her hair wet, her eyes a striking blue. And she was wearing an old, colorful bracelet.

"I hope it's waterproof," Kaylin said. She waited before adding, "Do you feel any different?"

The Aerian sergeant deflated. "No."

"Sometimes," Helen said quietly, "regalia is just that. All of its power resides in the symbolism. I am sorry," she added.

"You've made a home for me that I thought I'd never see again," Moran replied. "You've kept me safe. You've told me nothing but truth. You've got nothing to apologize for."

"It's not considered good manners to tell people truths they haven't asked to hear."

Moran's smile was brief, but genuine. "No, it isn't. But

you're Kaylin's home, and while Kaylin is valued for many things, good manners aren't one of them."

"My manners are better than they used to be," Kaylin protested.

"Vastly better," Moran agreed. She stood. Water ran instantly off her wings, but the rest of her required towels. Helen didn't magically appear to hand them to her, but Kaylin was closer, and did.

"What are you going to do?"

"I'm going to sleep," Moran replied. "And then I'm going to wake up, eat breakfast, and go to the Halls in the morning."

"You're certain? You said you were taking a leave—"

"I've changed my mind." She grimaced as if at old pain. "Helen is probably right. About me. About how I feel about my own people."

"And dinner?"

The Aerian Hawk winced. "I'll come to dinner, if the Emperor allows it."

"He said it was a casual meal—"

"The Imperial version of *casual* was out of my reach when I was growing up. And angry Aerians have nothing on angry Dragons."

Kaylin did not sleep well. The familiar spent the entire night nattering in his sleep—and smacking Kaylin in the face with his wings. And his tail. The fourth time she woke up, she considered opening a window and dropping him out of it.

Helen considered that idea to be unwise and unkind.

"If I haven't done it yet, I'm not likely to start—but we all have to have daydreams."

She woke, dressed, checked to make certain there were no emergency mirror messages waiting in Helen's queue, and headed down the stairs. She remembered, halfway down, that she was still in possession of the blessing of air, and forgot it again five steps later.

Annarion was shouting.

Had he been shouting at Mandoran, she would have grimaced, massaged her temples—she was working on a headache—and continued toward the breakfast room. Unfortunately, the voice that returned that shout in both volume and length was not Mandoran's.

"No, dear," Helen said, her voice more subdued than usual. "Lord Nightshade is here."

"Why didn't you tell me?"

"You were trying to sleep, and I didn't want to add to the interruptions."

"I don't think I've ever heard Nightshade shout like that."

"No, probably not. Let me do something about that."

"Short of throwing them both out, or shutting them in the training rooms—I'm assuming that's not where they are—I'm not sure you *can*. They're almost as loud as Dragons." And about as safe, Kaylin thought. "I can't actually understand them."

"No, dear. I can't completely diminish the volume, but I am trying to give them some privacy."

Bellusdeo looked about as amused at the shouting as Kaylin felt. "You look terrible," she said when Kaylin entered the dining room.

"I look better than I feel. Have they been shouting like that for long?"

"No. That just started. When I regret my lack of family," she added, somewhat sourly, "I remind myself that there are some things I don't miss."

"You had fights like this with your sisters?"

"I had worse fights with my sisters, if you must know. We were younger, and Dragons are not famously restrained when they lose their tempers."

"But you were mostly human."

"I'll thank you never to repeat that. But I will then add that the elders don't interfere much with children's fights if they're female children. The possible damage is so insignificant it doesn't warrant constant supervision. That, and they generally have their hands full with the rest of the clutch because the males can cause irreparable damage when they lose it."

"I don't think that's good parenting," Kaylin replied.

Golden brows rose. "Our concept of parenting is not yours. In the old days, it was considered perfectly reasonable to let clutch-mates murder each other in fits of aggression and rage. It thinned out the weak."

"You're joking, right?"

"Do I look like I'm joking?"

"She's not joking," Mandoran added. He entered the dining hall and draped himself across the table, after first dropping his butt into the nearest chair.

"And Barrani parenting?"

"More careful—but our next generations weren't born in clutches. Or very often." He grimaced as he glanced at Bellusdeo. "However, our 'more careful' wouldn't pass your parenting muster, either. Remember why you met us. The cull-the-weak mentality exists everywhere in the immortal world." His eyes fell to breakfast with clear distaste. "They've been talking for a couple of hours."

"What are they fighting about?"

"Initially?"

Kaylin nodded.

"Kaylin, dear, they are allowed some privacy—"

"Which one of us never gets," Mandoran snapped. "Annarion told his brother that he's going to take the Test of Name in the High Halls."

Kaylin, whose appetite had already been severely compromised, joined Mandoran in his contemplation of breakfast. "Has he lost his mind?"

"Funny, that's what Nightshade said."

"Was that the shouting part?"

"No—that came later."

"Do I want to know?"

"Yes, obviously. You just want it to be a big misunderstanding that will resolve itself with mortal-style hugs and kisses."

This was true. Kaylin flushed. "I know that Nightshade spent a lot of years searching for a way to find—and free—his brother. I don't understand him. He seems very Barrani in other ways, except for the outcaste part. But if he cares about anything outside of himself, it's his family."

"No," Mandoran replied, picking up a fork as if it weighed more than his entire arm. "It's his *brother*. He considered the rest of his family responsible for Annarion's loss. He did not, and would not, forgive."

"That's why they're fighting."

"More or less. Annarion is not outcaste. He is considered Barrani, inasmuch as that's possible for any of us anymore."

"What do you mean?"

It was Bellusdeo who answered, which surprised Mandoran, judging from his expression as he turned to stare at the Dragon. "Dragons, Barrani, almost any person of any race who is considered to be a power, hate to admit that they've made mistakes. They will avoid referring to their mistakes—because of course, anyone who lives and breathes makes them—with a determination that might seem stupid, when seen from the outside.

"Annarion is therefore considered Barrani—and only Barrani—in every legal way by his Caste Court. The Barrani Caste Court is somewhat elastic; it is political. Barrani outcaste lords have been repatriated, historically, with a change of leadership."

"Not often," Mandoran said, frowning.

"More often than Dragon outcastes."

Mandoran shrugged. Obviously he believed her statement was both true and irrelevant.

"Annarion is not, as you are well aware, what the rest of the Barrani are. He has to struggle to retain even his shape. He's willing to make that effort. The polite fiction is that he has returned. Because he has—and I'm sure Mandoran will correct me if I'm mistaken—he is a legitimate member of his family line. He cannot hold or take it back if he is not a Lord of the High Court. He cannot be Lord of the High Court—"

"Without taking the Test of Name."

Mandoran did not argue or correct Bellusdeo.

"He's not ready for that," Kaylin said.

"You're not going to tell him that," Mandoran said. "First of all, he probably wouldn't hear it, given the argument he's having now. Second of all, it's not going to matter. He thinks that his brother abandoned his duty to the family and the line, surrendering it to distant cousins because he made himself outcaste. He believes that the *only* responsible thing he can do is establish himself as a Lord of the High Court and retake what is, in theory, his.

"You can imagine the cousin in question, who is a Lord of the High Court and has been for centuries—that timing coincidentally around the same period in which Nightshade was made outcaste—is not thrilled. Although Annarion is in line, he has no legitimate claim if he can't pass the test. If he takes the test and passes it, he *does* have a claim.

"Claims are theoretical. The law would give him the ancestral home, lands and title *if* he survives, but they would be slow about the grant. It's quite possible—quite probable— that he would not survive becoming a Lord; there would almost certainly be assassination attempts."

"I'm still stuck on the taking-the-test-and-surviving-it part."

"So is Lord Nightshade. I believe that's the core of his argument. If his brother has returned, he is not what he was. But Annarion's argument is the same. Nightshade is not what he was, either."

"And that's caused all the shouting?"

"No, dear," Helen said. "Annarion is angry with his older brother. He feels betrayed."

"But Nightshade did so much of what he did—"

"To find his brother, yes. Lord Nightshade feels that sacrificing the line—or his claim to it—was an acceptable cost if it meant not abandoning the only member of his family he truly cared for. Annarion, sadly, does not see this the same way."

Mandoran winced.

"What?" Kaylin asked him.

"Helen's understating things."

"You can hear them." Of course he could.

"Yes. Helen can't provide privacy for those who are Namebound." Mandoran's face was tight with pain. "Annarion is reminding his brother that duty—his duty—should never have been forsaken for something as trivial as brotherly affection."

Even Kaylin winced. She'd never had brothers or sisters. Her mother had died. She'd never had a father. But she'd yearned for family. She still did. Severn had once said that she built family wherever she went—and maybe that was even true. But she wouldn't want any of her made family to suffer for her sake. That wasn't supposed to be the point of family.

"Isn't it?" Helen asked softly.

"No!"

Mandoran snorted, some of his normal color returning to his face. "You walked into the heart of the green to try to help Teela. Yes, she was pissed off about it. She still is. You often do exactly what Nightshade did." He shook his head. "It's never wise to love Barrani, if you are one. For mortals—for you—you only have to maintain it for a couple of decades, after which you're too old."

"Too old to love?"

"Too old to shoulder the burden of it. Barrani are never too old. It's why we avoid the hells out of each other when we're older and smarter." He grimaced. "I won't repeat what Annarion just told me to do."

"Thank you," Helen said before Kaylin could ask.

"On the other hand," Mandoran added, "I think this makes me grateful that my own family line is ash and dust at this point."

Helen raised a brow.

"There's no pressure."

"I believe you could petition the High Court to have your line reinstated—you are, after all, alive, and you are demonstrably of your line."

"I was a useless youngest son," Mandoran replied, grinning. Kaylin was almost certain he was lying. "But I think I'm going to accompany Kaylin to the Halls today."

"Oh, no, you don't. Do you have any idea what my day is going to be like as is?"

"None at all. But I do know what *my* day is going to be like if I stay here."

"It's not like he's going to hurt you."

Mandoran laughed. "If you think this doesn't cause pain, you're not as smart as you look."

"You think I look like a mortal idiot."

"And your point is?"

"No one likes to watch their friends in pain when there's nothing they can do to help them," Moran said. Kaylin hadn't even heard her enter the dining room.

She turned, and then stopped short as she saw the Aerian sergeant.

Moran was wearing something Kaylin had never seen her in before. It was—or appeared to be, at first glance—a dress, but as she watched Moran walk, she adjusted that assumption. What had appeared to be skirts were separate but flowing legs; they moved as if they had a will of their own—or at least a breeze of their own. They were white and powder blue and azure and gold, colors that hinted at sky, at day, at light. The sleeves, however, were indigo, full draping cloth flecked with silver and gold and pale, transparent gauze. And the chest was the color of sunset—or sunrise. The bracelet was the only thing on her bare right arm.

"You can't go to work dressed like that."

"I can," Moran replied. "The tabard will cover it."

"That's not—"

"There are no rules to the contrary. You wear black because dirt and blood show less—but it's not necessary, either. You could wear any functional clothing as long as you wore the tabard."

"I couldn't wear *that*—I'd trip over the hem."

"No, Kaylin, you wouldn't. This is a dress designed for

flight, and possible fight. It will not trip me, it will not get caught in anything, it will not tear."

"But—but—" She exhaled. Met Moran's military blue gaze.

"This is the ceremonial dress of the *Illumen praevolo*. And that," she added, taking a stool and pulling it up to the table, "is what I am."

"I like the dress," Teela said. Both she and her partner were lounging in the foyer, having chosen to miss breakfast.

"Thank you," Moran replied. "I was concerned that it would be a little too much for the office."

"Not a *little*," Kaylin countered. Last night, Moran had planned to take a leave of absence, as requested. By the Hawklord. One conversation later—if Annarion and his brother didn't count—she was not only going into the office, but she was going in dressed as the *Illumen praevolo*. It should have been hard to look martial in that dress. It wasn't. Moran looked very much like she was prepared for the battlefield.

"You're going to cause a bit of a stir," Tain added, looking appreciative. "But it suits you."

"The stir or the dress?" Moran asked, the corners of her lips rising.

"Both, I think."

"I'm almost sorry we missed breakfast. But Annarion wasn't in the best of moods," Teela said. Tain's addition was lost, for a moment, to shouting. "They almost sound like Dragons."

"You think?"

"They really don't," Bellusdeo said, "but if you want a Dragon to compare it to, I'm happy to oblige."

"I bet you are," Mandoran said. "And I'd just as soon take your word for it."

"You're willing to take my word for something?"

"Given the alternative, yes. Don't get used to it."

Bellusdeo snorted smoke, but her eyes were close to golden. They left the house in a huddle the minute Severn showed up at the door.

"They sound like Dragons," Severn said as he reversed course and headed back down the walk.

"Don't you start, too," Bellusdeo told him. "They sound nothing like Dragons—they just happen to be loud."

It was Kaylin's turn to snort. "Having listened to your indecipherable discussions with the Emperor half a palace away, I'm going to say that loud isn't the only thing they have in common."

Bellusdeo looked down her nose at Kaylin, lifting a brow as she did.

The familiar was sitting on Kaylin's shoulder, his wings folded. He looked alert, but not alarmed. The Barrani were blue-eyed, which was pretty much normal. It was amazing to Kaylin how similar their eyes were to Moran's at the moment. Bellusdeo's eyes had settled into an alert orange, but it was a pale color.

Moran attracted attention. She hadn't chosen to don the tabard for the walk to the Halls, and people in the streets stopped to look—or, in one or two cases, stare—as they walked past. In part, it might be the bracelet and bandaged wing—Moran hadn't elected to remove the dressing that kept the damaged wing in place. Kaylin doubted it, though. Moran walked with a kind of bold confidence she'd never seen.

Not that Moran lacked confidence, of course; in the infirmary, she had more pull than the Hawklord. She certainly had more pull than any of her patients, and had even threatened to strap an angry, hurt Leontine to a bed on at least one occasion. But that was a function of knowing her job, and knowing it well. This was different. It was almost as if she'd spent the whole of her life flying under cloud cover, and had finally flown free of it. She looked younger.

No, not younger, Kaylin thought. But…brighter, somehow. As if the trappings of the *praevolo* that she'd disdained for all of her life had been a missing, and essential, part of her nature.

"I'd like to see her fly," Mandoran said—very quietly. Aerian ears weren't Leontine or Barrani; in that, they were much closer to human, so whispering was safe.

"So would I," Kaylin replied, just as quietly. And it was true. She wanted Moran to let her heal her wing. She wanted Moran to fly. She thought, if she flew today, the Aerian would own the skies.

Instead, as if she were human, Moran owned the streets. Maybe it was the dress. Maybe it was the brilliance of the colors. Usually, Moran—like any sergeant—seemed both definitive and gray, as if it was necessary to let the office determine her shape. Or rather, she had. Today was a revelation. The Aerian didn't look happy, exactly. From everything she'd said, being *praevolo* had not been pleasant for her. It had cost her her mother, her grandmother—the only family she had.

Kaylin hated winter and fiefs and disease, because those three things had killed her mother. But it was like hating rain. Railing against weather didn't change the weather, because the weather didn't care. It had no essential malice. It was something to be endured.

Moran had lost kin because of *people*. It was different. It was profoundly different. And she'd denied the wings that had been her unwanted birthright. She'd ignored them. She'd proved that she didn't *need* them to make a place for herself. She'd made one.

But it was a conflicted space—Kaylin saw that now, if only in comparison. She had been saying, in every possible way, *Ignore me, ignore my differences.* She'd forced herself to fit in. By denying what she *was*, she'd created a life in which everyone else did, or could, deny it, as well. And that would have been fine, if not for the Caste Court. Or so Kaylin would have said. Now, she wasn't certain. Moran had lived behind walls. Kaylin wasn't certain if she'd knocked the walls down or opened a door, and it didn't matter.

No one attacked her on the way to work. The familiar was alert. Everyone was alert, even Mandoran. But there were no more invisible attackers, no more magical assassins. There was just open, clear sky. There were normal Aerian patrols.

There was, when they reached the doors, Clint and Tanner.

Tanner blinked but otherwise held his post. It was Clint who froze in place.

"If you don't close your mouth," Kaylin told him cheerfully, "you're going to end up swallowing flies or other large insects."

His hands had locked around the halberd's pole; his eyes were purple. Fair enough. Purple was Aerian surprise, and Kaylin expected to see a lot of it today. Tanner's eyes remained their normal color. He didn't whistle—it wasn't worth his job.

Kaylin expected Clint to say something to her; he'd gone out of his way to warn her to stay out of things. Or maybe she expected him to be cold, once the shock had worn off. Or—hells, she had no idea what she expected. She only knew that she hadn't expected him to fold at the knee, to spread his wings—into Tanner, since the Aerian wingspan was actually far greater than the span of the door frame.

And Moran accepted what was an obeisance. She let him hold it for what felt like minutes—and Kaylin's eyes would have been purple had she been Aerian, because she realized that Clint had no intention of rising until given permission. Which Moran finally did.

"If you do that once I've entered the Halls," Moran said pleasantly, "I'll see you busted back to private."

He rose, and reality reasserted itself. His eyes shaded from purple to a different Aerian color. Kaylin had expected that color to be blue, because she expected that this act of defiance on Moran's part would be considered trouble. But they went to gray instead. Honestly, racial interactions always contained hidden complications that made Kaylin feel stupid.

They entered the Halls.

Moran went to the infirmary—it was hers, after all— where she donned the version of tabard designed to accommodate Aerian wings. She allowed Bellusdeo to help her, glaring Kaylin out of the room before she could offer.

"I'm not the sergeant you have to worry about while you're here. And I can practically hear the other one growling."

There was a division in office space between the Aerians and the rest of the groundbound Hawks, because Aerians and the run-of-the-mill chairs and desks didn't combine well. They required more space, different chairs and less-confining desks; they worked at tables, without the drawer real estate, and they generally preferred to stand, although they'd take the sturdy stools created for their use.

Comfortable or not, they were required to turn in the same paperwork anyone else was; in that, Marcus was an equal-opportunity sergeant. If *he* had to suffer through paperwork, he made sure the suffering was shared.

Kaylin therefore missed some of the early Aerian reactions.

Marcus, however, with Leontine hearing and general paranoia, didn't. The growl was so loud, Kaylin missed the fact that her name was wedged somewhere in its depths. His eyes, of course, were a bright orange, which appeared to be darkening into the bad color for Leontines. She made her way to the front of his desk. Hardwood was definitely better when it came to Leontine claws; given his mood, there should have been runnels in the wood. Fortunately, there were only visible scratches so far.

"What," he demanded without preamble, "did you do?"

Kaylin considered the truth, which was bad. She considered the Leontine bristling in front of her: also bad. And she considered being caught in a lie while the Leontine was in this mood. She settled for less bad; there was no good here.

"I returned an item to Moran. It belonged to her," she added, keeping her voice as flat as possible.

"And this item wouldn't happen to be the bracelet she's wearing, would it?"

"Sir."

"It looks a lot like the bracelet in the Records transmission."

"Sir."

"Which would generally be considered *evidence*."

"Sir." She stopped herself from wilting, because it never actually helped.

"And the sergeant's dress?" He spoke the last word with clear distaste.

"Is hers. It's not against regulations. She has full freedom of motion in it, and she's wearing her identifying colors. Sir." *Shut up, Kaylin. Just shut up.*

Marcus said, "The Hawklord wants to speak to you. Now." His mirror was flat and reflective. Seeing her glance move—it was the only thing about Kaylin that did—he said, "Over your left shoulder."

Hanson stood in the arch that led to the Tower stairs, arms folded.

CHAPTER 12

"No," Hanson said, as he led the way back up the stairs—where his office, among other things, was located. "My mirror is not broken. Nor is the Hawklord's." He was grim, but Kaylin expected that. He was worried, which she hadn't. "No, don't speak to me." When she raised both brows, he said, "Plausible deniability. My desk is the ugliest it's been in years and I *do not* want any more involvement than I already have. I don't care what you did. I don't care what you do—don't repeat that where anyone can hear you. I have more than enough emergencies on my plate without you adding to them."

"Is the Hawklord angry?"

"Which part of 'don't speak to me' wasn't clear?"

Which was, Kaylin assumed, an answer. It was the wrong answer, as it turned out.

When Kaylin hit the Tower's top floor, the doors were open. She hesitated at the top of the stairs. In general, when the Hawklord was angry, they were shut; he made her open them the normal way, which always caused some pain.

Severn said a single word under his breath. It wasn't particularly polite.

"Private. Corporal. Please come in." The Hawklord's wings were high, which was all she could see of him, his eyes and their color facing away from them. He stood in front of his mirror, which was not reflective. Although he spoke softly, he enunciated just a little bit too well.

He was staring at a Records capture of Moran at the front doors. In her dress. With her bracelet. And her expression as she looked down on Clint's bowed, lowered head.

"Do you recognize Clint's posture?" he asked without turning, his voice soft, the syllables still a shade too pronounced.

"No, sir."

"Be more expansive. What do you think he is doing?"

"Kneeling."

"And his wings?"

She'd wondered about that. They were wide and high in a way that would have suggested aggression—if he'd been standing. "I'm sorry, sir. This was definitely not taught in racial integration classes, and I paid attention to everything I was taught about Aerians."

"The qualifier is—and was—noted."

Kaylin waited for the question Marcus had asked. Significantly, the Hawklord failed to ask it.

"You will not recognize the dress," he continued. "You will not recognize the significance of the bracelet."

"Sir." She chose the safest syllable.

He chose to let her. "There was no trouble on the way to the office this morning."

"No, sir."

"Did that surprise you?"

Had it? Yes. If she thought about it, it did. "Because of the dress?"

"Yes, Private. Because of the dress." His eyes were a shade

of gray that was tinged with blue. "I saw her fly once. When I was younger. I am not dar Carafel. I could never presume to rise so high." The words were said with only the faintest tinge of bitterness—and Kaylin recognized, in them, some part of her own envy and frustration at the unfairness of the universe. It was unsettling; she'd never heard it in the Hawklord's voice before.

"Flight," he continued, "has a meaning for you that it does not generally have for those who *can* fly. Valuing it, idolizing it as you do would be like idolizing breathing, for humans. Or walking. It is something we take for granted—until it is lost, and we are groundbound. Humans who lose the ability to walk have similar difficulties.

"But, Kaylin—when the *praevolo* flies, we feel it. All of us."

"She can't fly, though."

"No, not yet. But seeing her today, I cannot believe that she will never fly again." And he smiled. "Things are about to become interesting. The human in the holding cell is not dead. There has been only one attempt to poison him since yesterday—but the Aerians are not fools. Those who are complicit in the previous difficulties became so because they were afraid. Their families, where family exists, are in the Southern Reach, and dar Carafel rules the Reach." He shook his head, lifted his hand toward the mirror's surface and stopped, motionless and silent as he looked at Moran's image.

He then turned to face Kaylin, the undispelled image of Moran at his back.

"You will be having dinner guests this evening."

Kaylin nodded.

"I would like to invite myself to dinner."

And froze. When it became clear that the Hawklord was

not going to add any more words until she answered him, she turned to Severn, who predictably shrugged.

What should I do?

It's not my house, he replied. He wasn't nearly as disturbed about this as Kaylin was—but she saw that he hadn't really planned on attending dinner, either.

Coward.

You'd avoid it like the plague if Helen weren't your home.

This was more or less true. *It's supposed to be an informal dinner. With mostly just the Emperor and Bellusdeo. If the Hawklord comes, that changes everything.*

Oh?

It'll be political.

It's always political, Kaylin. When there are more than two people in any gathering, it eventually becomes political. Politics is just another way of saying, "I want something and I'm going to get it." There's more finesse. The rules of the game change, depending on the participants. But people are political.

I don't want the Emperor to kill me.

Neither do I. But Bellusdeo, at least, will find the Hawklord's presence amusing—and I think the Emperor has proven that he does care about her.

He's got a really stupid way of showing it.

People, Severn said again, as if that explained everything. And maybe it did. Kaylin cleared her throat, thinking that Severn was right. If Bellusdeo was amused, if Bellusdeo was not uncomfortable, the Emperor would forgive much.

"The thing is," she heard herself saying before she could close her mouth and choose words more carefully, "it's supposed to be an informal dinner. He's not there as—as…" The words trailed off, because speaking them out loud revealed the stupidity inherent in them. He wasn't there with his guards. He wasn't in his throne room. He wasn't wearing a crown—if he even wore a crown in his audience chamber. Kaylin couldn't remember.

But he *was* the Emperor. Nothing he did or said would change that.

"Is it about Moran?"

"Not directly," was the pleasant reply. "I am, of course, being watched. I am being observed. Any petitions I make to the Caste Court will be summarily shelved—with much more politic wording, and no doubt a few veiled threats."

"I don't consider assassins to be much in the way of 'veiled,' sir."

"They were not attempting to kill me. Any petition I make to the Imperial Courts on behalf of the Imperial Law will likewise be known to, and examined by, the Aerian Caste Court. They will have warning, if I choose to act against their interests. Remanding this to the Imperial Courts would be against their interests.

"Their use of a human, however, opens the door to that remand. I do not understand why they chose to do so. I have been considering how to best approach what is a delicate situation. And you have a dinner guest who might be able to help. I don't believe in coincidence," he added.

Kaylin, at this point, didn't believe in luck. Or at least not good luck. "Yes," she said. "If you want to come to dinner, please feel free. It'll give us all something to talk about that isn't mostly awkward."

I'd hate, Severn said, *to see your idea of awkward dinner conversation.*

She snorted. *Mostly it involves fire, or knives. Or spoken Dragon.*

Work was not exactly comfortable for the rest of the day. Kaylin could focus and forget about the looming dinner while she was on her beat, Severn by her side, but every other thing was lost to the growing stress. She did manage to enter Margot's without kicking her sign over, and she did thank Margot for sending the Records transmission that was about to spoil a lot of Aerians' days.

But she wasn't at her best, and by the time she returned to the Halls for the brief end-of-day report, she was so tense her shoulders were practically bunched up around her ears. The familiar registered his objection by curling up in a pile on top of her head.

"Are you going to come to dinner?" she asked Severn. She tried to sound casual, and managed extremely anxious instead.

"I wasn't going to."

"That means you've changed your mind?"

"Kaylin, he's not going to eat you."

"I know—Bellusdeo would hate him forever, so he won't risk that."

"I doubt anything you could do or say could materially alter his perception of you."

"I don't," was the glum reply.

I can be there without being present, if that's what you want.

She shook her head. What she wanted was her partner by her side when she went in to face danger. "It's just—the Hawklord's going to be there, as well. I'm due that promotion, and I don't want to mess it up."

"You can't."

"I can. I've done it before."

Severn shook his head. "Yes, if you want. I'll come to dinner. But I'm not coming dressed like this. I'll meet you at home."

"Do you have better clothing?"

"Yes. So do you."

"Not better," Kaylin said. "Just different."

★ ★ ★

Moran and Bellusdeo were waiting just outside the infirmary doors.

"You're late," the Dragon pointed out.

"No, you're early."

Moran nodded. "We are. But you and Lord Bellusdeo have an important guest this evening. By all accounts, he's visiting as a private citizen."

"A private citizen who is probably punctual to within seconds."

"And can destroy a city block just by breathing on it, yes." Moran's smile was slightly strained, but Kaylin thought it was genuine. The Aerian Hawk removed her tabard, folded it carefully, and set it on her desk. She removed the regulation belt that came with it, transforming herself into the bold, colorful woman who had walked with so much confidence and purpose toward the Halls of Law in the morning.

"How were things here?"

"They were very quiet," Moran said, grinning. "Apparently the Aerian Hawks have been superbly careful in their drills—as have the applicants for the Sword division. You'd almost think they're afraid to come to the infirmary. At all."

"I doubt it's fear," Bellusdeo said, stepping into the hall.

"No?"

"Shame. Guilt. Self-loathing. But fear? No. And before you ask, I have no issues with that. I think they should be ashamed of themselves."

Moran shook her head. "You don't know what it's like."

"No. But I know enough to know that their behavior is execrable. Don't bother defending them. Don't bother giving me reasons. They swore an oath to the Emperor's Law—and their failure to uphold their oath is unacceptable."

"Back in your day, they'd be dead?"

"If they broke their personal oaths to me? Yes. And ash, so Shadow couldn't use their corpses against us."

By the time Kaylin made it to her own front door, the familiar was chittering like an angry parrot. She couldn't understand him, and would have just ignored him—but he didn't like it when she ignored him because she was too absorbed in other thoughts. To be fair, he didn't like it when she ignored him on purpose, either, but this was different.

Helen was waiting for her at the front door. She had, in fact, opened it. But Helen's actual physical body started at the gatehouse, not the building; she was of course aware of everything Kaylin was thinking the minute she passed the fence line.

"You have two hours, dear." To Moran, she said, "I think you look lovely. You won't be joining us for dinner?"

"No, if that's acceptable to you."

"Lord Grammayre will," Helen pointed out.

"...Pardon?"

"Did Kaylin forget to tell you? I see that she did. The Hawklord will be joining us for dinner."

Dragon eyes and Aerian eyes both drilled into the side of Kaylin's averted face. Which was probably redder than it had to be. The big advantage to being Leontine, in Kaylin's opinion, was that humiliation or embarrassment wasn't instantly trumpeted to everyone with working eyes by the color of fur.

"When were you going to mention this?" Moran snapped, in her annoyed-sergeant voice.

"She wasn't, if she could get away with it," Bellusdeo replied. Kaylin still hadn't groped her way toward a coherent reply she thought Moran could live with.

"Why did you invite the Hawklord?" Moran demanded.

Demand was going to be her mode of conversation for at least the next few minutes.

"I didn't. He invited himself."

Moran's eyes narrowed.

"She isn't lying," Helen told the Aerian in a very mild voice.

Moran accepted this. She probably wouldn't have accepted it as easily coming from Kaylin, and Kaylin tried not to resent it. "How did he find out about your dinner?"

"I've been wondering that, as well. I certainly didn't tell him. I didn't tell anyone at the office." But people at the office had also been guests in her home, inasmuch as she'd ever had guests. She considered Teela and Tain. "It's political."

Moran's expression said *no kidding*, but more emphatically. "So you're having dinner with the Emperor and the Hawklord." She shook her head.

"You could join us."

"Not a chance. If I could actually fly, I'd spend the evening in training exercises, just to make sure there was no possibility of overlap." She exhaled, and some of the tension left her shoulders. It had lodged pretty deeply in her face, though.

"The Emperor would be coming to dinner regardless of where you were living," Helen told the Aerian. Kaylin was perversely happy to see that she wasn't the only person whose private thoughts were addressed out loud. "The Hawklord would therefore invite himself to dinner, again regardless of your residence. It is the Emperor he wishes to—informally, off-Records—engage. Your presence may indeed be causing difficulty for the Hawklord, but it is not causing difficulty for Kaylin. Or for me.

"Kaylin, however, now needs to take a bath. I will accompany her," she added. "She will need to dress. I will remind her of the etiquette required when entertaining guests of note."

"How do you know etiquette?"

"My last tenant was alive when the Dragon Emperor ruled," Helen replied. "And in his fashion, he was impeccably polite and considerate."

"Meaning I'm not."

"You are very considerate," Helen told her gently. "When you are aware of the need for consideration. And you have had several lessons with Lord Diarmat."

This caused smoke to billow out of Bellusdeo's nostrils, mostly because she was keeping her mouth shut. Mention of Diarmat did nothing helpful for the color of her eyes.

"Will Maggaron aid you in dressing, or may I?" Helen asked the Dragon.

"I don't need help with my dress. I'm not going to wear court clothing to the dinner table. If I were in a slightly worse mood, I wouldn't wear anything. At all."

Moran's eyes widened.

Kaylin's closed. "I think the Arkon is also coming for dinner."

"Lannagaros—"

"You told him, the last time we talked, that you wanted him to come. He hates leaving his library for anything less than an all-out battle, but I think he'll be here, because you wanted him to be here."

"You think I'm being unfair."

"Not really. But the Arkon has never treated me the way he treats you." The oldest of the Dragons was, and had always been, fond of Bellusdeo. What he found amusing behavior from her would have been cause to reduce Kaylin to ash.

Helen informed Kaylin the moment the Emperor reached the gatehouse. "You were correct," she said. "The Arkon is with him."

"Does he look happy?"

"Which one, dear?"

"Either of them." Kaylin tried not to sound glum. She mostly failed. "But I was talking about the Arkon. I can't imagine the Emperor ever looking happy. His face would break."

"The Arkon looks irritated."

Great.

"The Emperor does not."

"He doesn't?"

"His face is almost entirely without expression. Ah, I think the Hawklord has also arrived. Did you not tell him to use the tower entrance?"

"He's used to doors," Kaylin replied. "And no, I didn't tell him to use the tower entrance. That's fine for Dragons in flight form—they can't get through our doors without destroying them. Aerians can land and walk in. It's what they do everywhere else in the city."

"I shall be sure to mention the aperture above. He flew, after all." Helen cleared her throat, which was entirely an affectation, as she didn't really have one.

Kaylin understood this to mean that she had to bust her butt to get to the front door before the guests did. The small dragon sat gracefully on the shoulder of the one good dress she owned that she hadn't destroyed. It was a white dress; it covered a lot less than was ideal—which in this case meant her arms were exposed. She'd considered the other dress she owned, but Helen's glacial frown made clear that she considered it unsuitable.

"I don't have a lot of call to wear dresses," Kaylin had said.

"No, dear. But this one is perfectly serviceable." And she had lifted a dress that Kaylin had only worn once.

"I'm not sure—"

"I am. If you are to entertain the Emperor in future, you might consider speaking with Lord Grammayre about your rate of pay. The clothing you do possess is perfectly functional—but not for meeting royalty. And while I do not get out of the house much—" By which she meant at all. "—I understand that more appropriate clothing *is* a not-inconsiderable expense."

"But he's not here as royalty—that's the *whole point*, Helen."

"And if you honestly think that royalty is something that is donned and discarded, as if it were mere clothing, you are making a grave mistake. No matter what he calls himself, he is the Eternal Emperor. You are part of his collective hoard. Most people would consider it an honor—an undreamed-of honor—to entertain him."

Kaylin considered it a nightmare, but she knew Helen was probably right. "You can't make dresses? You can make everything else."

"Yes—but any dress I made for you would vanish the moment you stepped off the property."

"I'll be here the entire time."

"I'm sure you thought that the first night we met as well—and you ended up flying off to fight ancient sorcerers by the side of the Dragons. You would not have been happy to have spent any of your necessary time changing clothing."

Kaylin surrendered. White dress it was. But she wasn't particularly comfortable as she ran down the stairs, taking them three at a time. It wasn't so much the skirt—it was the feeling of exposure. When she was in her normal clothing, even without her tabard, she still felt like a Hawk.

Right now, she mostly felt half-naked and uncertain. She preferred the Hawk. The familiar warbled in her left ear, as if trying to be encouraging. She appreciated it.

"You have very punctual guests," Helen said, radiating approval. She was waiting beside the closed doors.

"Go figure," Kaylin replied. Punctuality was an almost mortal enemy, although she'd spent a lot of her life trying to make it a friend. She checked her wrist to make sure her bracer was in place. It had come from the Imperial treasury, and she was required, by equally Imperial command, to wear it At All Times. While the definition of *always* was constantly being stretched, the Emperor would be in front of her face for most of the evening, and Dragons weren't famously forgiving when their commands were flouted.

She inhaled, held her breath, and nodded to Helen. Helen opened the doors, but she did it the normal way: with her hands. She stepped back after smiling at the first visitors at the door.

Kaylin's smile was more stilted than Helen's, but it was far better than the smiles on the faces of the two Dragons, since they didn't even bother to make the attempt. They might have been coming to a funeral.

"Arkon, Darranatos." She bowed. It was stiff and graceless, but the end posture would probably have garnered no more than perfunctory criticism from Diarmat. "Welcome."

The Arkon offered her a shallow bow; the Emperor merely nodded. He did, however, bow to Helen.

It was customary, Helen had told Kaylin as she had dressed, to invite guests to take tea—or something stronger—when they first arrived.

"But they're coming here for dinner," Kaylin had pointed out while fussing with her hair, "not tea."

"Dinner generally takes a while, and there's usually some polite socializing before people are seated for the meal."

Drug addicts, pushers, and frauds were a more welcome part of Kaylin's day than polite socializing.

"You socialize all the time, dear."

"We lounge around the dining room table because it's the biggest, and we mostly trade insults and whining," Kaylin had pointed out. "And offending anyone at my breakfast table isn't career-limiting. I have to care what these guests think of me."

"They are not going to harm you in your own home. It would be a disgraceful breach of etiquette."

"And impossible, because you're my home."

"I am talking about their behavior, not my own—but yes, if it somehow came to that, they would not be able to harm you. There is nothing you could do that would necessitate that."

So Kaylin now invited the two Dragons to sit in the parlor. It had changed both size and shape. Helen frequently adjusted spaces as she deemed necessary. Kaylin wondered what people without Helen did, but she knew. They didn't have the bloody Emperor as an informal guest.

Helen, however, rescued Kaylin by taking on the duties of a servant. She didn't instruct Kaylin in the pouring of tea or the offering of drinks or anything else; she did that all herself. Kaylin should have appreciated it more, but the menial and necessary tasks would have given her something to *do* other than feeling awkward and incompetent.

She was rescued by the arrival, minutes later, of the Hawk-lord. In theory, Helen was to answer the door and lead the new guests in; in practice, Kaylin leapt to her feet, grateful to leave the awkward, silent room. When she was almost at the door, Bellusdeo drifted down the stairs. She stopped, her eyes shifting into the color of Dragon surprise.

"Is that you, Kaylin?"

Kaylin said, "Answering the door now. Are you sure Moran isn't coming?"

"I'm absolutely positive. Is that dress new? I've never seen it before."

"And I wish that had continued."

"It's very striking, and it suits you."

"It doesn't suit me at all—"

"Kaylin, dear. The door," Helen's disembodied voice said. To Bellusdeo, she added, "Kaylin is nervous because she is not accustomed to guests."

"I have guests living with me all the time," Kaylin pointed out, as she reached the closed front doors.

"Yes and no, dear. They are technically guests, but you treat them very much as if they were family. Siblings. You are not used to *guests*."

Bellusdeo, however, said, "Let me entertain the Dragons while you greet the new arrival." She didn't look nervous. At all. Kaylin was too grateful to feel resentful.

The Hawklord was waiting at the door. He was not dressed as the Hawklord; he was entirely more colorful, although not as colorful as Moran's ceremonial garb had been. He wasn't wearing a dress, but the vest that overlay the long, belled sleeves of an emerald green shirt ended a good six inches below his knees. The vest itself was a mixture of purple and blues, with gold stitching, gold trim and white interlaced ribbons.

Only his boots looked normal, for a value of normal that involved the Emperor, the Arkon and the Hawklord at the same table.

Lord Grammayre smiled as he no doubt correctly read her expression. "Kaylin."

"Lord Grammayre." She remembered to bow. It was not as

stiff a bow as the one she'd offered the Dragons. If she wasn't at home with the Hawklord, she was vastly more comfortable in his presence. He'd seen her at her absolute worst, and had found it in himself to make the beginnings of a home for her.

She'd had to do the rest, but the rest hadn't seemed so hard given the alternative: a life spent in Barren. This man wasn't Caitlin—but he wasn't the Emperor, either. And neither of the men were Barren. Neither of them ever would be.

"May I compliment you on your appearance?" Lord Grammayre asked.

"If you absolutely insist."

Helen cleared her invisible throat.

"…I mean, thank you. Do you recognize the dress?"

"I was about to ask." The Hawklord smiled. "It suits you."

"It doesn't."

"It would if you didn't look so uncomfortable in it. It is very simple," he added. "The Aerians do not value simplicity in their formal dress, but there is much to be said for it."

"My normal clothing is simple, too."

"Ah. Yes. But perhaps not suited to entertaining."

Severn came last.

When the door opened—and yes, Kaylin had all but leapt out of her seat in her eagerness to take advantage of any excuse to be out of that room—she was so happy to see him she could have cried.

Severn, however, froze in place. His mouth was half-open, as if he'd been about to say hello and forgotten what the word meant. He did, after a few seconds, remember to blink. She was confused for that same few seconds, and then looked down at the white dress. She looked up again.

Severn was dressed more formally, but human male formal was just a fancier, more expensive version of normal.

"If you bow," she told him, "I'll kill you, I swear."

His smile was, at least, familiar. "I didn't expect that dress."

"Helen made me."

"I did not make her, as she said, do anything. She is an adult. She makes her own choices," Helen added.

"You'll notice Severn's not wearing a dress." Kaylin held out both of her hands; Severn hesitated before placing his on top of them. "We could trade."

"I don't think the dress would fit me."

"Betting?"

"Not while the Emperor is a dinner guest, no." His smile deepened. "I'll take that bet when he's gone, though."

"It's irrelevant," Helen told them both, "because Severn's clothing would *not* fit. In any way. Your guests," she added, "are waiting."

Bellusdeo was holding court when Severn and Kaylin made their way to the parlor. The Hawklord glanced in their direction, but it was brief and appeared to contain more amusement than censure. Severn made his bow to the Emperor; it was not up to Diarmat's standards, but then again, his whole demeanor had been so much more graceful than Kaylin's, it probably didn't matter.

He didn't appear to be uncomfortable in this roomful of people, two of whom could destroy his life just by lifting a pen. Or a voice.

Kaylin, relieved of the need for idle conversation, watched the Dragons. The Arkon's eyes were gold, pure gold. He was speaking with Bellusdeo, and her eyes, tinged lightly orange, rested in a relaxed, and even affectionate, expression. The Emperor might as well have been Kaylin.

And that was an odd thought. The Emperor was arguably

the most important man in the Empire—but he was just as uncomfortable, felt just as out of place, as Kaylin did.

As if he could hear the thought that not even she was stupid enough to put into words, he raised a dark brow in her direction. His hair had been oiled and pulled back off his face; it fell down his back in a series of intricate knots that did not scream "informal" to Kaylin.

But he had no Imperial Palace Guards with him, and for that, she was profoundly grateful.

"Dinner," Helen came in to announce, "is served. If you would follow me?"

CHAPTER 13

The parlor was not the only room in the house that had undergone transformation; the dining room had also been changed. Although the shape and size of the room was roughly the same as it had been at breakfast this very distant morning, the ceilings had sprouted a few feet of height, and the windows had grown to match them. They'd also gained both width and stained glass. The table, however, had shrunk, and the chairs had been replaced; they were darker, heavier, and flawless.

Helen did not tell people where to sit, and that was slightly awkward, because both Kaylin and Bellusdeo attempted to take the seat farthest from the Emperor. They would have collided had it not been for Severn, who slid a hand to Kaylin's elbow.

She felt a little shock of warmth as his palm touched her skin. He guided her to a chair and pulled it out for her. What she really wanted was to sit Teela-style—with the chair back against the table, while her arms were draped over the top rail.

The top rail of *these* chairs, however, would have been too much of a stretch. She sat. Severn sat beside her. Bellusdeo sat opposite the Emperor, but this table was short enough that she wasn't halfway across the room. The Arkon sat to one side of the golden Dragon. The Hawklord sat between the Arkon and the Emperor.

As a dinner, it felt a lot like an awkward council of war.

"Lord Grammayre," the Emperor said. "It has been some small while since you have graced my presence in person."

"I was surprised to hear that you were kind enough to join Kaylin for dinner. I have been, as you must imagine, embroiled in racial difficulties. I would never otherwise forgo the pleasure of your company." The Hawklord said this with a completely straight face. Kaylin thought he sounded sincere. It wasn't the first time she'd had questions about his sanity—he'd taken her on, after all—but it was close.

Bellusdeo's eyes were orange-tinged gold, but they were as gold as they ever got when she was in the presence of the Emperor. Kaylin prayed—in that nonspecific way that people did who weren't religious—that they'd remain that way.

The Arkon snorted smoke. "We are then to turn dinner into a political discussion?"

"Hush, Lannagaros," Bellusdeo said. "For some of us, politics *is* polite dinner conversation."

Although the Arkon grimaced, his eyes remained pure gold. He frowned—deeply—at Bellusdeo, who surprised Kaylin by laughing. She considered approaching the Arkon's disapproval the same way, and decided against it; if Bellusdeo ever misread the situation, the fire that resulted wouldn't turn *her* to ash.

But she felt herself relaxing as she watched the two Dragons, and she reminded herself that the Arkon was family to Bellusdeo, inasmuch as Dragons ever claimed any.

"And you're involving yourself in the politics of the realm now, are you?" the Arkon said.

Bellusdeo's smile was almost feline. "Only so far as the politics affect my home."

"Meaning?"

"Sergeant dar Carafel is living with us, as I imagine you know."

The Emperor said, "I did mention it. He was, however, deeply involved in the study of something long dead; it may have escaped his hearing."

"I'm surprised you'd interrupt him when his concentration was that intense."

"Had I not, we would not have arrived for dinner within a week of its actual time."

Bellusdeo chuckled.

The Emperor's eyes, Kaylin noted, were the darkest shade of orange in the dining room—but they lightened at her obvious amusement.

"He has always been like that. I was told he was like that when he emerged from the egg. Did they ever tell you about his shell?"

The Arkon actually flushed, which in a man of his apparent age was almost shocking. "Bellusdeo, please. I was a hatchling; it is not relevant now."

"No. I was not privileged to speak with those who had known him from birth. What did they say?"

"He very carefully collected all the pieces he could find of his own shell, and put them into a tidy pile. He also bit anyone who came near them—and that would include the clutch workers. They were all," she added, to the non-Dragons in the room, "significantly larger than he was."

"I see now," the Arkon said, "why my presence was deemed necessary."

Kaylin almost laughed at his expression. But she understood, watching, that it *was* necessary. Bellusdeo was mocking him—but she was mocking him the way she mocked Maggaron. There was no edge in it, just affection and the expectation that she would be forgiven.

"It seems you have remained true to yourself," the Emperor said gravely.

"And you?" Bellusdeo asked, surprising everyone at the table. "Have you?"

The Emperor stiffened; his eyes became more orange. The line of his lips thinned. His hands didn't become fists, but they rested on the table, stiff as boards.

The Arkon reached out and placed one hand over Bellusdeo's. "That is perhaps not a question for the dinner table." His voice was gentle; a brief eddy of pain marred, but did not eradicate, his affectionate expression.

"And am I to speak only of trivialities and things that do not concern me?" she demanded. Her eyes were more orange, too.

"No," Kaylin said. "We can talk about Caste Court exemptions instead. Because at the moment, those do concern you."

"I am not—"

"You're the one standing guard in the infirmary."

Bellusdeo bit back a reply, and nodded. She was, to Kaylin's surprise, spoiling for a fight. But she wasn't four. She reined in her temper, biting back words. Kaylin was going to be grateful if the evening ended without any of the Dragons resorting to their native tongue. "Yes, you're right. And Lord Grammayre is no doubt being polite in his interest about the Arkon's early years."

The Emperor was more than willing to leave the subject behind, even if the one he was retreating to was tangled and political. He did glance thoughtfully at Kaylin before transferring his pointed gaze to the man who was commanding officer of all of the Hawks, ground or sky.

"You have always disliked Caste Court exemptions, Lord Grammayre."

Every Hawk—no, every person who worked in the Halls of Law—hated Caste Court exemptions. Admittedly, it was the Barrani who made the most use of them; it was life-threatening to be involved in any investigation that pointed at Barrani criminals, which was most of the reason the force had Barrani Hawks to begin with.

Before the Hawklord could reply, the Emperor said, "As I am here informally, the general rules that govern behavior in the audience chambers need not apply here. You may address me as 'Majesty.'"

It was Severn who choked on his soup, which surprised her. *I find the Draconic idea of informality…ridiculous.*

So did Kaylin, for what that was worth. Given that the Emperor had all the power, she didn't labor under any misconceptions.

"Thank you, Your Majesty. As you are aware, some difficulty has arisen in regards to a member of the Hawks who serve the Imperial Law."

"I am *exceedingly* aware, yes. My secretaries and their undersecretaries dread even activating their mirrors at the start of their shift. It appears—and I have failed to ascertain the truth of this—that they have taken to referring to the Caste Court collectively as 'the harpies.'"

The Hawklord choked on his soup, just as Severn had. Kaylin took comfort from the fact that she hadn't. Maybe Diarmat's forbidding, ridiculous, humiliating lessons had some value, after all.

"My apologies, Your Majesty. I was not expecting that."

"You feel it is inaccurate?"

"I feel it is unfortunate." He smiled as he said it. "I will not vouch for accuracy but feel compelled to point out that my secretary refers to these particular communications in a way entirely inappropriate for repetition at the dining table."

"Then we are in accord. They will no doubt note your attendance at this dinner."

"They will. Moran dar Carafel is currently in residence. But they have no recourse to forbid it."

"I take it, from your private's expression, that you wish us—ah, apologies, me—to remand this case to your jurisdiction. You will, of course, have grounds for this request."

"I do."

"You understand that the Caste Court will demand your flight feathers—if not your entire wings—should I condescend to do this."

"They are demanding my wings now. But they are inconvenienced in this demand by Imperial Law. Even were I to be considered a traitor to my flight and my race, they would have to have grounds on which to make that accusation. If they did, they could of course try me and have me executed."

"If you agreed to be tried by the Caste Court, yes."

"I do not think I could perform my duties as an outcaste." And Kaylin remembered that the outcastes lost their wings. "There is some possibility that charges will be forthcoming," Lord Grammayre continued.

"So I've been told."

Kaylin, however, had not, and she almost pushed herself out of her chair and across the table in angry outrage.

Helen's hand—Helen's physical hand—clamped down on her right shoulder. "The next course," she said, "will be served now."

Over the next two courses—none of which were the main meal, and all of which were distinctly unappetizing because they were too fancy—Grammayre and the Emperor danced around the question of the remand. The Emperor made no commitment, and the Hawklord was wise enough not to demand one.

"I had word that Moran dar Carafel has donned the ceremonial raiment of her position."

"Yes, Your Majesty. As of this morning. She came to the Halls in almost complete regalia." He deliberately avoided looking at Kaylin. "I do not know if you have seen the Records capture that arrived yesterday afternoon."

"In theory, I have not. The Caste Court has demanded its embargo."

The Hawklord didn't seem to be surprised that the Emperor had, theoretically, chosen to respect any part of this demand. Kaylin, however, was.

"Theoretically, then, a human male is involved. He is currently in the holding cells for attempted assault—magical in nature—of Hawks."

"Actual assault of a resident of Elani," Kaylin helpfully added.

"I fail to see how an assault of that nature could be under the rubric of caste exemption," the Emperor said. His eyes, which had been orange, now shaded into a more familiar orange gold. The Emperor's eyes were never pure gold, in Kaylin's experience.

"Oddly enough, Your Majesty, so did I. I have," he added, "examined extant Caste Court Records—where they are available—and the man in question is definitively human; he is not outcaste Aerian."

"They couldn't make that claim of outcaste Aerians," Kaylin interrupted, thinking with a pang of Lillias and the blessing she had procured for Moran, a gift Kaylin had still not given to the Aerian sergeant.

"Outcaste Aerians remain, for the purposes of Imperial Law, Aerian," the Hawklord replied.

"Since when?" Before he could answer, she continued. "I know the actual laws. I know the actual laws better than half the older Hawks. Outcaste means something. You make someone outcaste, you're essentially saying they're no longer part of your *entire race*."

"That is not entirely true," Bellusdeo said. "The Barrani outcastes—"

"Aren't Aerians," Kaylin snapped.

Careful. She looked across the table and met Severn's gaze. Swallowed.

Bellusdeo, who was used to Kaylin, didn't even seem to notice the interruption. But the Emperor, who wasn't, did. Kaylin slammed into the wall of his orange eyes, but the Eternal Emperor's expression was neutral. She glanced at the Arkon; his eyes were still golden.

"You speak," the Emperor said, "as if you have actually met outcaste Aerians."

This time, it was the Hawklord whose eyes shifted color; his wings definitely rose. He was far too well-bred to spread them at the dining table.

"I have," Kaylin told the table.

"And I would like to know *who*," a voice said from the hall. Kaylin looked past the dining table—everyone probably did—to see Moran dar Carafel, framed by the door.

She was dressed as she had been for her martial and defiant walk to the Halls of Law, with a couple of essential differences. The first: her hair. She had bathed, and it was a shiny, straight fall down her back. Her eyes were blue, but given the tone of her voice—appropriate for the infirmary and a sergeant—Kaylin expected that. Her injured wing had not yet been rebound; it was high, in all its damaged glory, the spots that had defined her life hidden from view by the rest of her.

"Private?"

"Kaylin," Kaylin replied. "I'm not on duty."

A very fancy stool appeared at the table. Apparently Moran was going to join them for dinner, after all.

Everyone at the table except Kaylin rose. Kaylin belatedly remembered that this was something people did at a dinner table when someone significant joined the party. That was the frustrating thing about so-called manners. None of them really made any *sense*. Then again, neither did Caste Court exemptions, as far as Kaylin was concerned, and she'd learned to live with those. She rose, as well.

She could feel an apology hovering in the air—Helen's. She willed Helen not to say it out loud until after the guests had left, and Helen, hearing everything that Kaylin could think, remained silent.

Moran glanced at the stool, and then at the gathered, standing guests. Some of the swell of what Kaylin had assumed was rage left her—or at least it left her wings. Her eyes remained very blue as she marched toward the stool and sat on it. She was about as graceful as Kaylin would have been had she been angry.

And she was also now the angriest person at the table. In general, angry dinner companions were never a good thing if one liked uninterrupted eating, but at the moment, her anger eased the tension between Bellusdeo and the Emperor. Since that was the theoretical point of the dinner in the first place, Kaylin accepted the angry Aerian with far less discomfort than she normally would. Even when the Aerian's glare was turned, like a giant, blunt weapon, on her.

"I'm not sure this is the place to discuss it," Kaylin began.

"Don't stall."

"I'm not stalling. I'm being serious."

"She is not incorrect," the Hawklord said, coming to Kaylin's rescue.

"It involves me," was Moran's flat reply.

Not even the Hawklord could argue with that, although Kaylin's first instinct was to do so. The problem with that instinct was that she'd have to lie. She would never have met an outcaste Aerian if it weren't for Moran, and clearly both the Aerians knew it. "It does," Kaylin admitted. "But not in a bad way. And I think Lord Grammayre is right—this isn't the place to have this conversation."

"Given the conversation you were about to start," Moran replied, "it can't be any worse."

"For me? No. For you? I thought you weren't—"

"I heard what you said. Helen was kind enough to repeat it. I thought my intervention would be welcome."

Kaylin highly doubted that. But the truth was, the Hawklord seemed genuinely pleased to see her at the table. Grammayre, like the Emperor, was not a man known for his ability to mimic pleasure or joy—at least not in the office, which was the only place they interacted.

"Your company," the Emperor said, "is always welcome."

Blue faded into purple and then returned. Moran inclined her head. "Your Majesty, you do me too much honor."

"We all, to some extent, bear the burdens of our office," he replied. "And yours was, is, and has always been, significant to your people. It has been many years since I last saw those robes or that bracelet."

Moran's head tilted slightly, as if she were leaning in to catch the echo of words she hadn't expected. She glanced, once, at her familiar table-mates, and then spoke. "You knew my predecessor?"

"Not well, no. I had occasion to meet with him, of course."

"You did?"

"He was dar Carafel by birth, a member of the Caste Court."

She grimaced, just as Kaylin would have done. Kaylin had always assumed that Moran was a decade and a half older than she was; she lost that certainty, watching the off-duty sergeant. "I see."

"You are dar Carafel."

"I was adopted into dar Carafel, yes. I am not a member of the Caste Court." Her voice implied strongly that she would become a member over her dead body. Then again, she was a Hawk.

"No, you are not. You are a sergeant in the Hawks. There are no Aerians I prize more highly, if that is an acceptable word. You serve my Law, and my city, almost as if it were your own."

"It kind of is," Kaylin said quietly.

"The injuries you have taken," the Emperor continued as if Kaylin hadn't spoken, which was probably for the best, "were taken in defense of the city. Those injuries are responsible for your current predicament. And mine. And Lord Grammayre's. They are not, however, a source of shame. Nor should they ever be. Were it not for the sacrifice of the Aerians, many, many more would have died.

"I would vastly rather meet with the Lord of Hawks than the Caste Court. I will overlook the fact that you are dar Carafel, in this room."

Moran's eyes widened, and she bit back a brief laugh; her cheeks reddened as she lowered her chin.

Bellusdeo was staring at the Emperor's profile, almost arrested. He noticed, raising one dark brow at her expression.

"Surely you did not think I possessed no sense of humor, Lord Bellusdeo?"

To Kaylin's surprise, Bellusdeo also reddened. She was, however, more defiant—probably because she could be. Nothing short of attempted assassination was likely to lead to her death at the Emperor's hands. "I can be forgiven for that, I believe. You have evinced none of that humor in my presence since my arrival in Elantra."

"Some things are too important for humor," the Emperor replied. His eye membranes lowered. "Humor requires a certain detachment, implies a lack of concern."

The gold Dragon snorted. This time, there was no smoke in it. "Is that how you see it? Humor is grounding. It steadies troops, it eases tension."

"I am not a man famed for my sense of humor."

"No, I can see that. I rather considered you might be famed for its lack."

"That is harsh."

She smiled. "Yes. It is, and I will tender apologies for it, now." She turned to Moran. "As I will tender apologies to you, for interrupting."

"I imagine," the Hawklord said, "that she was grateful for the interruption."

"By law," the Emperor then continued, "the outcastes *are* considered a matter for and of the Caste Courts. If the outcaste chooses to do so, they can throw themselves onto the mercy of the Imperial Courts—but that is not easily done if their position and their relative power is not secure enough to begin with." Seeing Kaylin's expression, he added, "The outcastes are protected by Imperial Law if they request such protection. I do not believe such a petition has ever been made by an Aerian."

"I told you—I asked you—to stay out of this," Moran told

Kaylin, her tone at odds with the words themselves. The former verb was the more correct one.

"I did. I didn't search the streets for outcaste Aerians—you know as well as I do now that I wouldn't have even noticed them if I'd passed them in the streets. They don't have *wings*, Moran. They look human to the casual eye. You have to speak with them to notice that their eye color changes—and most people in the city aren't going to do that if the Aerian doesn't want to be social."

"Then how did you meet an outcaste?"

"Evanton."

Moran frowned. "Evanton? The one that sells garbage and surprisingly useful enchantments from time to time?"

"Yeah. Grouchy old guy, but makes good tea. And cookies."

Bellusdeo did exhale smoke then. Her eyes were tinted orange as she dragged her gaze from the Emperor to Kaylin, and dropped it on her head.

"What? Everything I've said is true. He *is* a grouchy old guy. He does make good tea, even if he doesn't like tea."

"There are days," Bellusdeo replied, "where I understand perfectly the abominable lessons you are forced to take under Lord Diarmat. Informality is one thing. Disrespect is quite another."

"Your meeting with Evanton?"

"Evanton had been approached by a woman. She wanted him to make something for her. Don't look at me like that—you know he enchanted my daggers so they don't make noise when they leave their sheaths."

"I am not entirely certain I approve," the Dragon Emperor said. The Hawklord stiffened.

"Is it illegal?" Bellusdeo's voice was chillier.

"Not yet."

"Well then, carry on," she said—to Kaylin.

"I'm not usually called in as a delivery service." She hesitated, looking at the table. This was a far larger crowd than the one she'd originally envisioned when she'd agreed to deliver what was, in essence, a gift. "But the woman wanted the item delivered to Sergeant dar Carafel of the Hawks."

"Did you meet this woman?" Moran demanded.

"Getting there," Kaylin said. "And yes, I did. I wasn't willing to deliver anything without at least meeting the person first. I trust Evanton," she added quickly, in case it was necessary. "There's no way he would make something harmful and ask me to pass it on—and he made it clear that *he* was making it.

"She looked like an older woman. Maybe in her fifties? Sixties? Maybe younger, but under some stress. I didn't—" Kaylin inhaled. Exhaled. "I didn't realize she was Aerian because she had no wings."

"How did you recognize what she was?" the Arkon asked quietly.

"Her eyes. Her eyes changed color. And I know Aerian color shifts like I know the back of my own hand."

She turned, then, to the Hawklord and Moran; both were still and silent, as if Kaylin's words had pinned them irrevocably in place. Moran broke that silence with difficulty; her eyes were a complicated color, a mix of purple and blue—a pale shade that implied sorrow and surprise in equal measure. "Did she tell you her name?"

"What did she ask Evanton to make?" the Hawklord demanded at the same time. The collision of Elantran questions caused an awkward pause, but it was to the Hawklord that Kaylin replied.

"A *bletsian*, she called it. Evanton said it's a blessing of air."

Moran closed her eyes. This was not uncommon among races whose eyes gave away their base emotional state, but it took Moran a full, silent minute before she opened them again—and the left side of her jaw was twitching. "And her name?"

Kaylin thought Moran knew. "She said her name was Lillias."

Moran rose.

The Hawklord rose, as well. "Moran."

"I want you to take me to her," the sergeant said to Kaylin.

"I have no idea where she is," Kaylin replied, uneasy now.

"Then I want you to take me to Evanton."

"Moran—" Lord Grammayre said again.

The Emperor, however, raised his voice—without apparent effort or strain. "Dinner is in progress. I am certain that Lillias will also be dining, if in different circumstances. The Keeper is unlikely to consider a sergeant's desire an immediate emergency. You will visit *tomorrow*, if you must do so at all."

Both of the Aerians sat.

Bellusdeo said, gently, "What is a *bletsian*, Moran?"

Moran swallowed. After a longer pause, she said, "If it's a blessing of air, it's meant as a gift. It might allow me to…fly. It won't allow me to fly naturally or forever, unless Evanton is vastly more powerful than any of my own kin. But such blessings were conferred by my people in very rare circumstances—and not always to the flightless or those who had been crippled." She used the last word bitterly, angry at herself. Or her people. Or the world.

The Hawklord said nothing.

"You knew," Moran said, accusation giving the words an edge that was never going to make a dinner table fun or relaxing.

Lord Grammayre said very, very little.

"You *knew*."

"Your life was difficult enough. She was—and is—out-caste."

"She did *nothing wrong*. She committed no crime by the laws of the people! She—"

"She thwarted the powerful." The Hawklord's voice was soft. "Your Majesty, forgive us."

It was Kaylin who spoke next. "The *reason* we have laws is that legally thwarting the powerful shouldn't *be* punishable by death or—or dismemberment. The laws are supposed to speak for people who don't have the power to speak loudly enough for themselves!"

The Emperor smiled. His eyes were, to Kaylin's surprise, an orange gold, but more gold than they had been all evening. "This perhaps leads directly in to Lord Grammayre's interests. I *am* the Emperor," he continued, his voice softening in a way that did not imply kindness or gentleness. "My word *is* law. You understand that, do you not, Private? If I chose to have you dismembered, or if I chose to reduce to ash where you were sitting—"

"You would have to go through Helen, and if you managed that, through *me*," Bellusdeo countered.

The Emperor lifted a hand, demanding at least temporary silence.

"I point out to the young and optimistic private a truth she has perhaps overlooked. Should I desire it, I could lay waste to half the city before I could be stopped—and it would be legal. I am the Emperor. The Empire is *mine*. The laws were created for my convenience. I can change them at any time."

Well, yes, because he was the Emperor. Kaylin held her peace, but it was very hard. Bellusdeo's eyes were orange.

The Arkon's, however, remained gold. The Arkon trusted and served the Eternal Emperor, and in the end, Kaylin trusted the librarian. She tried not to panic, and mostly succeeded.

"The laws are not always convenient to me," the Emperor continued. "There are times when I desire to reduce whole delegations that affront me in the audience chambers of the palace to their composite ash. There is one group in particular I would like to eat, but I fear they would be unpalatable to even a Dragon.

"I have chosen not to do so. I have made laws that can be safely enforced, and in order to ensure that they are, the enforcement is left to the mostly mortal, whose understandings of the frailty of mortals are more visceral, more personal.

"I did not make this choice out of the 'goodness of my heart.'" He used the Elantran phrase here; he otherwise defaulted to High Barrani. "Perhaps you do not understand this. I will now endeavor to explain. The Empire, as I stated emphatically, is mine. If I do not choose to destroy its citizens, if I do not exercise the prerogative of both rulership and anger, I will allow no others to do so—not without great effort on their part.

"And I do not so choose. What I will not allow myself, for the sake of my hoard, I will allow no others." He pinned Kaylin to her seat with the steady, unblinking orange of his eyes. "You fail to understand the value of the respect that comes from fear. I did not expect that."

"Respect doesn't come from fear. Obedience and terror do. I didn't *respect* Barren or Nightshade. I was terrified that they would kill me if they noticed me at all. I did whatever I was *told to do* because of that fear.

"I don't obey my sergeant because I'm *afraid* of him. I'm afraid that I won't live up to him. I'm afraid that I'm no good at my job—but I try. I try to get better. I want his *re-spect*, because he's damn good at what he does. His job is his duty. My job is *my* duty. And I'm not doing it because I'm afraid *of you*."

CHAPTER 14

"I begin to understand why Lord Diarmat's lessons were considered necessary. I also begin to understand why Kaylin has never been formally introduced at court, even if she is Chosen," Bellusdeo said. Her eyes had drifted toward the gold during most of Kaylin's speech. She was no longer on the edge of rage at the Emperor.

"Even so," the Emperor agreed. "I do not despise you because you are ill-mannered or common. I cannot, however, afford even the appearance of favoritism in front of the combined might of the representatives of the Caste Courts, and what remains of my flight. Most of the weight of stable rulership requires respect—and much of that respect comes, in the end, from fear.

"You are afraid to fail. That is both understandable and admirable. Fear, however, motivates many. In your case, you have something to lose; you do everything you can to avoid the shadow of that loss. It is the same with the Caste Courts of the various races, saving perhaps the Leontines and the Tha'alani. They have something to lose: position, life. If they enrage me enough that I take action against them, the ire of their compatriots, the peoples of their race, might well be enough to destroy them.

"They do not wish this. They must act with care. If you are seen to act carelessly, without even the minimum of courtly respect, they will challenge me. Or resent you. Possibly both. They will believe they can escape such challenge unscathed because you do.

"I cannot allow that. I am cognizant of your role in the protection of my city and my Empire. I am grateful for it. But the instability you might introduce by being, as you so quaintly put it, 'yourself,' is just as much of a danger; it is just quieter and more subtle.

"In the words of Lord Diarmat, you are dangerously self-indulgent and lazy when it comes to things outside the purview of the Hawks. You do not understand that proper behavior *is* a job. That it is learned the way you once learned the laws, or Barrani, or Aerian. You believe you are despised because of your mean birth and your life in the streets of the fiefs. Perhaps that is even comforting to you—I do not myself understand the comfort to be taken from that belief."

These were more words than she had had from the Emperor in her life. They weren't, sadly, the ones she had daydreamed of hearing. Maybe they were the ones she deserved.

Her silence seemed to goad him, which wasn't at this point her intent. Mostly her intent involved shrinking so much she was barely visible above the table line, and crawling away. She wanted to defend herself. But she looked at Severn, her partner, her onetime protector, and she realized that *he'd* learned. He'd learned all of this stuff. He was older, true. But he'd never been as prickly, as self-conscious, as she'd been.

I was, he told her gently, and privately. *I was just as concerned. But the five years does make a difference. Whatever you fear now, it will change in five years. Trust me.*

But the Eternal Emperor hadn't finished yet. "If, for some reason, I chose to be so indulgent—and you have value to my Hawks, and to the Empire itself—consider the changes wrought in your own life. You would be perceived—by men and women of power from all races—as a favorite. As a person who has the Emperor's ear. As a person who could tell the Emperor—or ask the Emperor for—anything.

"They would seek you out. They would seek to make use of you; to make you a pawn in the games that they play in the interracial courts. If I am to follow my own Laws, I could not simply destroy them in my irritation."

"I would have," Bellusdeo said quietly.

"Yes. But your Empire was not your hoard," was the Emperor's equally quiet reply. "You value the Chosen. That has been clear since you first returned to our world. Do you not see the danger to her?"

It was clear from the golden Dragon's expression that she did. But it was clear as well that almost everything the Emperor had said had surprised her. She was watching him closely now, her expression one of concentration. Or confusion. The confusion was slow to clear; it hadn't by the time the Emperor started to speak again.

"If you were so approached, how would you handle that approach?" His smile was knife thin. Sharp. "You are, of course, yourself, as you perceive it. You would handle it with outrage, and possibly insult." He glanced at Bellusdeo as if for confirmation. Her lips compressed and then, after a pause, she nodded. "And thus you would offend men and women of power. You have friends in high places, Private Neya. You have the Consort and the High Lord of the Barrani; you have Ybelline of the Tha'alani. I do not think you have made many friends among the Leontines, but perhaps I am less cognizant of their role in your life."

Kaylin thought of Marcus, but said nothing.

"Those connections might be embarrassed. They might not. They have clearly chosen to accept your behavior in the past. But it is simple to maintain a friendship that is *irrelevant* to your responsibilities, and their friendship, for you, a mortal woman who serves as a Hawk, is irrelevant.

"It will not remain so if you are given free rein at court. You believe that the Dragon Court seeks to preserve your life; you believe that that is the reason you have been assiduously kept from the royal presence. And it is. But not solely for the reasons you believe. You will be even more of a target than you have been in the past if you cannot learn to behave."

The familiar, who had been indolently listening in, squawked loudly.

"I do believe you have the capacity to protect her from most assassination attempts," the Emperor replied—with far more gravity. "But the power of the familiar is, legend would have us believe, directly proportional to the will and the power of the master." His tone made clear what he thought of at least one of those things, but then again, so had his whole monologue.

"You have no friends in the Reaches," he continued. "Moran dar Carafel, should she survive the public claim she has now made, would be one—and you have a Dragon as escort while she is on duty because of that. The Aerian Caste Court is almost in a political frenzy. I imagine that there will be a shuffling of positions when it is clear that the pawn they used to entangle the Elani merchant was, in fact, human. You are certain he was not also outcaste?"

Moran went white.

So did the Hawklord.

The Emperor effected not to notice—or perhaps he just

didn't. Most things that could threaten Aerians weren't going to be much of a danger to a Dragon.

"You've seen—pardon me, Your Majesty, you haven't seen—the Records capture Margot sent to the Halls of Law. At no point during the conversation in capture did the man's eyes change color—and his eyes were *brown*."

"That could be the effect of glamor or enchantment."

Kaylin bit down on her first words—which was hard, because she was annoyed. She was also uncomfortably too aware of herself, because of everything else that had been said. She felt, as she sometimes did, like a total, complete failure.

Think. Just think. "You believe the Aerian Caste Court will put that forward as an explanation?"

His eyes shaded, for the first time, toward a much more prominent gold as he inclined his head. "It has already begun."

Lord Grammayre's eyes were what Kaylin privately referred to as Barrani blue. "Has it?"

"Indeed."

"The Records transmission was embargoed."

"Indeed." The Emperor sounded bored, but he smiled. "Private Neya is on Records as having a strong sensitivity to magic and its use. We do not doubt you," he added, his voice softer than it had been all evening. "We fully believe the man who spoke with the Elani merchant was human, as you do.

"But the Elani merchant was not, in our opinion, meant to survive her encounter."

Kaylin didn't even regret saving Margot's life.

"She did, thanks to the intervention of the Hawks." He turned now to Lord Grammayre. "I will block the remand to the Caste Court in this instance." His smile was slender, sharper, but it still conveyed amusement. Kaylin decided that amusing the Emperor was career-threatening, because she probably wouldn't survive it. "I will also point out that, although no formal complaint has been made, rumors abound that an item of great import to the Aerians has been stolen."

Kaylin blinked. It took her about five seconds to understand what that item was, and then she was simply outraged.

Moran, however, although she was pale, was resolute. "It was not stolen," she said, although the Emperor hadn't actually named the item. "It belongs to me, while I live. That is the law of the Aerians. I am not dead; it is my *right* to bear it." She held up her hand in a clenched fist, and the bracelet she had donned slid down toward her elbow.

"Yes, *praevolo*, it is," the Emperor replied. "I am conversant with the laws of the Aerians. It appears they are less conversant with Imperial Law. Grammayre," he added. "You will find your information leak. But spread your net widely; it is likely, in my opinion, that the Aerian Hawks will not act against Moran dar Carafel at this point. She has declared herself.

"As has been proven, however, mortals are more than willing to accept the offer of coin for very unwise actions." He finally turned to Bellusdeo, who had remained mostly silent—and golden-eyed, which was almost shocking—during the Emperor's part of this discussion. "My apologies, Lord Bellusdeo. This is not what I envisaged when I requested the honor of a private, informal dinner."

She smiled. She smiled in a way that did not expose fangs. If Kaylin's eyes could change color, they'd have shifted all the way to whatever meant surprise in the race she'd otherwise have to be.

"It is not what I envisaged, either. But I find myself enjoying it far more than I have any encounter in the throne room. It has been both surprising and informative, and I have much to think about. No," she added, her voice softening.

"My kingdom was not my hoard. I have never felt that calling, that certainty of desire. But you have—and you have not let that desire or that calling madden you, as it historically has so many of our kin.

"Kaylin would be safe; she has Helen, she has me. She has, for at least a few years, Mandoran and Annarion. But she cannot live in isolation; being a Hawk is both what she does and who she is. If you would like, Your Majesty, I would be very much honored to dine with you again."

The Emperor's eyes shifted into a deep brown, the color of Dragon surprise. Kaylin had never seen it in him—as if his role as ruler had destroyed all ability to feel such an emotion. Or perhaps that was just her interpretation. She was a Hawk. She understood that the Hawks had hierarchy. Lord Grammayre did not stammer or curse, the way the rest of the rank and file could. He was their leader—and it wasn't a nominal leadership.

Marcus cursed like a groundhawk, and frequently tore chunks out of his desk—he said it prevented him from tearing them out of his idiots. But he was sergeant, and when he gave orders, you obeyed them. Even if you weren't a Hawk. Leontines of his size and weight made an instant impression on everyone mortal who had less in the way of fur and fangs.

It had never occurred to her that the people who ruled her working life were just like she was; that they could feel doubt or hesitation, that they did not know everything they needed to know, that they could—and probably did—make mistakes.

They gave orders, and she more or less followed them.

She needed that. She needed someone to make those decisions. She wasn't without freedom of choice; she made decisions of her own when she was in the streets or in a situation that none of the rulebooks covered. Marcus expected her to, as he put it, use her head as something other than a pathetic battering ram.

But the big decisions, or rather, the long-term decisions, weren't in her hands. All the *big* decisions about city-threatening events had been neatly tied into the visceral need to survive. There was thought in them, but it wasn't the kind of thought that led to political entanglements.

She tried to imagine what her life would be like if she woke up tomorrow and she was the Hawklord. Or worse, the Emperor. She couldn't do it. Everything in her rebelled. She didn't *want* to be corporal so she could order the privates around. She wanted to be corporal because it meant she was valued and acknowledged by the people in her life who mattered.

She didn't actually want to order people around at all. Because to do that, she would have to be responsible for them. It was a humbling, uncomfortable thought. What had the Emperor said? She was lazy? She cringed.

"Kaylin?" Bellusdeo said, in the tone that implied this was not the first time.

Kaylin blinked. "Sorry," she said, her cheeks flushing. "I was thinking."

"And I am certain," the Arkon added—before anyone else could, but there probably would have been some competition, "that we do not wish to interrupt you when you are making an effort you seldom make. It is often difficult to think and talk simultaneously." His eyes were, as they had been for most of the dinner, pure Dragon gold.

"What did I miss?" she asked, surrendering.

"Lord Bellusdeo—"

"Bellusdeo, please," the gold Dragon said, correcting him without irritation.

"Bellusdeo, then—it seems improper, when we are in

mixed company, but I am an old man—has asked when we might next convene. For an informal dinner."

"We're due to return to Diarmat in two days, if he's sufficiently recovered. So anytime after that, assuming I survive it."

The Arkon pinched the bridge of his nose. "*Lord* Diarmat will not reduce you to your component parts. He may be a bit out of sorts, but he is recovering. He will, however, break at least one of your arms if you so much as hint at an offer to finish the healing process for him; I do not recommend it."

"Drinks," Helen said, as she entered the room, "will be served now. I have taken the liberty of procuring refreshments more suitable to Dragons, if any of our guests would care for a beverage."

Kaylin privately wondered who—or what—Helen had slaughtered.

"Lord Diarmat," the Emperor said, "is that rarity: a completely loyal man. He has never found his hoard," he added softly, "and it is to be hoped that when he does, it does not conflict with me and mine—but until then, he pursues his duty logically and with a very particular…passion. You do not feel he values you. He understands your value to me, and to my Empire. In time, he will come to appreciate you."

"She won't live that long," Bellusdeo said. Kaylin wasn't the only person who found Lord Diarmat pompous and overbearing.

The Dragon Emperor rose. It wasn't his house, but it didn't matter; when he rose, everyone followed suit. *"Praevolo,"* he said, bowing to Moran. In Aerian, he added, "You have returned to the skies which birthed you." It was a stilted phrase; Kaylin suspected that it was ceremonial. It certainly didn't sound natural, given Moran's injuries.

Moran, however, understood and accepted it.

The Emperor then left the table, following Helen's Avatar.

Moran and Lord Grammayre remained. "As host," the Hawklord said in his mildest voice, "it is your responsibility to precede your guests."

Was it? Kaylin couldn't remember, and wondered if this was an Aerian custom, or a custom she'd never had to learn until now.

"You understand," the Hawklord said, while Kaylin hovered close to Moran, "that the political situation will become ugly and heated." It wasn't a question.

Moran lowered her head and drew her wings in toward her body. "Yes. I'm sorry."

"I am not, Moran. I am not sorry at all. You are aware of the possible costs. All of the possible costs. I will join the Emperor now. I believe you have something you wish to ask of Kaylin."

And Kaylin remembered Lillias, the outcaste Aerian, and the blessing that Evanton had created at her request. She would have to remember to ask Evanton how Lillias had paid for it—even if Evanton wasn't inclined to answer.

"I want you to take me to speak with Evanton. Give the *bletsian* back to him. Tell him to give it to Lillias—she can give it to me herself."

The only small hitch in the dinner entertainment was the arrival of an unexpected guest. He wasn't there for Kaylin, but it didn't matter. When Helen materialized in the parlor, she had everyone's attention. It was her expression; her lips were a compressed line.

"Lord Nightshade," she told Kaylin, "is at the gates."

This predictably caused a shift in the eye colors of the room, except for Kaylin and Severn, who had to make do with the usual facial expressions.

"He's here to visit his brother," Kaylin said quickly, leaping out of her chair.

"Ah. His brother would be Annarion?" the Arkon asked. He rose, as well.

"Lannagaros." Bellusdeo's use of the name implied either a request or a criticism.

"I feel the need to stretch my legs. Dinner was excellent, but I am not young anymore."

Kaylin almost snorted. She managed to cough instead. The Arkon was old, it was true. But old Dragons were generally *strong* Dragons. Age didn't diminish the immortals. Anyone who'd survived to be old was generally more powerful, not less.

"Kaylin," Bellusdeo then said, "Lannagaros would like to accompany you. He is clearly concerned for your safety." The golden Dragon obviously didn't believe this. Fair enough. Neither did Kaylin. "If you wish, I will join you."

Kaylin shook her head. "It's not me he wants to see."

"Is his visit entirely coincidental?" the Emperor asked; his eyes were orange.

"Likely. He comes here all the time to visit Annarion. And then they argue. Loudly. It's almost like they're Dragons."

The Hawklord winced.

Bellusdeo, however, chuckled—which meant the Emperor was under some pressure not to find the offhand comment offensive.

"I feel," Bellusdeo added, "that that is somehow a challenge." She turned to the Emperor, smiling. "Shall we?"

Kaylin fled the room before he could answer. It was, again, poor manners. Manners were difficult.

"I feel," the Arkon said, "that in spite of everything, the evening was a success. It was not a success in the particular way one might hope—but the addition of the Aerians added something necessary to the interaction." He wasn't smiling, but his voice implied that he might. "The appearance of Nightshade, however, will possibly add complications."

Nightshade was nothing but complication. "He's only here to see his brother."

"I do not doubt that. No one in that room does. But it is not the people in the room who will be adding those complications. It is the people who observe your house because Moran resides here."

Aerians.

"The Hawklord will be flying in the face of his Caste Court. If you think that his position will protect him from consequences, you have failed to understand how the Caste Courts feel about Imperial Law. They are willing—of course they are—to accede; the alternative would involve a winnowing of their race. The Emperor's Laws are the law—but never forget that the Emperor is the ultimate arbiter. He *is* the law."

"And he's meeting a fieflord in private at my house."

"Very good. Yes. He is meeting a fieflord, in private, at your house. I am not completely certain that the spies will recognize the Emperor's actual person. Or mine, for that matter. But they will research, and they will—eventually—know. Lord Nightshade's timing in this matter could not be less fortuitous. It will not, of course, harm the Emperor."

"...The Hawklord."

"Yes, Kaylin. The Caste Court is allowed, by law, to cast out constituent members of the race it rules. Its rules must abide, in some fashion, by the laws laid down by the Emperor—but in matters of racial inclusivity or exclusivity, they are given a free hand."

"I hate that."

"Believe that no hatred you feel for it could be as deep, as profound or as difficult as the Emperor's. He did not wish for the citizens of this Empire to be slaves. Ruling the weak is difficult. They are fearful, and fearful people are often very—what is your word?—ah, stupid. Stupid?"

"That's the word."

"He could rule as the Dragons once did, as the Barrani once did. But there is a delicacy to the mortal races that would consume most of you were he to significantly shift his style of rulership."

"The Barrani wouldn't like it much."

The Arkon snorted. "Some of the Barrani would like it very much; they are young, brash and foolish. Having lived through only a small part of the Draco-Barrani wars, they would welcome a chance to test themselves in the same arena as their forebearers once did."

"That would destroy the city."

"Yes. It would not destroy the Dragon Court. It would probably destroy the younger fools among the Barrani High Court, but I am not certain that that would be a great loss." At her expression, he added, "I *am* old, Kaylin. The old are famously impatient with certain youthful foibles." They had reached the doors. "I am impatient with the idea that glory is won by slaughter—because of course it is not slaughter that glory implies. The Elantrans have a phrase that is apropos."

"Please don't repeat it," Kaylin told him; she could guess which one, or at least which dozen, might apply. "You can get away with saying anything to the Emperor. I can't."

The door opened. Lord Nightshade stood in the doorway.

It was evening, but the foyer lights were bright; Kaylin could therefore clearly see that light reflected in eyes that were a shade too blue. That blue darkened as he met not Kaylin's eyes, but the Arkon's.

The ancient Dragon whose library was his hoard inclined his chin. "Calarnenne," he said.

"Lannagaros. Ah, no, Arkon." Lord Nightshade recovered first, and this time he bowed. It was not a superficial gesture.

"You did not bring your blade, I see."

"*Meliannos* is not a trivial weapon, and it is not much required in the streets of your city; no. I do not have it."

"Good. I will therefore endeavor not to find offense at your presence." The Arkon's eyes were orange. They'd been gold all evening.

"Had I known that Lord Kaylin was entertaining guests of such obvious import, I would have chosen a different evening to visit."

"You visit often, do you?"

"I visit my younger brother; he is currently in residence here."

"Yes. Annarion, I believe." The Arkon's smile had teeth in it, and not much else.

Nightshade stiffened.

"He reminds me," the Arkon added, "of you, in our distant youth."

"I do not believe I was ever as he is."

"Not physically, no—but he has a youthful optimism that veers dangerously close to naïveté."

Kaylin had said many things about Nightshade in her life. Naïveté was no part of them.

"Am I to be refused entry, then?"

"No. It is not my abode. I would counsel it, but Kaylin is somewhat like your younger brother in that regard. I will be blunt. Things are politically difficult for the Emperor, and your presence here increases the difficulty—for Lord Kaylin," he continued, ignoring her cringe, "and for another of her guests. This difficulty has involved Lord Bellusdeo."

Nightshade's eyes cleared somewhat.

"You understand, then."

"You refer to Moran dar Carafel."

"I do." The Arkon did not appear to be surprised that Nightshade knew Moran's name or situation. Then again, the Aerian Court probably wasn't the only one that was spying on this house.

For the first time since the door had opened, Nightshade turned to Kaylin. "Has the situation changed since her visit?"

"No." She exhaled. "Yes. But I don't understand why. If I had to guess—"

The Arkon cleared his throat. Loudly. It wasn't a roar, but it reverberated. "She has accepted the mantle of the *Illumen praevolo*. She has accepted it publicly."

Nightshade smiled. There was no ice in it, no malice; it made his face look young. All Barrani looked alike to mortals who weren't familiar with them; Kaylin had that familiarity. But it seemed to her, watching, that the Arkon was right. There was something of his brother in him.

"Lord Grammayre is also here," Kaylin told Nightshade.

"That is the reason for your dress?"

She had almost forgotten she was wearing it. "...Yes."

"It is a very fine dress. I would think you might more appropriately wear it in the presence of royalty."

Silence.

"...Arkon, you did not come alone." It was not a question.

The Arkon's smile was genuine. "No."

"Lord Kaylin, you have always decried politics as a game played by powermongers. You understand that your current dinner table would be considered exceedingly political at this time?"

"I didn't plan that!" She flushed and snapped her mouth shut.

"Very well. What would you have me do?" Nightshade

asked the Arkon. "It is likely my presence will be noted, re-gardless. It is not the first time I have communicated with Lord Grammayre; it will, no doubt, not be the last. He will support the *praevolo*?"

"I am not mortal," the Arkon replied—before Kaylin could. She considered this significant enough that the out-raged words that had been about to fall out of her mouth died. "I do not always understand the games that mortals play. But I understand something of loyalty and service, and it is my guess—and it is only a guess—that he intends to do so." The Dragon exhaled smoke; none of it reached Night-shade. "You are correct, however. The damage your pres-ence might do—to his cause—has already been done. Is your brother expecting you?"

"Not exactly."

"But he knows you're here," the brother in question said.

CHAPTER 15

Annarion stood at the height of the foyer's grand, curved staircase, just beneath the level of the ostentatious chandelier Helen had insisted was appropriate for their visitors. His face was pale, and his eyes were ringed; he looked very much like a mortal recovering from a significant bender.

More important at this very moment was that he didn't look happy to see his brother.

The Arkon noticed as well; it would have been impossible not to. At least he'd left Mandoran behind.

"Hello, older brother," a cheery voice said from up above on the second floor.

Or not.

"Are you guys done with dinner?" Mandoran asked. He was the only Barrani Kaylin had ever met who spoke almost exclusively in Elantran, her mother tongue. She was fine with it; the Barrani Hawks at the office often slid into Elantran when looking for appropriate phrases. She could see that neither the Arkon nor Lord Nightshade considered it a plus.

"Not yet," Kaylin told him as he appeared at the head of the stairs, a few steps up from Annarion. They shared no blood, no family line, but they were more kin than Annarion and Nightshade, who did.

Annarion turned a glare on Mandoran. Kaylin had no doubt that he also had words—but he kept those words private. It was Mandoran who usually dragged the rest of them into that private conversation by answering the unspoken out loud.

"What?" he said, continuing this trend as he met Annarion's chilly glare.

"Perhaps," the Arkon told the foyer at large, "we will attempt to convene an informal, intimate dinner at a third location. This one appears to have become dangerously crowded." He turned, and then turned back. "It is dangerous when dream becomes reality, Calarnenne. But I, too, have had the lost returned to me. It has complicated my life enormously—but it has given me both hope and joy."

Kaylin highly doubted that there was much joy to be found between Nightshade and Annarion, but kept this to herself; Annarion's glower made it clear enough that her words would have been superfluous.

Nightshade, however, looked surprised. As the older Dragon walked back toward the parlor, he said, "Thank you, Lannagaros."

"You know him?" Mandoran asked, heading down the stairs and leaving Annarion frozen on them. "You met him after the end of the wars?"

"Between," Nightshade replied, meeting Mandoran on the level of formality Mandoran had chosen.

"Between?"

"You did not fight in the wars," Nightshade said, voice chilly. He was watching his brother. "But the war transformed you regardless. We fought. We survived."

"He's a *Dragon*."

"Yes. Good of you to notice." He exhaled. "After the second war, there were no dreams of glory left in those of us who had survived. The Dragons destroyed much of our ancient lands—and we, in turn, destroyed their clutches, their flights. But we did not do so for our own individual purposes. We were commanded, and for the most part, we obeyed. Those who did not..." He shrugged. "The practice of making outcastes differs greatly among the various races. The Barrani model is more similar to the human one than any other.

"Lannagaros and I had much in common. Were it not for the war, we might have done our exploration, our researches, side by side. He is learned and knowledgeable in ways that I am not. He was a formidable opponent; he was cunning, canny and unpredictable.

"At the remove of centuries, that Dragon and I have more in common than I have with most of the Barrani of my acquaintance. We have shared similar experiences, have experienced similar losses. I almost killed him once," he added, smiling. "It taught us both respect."

"I am never going to understand my own people," was Mandoran's almost morose reply. "Helen said we can use the small dining room."

Kaylin wasn't aware that they had one.

"We didn't, technically," Helen said. Nightshade was not a guest in the way the Dragons or the Hawklord were. And Mandoran and Annarion were residents. "It is a small room meant for family, and was used for regular meals. We don't use it often because at the moment, the house is so full; it's not very roomy." Her disembodied voice paused. "Mandoran, I don't think your presence is needed."

"Of course it's not," was his cheerful reply.

"I don't think it's actually wanted, dear."

"No? Well, I suppose I could go say hello to the Emperor. Or Kaylin's boss. I've heard a lot about him, but I've never met the man."

Kaylin was almost frozen to the floor.

Mandoran laughed out loud. It was both a wonderful sound and an annoying one. And that probably summed up Mandoran in total: wonderful and annoying. "It's a *joke*. Given the lectures we overheard Helen giving you, it'd be as much fun as pulling teeth. My own teeth," he added, as if this wasn't clear.

Kaylin breathed again. She turned to follow the Arkon, and then turned back to touch Nightshade's sleeve almost hesitantly.

He looked down at her, because he was taller.

"You could try being honest," she told him softly.

"Why do you assume I have not been?"

"I'm not saying you've lied to your brother." She didn't think he had. "But you—you don't tell him everything. Just—try. What is there to lose?"

Annarion was silent.

To Annarion, Kaylin said, "The Arkon says you remind him of your brother when he was younger. I think he liked your brother."

"And now?"

"Now doesn't matter. But—I think he likes him now. Which surprises me. A lot." This was true. She could not recall the Arkon speaking of Nightshade with any affection in the past. "I'd appreciate if you two didn't start yelling at each other until after the rest of the guests have left."

"No," the Emperor was saying when Kaylin made the door frame. "She is not boring. I will concur. I will also, however, point out that if you are bored, you are too unoccupied. I am seldom bored, and I do not require excess excitement."

Bellusdeo laughed. Kaylin froze again; she felt like she'd spent a lot of the evening frozen in place. "It's not excitement, not precisely—but you never know exactly what is going to happen if you're with Kaylin. And some of it requires the whole of my concentration and power just to survive, which can be exhilarating."

"You cannot possibly expect that I would find that appealing?" The Dragon Emperor seemed mildly offended. "Were I to be in such a position, my city, my Empire, would almost certainly perish."

"My understanding is that you are correct. But she *is* Chosen, Darranatos. She has some part to play—or perhaps several—before she dies."

"Agreed. I have accepted her presence amongst my Hawks. My Hawks appear to have survived it."

"She is, and has been since she was allowed to formally join the force, exemplary in her work. She is not terribly adept at politics, because she cannot see it as part of that work," the Hawklord said, clearly part of the conversation.

"Then perhaps your situation," the Emperor said to Moran, "will be of some aid in that regard. Apologies," he added, "for implying that that is the only benefit of it."

"No apologies are necessary, Your Majesty. I think where Kaylin Neya is concerned, we are probably too protective. We see her, and we remember her as a child—Aerian, Leontine, human, it doesn't matter which variety. Only the Barrani are different in that regard, except Corporal Danelle. Her view tends to carry the rest of the Barrani Hawks, on the other hand."

Kaylin slunk out of the doorway, but not into the room. She was trying not to be mortified, and failing.

"They mean well, dear," Helen said. "They are not speaking poorly of you, and they wish you no ill. At times it is helpful, in informal situations, to have something in common. What they have in common—with the exception of the Emperor—is you. But the Emperor has evinced some flexibility where you are concerned that Bellusdeo thought he couldn't.

"Do not feel embarrassed that people care for you."

"It's not the caring that's embarrassing. It's the thinking of me as a child part. I know how to handle myself in the city streets. I'm not helpless, and I'm not ignorant. Maybe I was, when I was thirteen—but that was *then*."

Helen, however, had something other than Kaylin's personal dignity on her mind. "Did you hear, dear? Bellusdeo called the Emperor by his given name. That's a very positive sign." Kaylin couldn't see her—Helen's Avatar was in the parlor, after all—but she didn't need to. She could hear Helen's beaming smile. "But I'm not certain now," Helen added, her voice softening.

"Not certain about what?"

"I'm not certain the Emperor is right for her. Or rather, that she is right for the Emperor."

"Helen, you're giving me whiplash. Right for what?"

"As a mate, dear."

Kaylin was never going to understand her house. She personally agreed with the sentiment, but couldn't follow the path Helen had taken to arrive at it.

"He has his hoard," Helen explained.

"Well, yes—it's us."

"Yes, dear. But Dragons do not share."

"He's sharing the entire Empire."

"No, dear, he is not. The Empire is *his*. There is very little room, in Dragon thought, for *ours*."

"But Tiamaris shares the fief that bears his name. He shares it with Tara."

"Is that what you think?" Helen asked, obviously very surprised.

"I've been there. I've seen them. He does share."

"Kaylin, he *doesn't*."

"You haven't seen them."

"I've seen what you see. I see what you're seeing now, when you think of them. You think that he cares for Tara—and he does. But, Kaylin, Tara *is* his hoard. He does not share her."

"He shares her with the rest of the fief," Kaylin argued.

"No, dear. I understand how you have arrived at your conclusion, but no. You are misinterpreting what you see."

"How?"

"He understands Tara. He understands why she was created. He understands what went wrong for her. He does not intend ownership to be complete and impersonal—that is not the way Dragon hoards work. He allows the fief to share her time and her attention because it is what *she* requires. It gives her both joy and strength. The Emperor does not—and in my opinion, could not—see Bellusdeo the way Tiamaris sees Tara."

"Because he can't own her?"

"Because he has his hoard, dear. It will come first. It must come first. He is a Dragon, not a Barrani Lord. The Dragons do not swerve when they have finally chosen. But Bellusdeo requires an autonomy, a freedom, that would clash with the Emperor's focus and attention. I do not think they are right for each other."

Kaylin had never been the person that people came to for romantic advice.

"The Emperor did."

"You're telling me that's not romantic."

"It is not. If the Emperor has his hoard, he is cognizant of the need for Dragon children. He understands Bellusdeo's significance to the race—and at the moment, the race is confined to the Dragon Court and those who chose to sleep rather than serve. The Emperor understands duty."

"The Arkon's too old."

"As you've noted yourself, age does not mean for the immortal what it means for the mortal—but I concur. The Arkon feels that Bellusdeo is a child. He treats her as if she were one, although he is remarkably clear-eyed in his interactions and expectations."

"Who does that leave? Tiamaris is out. Sanabalis is probably out. She'd kill Diarmat if she could."

"I do not believe that to be the case, but Lord Diarmat is even more formal and rigid than the Emperor."

"Then who does that leave? If she has to have children—and she thinks she does, even if she hates the idea—she doesn't have a lot of choice. She asked the Emperor if she could wake one or two of those who chose to sleep, and he refused her."

"You are possibly overlooking someone, but I will leave that for the future. I am feeling much more optimistic about the present for the Dragons than I have since Bellusdeo came to live here. I will miss her," she added, "when she chooses to leave. You should join your guests, dear—they're probably going to wonder what's happened to you."

"Have they stopped talking about me yet?"

"I imagine they will once they're aware that you're listening."

The parlor discussion, during which dessert and a variety of drinks were served, went on for the next two hours.

Kaylin had never seen the Hawklord in an informal gathering before—if the gathering had started out stiffly, it had mellowed—and was surprised when he laughed. She could not remember ever hearing his laughter before.

She found it almost disturbing.

The Emperor's smiles were similar. She had discovered that he was possessed of an actual sense of humor—but it was bone-dry, easily missed. She found it comforting to know that everyone seemed to like each other, and even more comforting to know that they had enjoyed being guests in her home.

It wasn't that she wasn't used to guests—she knew Teela, after all, and Teela pretty much dropped by whenever she felt bored. But this was different. The Emperor and the Hawklord were not men who simply made themselves at home whenever the mood struck them.

She thought the Arkon might be, but he resented deeply being pried out of his library, and in general left it only in emergencies. He clearly considered the state of relations between his Emperor and Bellusdeo to be one, but his eyes had taken only very brief jaunts into orange through the evening.

She saw her guests to the door, thanked them for coming and meant it, and relaxed only when they were finally gone.

Nightshade was with Annarion. "Tell them," Kaylin said to Helen, "that they're free to shout at each other now if they absolutely have to—the Emperor's gone home."

After Kaylin had ditched the dress and returned to comfortable clothing, they convened in the dining room. Mandoran joined them.

"They're not shouting," Bellusdeo pointed out.

"Yes. Some people would consider that an improvement."

"I would, in general. Why don't you?"

"They're not speaking."

Kaylin wilted.

"At all."

"What is the problem?" the golden Dragon asked Mandoran. She was lounging across the nearest chair, in stark contrast to her very proper carriage and bearing during dinner. Apparently Kaylin wasn't the only person who found propriety almost unbearable at times.

"Hasn't changed any. Well, no, that's not true. I think Nightshade's biggest problem is the Test of Name in the High Halls. Annarion is insisting he'll take the test; Nightshade is insisting that he can't. If Nightshade weren't outcaste, there'd be no question—Annarion would obey. He'd hate it, but he'd obey.

"Nightshade, however, *is* outcaste. He isn't the head of his line, and he has no moral power over his younger brother. He has familial power—and Annarion hates it, but can't quite let that go—but no hierarchical claim. If Nightshade weren't outcaste, on the other hand, Annarion wouldn't be so insistent on being tested."

"I don't think it's a good idea," Kaylin told Mandoran.

"So Helen says."

"I've undergone the Test of Name."

"So Helen also says." Mandoran folded his arms and tilted his chair back on two legs. "If Annarion goes, I'm going with him." He grinned. It was not a comforting sight.

"You can't. The Test of Name is faced alone."

"According to Teela, you went with Severn."

"Yes—but we didn't intend to *take* the damn test, Mandoran. We stumbled into it by accident. This isn't a game."

"No. For Annarion, it isn't. Just between the two of us, I don't give a damn about my family line. I don't give a rat's ass about the High Court. They sent us to the green. They didn't care if we died there."

"I think they hoped you'd all become more powerful."

"Yes, and that's why they sent their younger children, their youngest sons or their daughters." Mandoran was not buying whatever the High Court of old had tried to sell him. Frankly, Kaylin didn't buy it, either—but she wasn't Barrani. Her opinion was irrelevant. "Also, frankly, Annarion finds his older brother's attitude condescending. He dislikes being thought of and treated as a child."

"By Barrani lights, he sort of is one."

"Yes. But by our lights, so are you, and you hate it. You should have some sympathy for him."

She did. But she remembered the godlike Shadow that lay in wait at the base of the Tower of testing, lord and prison for every single Barrani who had failed. He *was* the test. She wondered what Annarion and Mandoran could, or would, do when confronted with the captives, trapped in eternal hell. She thought Mandoran might be able to walk away, but Nightshade's younger brother? Never.

"The Tower," Helen said quietly, "is a test of many things."

"It's considered a Test of Name," Kaylin said.

"And it is that. But I think it is also a test of power. Or perhaps a test of hubris."

"I don't think *hubris* is the right word."

"You've been thinking that Mandoran would be wise enough to accept the power he could not defeat, and escape with his Name and his right to be called Lord."

"…Yes."

"But you were also thinking that Annarion couldn't walk away. He would challenge what he found at the base of the Tower, because he would understand the loss—to the race— of the Names."

Kaylin fell silent.

"But you are *also* thinking that Mandoran and Annarion are not Barrani in the traditional sense, or rather, that their abilities are not confined to the abilities granted them by simple birth and simple training. You are wondering what would happen if all of the twelve—or the remaining members, Teela already having passed—chose to take the test together."

"Funny," Mandoran said, grinning, "Annarion's been wondering that, as well. He hasn't seen what you've seen, of course, and the Lords are forbidden to speak of it. But Sedarias has also said that the tests—and the perceptions of them—are individual."

"How do you know what I've seen?"

"You might have mentioned something to Teela."

"And Teela *shared*?"

"Shocking, I know—but she does have that capability." He grimaced. "Now she's mad."

"I'm sorry, dear." Helen seemed and sounded truly apologetic. "When you think of the Tower of testing, you think, always, of the dead trapped beneath it by the ancient Shadows. You think of the High Lord's pain, and the Lady's."

"Yes, but that's supposed to be—"

"A secret. Yes. I cannot fathom why. Were I Barrani, I might train and teach my offspring and lead them to war to free my trapped kin."

"Teela has a thing or two to say," Mandoran interjected.

"She always does," Kaylin shot back.

"You don't need to throw yourself between me and Teela's anger—but I appreciate the effort."

Kaylin grimaced. "Share less."

Mandoran, predictably, laughed. "That's what Annarion said."

"And not you?"

Mandoran returned her steady almost glare with a cheeky gaze of his own. "I don't think his brother's wrong." He laughed as her eyebrows rose into her hairline, but the laughter drained abruptly. "Teela's given us some hint of what you saw. She's given us some explanation. She saw it herself, when she took, and passed, that test. She has the same burning desire as you have. The same desire, I'm certain, as the High Lord does.

"But she understands *why* the test exists. If the creature can take your Name, if he can bind you, if he can *transform* you, you cannot exist as a soldier in the fight against the Shadows. It's a test for—for corruptibility. Is that a word?"

"It is now. I understand what you're trying to say."

"It's not a test of anything else. If you can face that creature and walk away with your Name and your self intact, the Shadows will not be able to take you unless you give yourself to them. If you cannot walk away, the Shadows would otherwise devour you. Or worse. The High Lord is surrounded by the High Court. Even his guard is composed of Lords who have taken, and passed, that test.

"He is the focal point of all of our defenses in these benighted lands. He has powers that even the strongest of the Arcanists who grace his Court do not have. If he were to be corrupted, those powers would be turned against us in the worst case. In the best, they would simply cease to be used at all. I understand your desire to save the helpless," Mandoran added. He grimaced. "I'd have to understand it; at least half our cohort has the same desire. Sedarias surprises me, though. She was always the most martial, the most powerful, of our number.

"And by power I mean she understood politics, and was perfectly willing to play that game."

"And the others? The other half?"

"They're like me. Is it horrible? Yes. But, Kaylin: no one is forced to take that test. I'll go, if Annarion goes. I have to go. He's my *kyuthe*, my chosen kin. Teela can't go—she's gone. She'd need permission, and I don't think she'd be given it. But if Annarion chooses to go, Helen's going to get a *lot* more crowded."

"Why?"

"None of us would let Annarion go alone."

"You're here," Kaylin pointed out.

"Yes. And they would be here, as well. Even those who think he's being an idiot."

"Nightshade thinks he's being an idiot."

"Yes."

"…And Annarion thinks his brother has lost all sense of honor and responsibility."

"Yes. Got it in two." Mandoran slumped across the table and said, in a plaintive voice, "I'm starving."

Helen glanced at the top of his head with mild disapproval. "That is not how we ask for dinner," she told him. But food did appear to the left of his elbow.

"If I'd realized how complicated this was all going to be," Mandoran told the tabletop, "I'd've stayed in the green."

"You could have."

"Annarion's too straight and narrow to be left on his own. He was the best—or the stupidest—of all of us." He lifted his head. "He revered his older brother. Even when we changed, when we were altered by the *regalia*, his regret and desire was to find Nightshade and bring him home. And that was before his brother became outcaste."

"The current High Lord is not the one who banished him."

"Yes. We believe there may be avenues available to have

him reinstated. Nightshade, however, has professed disinterest in that."

"The Lady seems to like him."

"It doesn't matter, Kaylin. He is outcaste until and unless the High Lord deems otherwise. He is alive—and was left alive—because he captained one of the Seven Towers; he was considered by many an ugly necessity. He is still considered that way—but his life is guaranteed by his position in the fiefs. And Annarion has opposition, regardless. Annarion's line did not end, but it passed into the hands of distant cousins—and they are all Lords of the Court. They have no desire whatsoever to see Nightshade returned to prominence.

"They've even, according to Teela, made moves to demand the return of *Meliannos*, his great sword, to the Court."

She snorted. "Good luck with that."

Mandoran grinned. "I believe Teela's suggestion was that anyone who felt they *could* take the sword that he'd earned was free to try. She refused—as a wielder of one of the three—to join in the attempt. I don't think Teela hates Nightshade, either. Or she didn't, until he marked you."

"I think—I think he did that because—"

"Because he wanted to keep you? Because he thought you'd be useful in finding and, possibly, finally rescuing his long-lost younger brother?"

"Something like that."

"Do me a favor. *Don't* say that to Annarion, if you haven't already. He's blaming himself enough; he doesn't need to add that mark to his score."

"Score?"

"Isn't that the Elantran word I want?"

Given Mandoran, it probably *was* the word he meant. Given the gravity of the situation, she said, "I'm sure it's not."

"Well, anyway. He feels guilty. We'd like him to stop that; it's painful and yet at the same time almost boring."

Bellusdeo snorted smoke. "You are impossible. You are not—quite—boring, and yet I occasionally feel the strong desire to end your existence. Or at least make it vastly less comfortable."

"Right back at you," Mandoran said. He propped his head up on his hands, his elbows braced against the table; he then noticed the food and thanked Helen profusely. "You have saved my life," he told her.

"Yes," Helen agreed, in a more severe tone. "I would appreciate it if you didn't go to such lengths to waste my efforts."

He laughed.

Bellusdeo surprised Kaylin; as they were heading to their rooms for what Kaylin felt was a much-deserved rest given the stress of the evening, she said, "Thank you."

"For what?"

The gold Dragon smiled; it was almost rueful. "I didn't think much of your idea for an informal dinner at first."

"It wasn't actually my idea."

"I know. But you agreed. The Emperor didn't *command* you; he asked."

"I like not to be ash. It's not actually against the law for the Emperor to breathe on me."

Bellusdeo smiled. "No, it isn't. As was pointed out. I did not expect to enjoy myself—but, Kaylin, I did. Lannagaros seemed happy as well, and that is important to me."

Kaylin exhaled. "He cares a lot about both of you. The you part, I can understand. But the Emperor doesn't seem like the type of person it's easy—or even smart—to love."

"If we're being honest," Bellusdeo said, "neither were we,

when we were young. I think half the clutch-fathers would have reduced us to cinders without a second thought, had we been male. We were—and please, don't feel it necessary to repeat this—probably a lot more like Mandoran than like Annarion. Lannagaros was so stuffy and so proper, we often targeted him for mischief.

"And yet, he remembers us fondly. Thank you," she said again. "In a strange way, this evening gives me hope."

In the morning, Moran came to the table dressed for war. She wore the very colorful dress, she wore the bracelet, and she had adopted a long spear. She had arrived, Helen said, at the table early, and intended to accompany Kaylin to work.

"Doesn't that normally work the other way around? We accompany her?"

"Ah. I believe she intends to accompany you to work on a more roundabout route."

"She wants to see Evanton." It wasn't a question.

"Yes, dear. She believes he will be more helpful or more sympathetic if you are present."

"She's dead wrong about that."

"I'm not sure she is."

"If Lillias wanted to meet with Moran, don't you think she'd've given her the gift herself? She approached Evanton, who approached me."

"Yes, dear. I did mention this to Moran."

"Who doesn't care."

"No, dear. Lillias saved Moran's life when she was much younger. It is highly likely that's the reason Lillias was made outcaste and stripped of her wings."

Kaylin let out a volley of angry Leontine, which was best when one felt like raging. It had growling built in.

"I don't suppose you could tell Moran that I'm sick and staying in bed today?"

"Not convincingly, no. If you insist, however, I will try."

"Never mind. Evanton's really cranky in the morning, you know that?"

"I thought you believed he was always cranky."

"Only at me."

CHAPTER 16

The good news for the morning was that the Emperor's decision to deny the remand had not quite reached the Aerian Caste Court in time for them to really martial their forces of assassination. This meant the walk to work was theoretically as safe as yesterday's. A remand to the Imperial Courts would probably change that, but Kaylin wasn't certain how.

It did make her uneasy.

The bad news for the morning was that Evanton was *not* awake by the time Moran had marched them to his front door. Grethan was, poor sod, but he greeted the guests with both respect and bleary-eyed affection. Well, the affection part was mostly aimed at the familiar, who, as usual, leapt off Kaylin's shoulder at the first opportunity to land on the apprentice, chattering away in his happy squawk, as opposed to his outraged one.

"Evanton's asleep?" Kaylin asked, perhaps a shade too eagerly.

Teela and Tain had shown up at the house, as had Severn. They all understood that they were the unspoken bodyguard while Moran traveled to—and from—the Halls. Evanton's doorway was therefore crowded with Bellusdeo, the Barrani,

the Aerian and the two human Hawks. It was practically a
racial congress; all they needed was a Leontine, given Grethan was Tha'alani.

"Not anymore," Grethan replied apologetically. "Normally
I'd let him sleep—but he seemed to be expecting someone
this morning, and made sure I knew to wake him up."

Kaylin's wince was genuine. "I don't envy you."

"It's all right," was the surprisingly cheerful reply. "I'm
not the person he's going to be annoyed at."

Grethan didn't usher them into Evanton's unofficial office—the kitchen—because there wasn't enough room. He
left them in the second half of the storefront. It was about
as clean as it had been the first time she'd been ushered into
Evanton's presence—some of the cobwebs were old friends.
They hadn't, as far as she could see, accrued more dust over
time, but they certainly hadn't shed any of it, either.

Evanton could be heard clumping his way down the stairs.
Which meant he was using a cane. He didn't always require
one, but said he found them useful to maintain his balance
when he'd had a particularly trying day—which generally
meant he'd been arguing with the wild elements in his garden.

He paused in the doorway. His face, always lined and im-
printed with age, was pinched. "I see," he said, clinging to
his cane as if it would help him hold on to his temper. "It's
a busy morning." He glared at Kaylin. Of course he did.
"What have I told you about me and mornings?"

"I've come here in the morning before."

"Not *before* you start work. This is practically assault, and
you're a Hawk." To Teela he added, just as sourly, "You, at
least, should know better."

Teela's smile was genuine; she was amused. Then again, the Barrani didn't technically require sleep, which made them enormously smug around races that did.

Evanton's crankiness bounced right off Teela, and hit Kaylin in the side of the figurative head. "You're not a morning person, yourself."

She really wasn't. "It wasn't my idea."

"Imagine how much that comforts a tired, exhausted old man."

"Her imagination is not that good," Teela told Evanton. "I believe you're acquainted with everyone currently in the room."

"You are incorrect," Evanton snapped. He really *was* in a mood. Grethan had—as he so often did when Evanton was like this—vanished. He'd taken small and squawky with him.

Kaylin exhaled. "Evanton, this is Moran. Moran, Evanton."

Moran was staring at the old man, her mouth half-open. She hadn't spoken a single word since she'd entered his shop. In and of itself, this wasn't unusual; Moran wasn't big with words and used them sparingly—unless she was angry, in which case she could curse like a Hawk. She wasn't angry now.

"Moran? Moran dar Carafel?" Evanton asked. He was good, Kaylin thought. If she hadn't known better, she would have said he hadn't actually recognized her.

Moran stiffened at the use of her flight name—no surprise there. "It was my idea to come this early in the morning; please don't be angry with Kaylin or Teela."

"I am not angry; I am merely annoyed. And underslept. Kaylin is not notable for her observational skills if there has been no technical crime, or if the crime itself is largely social in nature." He offered Moran a formal bow, which was a surprise. *"Illumen praevolo."*

Moran returned the bow after another pause, in which her eyes lost their purple and returned to a more natural Aerian gray. With blue in it.

"You wished to speak with me."

"Yes, I did." She shook herself free of whatever it was she'd seen to distract her, and returned—with the force of a sergeant—to the job at hand. "One of your clients is a woman named Lillias."

Evanton gave Kaylin the side-eye, but didn't deny it.

"I'm sorry—the Emperor wanted to know, and I don't tell the Emperor to get stuffed." But that was mostly a lie. Moran had wanted to know.

"Did you not stop to consider that perhaps Lillias did not wish to be known? Did you give her gift to the *praevolo*?"

"No."

"I wouldn't take it," Moran said, picking up the answer before Kaylin could fumble it. "I haven't seen Lillias in years. I was told that she had passed away."

"You did not believe it."

"Oh, I believed it." Moran's eyes were definitely blue now. "Death might have been kinder."

"Might it? You yourself cannot fly, or so I have been told. Would you prefer death?"

"On some days? Yes."

Silence.

Evanton cleared his throat. "You are younger than you look, *praevolo*. If you desired flight, I am certain that Kaylin could heal your wing. She has healed more difficult injuries before, and the healing is harder the farther out from the original injury. You have not elected to do so."

Moran said nothing.

"Why do you wish to speak with Lillias?"

Moran said more nothing.

"If you cannot answer that simple question, I am afraid I will send you on to your day's work, while I go back to bed."

"She saved my life," Moran said. The words sounded as if they were being pulled out of her mouth by main force. "She saved my life when I was young. I should have died. I would have died. My grandmother did."

"Ah."

"I wasn't old enough to understand the politics. I wasn't old enough to understand the need for adoption. I wasn't old enough to understand legitimacy, or more precisely, illegitimacy. I'm not sure I truly understood what had happened. Lillias grabbed me and *flew*."

"To where?"

"To the ground. To the ground far beneath the Southern Reach. I want to speak with her because—" She paused. "I want to apologize to her."

"For that, I will not break my own rules of good business." He was frowning at Moran as if she were Kaylin in disguise. "You will have to do better, Sergeant."

Moran looked almost as helpless in the face of Evanton as Kaylin felt in the face of most of life. It didn't last. She shoved her inner sergeant to the forefront, straightened her back, her shoulders, the fall of her wings—even the injured one—and said, "I want to thank her."

Evanton smiled then. "For?"

"For all of the obvious reasons. For saving my life, first among them."

"In order for that to have value, you must consider your own life to have worth. Do you understand?"

She exhaled. "Yes, sir."

"Good. As you can imagine, I cannot snap my fingers and immediately produce Lillias. But if you will return to my store at closing time she will be here—if she is willing to meet you at all." As Kaylin drew breath to speak, Evanton said, "Lillias accepts what was done to her, inasmuch as she can. She can pass for human if she is calm, and she has managed to do so. But she avoids Aerians; she wants neither their pity nor her own fear of being lesser, being mutilated.

"Your sergeant is the Aerian she most reveres; to appear before her when she herself is wingless will take a great deal of determination and courage—and I am not entirely certain she has either in her. She would consider it humiliating."

Moran flinched over different words in Evanton's sentence. "She shouldn't," was her flat reply at the end.

"No, she should not. But if a Hawk loses his or her right arm—or leg—they are no longer fit for active duty. Although they once shared the same responsibilities and risks as the rest of the Hawks, they might consider being with Hawks to be an emphasis of everything they have lost." He was looking at Kaylin as he spoke. "Some people will see what they aren't. They will pity them for it; they will see nothing but the loss."

He meant Kaylin.

"And some people pretend that they've lost nothing," the private countered.

"Indeed. And that is difficult in a different way. Why?

Because neither of them involve seeing the actual person as he or she is *now*. I am not saying that it is a simple problem; it should be, but people complicate everything they're involved in. Lillias has lived a great deal of her life on the ground. She has not committed suicide. She has lost the use of her wings—as you yourself might, Moran, if you continue to be stubborn—and the loss was an experience that devastated her. She chose, as she could, to heal.

"I will not have you consider her as only the sum of her injuries. Do you both understand?"

Kaylin froze. Moran said nothing.

To Kaylin, Evanton continued, "Your mother died when you were five. Five years old in the fiefs, I believe?"

Kaylin nodded. She wasn't certain where this was going, but could guess that she probably wouldn't like it.

"If every single human you met looked at you with horror, called you a 'poor dear' and treated you like an orphaned child now, would you be fine with that?"

"No!" She stopped. "…No."

"You will probably be more of a disaster in that meeting than your sergeant. Your sergeant's sense of guilt and responsibility is too personal, true, but she is older. You have daydreamed of having wings—and flight—since I first met you. Understand that these *are* daydreams. You have also daydreamed of great wealth—but you do not pity those that are not greatly wealthy. Do not pity those who cannot fly, even if they once could. Flight did not make them safe. Flight is not, in and of itself, ennobling—as I am sure you are discovering in the current, somewhat charged political arena. And now, I am going back to bed."

He put action to the words and left them all in the store without another word.

★ ★ ★

They made their way to the Halls of Law. Kaylin was silent as she considered Evanton's words—and his particular example.

"What are you thinking?" Teela demanded, elbowing her in the ribs to get her attention.

"I'm thinking that you almost knocked me over." Which was true. She righted herself as her familiar started to chew her hair. "And I'm thinking that Evanton was right. Or is right."

"Oh?"

"This grown-up thing? It's hard." Teela looked both amused and slightly surprised. Kaylin latched on to the latter. "Is there something on my face?"

"No. It's just the first time I've ever heard you imply that you're not a grown-up. Tain?"

"There's a first for everything."

It was Moran who said, "You weren't the only one he was disappointed in, and I don't have half your excuses." Her smile was wan. "I think he meant to imply that what I want from Lillias is absolution." At Kaylin's expression, she added, "Forgiveness. My mother died. My grandmother died. I thought Lillias had died. All of them, because I exist. My mother and grandmother have nothing left to give me, no matter how much I think I need it. Lillias might—but Evanton's right." She grimaced. "It's been years since I've been lectured like that. I felt like I was four years old again."

"Me, too."

"So—it is hard, this grown-up thing, yes. But the alternative is not acceptable, either."

The discussion of their relative immaturity stopped by unspoken agreement well before they reached the Halls of Law, but Kaylin looked up frequently. The Aerian Hawks were on the move; they were flying in tight formations, practicing aerial drills. They didn't appear to notice the people passing beneath them, but Kaylin figured there'd be a test at the end of the day. They couldn't be Hawks and fail to note the significant things.

Then again, she'd never been directly under an Aerian corporal or sergeant. Moran's infirmary was staffed by Hawks, which made it part of the Hawks—in theory. In practice, the Swords used it, as well.

Clint and Tanner were on duty at the door. Clint said something inaudible—at least to the mortals present—to Tanner, set his polearm against the nearest stretch of wall and then leapt down the stairs in a bound that used wings.

He landed in front of Moran. He landed almost on one knee. It was impressive, and Kaylin wondered if any of the Aerians learning their drills above them had seen it, noted it, marked it.

Moran said something in Aerian. Kaylin didn't actually recognize the word or phrase. Although she understood most day-to-day Aerian, she knew she was missing something cultural. And knew as well that it wasn't taught in racial integration classes.

Clint replied. He replied, however, in Elantran. "*Praevolo*. We are yours to command."

"Technically," Moran replied, sliding into Elantran as well, "you're the Hawklord's to command. When I walk through those doors, I'm a Hawk." She didn't tell him to stand. She spoke to his bent head.

He raised that head and met her gaze. "While you wear those robes, you are *praevolo*."

"I'm *praevolo* regardless," Moran countered. "You've always known it."

Clint shook his head. "You were born with the wings. You were not—you were never willing to acknowledge what that means. Until now."

"It changes nothing," Moran told him.

Clint's eyes were a pale, steady blue. They weren't angry blue, though; in the light, if one weren't careful, they'd seem closer to ash gray. "It changes everything."

"It doesn't. The risk to you—and to your families—remains the same. In the current climate, it isn't safe."

"If it was safety we wanted, we would never have joined the Hawks. We would never have sworn to surrender our lives in the attempt to uphold and enforce the Emperor's laws. You are *praevolo*, now. Even those who doubted before have fallen silent. You are our flight."

Moran motioned, and Clint rose. "I don't want anyone to sacrifice their lives in anything but pursuit of the law."

"That decision is not yours to make," he countered.

"If you are mine to command, yes, it is."

He grinned, his teeth a slash of even, perfect white. "How long have you been a Hawk? You understand exactly how command works behind those doors."

Kaylin shrugged. Clint was right. Marcus was technically in charge; the Hawklord was technically the ultimate authority. But Hawks since the dawn of time, or at least the start of the Halls of Law, had ways of doing what they thought was the right thing. They understood the chain of command. They understood the rules. They also understood that, for small things, rules were flexible. You could stretch the hell out of them without ever actually breaking them.

People, she thought, just were not *good* at blind obedience.

Moran surprised Kaylin; she smiled. It was rueful, but genuine. "Fair enough."

★ ★ ★

The tenor of Aerian interactions within the Halls of Law had changed; Clint wasn't the only one who seemed affected by Moran's decision. The very colorful dress that Moran wore looked entirely out of place in the office; even with the Hawk's tabard hanging over most of it, it couldn't be disguised. Nor did Moran make that attempt. She was as good as her word; when Bellusdeo preceded her into the infirmary, she shooed the rest of her unofficial bodyguard away.

The familiar screamed.

Moran stared at him, her eyes beginning to widen, as Kaylin, obeying instincts she hadn't realized she'd developed, turned back toward the Aerian sergeant, and leapt—literally leapt—the distance that divided them. Her hair had time to stand on end, and her skin felt as if it were being flayed from the rest of her in one damn piece.

As the door opened and the world exploded in a flash of painful, painful color, Kaylin's ridiculous first thought was *Marcus is going to be so pissed off.*

The familiar's golden bubble extended to cover only Severn and the Aerian. Bellusdeo was beyond its range, as were the Barrani corporals. They were thrown back—Bellusdeo into Kaylin and Moran, Teela and Tain down the hall. There was a moment of silence—the kind of silence that happens in the wake of something loud—and then noise returned, at a remove.

Teela was already on her feet, her eyes midnight blue. Tain was half a step behind her—but Teela had always had the best reflexes on the Barrani side of the department. Their tabards and their leathers were going to need either major cleaning or repairs.

Bellusdeo's clothing was going to require complete replacement. She shed it without much regret, armoring up instead; the scales that adorned her Dragon body became small plates behind which the human form could shelter. All Dragons could do this—and were generally forced to it if they'd chosen to adopt their Draconic shape without enough preparation or warning.

"Fail to mention this to the Emperor," the Dragon said. She wobbled.

"I can't."

"You can fail to volunteer the information. I've seen you do that a hundred times."

"I write it all up in the reports."

"The ones that Marcus shreds rather than reading?"

"Yeah. Those ones."

"Fine. Write it up in a report."

"Marcus'll read this one."

Bellusdeo impressed Kaylin with her command of the Leontine language—or at least the important bits. Also? Dragons could growl. Human throats didn't do justice to Leontine, but Dragon throats clearly did.

"Are you all right?"

"Nothing is broken." Bellusdeo winced.

"Ribs?" Moran asked.

"Possibly cracked. I've certainly suffered worse in my time." She righted herself, stepping back from Kaylin and the familiar. Teela had already made it to what remained of the infirmary's door—about a third of the door frame, at knee height or below. "I think it's safe," she told Moran. "There's no longer obvious, active magic." She was frowning.

So was Kaylin. "I didn't sense anything."

"No. It's not as impressive as the Arcane bomb that destroyed your home," Teela observed, "but it wouldn't have to be. It wasn't meant to kill a Dragon. It was, as far as I can tell, a very traditional explosion. You felt nothing at all?"

"Not until the explosion was already happening, no."

Teela shook her head. "Corporal," she said to Severn, "can you keep an eye on Kaylin while the rest of us stand in front of an outraged, angry Leontine for a few minutes?"

Severn nodded.

So did Kaylin. Teela meant for her to examine the room for magical sigils and signatures. The Imperial mages would no doubt be called in as the experts, but Marcus would want as much information as he could get his claws on, as quickly as possible. And Imperial mages were not terrified privates under his command.

"I don't understand how I missed this," Kaylin told her partner, as she picked her way through what remained of the room's bedding. "I think it must have been hidden in the cupboard to the left."

Severn nodded. The cupboard in question had ceased to exist. There was a large indent in the wall where the cupboard had once been affixed. There were a lot of splinters, and some impressive charring around the hanging bits of wood and glass that had been farther away.

The mirror—the large mirror—was shards.

Moran wasn't going to be able to reclaim anything that had been in the infirmary at the time. Luckily, there had been no patients strapped to beds, because they wouldn't have survived it, either.

"Anything?"

Kaylin nodded, frowning. "It's a single sigil, a modest one—I don't think I've seen it before."

The familiar squawked loudly.

"It's surprisingly small, is the thing. An explosion of this nature should have splashed magical signatures across most of the walls, or anything left standing." Which was probably why Teela had left them behind. "This one didn't." She froze.

The familiar sighed loudly and lifted his left wing—he was perched on her right shoulder—to cover her eyes.

Kaylin's Leontine was not as impressive as Bellusdeo's, but she was certain she meant it more. "You know that don't touch anything at a crime scene rule?"

"I haven't touched anything at all."

"I don't think it's necessarily completely safe for anyone to be in this room."

Severn was unwinding his weapon chain.

"It's not—it's not quite like that. I think—" She shook her head. "There's Shadow here, or the corpse of Shadow; it's spread across everything like it's blood."

Sergeant Kassan was not happy. Given the color of his eyes, there was barely room for *more* anger, but he managed it. He didn't blame Kaylin, because it wasn't her fault—but when he was in a mood, fault didn't matter. Convenient targets did.

"I want the Dragon sent home," Marcus said, dispensing with all pretense at formality.

"I'm not in command of the Dragon; technically, the Hawklord could ask to have her removed. But the Hawklord has been told that Lord Bellusdeo has Imperial permission to be here. By the Emperor."

"That's why I'm telling *you* to do it. I want the Dragon sent home. We're going to be ash and body parts if she's injured."

"The Hawklord—"

"The Hawklord is in conference with the Wolflord and

the Swordlord. And the Emperor. Security in the Halls should have prevented something like this from happening here. Clearly the breach was deliberate."

That was what was upsetting him. Stupidity could—and sometimes did—enrage him, but he didn't consider stupidity malice. He figured he could scream it out of the new recruits—and in general, he could. This wasn't a problem caused by new recruits who needed to learn the rules.

This was done by someone who already knew what the rules were, and had circumvented them. It implied actual knowledge. Maybe.

"You're thinking," Marcus growled.

"I couldn't feel the magic. At all. It's possible that someone—anyone—carried it in; it would be unremarkable. It was in the supplies cabinet. Moran might know which supplies it was hidden in. There wasn't enough left over for me to take an educated guess.

"But...the Shadow is disturbing. It's the second time we've seen it. The man in the holding cells wasn't aware of it—it seems inert, somehow, and about as sentient as—" She bit back the comment. "It didn't seem to have a will of its own, and that's a lot more common with Shadow."

"I think," Marcus said, rising as something over Kaylin's shoulder caught his attention, "it's time to speak with our prisoner."

Kaylin turned in the direction of Marcus's glare; he was incapable, at this point, of anything else. And she recognized the man who stood on the office side of the doors, waiting, his expression dour but otherwise inscrutable.

It was Nevoran, a young member of the Tha'alanari, the small branch of the race of telepaths that was judged strong enough to experience the insanity of outsiders without flooding the group racial memory with it. He was bronze, blond, and his eyes were very, very green, which in the Tha'alani was the equivalent of Barrani blue.

They lightened slightly, gaining some gold, as he saw Kaylin. He bowed to her, not to Marcus, and she saw that beneath the tan, his color was bad. And it would be. Of course it would be. The Emperor demanded—and she remembered, once again, that she hated him for it—that the Tha'alani surrender members for the use of the Halls of Law and the Imperial interrogators. Nevoran was one.

She wished it had been Scoros instead. Or even Ybelline. But that's not who they'd sent, and perhaps the older two were unavailable.

She crossed the room before Marcus could, reached Nevoran and lifted her face, her forehead. He hesitated only briefly; the flexible stalks that graced the foreheads of every member of his race then danced a moment in the air as he bent toward her. He touched her forehead with those stalks— as he would have to do with the criminal—and she heard his voice. He heard hers. No words were necessary.

She heard more than that, though. She heard Ybelline, the castelord of the Tha'alani—the only castelord Kaylin trusted. The only one she was certain she could.

Kaylin.

Ybelline.

You have not visited us in a while.

Things have been a little hectic here.

Yes. I see.

Kaylin heard an immediate plethora of voices, most of them young. She made field trips to the Tha'alani quarter with the foundlings, and had discovered that children of any race had a lot in common. Although the Tha'alani young could have attention whenever they wanted it, they seemed to want an endless supply, and the foundlings had not yet learned to fear and hate the mind readers. Kaylin wanted to make sure they never did, but that wasn't in her hands. She could only offer them the experience, and hope.

Kaylin, Nevoran said, a hint of amusement in his tone, *I believe your sergeant is about to rip out your throat.* There was no fear in the words. *Is there anything I should know?* This was a very polite way of asking permission to sort through Kaylin's understanding of events, and she gave it instantly. It was much easier than trying to come up with the right words, and it allowed for very, very little misunderstanding.

Kaylin blinked and opened her eyes as Nevoran withdrew his stalks.

Marcus was growly. "When you're finished?" he said. There were other words he wanted to add, but Nevoran wasn't a Hawk, and in general he tried not to humiliate his subordinates in front of outsiders. On the other hand, he'd had a very bad morning, and the day wasn't looking up.

Caitlin waved to Nevoran and asked how his mother was. Kaylin knew he had a mother—obviously, everyone did— but it had never occurred to her to ask. Nor had it occurred to her to ask about Nevoran's new, and first, child.

Nevoran's eyes were almost gold by the end of Caitlin's barrage of friendly questions; Marcus's eyes were distinctly orange. But he tolerated it with only a background growl of general irritation.

Nevoran had been well trained. He knew what Leontines were likely to do or be. But he also clearly understood Caitlin's role in the office; he knew that answering her questions would not be considered insubordination of any kind, because it was Caitlin who asked. It made him comfortable—

or as comfortable as he could be, given his job here. Kaylin was grateful for the office den mother as Marcus impatiently took the lead.

CHAPTER 17

The Barrani guarding the prisoner were playing dice. It wasn't, strictly speaking, a cultural pastime of the Barrani, but they'd adapted well to it. Humans didn't play with them, though, as the Barrani had a fairly rarified concept of cheating: It didn't count if you won. Since the Barrani had an aptitude for magic, and the type of magic that helped dice stop on certain faces was so trivial it wouldn't be worthy of note among their own kin, it was a great way to throw money away. No Hawk, no matter how green, was willing to lose their temper and start a brawl when the opponent was Barrani.

Well, unless they were drunk. Or young. Kaylin winced, thinking about being young and drunk, and decided to think about the prisoner instead.

He was skittish. Of course he was. Nevoran was here.

"I've cooperated! I've answered all your questions!"

Fear, Kaylin thought, was the contagion that the Tha'alanari were trained to keep away from the racial mind. Fear was, to the Tha'alani, a particular type of insanity; if left untended, unquieted, it spread like fire through dry grass, with about the same results.

She had hated the Tha'alani when she had first come to the

Halls of Law. She didn't hate them now. But she understood the man's fear and tried—very hard—not to judge him. Her natural protective instincts made this harder than it should have been. He'd come to threaten and control Margot. But... Kaylin had done worse, in her time.

"Yes. You have. But there are elements of your story that require further investigation. Before you start whining," the Leontine growled, "I don't believe you've lied. But an Arcane bomb destroyed an important room or two in the Halls and everyone is on edge.

"You were carrying Shadow."

The man blanched. He had seen it with his own eyes; he couldn't deny it. It was, Kaylin thought, the heart of his fear. He didn't *feel* different. But what if he was? What if the Shadow had transformed him, somehow?

"Well, so was the bomb. Private Neya has experience with Shadow. None of that prior experience is useful. We don't know how you were infested with Shadow; we know that you were, and that it was purged. By the private. What we need to know, now, is who hired you—"

"I *told you* that!"

"And what they gave or exchanged with you that might have been a way to convey that Shadow. It's obviously not something you noticed."

The man's eyes were wide; he was almost green and sweating. Kaylin understood this, as well. She turned to Nevoran, lifting her face. Nevoran's eyes rounded, and then his lips quirked in an almost bitter smile. But he dropped his stalks to Kaylin's forehead.

I'm really, really sorry.

I am not aware that you have anything to be sorry about. The decision was the Emperor's, or the Hawklord's. It was not, and is not, yours. You wish him to witness this contact, yes?

Yes. I can't tell him that you're not going to read his mind—of course you are. He'd have to be dead not to notice. This is all I've got. I can let him see that you touch me, and that I'm not noticeably insane—stop laughing.

Sorry.

I don't think that word means what you think it means. And you know what? He doesn't deserve the consideration. I don't care if he's terrified—he should damn well be terrified. He should never have agreed to work for Aerian assassins, and maybe—if he survives this, and you'll note the Barrani guards—he'll remember never to do it again. I'm not doing this for his sake.

No. You are attempting to lessen his fear for our sake.

Yes. And I resent it.

She heard Ybelline's laughter. It was bright and full and it permeated the entire mental space with a kind of wry, affectionate approval.

Nevoran withdrew his stalks; Kaylin was smiling with an echo of Ybelline's amusement. There was no edge in it. There was never an edge in the Tha'alani castelord's laughter.

The man had watched, openmouthed, as Nevoran had touched Kaylin's forehead. Kaylin, who resented him, nonetheless said, "Don't fight it. The only thing the Emperor wants is information about what was done to you—and how it might have been done. If you let him see that without struggling to hide it, there won't be any pain, and it'll be over before you know it.

"He's not going to look for all the other crimes you were involved in. He's not going to look for anything about your past that isn't directly related to the Shadow incident. Got it?"

"What did he want from you?" The man's voice was shaky, and his color was still terrible—but it wasn't *as* bad, which was probably as much as anyone could hope for.

"To say hello, more or less."

★ ★ ★

Nevoran had not been fitted with a memory crystal; they were very, very rare, and very, very expensive, and the Imperial coffers did not extend to their common use. He therefore touched the prisoner's forehead—and the prisoner did have to be restrained—and extracted information. Whether or not it would be useful would be determined later. Kaylin watched Nevoran brace himself against the contact, and she looked away.

The Tha'alani didn't want this any more than the human man did. Standing over them both was the Emperor—or the shadow he cast.

The man, however, stopped struggling. He had not passed out. He spoke to Nevoran; Kaylin couldn't hear the Tha'alani's reply. But she saw the prisoner relax, marginally; she was very, very surprised when he started to cry.

They were not tears of terror.

He spoke again. He told Nevoran what to look for. He volunteered the information—and although it was unnecessary, as Nevoran was trained well, Kaylin was almost impressed. The only time she'd been given to a Tha'alani interrogator, she had fought every step of the way.

In the end, he dropped, slowly, to his knees—forcing Nevoran to follow to maintain physical contact. When Nevoran stepped back, the man lifted his face to stare at the Tha'alani, whose eyes were not green, but not gold, either. He said nothing. Nevoran, however, offered him a sad smile. "Thank you, Caven."

"What did you *do* to him?" Kaylin asked, when they left the cell.

"I found the information the Emperor requires." The answer was smooth and uninflected—it was almost human.

He hesitated, and then said, "Ybelline feels that some—not all—of your criminals are insane. I feel that *all* of them are insane; there is some argument about this in the Tha'alanari. But our own, when isolated because of injuries or birth defects, become as insane as every other race. It is the isolation.

"And the fear. I attempted to find and comfort that fear. I am not certain that I did what was necessary—but it seems to have had a positive effect." He hesitated. "I remember Grethan."

Kaylin was silent for a long moment. "He's happy, I think."

"He is as happy as he could be, yes. He talks to the *Tha'alaan* now, with the help of the water. We hear his voice. It is not our voice; it is not influenced greatly by our voice— but there is no rage and fear in it. Well, perhaps not no fear; his master seems temperamental. I must speak with your Hawklord and the Imperial mages now."

The second surprise of the day was presented to Kaylin when she returned to the office and took a stroll past the duty roster. She was on the Elani beat, which wasn't unusual, given it was her beat. She was not, however, partnered with Severn. Teela had been penciled in.

Tain was put out, and Kaylin didn't blame him. Apparently sidelined in order to write the reports that Marcus habitually ignored, he was about as friendly as a sick, wet cat. "Where's Severn?"

"I'm not sure."

Marcus, a Leontine, could hear the entire conversation, such as it was. "Corporal Handred has been seconded to the Wolves."

Kaylin froze. "Why?"

"Ask the Hawklord. He wants to see you in the Tower," Marcus growled. "Let me rescind that. *Don't* ask the Hawklord. His day is going to be end-to-end stupid questions, or worse, political ones. And don't bother the corporal, either."

Hanson, the Hawklord's personal aide, looked about as happy as Tain had, but with mortal variations.

"If you're going to do such a good job imitating a hang-over, you should just give up and go out drinking with the rest of us," Teela told him.

"Thanks, but I like my limbs where they are. On most days." Clearly this wasn't one of them. "You're here to add to my workload?"

"Marcus said the Hawklord wanted to see us." Kaylin stepped out from behind Teela.

"I question the use of the verb, but yes, it appears that he feels it necessary to speak with you before you escape the Halls of Law."

"We're heading out to Elani."

"Normally you'd have my sympathies. Today, you have my bitter and undying envy. He's not having a good day. If you could avoid asking stupid questions or demanding an-swers he is not allowed to give, you might still be on track for promotion at the end of the interview."

The Hawklord's eyes were a midnight blue when Kaylin and Teela entered the Tower. Lord Grammayre was standing in front of his mirror; the mirror was reflective, not active.

"Did you speak with Nevoran before he left the Halls?" was the first question out of his mouth. "Did he tell you what he witnessed?"

"No. I didn't ask."

"I am almost shocked. The prisoner, according to Nevoran, was approached by a friend."

"A friend, or an acquaintance?"

"Let us say a former friend. He knew the man, and had known him for a number of years. The man in question often has odd jobs for him."

"Legal jobs?"

"Not all of them. Most of them, however, are. Before you ask, this information was volunteered by the prisoner, not the interrogator."

Kaylin looked slightly offended at this preemptive correction. "Nevoran is *Tha'alanari*. He understands the laws involving disclosure better than almost anyone here."

"Yes. Well. Hawks have been sent to question the friend. Regardless, the prisoner was offered the job for a sizeable sum of money. He was told that he was to do exactly what he did with Margot."

"Was he supposed to kill her afterward?"

"No. That was not part of his original remit."

Kaylin frowned thoughtfully at the tone of the Hawklord's voice. "You think someone else was going to kill her and he was supposed to take the fall for it?"

"I think that likely."

"Did he ever speak to an Aerian directly?"

"No. He spoke only to the go-between." The Hawklord waited.

"You think an Aerian was present."

"Yes. It would not be the first time some form of invisibility has been used. Nevoran is entirely caged by the man's perceptions, and he perceived nothing. He was slightly confused—the amount of money seemed high for the job at hand. He was also slightly suspicious.

"But if our unknown adversaries could command Aerians to assassinate Moran dar Carafel, they could not command Aerians to steal the bracelet that the man held. It would be safer—by far—to command Aerians to steal the Emperor's crown. While he's wearing it.

"I have spoken with Master Sabrai of the Oracles. No one approached the Oracular Halls with a similar request—but to speak with the Oracles requires the tacit permission of the Emperor. Again, it is unlikely that permission would have been forthcoming."

"Why do they care about Oracles at all?"

"That would be the question. At the moment, it is the only question worth asking." At Kaylin's expression, the Hawklord continued. "The facts as we know them are simple. Someone Aerian wants Moran dar Carafel dead. The reasons are less clear. On the surface of things, if Moran dies, the power of the *praevolo* returns to the race. But it is not a predictable return; I cannot see why or how her death would be of use.

"But clearly, it is of enough use that assassins have been sent against her." His eyes lightened a touch, although they retained their base blue. "They will not find willing volunteers again while she lives. She has declared herself in a way that is undeniable."

"How so?"

"She can wear the bracelet."

"Pardon?"

"She can wear the bracelet. Did she not tell you?"

Kaylin frowned. "Are you telling me that no one else could wear it?"

"That is exactly what I'm telling you."

"But—it didn't feel like *magic* to me." Kaylin felt the ground give way beneath her feet. She had taken the bracelet—which was technically against the rules—and *handed* it to Moran. "What—what does it do to Aerians who aren't *praevolo*?"

The Hawklord did not reply. But he didn't glare her into

stammers and eventual silence, either. "I am not of significant enough import in the Southern Reach to know that for fact. What I know is what the rest of the Hawks and Swords know; it is based in story and perhaps even myth, not fact. I dislike story and myth as the basis for an investigation.

"But I understand that, in some ways, they have a life of their own. In the stories I was told while a child in the Reaches, and in the stories that the rest of the Aerians here were also told, anyone presumptuous enough to claim it died. The *praevolo* was said to be incorruptible; he—or she—was the heart of all the flights. The rest of the Aerians were not.

"When our ancestors escaped our dying world—and the reasons for its death vary between tellers—it was the *praevolo* who preserved our gift of flight. If the *praevolo* flew, the Aerians flew."

Kaylin nodded; this was in keeping with what she'd been told.

"Modern theory, of course, considers this to be a metaphor."

"What else does modern theory say?"

"It varies. The current thought is that Aerians require a base level of actual magic if their wings are to function as more than mere decorations. The *praevolo* would, in this scenario, be an Aerian who has the ability to contain that base magic within a local area. They would radiate enough magic that the wings could function. They are essentially a repository of power. The magic required is like sun or rain," he added. "It is an essential part of the locale. Elantra, and the Empire, has that magic. There are two known places that do not.

"In theory, were Moran's wings whole, she could fly in either of those places. And in theory, if she were present, we could join her. But only then."

"And the bracelet, in modern theory?"

He grimaced, but his eyes lightened enough that she could see the gray in them. "In modern theory, it would be a repository—a complicated repository—of magic. It cannot be used by any but the *praevolo*. Anyone else who attempts to wear it is destroyed by the influx of magical energy. It is not, according to story, subtle or pretty."

"So…Moran had the wings."

"Yes. But she did not have the bracelet. She did not wear it. It was the only test of her legitimacy that could be offered, and she declined to take it."

"And now that she's wearing it…"

"Yes. To the Aerian Hawks, Moran dar Carafel *is* the *praevolo* now. Arguments could be made in the past—and were—that without that proof, she just had unique wings. Those arguments have now been slaughtered."

"Did she *know* what she was risking?"

"What do you think, Private?"

"I think I understand why Hanson thinks Elani looks good today. If, somehow, the Arcanists have isolated a way to capture, to direct, the power of the *praevolo*, Moran's death would mean that they could choose a suitable host."

"Yes."

Kaylin considered this. "They want information about the possible future because if it doesn't work, they fear disaster?"

"That would be my assumption. Go back to work."

"I'm still stuck on the Shadows."

"Yes, I know."

"I mean—" Kaylin exhaled. "Shadow *is* magic, of a kind."

"Now you are crossing into dangerous, theological territory." His eyes were blue again.

"But it is. It's like fire or water or earth or air—but not elemental in the same way. Gilbert was Shadow. Gilbert's power was of Shadow. But he wasn't inherently evil. What if Shadow is the magic?"

Teela cleared her throat. Loudly. She saluted the Hawklord and dragged Kaylin out of the room.

"I don't understand why that was a bad question."

"Given the Imperial Laws, the existence of the fiefs, the Towers and their fieflords, you don't understand *why* it was a bad question? The Emperor allows lands that are *not* his in the very heart of his hoard, to defend and protect *against* Shadow, and you don't understand why it was a bad question?" Her words were sharp; her voice was soft.

The small dragon squawked.

"But what if—what if we're not looking at Shadow the right way? What if the Shadows we fight don't represent *all* Shadows? Humans sometimes kill people, but not all humans are murderers. Barrani can prey on mortals, but not all Barrani do. I mean, the list could go on and on. What if Shadow is like that?"

"You are not going to tell the Hawklord that you believe that the power of the *praevolo* is based in, or upon, Shadow. Just…don't. Things are politically ugly enough as is, even for mortals."

"All right. I won't. But—do you think I'm wrong?"

Teela exhaled. "Kitling, did I mention political ugliness?"

"Yes."

"I do not think you are entirely wrong. There is a distinct possibility you may be right, which is profoundly disturbing. Shadow is not the only transformative magic—or perhaps, as you've said, we don't clearly understand its power. What controls Shadow, what attacks from Ravellon, is one thing in many parts, but Gilbert was not *of* it.

"If you did not despise Arcanists so much, that is the place I'd start my inquiries."

"No way. If they haven't thought of it themselves, they'll start. Arcanists can take anything and make it worse. For us."

"And that leaves the Arkon."

"I'd rather talk to the Arkon."

Talking to the Arkon involved a delay. Kaylin mirrored the Imperial Library from Caitlin's desk on the way out to patrol Elani. She then went in search of Bellusdeo, whose unofficial position had become bodyguard to Moran dar Carafel.

Given the destruction of the infirmary, Moran was at large, or should have been. In practice, Moran had commandeered a conference room meant for larger gatherings of senior Hawks. It was a space that had been designed for quiet, at least from the outside. Magic was woven into the carpets that lined the scratched floors and the cushions that covered the chairs. Those chairs had been dinged and scratched, but they were solid enough that the damage was entirely cosmetic. Even Marcus would have some trouble disposing of them the Leontine way.

Bellusdeo was standing by the door when Kaylin peered into the room. Moran had some supplies—no doubt wrangled out of the quartermaster—on the large table. There were no beds, but the infirmary had been empty of patients when the bomb had exploded. The gold Dragon looked up.

"I've asked to speak with the Arkon," Kaylin told her. "And if he says yes, I'll be heading directly to the palace from work."

The Dragon nodded, half her attention on Kaylin. The other half was on Moran. "You know," she said quietly, "if I had had people of her caliber under me, I could have—"

"Ruled the world?"

Bellusdeo shook her head, her expression going pensive. "Maybe saved it." She shook herself. "Why do you need to speak with the Arkon?"

"It's about Shadow. Teela says it's political."

"I see. I'm certain he will speak with you."

"You want to come, too?"

"Yes, I think so. We will have to detour to see Moran safely home."

Kaylin nodded and left.

When Kaylin and Teela returned at the end of the day, Moran was adjusting a standing mirror that she must have commandeered from somewhere. The sergeant clearly wasn't comfortable with the lack of beds or a proper desk, but fortunately, there had been few visitors to Moran's improvised infirmary that day—only three, and none of them had been Aerian. One, a new Sword, had had his foot broken—but not crushed—by a horse. A horse that was meant, of course, to be used by the Halls of Law. Kaylin privately felt a deep sympathy for him; he, like Kaylin, had not been raised in an environment where money—and land—was a given, and had therefore never learned to ride.

Moran's angry energy and the need to martial her forces—such as they were—deserted her as the group made their way home. Her wings were drawn in tight; her shoulders were bunched together, as if to ward off blows.

Helen was waiting for them at the open doors. She handed Moran a mug and the Aerian took it with silent gratitude.

"Come," Helen told Moran. "I think a bath—and a change of clothing—is in order. You are *praevolo*, but here, the regalia is not necessary. There are no more tests to pass or fail today." To Kaylin, she said, "The Arkon sent you a message."

"He mirrored?"

"Yes. He has, I believe, rearranged his personal schedule to include time for you, and asks that we ask Bellusdeo to cause less fire. I'm not sure I understand the request."

Bellusdeo snorted a small stream of smoke. "He has clearly become addled with age if he thinks *that* was a fire. I'm almost of mind to set something alight just to remind him of the difference."

"Please don't." Kaylin rushed in to wedge the request between Bellusdeo's annoyed sentences. "I *am* interrupting his work. He hates that."

"He also hates to be left out of anything that might—just might—require his expertise. Honestly, I think we would have been better off visiting Tiamaris."

Given that Tara's job was to guard against *any* incursion of Shadow, Kaylin wasn't nearly as confident. "We're going to be late."

"Yes, probably. But if I show up at the palace in full armor, there'll be a ruckus, and I don't feel like dealing with that today."

By unspoken agreement, the bomb at the office was not to be mentioned, but Kaylin wasn't stupid. It would be on Records, and an investigation or ten was currently underway. There was about zero chance that the Emperor did not know what had occurred. There was a higher chance that the Arkon had managed to avoid the information.

Kaylin, with Bellusdeo as sole escort, walked to the Imperial Palace. It was closer to her new home than her old one, but given how little she generally enjoyed her visits, she didn't consider this a plus. Bellusdeo, however, seemed calm. The informal dinner that Kaylin had dreaded had, in the end, all interruptions aside, had a positive effect. Bellusdeo no longer went orange-eyed at the mention of the Emperor.

Lord Emmerian was waiting for them in place of the steward, a young page by his side. "Lord Bellusdeo," he said, sweeping a very Barrani-style bow.

"Lord Emmerian. The Arkon has now sent you out as a glorified page?"

Emmerian's grin was rueful. "The Arkon? No. Some rumor has reached the Court of the morning's…excitement."

"And you were sent to make sure that I was materially unharmed."

"Indeed. The Emperor was not best pleased, and has been martialing the full force of his concentration."

"He is not investigating, surely. That is what the Hawks are for."

"Ah, not investigating, no. But there were some concerns, when the report was delivered—verbally, by the Lord of Hawks—that he would fly himself out to the Southern Reach and reduce the Caste Court and the dar Carafel flight to such small parts none of it would ever be found again."

"I'm somewhat partial to that idea myself, at the moment."

"Yes. The Arkon felt you might be."

Bellusdeo's eyes lightened, and a grin caused the corners of her mouth to twitch. "And so he sent you to head me off?"

"To escort you, Lord Bellusdeo," was the grave reply, although it seemed to Kaylin that a smile lurked in the Dragon's eyes. "I am not certain why, but he believes you have a mercurial and unpredictable temper. I have never seen you destroy things in a sudden rage; nor have I heard stories or rumors that have any merit in them."

"He knew me when I was just out of the shell," she replied.

"Perhaps that would explain it. Will you tell me a little of your current work with the Hawks?"

"I am not a Hawk," was Bellusdeo's careful reply; she had just given Kaylin the side-eye. "But I have been given permission to accompany Lord Kaylin while she does her duty. My laws were similar in spirit, but there are material differences in their execution; I felt that this would be the best way to learn about the Imperial Laws." She took the arm he offered, and they preceded Kaylin down the hall toward the Imperial Library that was the Arkon's den.

The Arkon was frazzled—or at least his hair was—but on closer inspection, his eyes were almost gold. Some hint of orange had shifted their hue, but it was slight, and it vanished as he caught sight of Bellusdeo. "I honestly do not see the point in rumor," he told her, nodding to Emmerian.

"There is a reason it is called 'rumor' and not 'fact,' Lannagaros. I have survived much, much worse than a tiny, mortal bomb. And far more Shadow than the bomb is reputed to contain."

At that, the orange that had nearly disappeared returned in full force.

"...I see the rumors did not trend in that direction," Bellusdeo said. She released Lord Emmerian's arm. "Thank you for the company. And thank you," she added, "for asking questions and listening as if you actually had some care for the answers."

Emmerian's eyes were golden. "I am not considered particularly possessive or aggressive," he told Bellusdeo. "And the clutch-fathers were absolutely certain I would never find, never make, a hoard of my own."

"I would bite them myself, if I thought they still survived. That is a terrible thing to say to a child."

"They spoke their minds," Emmerian replied. "And in truth? They were not wrong. It is significant, I think, that Lord Tiamaris found his hoard; he is the youngest of us. But he is Tiamaris, and remains so."

"You've visited him?"

"Yes, at his invitation. And once at the Emperor's directive. I was not certain what to expect—it has been centuries since a Dragon has declared his hoard. Once, there might have been ceremony—but perhaps not. It is hard to dress up or civilize the very visceral *mine* that seems to reside at the heart of the choice.

"He is not unchanged, not precisely—but he is brighter, stronger, more certain; he is confident in a way that he was not before. It is…illuminating."

"Oh?"

"He is not the first Dragon I have seen make such a declaration. But I have seen the way it breaks the weak, in the end. I have seen the fear of, the fear for, *hoard* push greater Dragons into madness. Tiamaris is not broken, but strengthened. And I am wasting the Arkon's precious time."

"But not mine," Bellusdeo countered. She bowed to him, and said, her back to the Arkon, "I am certain Lannagaros is grateful that you took the time to escort us personally." There was an edge of command in her tone.

Emmerian chuckled. "I am certain he is grateful, as well."

"And he would like to remain that way," the Arkon said. "I feel that the chances of that are diminishing with each passing sentence."

CHAPTER 18

The Arkon then led Bellusdeo and Kaylin to the far end of the many, many rooms in his possession. This was one of the theoretically safe rooms; it had no actual doors until the Arkon approached it, whereupon a door materialized in a stretch of unadorned wall. Kaylin's arms ached in protest, but she expected that; she'd been both surprised and grateful that the library's large doors had been open when she'd arrived.

The Arkon did not ask questions. He didn't speak at all until they were safely ensconced in the room and the door had been firmly shut.

"You will now explain," he said—to Kaylin. Of course. "The comment about Shadow."

"I didn't make the comment!"

"I did not say you did. I did, however, say that you will explain it."

Bellusdeo chuckled. If Diarmat had said something similar—and it was exactly the kind of thing he *would* say—she would have been orange-eyed and threatening fire with each breath she expelled. She seemed to expect it, and even to treasure it, from the Arkon.

Kaylin found it difficult to do the same, and reminded

herself that she actually liked the Arkon. Sometimes it was harder than others. "You know," she told him, "it's not that I mind answering your questions, but when I've answered them you come up with a hundred more, none of which I *can* answer."

"I will endeavor to keep that in mind. Your explanation?"

"The bomb was, in theory, an Arcane bomb—but tiny."

"It destroyed the infirmary."

"Yes."

"It damaged the bearing wall."

"Did it?"

The Arkon threw a significant and slightly accusing glance at Bellusdeo, who shrugged. "I have learned with experience," she told the Hawk, "that the Arkon is certain of his facts. He does not make statements of that nature frivolously."

"Fine. It did. At the time, I was focused on Moran."

"Continue."

"You know I've often been called in for investigations where magic is a suspected part of the crime. And that I've had some experience with the aftermath of Arcane bombs."

"Indeed."

"This one was, in theory, far too small to do the damage it did. The magical signature heavily implied—to me—that unless the bomb had been ingested, it wouldn't cause death, let alone the destruction it did cause. But the signature of the mage—and before you ask, no, I didn't recognize it, it wasn't familiar—wasn't the only aftereffect of the bomb's explosion."

"Continue."

"There was Shadow spread unevenly across most of the room. It follows the magical splash patterns, and it's strongest where we believe the bomb was planted." Now, she hesitated. She looked to Bellusdeo.

"I'm not a Hawk," the gold Dragon replied, "but regardless of your answers, I intend to continue to guard Moran." A thread of defiance bound the words of that sentence together.

Kaylin very much feared that any goodwill generated by the Emperor's informal dinner was going to be ash very soon. The Emperor was *not* going to be happy. "The Shadow wasn't sentient. At all. I'm not a mage—I can only barely light a candle—but I'd guess, given the splash patterns and the presence of Shadow, that the actual force of the explosion was provided *by* the Shadow the bomb contained."

"You've seen Shadow magic before," the Arkon said, voice flat.

Kaylin frowned. "Yes."

"Was it similar?"

"No."

"The differences?"

"The first time I saw what I'd identify as Shadow magic, there *was* a sigil. It was composed of black smoke with a little too much solidity, but it was a sigil."

"You do not consider the sigil or signature of most magic innately intelligent."

"No."

"You consider Shadow to be innately intelligent."

She nodded, still thinking, still frowning.

"What is the difference?"

"I've seen elementals summoned. The small ones are the ones that light candles. Summoning elementals doesn't leave signatures the way Arcane bombs do. The fire *is* the magic, but it's also fire. The same is true of the water or the air; I assume it's true of the earth, as well."

The Arkon nodded.

"This…is more like that. The first time I saw Shadow used for magic, there *was* a signature. I'm not sure I understand why the two are different. I can sense when someone is summoning elements; I can feel it *as* magic." Her hesitation was still thoughtful. "But mages who create Arcane bombs can also summon. Well, some of them. I don't really understand how magic works."

"Not even the Arcanists understand all the ways in which magic does—or does not—work. You are certain of the presence of Shadow?"

Kaylin nodded.

To Bellusdeo, the Arkon said, "Did you see the room after the explosion?" He tactfully did not mention that she had pretty much been blown into the wall opposite the infirmary door, and she didn't mention it, either. "Did you notice the Shadow?"

"No. Did the Imperial mages?"

"The Imperial mages are notably tardy when delivering anything other than verbal reports."

"Meaning no?"

"Meaning I do not know yet." He exhaled a puff of smoke.

"Can I ask a question?" Kaylin asked, before Bellusdeo could speak again.

"Demonstrably." The Arkon waited.

Kaylin fumbled with words in the silence, trying to put smart sentences together. She didn't have many in place when Bellusdeo snorted. "She is wondering if the *Illumen praevolo*'s magic is of the Shadow."

The Arkon did not immediately become orange-eyed, although there was a faint, almost copper cast to his eyes. His inner membranes rose. "Why would you ask that question?"

Kaylin hadn't, but felt no need to point this out; it never got her anywhere where the Arkon was concerned. "The story of the *praevolo*, and the presence of Shadow magic—

with the assassins the first time, and with the mortal agent the second time... Aerians apparently require a world that has strong magic if their wings aren't meant for anything other than decoration. The story is that the *praevolo* was somehow created or born at a time of great need, and he led his people across the endless space between worlds."

"I am aware of the variants of *praevolo* myths and legends."

"I don't know a lot about the death of whole worlds."

"You know more than most, and I include mortal scholars among that number."

"Bellusdeo's previous home was lost to Shadow. It was lost to the Shadows at the heart of Ravellon, because Ravellon existed on her world."

"Ravellon is believed to have existed on many worlds before the fall."

Kaylin nodded. "If the ability to use Shadow as if it were normal magic—or elemental magic—was known, maybe worlds wouldn't have fallen. The thing is," she continued, "if you summon a big-enough fire, all it wants to do is burn things. Anything. All the things. If you summon too much water, it's the same—except it wants to drop on things or drown them."

"Indeed."

"But there's part of the water that doesn't want those things. And when I'm in the elemental garden, the fire doesn't try to burn me."

"It's probably too terrified of Evanton," Bellusdeo pointed out.

"Fair enough. The Shadow wants to devour things—to alter them, to change them, to absorb them somehow. What if the Shadow is like the fire or the water?"

"Fire and water are necessary to life. They are part of the natural order."

"Yes, but—"

"But?"

"What if Shadow is part of the natural order, as well?"

Bellusdeo, who had lost most of what she valued in life to Shadow, did not bite Kaylin, but it was probably close.

"What if, on the original Aerian world, Shadow was simply used the way we use fire or water? What if Shadow was the only power they could call upon that could carry them across the sky, or the emptiness between worlds?"

"You are asking very dangerous questions."

"I'm trying to understand what we're facing. I'm trying to understand how it works. Even the Shadow that inhabited our human criminal wasn't transformative in the way Shadow normally is. What if that *is* the power?"

"It would be forbidden use."

"What if they don't understand it *as* the source of their power?"

"Ignorance in this case is not an excuse."

"It's an explanation."

"It is, and explanations often displace accusations of high treason." He exhaled. "The questions, while dangerous, are also somewhat perceptive. The dangers, I believe, outweigh the possible benefits in the use of this kind of magic. If Shadow is, indeed, an elemental force—"

"The thing is, Gilbert was Shadow. I'd swear he was. But…he wasn't like the one-offs we fought in the fiefs of Tiamaris. Or anywhere else. And I'm now wondering if that's because he *has* Shadow as power, the way maybe the *praevolo* did, but the power doesn't control him; he controls the power."

"Have you asked Moran dar Carafel about this?"

"Not yet."

"I would be interested in her answer, if you do ask. I believe that your Helen would be aware of the presence of Shadow within her own boundaries; has she mentioned any danger?"

"No."

"You understand that if this becomes a commonly asked question, it will doom the Aerians in the city." It was almost a question, but didn't rise at the end. "You are an officer of the Halls of Law, one-third of which is committed to keeping the peace, such as peace is."

Kaylin nodded.

"You understand that there will be *no* peace if even a whiff of this rumor reaches the general populace?" The Arkon frowned. "Clearly, the answer is no. I invite you to spend some time in thought. Fear makes humans incredibly unwise. Shadows—for good reason—breed fear in the populace of Elantra. I am almost certain that the Aerians do not use Shadow as their locomotive force."

Kaylin nodded.

"What now?"

"What if the Aerian mages—and there are rumored Aerian Arcanists in the mix—do use that power now, even if they don't completely realize what it is?"

The Arkon's eyes were burning a steady orange.

"I mean—what if they do? Or did? What if the Aerians that want Moran gone are somehow entwined with *our* version of Shadow?"

"Meaning?"

"If they summoned their power and got more than they could control. Fire elementals have reduced their summoners to charred flesh—or worse—before. At least that's what I've been told."

"You believe that something other is now driving the Aerian Caste Court."

"I believe that it *might* be. We know what happens when the other elementals are too much for the summoner to control. It's obvious. It involves corpses. But...what if that's not what uncontrolled Shadow does?"

The Arkon rose. "I have much to consider," he said. "I will see you out." This was a very polite way of saying *get lost*. Probably because Bellusdeo was in the room.

Only when they had crossed the fence line of their home did Bellusdeo choose to speak. "Lannagaros was upset."

"I'm upset, as well."

"Ah. I do not think he faults your reasoning—neither do I, if it comes to that. I think he hadn't considered it before. Not in the way you put it. He's right, however."

"About the cost to the Aerians?"

Bellusdeo nodded. "People always try to simplify their lives. Most humans do not interact with the Aerians—and of the ones that do so regularly, most are merchants or members of the Imperial Palace staff. They think of Aerians as people with wings who live outside of the city. And as Hawks.

"If rumors spread, the only thing most people will know is that Aerians are infested with Shadow. Nothing will balance the fear."

Kaylin slowed, as she sometimes did when she was thinking. "It's like me."

"Pardon?"

"It's like I was about the Tha'alani."

"You seem to like them."

"Now, yes. But I hated them for years. All of them. I identified them by their forehead stalks and their racial ability, and I hated them because I feared them." She squirmed, saying this out loud; squirmed thinking about that younger self and how stupid she'd been. It made her wonder how many other things she was *still* being stupid about without realizing it. This was not a comfortable thought.

"You learned," Bellusdeo quite reasonably pointed out.

"Yes—but that was almost a fluke. And that kind of fluke isn't going to happen to every other person who believes what I believed."

"No. People are always fearful, dear," Helen said, although they hadn't even reached the door. The door did open, and her Avatar stood in the frame, but her voice was much closer than the rest of her. "I have always thought it unwise to let fear be your personal guide."

"Which one would you prefer? Love has its problems as well, if you listen to old stories."

"Ah, but I would argue that that is not love—it is *fear*. It is fear of the loss of love. But we might spend idle hours arguing the definition of the word *love*, and I have dinner prepared. Moran," she added, "has been waiting for you."

"For me?"

"You are, I believe, to visit Evanton's shop tonight. With her."

Damn. "I forgot all about it."

"Well, the loss of the infirmary and its attendant difficulties would probably drive less pressing needs out of your thoughts," was Helen's very charitable reply. "But you don't have a lot of time before you have to leave."

Moran was nervous. Her eyes were shifting color with every second step she took. She wore the robes and the bracelet of the *praevolo*. During the day, she wore them as if they were a suit of armor. If she took no personal comfort from the act, the rest of the Aerian Hawks did. In a weird sort of way, it was a command decision.

Lillias, however, was not. She was part of Moran's history,

and entwined with the severely unhappy bits at that. But she had saved Moran's life. And in all probability, that decision had cost Lillias her literal wings.

There were a lot of questions Kaylin wanted to ask about that. A lot. How did it even *happen*? The wings were physical; they were like arms and legs. There existed no spell that Kaylin knew of that would allow someone to magically remove said arms or legs from anyone who had them. That said, swords and axes generally did the trick—they just didn't do it instantly or cleanly.

"Thank you," Moran said, as they reached the start of the Elani district.

"For what?"

"For coming with me. It's been a long day—I was afraid there'd been some sort of midwives emergency, and you weren't coming back."

"There was an Arkon emergency," Kaylin told her. "But at least it didn't involve fire."

"The Arkon was the older man I met at dinner?"

"Older Dragon, but yes. Bellusdeo insists that he actually likes me, but on days like this one, you wouldn't know it."

"How did you meet him?" Moran asked. Kaylin answered, realizing that if the discussion wasn't important for the information it contained, it was important for other reasons.

She was still talking about the Arkon when they reached Evanton's front door. Light could be seen through the windows. "Evanton wasn't certain she'd come," Kaylin reminded Moran.

"No. I guess we won't know if we don't knock."

Grethan met them at the door. In general, Kaylin approved of this because Evanton took a long time to reach the door, and he hated it when people either pulled the bell a dozen times or, worse, pulled it once and assumed he wasn't in when he didn't immediately answer.

Kaylin had once suggested that maybe, just maybe, magic be used on that door or that bell that would allow the visitor to recognize when Evanton was, or was not, receiving guests, which got her a long lecture, but changed nothing. She'd long since given up trying. If she wanted to see Evanton, she had to play by his rules.

Grethan, however, was not old; he was young enough that walking to the door and answering it wasn't at all taxing. He didn't despise interruptions; he didn't resent them. He smiled up at Kaylin's familiar as he saw who stood on the other side of the open door.

The familiar squawked and leapt off the Kaylin perch and onto the Grethan one.

"Is he in?"

"He's in the kitchen," Grethan replied. "But I think he intends to move to the garden when you're here. You're a bit on the late side," he added, half-apologetically.

"We had a bit of a day."

"It's you," Grethan said.

"What is that supposed to mean?"

"You always have a 'bit of a day.' Whenever I think it's hard being Evanton's apprentice, I think about being you instead, and it helps. Um, sorry."

The small dragon squawked.

"People destroyed her home once. She had to face the Devourer; she had to save the elemental garden from—from a mad man. She has an angry Leontine as a boss, she has a Dragon as a friend—and even that friend came only because she almost died in Shadow. I mean, seriously—she has a really stressful life. I only have to deal with sulky wild elements and a really grouchy Evanton—and he's not grouchy all the time."

Moran chuckled. "He's not wrong."

Lillias was waiting in the kitchen, her eyes a martial blue.

Evanton's eyes didn't change color; he had the rest of his very lined face to make up for the lack, and it did. She was late, yes, and clearly, at the moment, late was an almost unpardonable capital crime.

"I'm sorry we're late," Kaylin said before Evanton could speak. "It's entirely my fault; Moran was waiting for me. But I had a Dragon to deal with, and while you're like the Dragon in temper, you can't reduce me to ash without the fire's permission."

"The fire is not notably reluctant to burn things."

"No, but it would upset your guests."

Lillias had been watching Moran, and only Moran; the social dance of apology, groveling and possible forgiveness meant nothing to her. Her eyes were a complicated shade of purple and the deeper gray that was the Aerian norm. She rose from the chair she'd occupied, and froze, standing by the table.

Moran understood what had happened; Kaylin didn't, but could guess. Some greeting to the *praevolo* involved the spread or movement of actual wings, and Lillias, without them, couldn't perform the proper gestures.

Moran caught Lillias's hands before Lillias could fall to her knees. "I thought you'd died," the Aerian sergeant whispered.

Lillias bowed her head. She raised it again when Moran's hands tightened. "No, Moran." She didn't use the title.

"Why didn't you contact me?"

"I did not know how. I was stranded, grounded. Were it not for the kindness of another Aerian, I would have remained in the Southern Reach, in a cave that was once used for the outcaste and other criminals; I had no way of reaching the ground. But I could not return."

"But—I work on the ground—"

"Yes. I was not aware of that. I was given very little information about the Aerians." She spoke the word as if it no longer applied to her. "And I had to adapt to life here. I almost didn't," she added, but the words were spoken with a wryness that bordered on affection. She shook herself. "I wouldn't have recognized you, if not for the wings. You are a grown woman now, not an angry young child." She hesitated. "Evanton says you wished to speak with me?"

"Of course I did. I had no idea you were alive until Kaylin said she'd met you."

"We are going to the garden," Evanton declared, rising. "The kitchen is crowded enough that it feels cramped; the garden is quite pleasant at the moment. Come."

The elemental garden was, as Evanton had stated, pleasant. The breeze was gentle. The water was entirely contained in a pond that was deeper than the Imperial Palace was tall. Moss had grown across stones, but the earth was calm, and the grass that took root in it was lush and green, if a little unkempt.

Lillias had clearly seen this garden before, judging by her utter lack of surprise, but Moran had not. Given the cramped, rickety hall and the narrow closet-size door that led to this space, that wasn't surprising.

"You've been here before," Kaylin said to Lillias.

"Yes. Not often. Evanton is a busy man, and I don't like to intrude."

Moran was flexing her wings, although the injured one was slow to respond.

"How did you find out that Moran was here? I mean, on the ground?"

"Because I saw her," Lillias replied. "I saw her on the night the Dragons came out to fight. I saw her in the air, with the rest of the Hawks."

"You could recognize her from the ground?"

Lillias looked genuinely surprised by the question. She glanced at Moran, who was speaking, for the moment, to Evanton.

"I'm sorry if that was rude—it wasn't intentional."

"No. No, I forget myself." Lillias's smile was old and care-worn. "We can see her, when she flies. She could be miles off, and if we could see her at all as more than a speck in the sky, we would know, instantly, who she is. She is *praevolo*."

"You saw her get injured."

Lillias bowed her head. "Yes."

"That's why you had Evanton make the charm?"

"It is not a charm," Lillias's voice was even quieter. She stiffened and looked over her shoulder. "It is part of the voice of the wind here. Can you hear it?"

Kaylin couldn't.

"The wind knows its own," Lillias said in Aerian. It was a phrase Kaylin knew because the Hawklord sometimes used it. But he'd never meant it literally, and it was clear that Lillias did. "I have no wings," she continued. "Which you, of course, noticed. Most people don't."

"But your eyes—"

"Most people don't. They are not Hawks, and they are not accustomed to judging mood from the color of eyes; they look at expressions, and listen to tone of voice. Now hush, and listen."

"To what?"

"The wind."

★ ★ ★

The wind did not speak to Kaylin, not in words she could recognize. Sometimes she spoke to the wind, in this garden, and it did respond, but not often. And clearly not the way it responded to Moran and Lillias. As if aware of what was to happen—and how could he not be?—Evanton came to stand by Kaylin's side.

Lillias lifted her arms; Moran lifted both arms and wings, although the injured one twitched. Kaylin looked at the sergeant, and then looked away from what she saw in the Aerian's face. In both of their faces.

The breeze grew stronger, but it didn't gather debris in its folds, and in truth, it felt gentle. It sounded almost like a gale.

Lillias was the first to leave the ground. As if she had wings, phantom wings, she rose in the air, her feet breaking all connection with the grass beneath them. She moved as if those wings had never been lost, and she rose, looking up, always up, into the endless sky of the Keeper's garden.

Moran didn't appear to be shocked; she, too, rose. She had wings, but they could not carry her weight—not in the world outside this enclosed space. But in this space, it wasn't wings that were required. Kaylin's hands curled into fists, not because she was angry, but because she wanted instinctively to hang on to something.

The air didn't hold her. The air didn't lift her. It had never been her element.

She watched. She watched the wingless woman turn and spiral in the air, rising and plunging deliberately in a dive. She watched Moran join her, weaving complicated, tight circles around her. The Aerian Hawks practicing their drills would never, ever have been able to keep up with her. She looked…younger. Joyful.

Lillias laughed, was laughing, and Kaylin wondered then

how hard it would be to lose both of her legs, because that was the only comparison she could make. And yet Lillias had made a life for herself here. It wasn't the life she'd once had, and she didn't live without regret—but she did live.

"I met her," Evanton said, "some years ago. I recognized what she was, as you did. What she said, however, was not wrong: people do not notice. It is possible for Lillias to live as you live—but it was very, very hard.

"You do not think of the fiefs as a particularly pleasant place."

"I like Tiamaris."

"Yes. But Tiamaris was not the fief of your birth or your childhood, such as it was. Nightshade was. You think of it as disadvantageous, and primarily it was. You had neither a normal childhood nor a normal life; you had no certain sense of safety. But I will argue that your life there did provide you with one or two advantages that Lillias did not have."

Kaylin opened her mouth to protest and shut it again.

"You're getting better," Evanton said. "I had almost begun to despair. You were about to ask me what the advantages to you now are."

She nodded.

"You had no home, Kaylin. You had no family. You had no sense that survival was certain. In every possible way, you lived on the edge. Because you did, you have no sense of society, and your place in it. Lillias was not powerful. She was not born to a significant flight. But she had family, and home. She had a place she understood. She knew what the rules were, and she had a job that she took some pride in.

"All of these were lost to her the minute she made her decision. It was," he added mildly, "the right decision, in my opinion—but it was enormously costly. Sometimes, when the costs never end, the rightness of the decision is called into question. She lost what she had, when she fell.

"You found what you've built. You were not mired in the loss; it did not destroy you. You expected far, far less than Lillias had, until that moment, expected. Every comparison you made to your previous life was a good one. You did not pause to think that people were rude or graceless, because your sense of manners, such as they were, were very primitive. For Lillias, it was much harder. She had more to lose, and lost it all. She could not, at the time, see what she had to gain, because the one thing she wanted, she could never have again."

Kaylin thought, without resentment, that Evanton was right. "If it's all the same to you," she added, "I'd rather no other child ever had to live with my so-called advantage."

"It is a silver lining, Kaylin. It is not one to be desired, and where you survived, many in your position—and I have no doubt there *are* many—do not. But your entry into Elantra was vastly less painful and less complicated in the end than hers."

"Did Moran always fly like that?"

"I have no idea. Like Lillias, I saw her in flight only once."

"You saw her?"

"Yes, Kaylin. I am the Keeper; I am aware of many things that occur within the city itself, and so close to the heart of Shadow." He looked up at the two women flying in the folds of elemental air. "Do you understand what they're saying?"

"Not all of it. Some. My Aerian's not as good as my Barrani. This is what the *bletsian* was supposed to do for her. For Moran, I mean."

"Yes. It was what I gifted Lillias, when we first met." He shook his head. "It is hard, to make sacrifices. Harder when none of them seem necessary or relevant in retrospect. Lillias needed to see Moran as she is now."

Kaylin was frowning. "But…"

"But?"

"You said Moran wasn't allowed to see Lillias as only one thing—in this case, a tragedy, a cause for guilt."

"I did."

"But…Lillias doesn't really see Moran, does she? I mean, she sees the *Illumen praevolo*. But Moran as she is?"

"You know, there are days when I despair of you. And there are other days—like this one—when I realize that being a groundhawk *is* your calling. Yes, Kaylin. She sees the *praevolo*. She could hardly see anything else; Moran was a child when Lillias was made outcaste. She did not interact with Moran at any time; she did not visit her at the Halls of Law. She was only peripherally aware of the fact that Moran—no, that the *praevolo*—was still alive.

"But she gave up her life—as an Aerian—on the day that she saved Moran's, and she did it for the *praevolo*. And for the child. You would like Lillias, if you had met her in other circumstances. But she sees only some small part of what Moran is."

"And she didn't get the humiliating lecture."

"Ah. No. But I don't know her quite as well as I know you."

"You didn't know Moran at all, and you lectured her."

"True. But there is a type of self-aggrandizing guilt with which I am all too familiar, and I dislike it intensely." He had the grace to redden. "I may have been a bit too harsh."

But watching the two Aerians—neither of whom could take to the skies by their own power—Kaylin shook her head. "No," she said, a smile hovering across her lips. "You were exactly harsh enough." She looked at Evanton and added, "But don't feel a great need to repeat it anytime soon."

He laughed.

CHAPTER 19

Evanton left Lillias and Moran in the garden after first speaking to the wind. He escorted Kaylin out, and shut the door. "It is the one space in which they will be perfectly safe." His smile was sadder and more lined, but it often was when he left the confines of the Keeper's garden: age settled far more heavily across his shoulders anywhere but there.

"Did Lillias explain what the fancy dress means?"

"I understand the fancy dress, as you call it; I did not require explanations."

Kaylin hesitated. Bellusdeo's warnings—about panic, about fear, about the nature of people—were weighty and sharp.

"You are thinking so loudly I can practically hear you, and you are not thinking anything pleasant."

"No."

"I hesitate to ask you to share. In general, your unpleasant thoughts—or at least the ones that cause that particular expression—cause difficulties for everyone. On the other hand, some difficulties require intervention, and it is better to have an early warning."

"I'm not actually supposed to talk about it," Kaylin mumbled.

"Ah. But they can't stop you from thinking?"

"No. And you're smart, and you know things. I mean, different things."

"Than you?"

"Than the Arkon."

"You discussed this with the Arkon."

"Yes. Because—"

"He is ancient and has some affinity for antiquities." At Kaylin's expression, he frowned and added, "He knows more than you do. What did you ask him?"

"I, um, asked him if he thought there was any chance at all that Shadow was, like the elements, a source of power. I mean, not *like* elements, but *kind* of like them. You know how summoners get powerful enough to summon bigger chunks of elemental fire, and then they have to fight like hell to make certain the fire doesn't burn everything in sight?"

"Yes," was Evanton's dry response.

Kaylin reddened. Of course he knew. "What if Shadow was sort of like that? I mean, that some people could summon Shadow, and it would do what they wanted, and some could summon Shadow and it would…eat them."

"You asked the Arkon this."

She nodded.

"His answer?"

"He thought it was a very good question."

"*Why* exactly did you ask the Arkon the question?"

Kaylin told him.

"There is no Shadow in my garden," Evanton said when they had taken their usual seats around the now-less-crowded kitchen table. "There is, however, the Devourer of Worlds. I do not think he will awaken in any true sense for centuries."

"The Devourer isn't Shadow, though."

"No." Evanton paused. "Nor can he, in theory, be summoned the way the wild elements can. But it is possible that you are materially half-correct. It is not, however, a magic that I believe the Aerians know how to use, if anyone currently does."

"I think someone currently does. The human who bullied Margot into reading the future—which made about as much sense to anyone else as Oracles usually do before things actually happen—was somehow imbued with Shadow. Or infested by it. That Shadow was, I think, key to his ability to physically control Margot—but he seemed both surprised and genuinely upset to see it.

"Second, the Arcane bomb that destroyed the infirmary earlier today. Usually when there's that much damage done, you can see the magical splash across the bits and pieces of debris. There *was* some of that, but not nearly enough for a bomb of that power. There was also a lot of inert Shadow.

"And third..." Here she hesitated. "I don't know what you've been told about the *praevolo*. Probably a lot more than I have," she added in a rush when she saw Evanton's wrinkles begin to fall into his pinched, annoyed expression. "Third, the world the Aerians were originally from was somehow losing its magic. I don't understand how or why—I mean, how do you lose magic?—but that's what they believed. They need magic to fly.

"So they left it. But if the problem was magic—or lack of magic—I'm not sure I understand *how* the *praevolo* could be a vessel for enough magic to allow the Aerians to fly in their search. And yet, that's what they think the *praevolo* did."

Evanton nodded.

"The Barrani have what they refer to as a Test of Name."

"Be careful, Kaylin."

"I'm being careful. I'm only talking to you."

"Yes. With your usual subtlety."

She shrugged, fief shrug. "The *reason* they have the test is because of Shadow—our Shadow, the Shadow in Ravellon. What the Shadow touches, it alters. If altered, the person changed becomes part of that Shadow, subordinate to it. It changes something about the person.

"Those who survive the Test of Name *can* face the Shadow without being consumed by it. Those who fail can't. That's the theory," she added. "Look, I *hate it*. But no one is forced to take the Test of Name. Most of the Barrani Hawks haven't, and won't."

"One cannot be Lord of the High Court without undergoing it," Evanton observed. "And children of important lineages almost certainly consider they have no choice but to take that risk."

She thought of Annarion and fell silent for a beat or two.

"If Shadow is like fire, it's likely to consume those who can't control it." She hesitated again. "The bracelet Moran is wearing—"

"Yes," Evanton replied, as if the word was a wall.

"Only the *praevolo* can wear it. It apparently—"

"Destroys anyone else." Evanton's frown lines deepened. "Moran is *praevolo*. She was accepted—provisionally—as *praevolo*. She was adopted into arguably the most powerful and significant flight in the Southern Reach. Do you honestly think that adoption would have proceeded if the dar Carafel weren't certain?" His frown was familiar, and oddly comforting in spite of the fact that it was turned on her.

Did she? No. No, of course not.

"They may not have let her *keep* it. In theory, there are guardians who protect the regalia. In practice, it is historically unwise to have men of ambition and power as guardians to objects—or kingdoms—they might otherwise desire to possess. In general, the guardians become the kings—usually when their charges die."

"The *praevolo* didn't rule, though."

"No, perhaps not. But the *praevolo*'s power is considered close to divine. It is the *heart* of flight, to the Aerians. Moran is the mortal expression of it."

"And she can't fly."

Evanton said a quiet nothing. A quiet, significant nothing.

"She can't fly," Kaylin repeated. "Have you taken a closer look at her wing?"

"She is *praevolo*."

"Evanton—" Kaylin stopped. Froze. "You think—you think the assassination attempts started because she's *praevolo* and she couldn't fly. You think—"

"It is not my job to think," was his testy reply. "It's yours. In theory, you get paid for it."

"I'm off-duty," Kaylin pointed out.

"There's no reason you can't think on your own time."

No wonder Grethan was invisible. But Evanton's dour questions had kicked off thoughts that wouldn't stop once they'd gained traction. "If the power of the *praevolo* is the heart of flight—if the *praevolo* was meant to give flight to the flightless, her inability to fly proves she's a fraud."

He was silent.

"The dar Carafel—the ones doing the adopting—knew that she could wear the bracelet. You're right. They'd've had to know. They know she's not a fraud, and they know it would be hard to convince the rest of the people—you know, the ones who do the *actual* work—"

"Classism, Kaylin."

"I don't care. It would be hard to convince them that she was a fraud when they didn't believe it themselves. People like Lillias will give up their lives to protect her because of what she means as a symbol." She slowed down. "People like Clint or the rest of the Hawks. If they believed it, they would.

"But if she couldn't fly—in spite of injuries that would cripple any other Aerian—she becomes a fraud. And if she's considered a fraud, her death means nothing. No, probably more than nothing: it's like she's been lying, and she's been caught out, and she's facing justice. Ugh. You know, she's suffered because of those wings. She's lost a lot. I can't think of a thing she's truly gained. And no one else is going to believe that, unless they know her well enough that she's willing to talk about her life."

"No."

"But the thing I don't understand is *why?* The power of the *praevolo* is random. It's not predictable. It skips generations. Killing her means that in the future another *praevolo* might be born—with a better pedigree—but that future might be generations down the road."

"We circle back, then."

"It would only make sense if they had some way of passing that power on." Her frown deepened. "Or if they *believed* they had a way of passing that power on. If they could choose." She looked at Evanton. "Have you examined Moran's bracelet at all?"

Evanton smiled then. "Only in a cursory fashion. I do not deem it wise—or safe—to handle."

"But the mortal carried it."

"Yes. The mortal who was, as you have mentioned, imbued somehow with Shadow."

"Do you think it's possible that it's the *bracelet* that contains the power?"

"And that it's the *praevolo* who can house it?" Evanton opened his cookie tin and handed it to Kaylin, almost as if the question deserved a smidgen of reward. "I think it is possible, yes. I think, however, it is unlikely."

Kaylin deflated.

"But I think it very likely that men who are accustomed to power and its use, to rank and its use, to elevated birth and its rules, might well come to view it that way."

"But if they're wrong..." Kaylin hesitated.

"You think they may be attempting to unlock the power itself."

"And Moran is wearing it."

"And Moran is wearing it, yes."

"They're not getting it back unless they cut off her arm—and they're not doing that unless she's very dead."

"Indeed. Have a cookie or two. I always feel guilty when I tear Lillias from the sky."

Kaylin took two cookies. A thought occurred to her and she stopped chewing.

"You can think and eat at the same time."

She swallowed quickly. "I can't talk and eat at the same time. According to you."

"Yes?"

"The wind is only carrying Lillias."

Evanton smiled.

"But Moran is flying."

His smile deepened.

"You are a devious old bastard."

"Thank you. If I weren't, I would not be a very capable Keeper."

"But Grethan is your apprentice, and he isn't."

"Yes. It is a fear; there's only so much I can teach him. The Tha'alani are not naturally devious—they've no reason to be. Grethan, absent the *Tha'alaan*, is probably as close as one of his kind can come, and frankly..."

"He's terrible at it."

"Yes. When he is not being ridden by his fear and his insecurity, he is painfully honest." The Keeper rose. "Now, will you tell Moran, or shall I?"

"But the thing I don't understand—"

"We will never make it down this *very short* hall if you do not stop asking questions. There are so many things you don't understand I will expire of old age just making the attempt to alleviate your ignorance."

"The thing I don't understand," she continued, dogged now, because it was important, "is how the Shadow got where it did. I mean, Moran never touched the first guy. You could make the argument that he handled the bracelet, and somehow, Shadow spilled into him—but I think that's a pretty big stretch.

"And even if it weren't, and that's *how* he got the power, *he* didn't make the Arcane bomb."

"No. No doubt an Arcanist did."

Kaylin stared at the door at the end of the hall. "...And there is an Aerian Arcanist, or so I've been told."

"Yes. Are all Arcanists evil by default?"

"Yes."

Evanton snorted. "Your time in the Hawks has been an almost unalloyed good for you—but in this one regard, it is faulty. No single group is, by default, evil."

"You've met a lot of Arcanists, have you?"

"Only a handful. Your Teela was one." As Kaylin opened her mouth, Evanton glared. "No. Shut up now or we will never leave the hall, and I, for one, am a tired old man. It is past my bedtime and I need my sleep."

Lillias was on the ground when Evanton opened the door; she seemed to be waiting for them. Her eyes were filmed with tears, and clearly, some of those tears had already been spilled. She smiled at Evanton; Kaylin saw some hint of the younger woman she might once have been. To Kaylin, she said, "Can you see her?"

The answer was yes—but only barely. Kaylin knew that the skies above this garden were actual skies; they were not illusory. But Moran was a speck so small she might have been a tiny bird. A tiny bird with daydreams of being a hawk. She rose, she drifted, she dropped—the drop so sudden in its plunge Kaylin forgot to breathe—and she rolled. The Aerian Swords, the new ones, would have died of envy had they seen the ease with which she now covered the sky.

"How did she get hit at all?"

"She was carrying the netting," Evanton replied. He was cranky and tired—he hadn't been making that up—and seemed to feel that the answer was so obvious Kaylin shouldn't have wasted air asking the question. "If you recall the purpose of the netting?"

"...To dampen magic."

"Very good."

Kaylin stared. She felt a pang of resentment for the Halls of Law and the Imperial Hawks and the Barrani, because Moran should not have been carrying those nets. Moran should never have had to touch them. Because *this* was what it had cost her.

"You are thinking with your mouth open," Evanton said.

"You know, I really think you should leave your house more often. Go visit the Arkon; you're practically the same person when you're in a cranky mood."

"Her duty did not cost her anything. She is, as I said, flying entirely under her own power. You could rip the wings from her back—"

Lillias almost shrieked.

"—and she could fly. She cannot be made outcaste. She cannot be sundered from the ability you see now."

"I've never seen her fly like this."

"Almost no one has." Evanton's voice softened as he watched her. "She does so only here, because here, she has privacy. Lillias has seen her fly like this before, and neither you nor I are Aerian; we come with no baggage and no expectations."

Kaylin snorted. "You? No expectations?"

"She does not, perhaps, know me as well as you do." Evanton folded his arms. "But even I find it almost breathtaking. I hate to interrupt her."

In Kaylin's experience, this meant very little. And sure enough, he spoke to the wind in syllables that sounded like language but failed to become actual words to her ears. The wind clearly spoke to Moran, and Moran became larger and larger as she descended; when she landed, she was an Aerian woman of nominal height and build, and her wings were the same wings they'd been since the night the High Halls had been attacked by their ancestors.

"Evanton's grouchy because he's tired and he needs sleep," Kaylin said by way of explanation. Or apology.

"Evanton is, indeed, somewhat tired. He is grouchy because he has spent an hour listening to your private."

Lillias watched with a frown that meant she was accepting Evanton's version of events, which made some kind of sense. Evanton gave her the gift of flight she had lost—and it was clear that there was no greater gift. Yes, she had adapted to a wingless, human life. To hear Evanton speak of her, she had adapted well. But it was here that she could shed gravity and all of the pain of her past decisions.

And it was here, Kaylin realized, that she could watch

Moran fly, and understand that the choice that had cost her flight had been, in the end, for the moment, worth it.

Moran's wings rose and spread in a complicated way that spoke of respect or veneration as she turned to Evanton. She added a very human bow.

"You tell her," Evanton said to Kaylin. "I am going to bed."

Lillias left. It was late enough that she could refuse Kaylin's offer of hospitality; late enough that she could also refuse Moran's. And Moran did offer, assuming rightly that Helen would be just as happy to have Lillias visit as she was to have Moran.

Lillias thanked Moran profusely, which embarrassed the Hawk sergeant, who felt that gratitude, if it existed at all, should be going in the other direction. But, mindful of Evanton, she accepted Lillias's undeserved thanks with patience and only the hint of a blush.

"Praevolo," Lillias said, "it does my heart good to see you fly again. No one, ever, has flown the way you fly; no one could touch your flight, even when you were a child. No one."

"Could I see you again?" Moran asked.

Lillias hesitated. "You should not be seen," she finally replied, "in the company of an outcaste. It will do you no good."

"It will do *me* a great deal of good—and as you might imagine, I'm not fond of the Caste Court or the dar Carafel flight at the moment. What they need, I can't—won't—give them. What I need, they could never, ever give me." When Lillias once again fell silent, Moran added, "I ask as *praevolo.*"

Lillias bowed her head instantly. Moran caught her hands before she could fully fold to the ground, as Clint had so shockingly done. "Yes, *praevolo.* If I can be of use to you, even as I am, yes."

★ ★ ★

"That was a bit low, wasn't it?" Kaylin asked Moran after addresses had been exchanged and the two Aerians had parted.

Moran shrugged. "She would have said no for 'my own good,' and actually, I'm pretty sick of that."

"Maybe she thought it would be for *her* own good."

"Do you believe that?"

Kaylin's shrug was more defensive, a fief shrug.

"I'll take that as no. I—" She shook her head. "I was happy to see her fly. I know she can't, when she's not in Evanton's garden. How did you meet him?"

"Teela."

"Why did she introduce you?"

"He's willing to use magic for practical things, and I wanted daggers that made no noise when I unsheathed them. I thought Teela would know where to go for that. She did. I had no idea what his other job was. Teela obviously did, and couldn't be bothered to tell me."

"Do you think he'd let me visit again?"

"You want to fly again?"

Moran nodded. If she caught the shift in Kaylin's tone, she suspected nothing. Kaylin privately cursed Evanton in three different languages; Leontine was easier on the throat when it wasn't spoken aloud.

"You can fly."

Moran said, "Yes. The wind—"

"No. Lillias needed the wind. But Evanton said you didn't."

Moran stopped walking. Given the past few days, Kaylin wished she'd left this conversation for home, which was essentially a very welcoming, impregnable fortress. The small dragon was sitting on her shoulder in a state of alertness that didn't make Kaylin feel any safer.

"What did you say?"

Kaylin began to walk, and Moran caught up with her. Moran wasn't a groundhawk; she didn't know how to walk the streets the way groundhawks did. She did, however, know how to march.

"Kaylin."

"Evanton told me that the only person the wind was carrying was Lillias. You were never dependent on the wind for your flight."

"But my wing—"

"He said you could still fly even if they cut the wings off your back. I think that's what *praevolo* means."

"I've been in charge of the infirmary for years now. I've seen all kinds of injuries—Aerian injuries among them. I *know* my own people."

"Yes. But Evanton said that the wind wasn't helping you at all—and I tend to believe him when it comes to the wild elements. He said you were flying under your own power. If you want, we can go wake him up—but he'd likely bite heads off. Probably mine," she added.

Moran fell silent then. She kept moving. But her thoughts, such as they were, were turned entirely inward. It wasn't a comfortable silence.

Kaylin tried to fill it, which was beyond awkward. "Have you tried to fly since the—the attack?"

"No. I could barely lift my wing."

Kaylin swallowed. "Evanton doesn't think you'd have been injured at all if you weren't carrying the netting. It's—"

"I know what its function was. I know how important it was—that's why I was carrying it. You're a Hawk."

Kaylin nodded.

"You're proud of the fact that you're a Hawk. Your job is effectively the only life you want."

"I hate writing reports."

"Every Hawk hates writing reports. Except maybe Hanson. If you *liked* writing reports, they'd probably keep you off the streets because they'd question your sanity. But you're a Hawk. Does it surprise you to know that I'm not that different? This job was *mine*. Is mine. It's not about the Caste Court. It's not about dar Carafel. It's useful. I have a function, a role. I know what it is.

"We needed that netting. We knew the risks. Those spells took *Dragons* out of the sky. But Dragons are a larger target than Aerians. And there are a lot more of us. Did I love the injury? No. Of course not.

"But I got it doing something that needed to be done. Don't tell me what I should or shouldn't have been doing. I'm a Hawk. I'm a sergeant. I know my own job."

Kaylin lowered her head, although she did keep walking. After a silent block had passed, she said, "Sorry. I mean it. I'm sorry."

"You should be."

"...For how long?"

Moran's laugh was both genuine and frustrated. "About that long, I'd imagine."

"You don't believe him."

"I don't, but not in the way you mean. I have a lot to think about, and I don't want to test his words just yet."

Moran headed to her room the minute she entered the house; she said hello to Helen, but avoided everyone else.

Everyone else was in the dining room, except for Annarion.

"Nightshade's here?"

"Yes, dear," Helen said. She was standing in the doorway, or rather, just to one side of it.

"You don't like him?" Mandoran asked.

"She doesn't trust him," Kaylin countered. "I think she'd be willing to like him if he wasn't causing so much obvious pain."

"Annarion's causing his share of pain," Mandoran replied, brooding. "You know, I used to envy him. I used to envy his relationship with his oldest brother." He sat half-sprawled across the table, his elbows propping up what little of him remained upright.

"Less envy now?"

"My father," Mandoran replied, shifting into the High Barrani he so rarely spoke, "could cause pain simply by opening his eyes. We—the children who were chosen to go to the West March—were supposed to be the best, the strongest, the brightest. My father, however, did not entirely believe that the investment of power would be successful.

"He therefore chose to sacrifice—his words—his weakest, most disappointing son. That would be me. They died when I was gone, victims of the war. Different victims than we were. My brothers had no love for me—and I had three, Lord Kaylin. It was rare, among the Barrani line, to have four sons."

"Daughters?"

"One. Adopted. I believe our father had hopes that she could be trained to withstand the tests the Consort must take, survive and pass. He was an ambitious man."

Kaylin frowned. "But if you hated him—"

"—then why do I hate Dragons?"

"Something like that."

"Because they destroyed my home. I was like any other angry Barrani child; I daydreamed of returning to the father who had dismissed me and forcing him to acknowledge me. Probably," he added, sliding back into Elantran, "by killing him. I was not happy to be thrown away. But I found family in the others. I found companionship such as I had never known. I found people who *wanted* to trust as much as I did, even if they'd been told that it was foolish, stupid, weak.

"We didn't give each other our True Names by accident—but we didn't do it trivially, either. We'd all been told the same stories about the cost of it. I loved them. I still love them.

"Annarion was different. I think Annarion *was* the best and the brightest of his line. He said his brother had volunteered to come in his stead—because the risk to the line was too high if the experiment failed. You can't imagine how I envied him."

"Obviously their father didn't agree."

"Annarion refused. He refused because he was concerned and he was afraid—for his line—of the cost of Nightshade's loss. He won that argument, but it wasn't a short one, and Nightshade was not happy. And of course, you know what happened."

Kaylin nodded.

"Annarion didn't lie. He *was* afraid for his line. He thought—he believed—that Nightshade could govern and lead it, should their father fall. He never imagined that Nightshade would become outcaste—he never had nightmares about it, either. His confidence in his brother was absolute and unshakeable."

Kaylin winced. She wasn't sure if she winced on Annarion's behalf, or on Nightshade's. She could almost feel the anger of the younger; could certainly feel the guilt and the pain of the older. "Does family always work this way?" she asked.

"Not mine. And from the sounds of it, not most of ours." Mandoran exhaled. "Teela loved her mother, and...I think we all would have liked her mother. But her father had her mother killed, and you know how that turned out. It's easy to love someone completely for a handful of years—even mortal years. It's not easy to continue that with the passage of centuries. It's just not."

"But you and your cohort have."

"It's the Name, Kaylin. We can see each other's thoughts, feel each other's feelings, trade information so naturally we forget it's necessary to speak at all. We're not one person, but we're like one entity. Except Teela. No, don't make that face—Teela *is* part of us. But she's changed in ways we haven't. And she can hide herself, guard herself, keep herself out of our heart.

"Sedarias accepts it the most easily, but Sedarias was the oldest of us, and her family was highly, highly political. Not all of us feel the same way. We don't think Teela's happy."

"You think she would be if she relaxed?"

"Yes." Mandoran exhaled. "And no. Annarion isn't happy. He's been unhappy since his reunion with the brother he loved and revered."

"If it makes you feel any better, Nightshade's pretty miserable, as well."

"I thought it would," Mandoran conceded. "But actually, it doesn't. At all. I mean—if Nightshade had changed so much that he'd given up on Annarion, that he'd stopped caring about him at all, sure. But it's pretty clear to everyone except Annarion that he never did. That he does, in fact, love his brother—that he's never stopped. Sedarias believes that the reason Nightshade is outcaste is that he wouldn't give up on Annarion, and he pushed the wrong people in the wrong way far too often. What do you think?"

"I think she's probably right."

"So, on the one hand, Annarion, who was homesick for centuries. On the other, Nightshade, who surrendered the rest of his life and position in order to find a way to return his brother home. You were that way." Mandoran glanced at the mark on her cheek. "We can't prevent Annarion's pain. But we don't want to destroy Nightshade, either. Well, most of us don't. So mostly, it just sucks. It's like—there's all this warmth and family love and it's causing nothing but pain. It's a waste."

A very loud Barrani voice broke the quiet. Mandoran slumped against the table, turning his face to the side. "That's Annarion."

"I know. I'm heading to bed."

"You won't be able to sleep."

"That's just shouting. Helen can keep that level of noise out of my room."

"That level, yes. But they're just starting."

Kaylin nodded. "And I might as well get whatever sleep I can before nothing can drown it out. Who knows? I might be lucky. The midwives' guild might have an emergency."

CHAPTER 20

Kaylin did not consider this the height of luck four hours later, and cursed herself for her thoughtless, offhand comment. It was fine to complain *after* the fact. It was fine to complain if you *did* the work. But somewhere, some woman was struggling simply to survive the birth of her child—and Kaylin had made a joke about it.

"Why didn't you wake me up *sooner*?" Kaylin demanded of her home.

"I woke you as soon as I had evaluated the message, dear," Helen said.

Kaylin dressed in a rush of panic. "Where do I need to be?"

Helen's answer did not make things any clearer. The familiar landed on Kaylin's shoulders as she leapt out of her room and headed down the stairs, taking them two and three at a time until she could leap to the ground below without breaking anything. She headed straight for the only room in the house in which mirrors actually worked. Even then, there was a delay while Helen evaluated incoming communication for safety purposes.

Helen keyed the mirror to life; its center filled, without fanfare or visual effects, with a very familiar face, its lines structured around an equally familiar expression. Marya was the head of the midwives guild, the über den mother. She had a temper that was constantly being challenged by the stupidity and the unfairness of the universe, although she claimed to be far mellower now than she had been in her youth. Kaylin was grateful she had never met Marya in that youth.

"Where," she demanded, before Marya could open her mouth, "do I need to be?"

Marya said, "Keira is there. It's not—" Her lips thinned. It wasn't going well. Of course it wasn't. They didn't call Kaylin for normal births. They didn't call her for difficult births often, either. But catastrophic ones? Yes. "It's near Highpost."

Highpost. Kaylin closed her eyes. "How long ago did Keira mirror in?"

Silence.

Kaylin wheeled, turning on Helen in a kind of helpless rage that almost demanded it be passed on or shared. "How *long ago* did the message arrive?"

Helen was unflappable. "Less than half an hour ago."

"Why didn't you *wake me up*?"

"Dear, I did."

Kaylin was tying her bootlaces. The familiar was slumped across her shoulders, indifferent to the panic and the fear and the desperation that were fighting for control of her mind. She wasn't going to make it. She wasn't going to make it in time.

Teela had never understood this particular panic, although she'd seen it a few times; she'd been at Kaylin's apartment when the mirror had started its blaring appeal for attention. The midwives were not the Hawks; Kaylin's survival did not depend on them in any way. They didn't pay her; her work for the guild was strictly voluntary.

The women who were in the midst of a delivery that

the midwives thought was likely to kill them were strangers to Kaylin. She didn't know them. She owed them no loyalty. She owed them, in Teela's opinion, nothing. She could understand the mortal need to be of use—although this stretched the definition of the word *understand*, in Kaylin's opinion. She couldn't understand the panic. She couldn't understand the dread weight of guilt that accompanied the thought of *too late*.

That had been an early argument. If Teela still didn't precisely understand it, that didn't matter; she knew what it meant to Kaylin.

Kaylin opened the door with so much force it would have bounced against the nearest wall had it been a normal door, a normal wall. Because it was part of Helen, this didn't happen. She made a beeline for the front door, stopped, and rolled up her sleeve. The bracer was clipped around her wrist like a dead weight. It wasn't—but it was going to be worse than dead weight tonight. She pressed the studded gems across the bracer's length, and when it clicked open, she removed it and tossed it over her shoulder.

"Are you certain you should be doing that?"

She had her hand on the door handle; she had the door open a few inches. Turning only her head, she looked up the stairs to see Moran. She was not dressed for the office—which, in the past few days, meant very colorful clothing—but she was also not yet dressed for bed. She looked like her normal self: Hawk sergeant, undisputed ruler of the infirmary.

"I have to," she said. "I'll explain later."

"You don't need to explain later. Helen told me what's happening."

"Good. I'll be back when I'm back."

"Wait."

Kaylin wanted to shriek in agonized frustration. She waited instead, but it was very, very hard.

"I'll take you there."

"What?"

"I'll fly."

A different panic struggled for expression and attention, but failed to gain enough of a foothold that it formed an actual thought. "You can't."

"According to Evanton—and you—I can. I'll take you. That's not a request."

The desire to argue came and went, streaming past before Kaylin could catch it. "Fine. But *hurry*."

While night air pushed hair out of her eyes, Kaylin's second thoughts asserted themselves. Moran was larger than Kaylin, but not by a significant amount, and even Clint had complained about Kaylin's weight when he was forced to carry it while flying, admittedly in a sort of good-humored way.

Moran was mortal. Moran was Aerian. Kaylin was living with a *Dragon*, and while it was technically illegal for Dragons to assume their scaled, racial form without Imperial consent, Kaylin was fairly certain Bellusdeo would be forgiven if she happened to break that law. Her weight was entirely insignificant to a Dragon of Bellusdeo's size, and Bellusdeo had the grace, maneuverability and speed of the much-smaller Aerians while she was on wing.

Bellusdeo had been the target of assassins in the past—but Bellusdeo was harder to kill than any of Kaylin's other friends, and she included the Barrani in that number. Moran was staying with Kaylin *because* it was safest. No assassins could reach her while Helen stood guard.

And Kaylin had allowed Moran to risk everything by flying her to Highpost, in the desperate hope she could arrive in time. She hadn't stopped to *think*. She hadn't assessed the risk. She hadn't made the smart decision—wake up the Dragon—because she was still, on some gut level, used to working solo.

And if anything happened to Moran because of her own panic and her own inability to think on the spot…she couldn't finish the sentence, even internally.

Moran, however, seemed to have none of the fears that Kaylin did. And she didn't seem to feel Kaylin's weight at all. She flew like an arrow, but on a straighter trajectory, and her expression was a sergeant's expression. She understood what the job was and she understood how to get it done; nothing else mattered at the moment.

The familiar was no longer slumped across Kaylin's shoulder; he was seated, tail curled around Kaylin's throat for balance. He chittered like an angry bird but wasn't glaring at Kaylin while he did so; he didn't appear to be glaring at Moran, either.

"Do you know any useful words?" she asked the familiar; her voice was not loud in the rush of wind that followed Moran's flight.

He squawked.

Kaylin scanned the skies, but it was night, and late. The moon was not full, and the skies were cloudy enough that they flew by the pattern of streetlamps below their bodies. The darkness wouldn't have been a problem for the Dragon, either.

Please, please, please, Kaylin prayed. *If we get there in time, if Moran stays safe, I promise I will* think *before I rush into anything else. Please.*

Moran knew the city. She knew it well. She didn't ask for directions because she didn't need them. That was good, because the directions Kaylin would have given involved feet on the ground and the layout of streets. Running, she didn't have the option of ignoring the buildings in the way of the straightest path, although she'd leapt yards in haste any number of times in her career.

What would have taken at least half an hour at a brisk pace—Kaylin couldn't sprint for half an hour, no matter how much training she put in—took vastly less time by air. But she couldn't translate what her feet knew instinctively into the bird's-eye equivalent. She was grateful that she didn't need to. She would have had to give Bellusdeo directions.

Moran dropped her in front of the right house; it was a narrow, cramped space, a door with walls that extended to either side to encompass other doors, which opened into other homes. Moran knew it was the right house because it was the only one on the street that shed light; everyone in the immediate vicinity was sleeping.

Kaylin opened the door; it wasn't locked. "Keira!" she shouted up the stairs. She didn't bother to remove her boots; she did make certain Moran entered the cramped hall. The ceilings were low here—but low here was still better than the ceilings of her old apartment had been before the apartment had been reduced to rubble and splinters.

"Upstairs—thank god you're here."

Relief caused Kaylin's shoulders to slump; the breath left her in a rush. But she caught it again and sprinted up the stairs, because "on time" was only barely a guarantee, and it could change at any minute. "I got a ride," she said.

"Fine. Hurry."

"The ride's the best doctor the Halls of Law has."

"Good. Tell your doctor that the father has passed out and I think he hit his head on something on the way down. She can see to him. We need you."

★ ★ ★

The father had indeed hit something, as Keira had said, on the way down, and he wasn't particularly lucid when he woke to the grim face of an Aerian sergeant; he thought the wings were hallucinations. Moran, however, didn't look the angel that many religions seemed to favor; she was far too grim-faced for that. She was also annoyed. She considered the mother's condition to be an act of fate, given relatively healthy pregnancy; she considered the father's condition to be wilful stupidity.

Self-inflicted wounds were severely frowned upon in the Halls of Law, and the biggest frowns given were generally from the woman who had to deal with them. It made Kaylin, who was exhausted, want to cry sentimental tears.

The mother had lost a *lot* of blood; Kaylin had arrived only barely in time to save her. The loss of blood had caused trouble for the baby as well, and in all, the bed more resembled the aftermath of a bloody slaughter than it did a place of rest. Keira moved the mother when Kaylin said it was safe to do so. She was a good decade older than Kaylin, which, to Marya's eye, was young, but she was brisk and no-nonsense about anything she could actually affect.

"Have some tea," she told Kaylin. It wasn't a request. When Kaylin stared vacantly into the cup, Keira added, "You look terrible."

"I look better than I feel."

"Probably true. Have some tea." She turned to Moran, extended a hand and said, "I'm Keira. Thanks for dealing with the father. Normally someone would help with that—"

"You were occupied."

"He'll be okay?"

"He clearly has a very thick skull. Yes, he'll be okay. I'm going to take Kaylin home. We both have work in—two hours? Maybe three." To Kaylin, she said, "I better understand why our superiors tolerate your tardiness."

"Thanks."

"Do you do this often?"

"Probably not often enough. They only call me in when they know for certain things are going to get ugly—and sometimes, the call comes too late. I can't get there in time. I try," she added. "But—I don't normally have Aerians on hand."

"But you do."

"I've been called while at work maybe three times. And yes, I did get a ride, but in one of those cases, I actually needed it."

"You went to the Aeries?"

Kaylin nodded. Hesitating, she said, "How do your wings feel?"

"The injured one hurts—but it made no difference. I could fly. I flew." She spoke the last two words with a kind of bemused wonder.

She flew them back, as well. Kaylin was too exhausted to argue with her, but healing always had that effect on her when the injuries were severe. There had been no assassins, no magical attacks. It had been stupid to let Moran fly her out to the emergency—but Moran had been awake and ready. And if Kaylin had legged it the old-fashioned way, she wouldn't have made it on time.

Even a carriage driven by Teela wouldn't have made it on time.

Moran clearly wanted to stay outside in the night air, testing her wings. Using them. But Moran knew what the risks were and chose not to take them. From her expression, it was a close thing.

Moran, bright-eyed, was conversing with Helen when Kaylin dragged her butt up the stairs and deposited it heavily on her bed. The Aerian sergeant wasn't going to get a lot of sleep tonight, one way or the other.

Kaylin, on the other hand, couldn't keep her eyes open. Sleep mugged her, and she let it.

In the morning, Moran was once again colorfully dressed. She wore the bracelet. She spoke with Bellusdeo, who disappeared into the mirror room, which, in Kaylin's opinion, most resembled the holding cells in the Halls, and returned. Kaylin's face was an inch away from her plate, her eyes were circled so darkly she looked hungover, and she could barely force food into her mouth.

"I really think you should stay home," Moran told her.

"I'm awake. I'll work."

"Fine." *Fine* did not mean that Moran was content to let it go, which Kaylin discovered when Teela and Tain showed up at the front door.

"Kitling," Teela said, with obvious disapproval. "You went out drinking without us?"

"I went on a call for the midwives' guild." At Teela's shift in expression, Kaylin added, "We made it on time."

"We?"

Moran said, "I flew her out."

Discussion stopped—not that there was much of it—as the Barrani turned to Moran. "Did you, now?"

Moran nodded.

"Courtesy of the Keeper?"

"Indirectly, yes. But if you mean courtesy of his power or the blessing of the elements he both jails and serves, no."

"The meeting went well, then?"

Moran exhaled. "It went well." She flexed her wing—her injured wing—and grimaced.

"I'm surprised the wing could carry you both."

"You're surprised the wing could carry me," Moran said, voice dry as summer grass.

Teela shrugged. "It doesn't look like it's up to the task, and you certainly haven't been trying. If you could fly, we wouldn't be in this political tangle."

"I was thinking that, myself," Moran replied, grinning. It was a very, very martial expression.

Teela, whose eyes were mostly green, returned it, nuance for nuance. "We're not going to make great guards today— we can't keep up."

Bellusdeo muttered a single word that sounded a lot like derogatory Elantran.

"Pardon?"

"Tain might not be able to keep up; you certainly could."

Teela didn't deny it. "Let's go, shall we?" She frowned. "Mandoran's coming."

Kaylin wilted; Bellusdeo frowned.

"He's bored," Teela continued, "and Annarion is expecting Nightshade. Why, I don't know. If I were Nightshade at this point, I'd give his brother some space."

Kaylin had never had siblings, and had no comment, which was generally safest. "Tell him to hurry—we're going to be late."

"He says you're often late."

"Me? Yes. Moran? Never."

"He's hurrying."

Moran flew to work.

Bellusdeo joined her—in full Dragon glory. Kaylin assumed that the trip to the mirror cell had been to get permission, but didn't ask—it was better not to know.

The streets were therefore full of people who had momentarily forgotten their own business in favor of the aerial maneuvers of a large golden Dragon and her smaller Aerian companion. And they were maneuvers. There was nothing businesslike about Moran's flight paths, and nothing straightforward and simple, either.

Mandoran was making a face.

"What is it now?" Kaylin said, although her eyes were drawn to the sky again.

"Teela says I can't join them."

"Could you, if she weren't sitting on you?"

"I'm not certain—but yes, I think I could. You know, I haven't tried at all since I've been back?"

That wasn't remotely comforting. "Don't start now."

"I think it would be like swimming—but in air."

"We've got enough attention for the day. Don't add to it."

"You know, you shouldn't let Teela suck the fun out of your life."

"I haven't. I can't fly."

"Fine. You shouldn't let Teela suck the fun out of *my* life." He did, however, keep both of his feet on the ground as they made their way to the Halls of Law. "She's going to be late. You said she's never late."

"She's never been late in all my years at the Halls."

"And she's going to start now?"

"Probably."

Mandoran whistled at Moran's maneuver. "She really can fly circles around the Dragon."

"She can probably fly circles around the rest of the Aerians, too. I'm sure the ones who are watching her are pathetically grateful she's not in charge of their practice drills right about now."

"You think they're watching?"

"I'd bet all of last month's pay on it."

"No one here would be stupid enough to take that bet," Teela said. "We'd better get moving. The Dragon can handle anything stupid enough to take Moran on in these skies, and the Hawklord is going to want to speak to us."

Kaylin wilted. "We haven't done anything wrong."

"No, we haven't. And before you try to bite me, neither has Moran. But the Hawklord's the one who's been sitting in political debris since Moran was injured."

"You know, you should quit the late-night drinking binges," Clint said. He was speaking loudly, with the happy malevolence the very sober sometimes showed the very hungover.

"I wasn't out drinking. I was out carousing with the midwives."

His grin vanished.

"I made it in time, but only because—" She stopped.

Clint had never been particularly stupid. "The sergeant flew you out."

"How did you know?"

"I've been watching her in the skies since she took wing." His voice was almost a hush, which didn't suit his size or his general demeanor. "The Hawklord wants to see you."

Severn was at his desk when Kaylin entered the office and headed toward the Tower stairs.

"You're back."

Since it wasn't a question, he said nothing.

"What did the Wolflord want?"

He said more nothing, and Kaylin exhaled. "Sorry. That was a stupid question." If the Halls of Law could be said to be clandestine, it was entirely due to the Wolves.

She'd never been entirely comfortable with Severn as a Wolf. And he was a Hawk now. She opened her mouth again, but Severn shook his head.

"The Hawklord," he said, "is waiting."

"I want to know *exactly* what happened last night."

Kaylin was standing more or less at attention beside her partner, whose posture was perfect.

"You look like you haven't slept for a week. Did you go out drinking with Teela and Tain?"

Kaylin sighed. "No, sir."

"What did you do to Moran?"

She really resented the question, and was too exhausted to hide it. Being exhausted pushed her into one of two states, but since sleep wasn't an option, she settled into prickly and irritable instead. "*I* didn't do anything to the sergeant," she replied, using Moran's rank for emphasis, because hers was so junior in comparison.

The Hawklord frowned.

Kaylin attempted to straighten up shoulders that were probably sagging. Attention was not a natural posture. The small dragon was slumped across her shoulders as if he were absorbing her exhaustion. "We went to see Evanton, sir."

"And she returned, able to fly."

"We met Lillias."

He stiffened; he obviously recognized the name.

"He left Lillias in the garden with Moran, and Lillias told Moran that Evanton lets her fly there—in secret, in the folds of the elemental air. Moran was invited to join her— and did. Except she didn't need the elemental air. The injuries she sustained, which would cripple any other Aerian, apparently don't affect her ability to fly. Once she realized this…" Kaylin shrugged.

"She flew to work."

Kaylin nodded.

"Which means she could fly to the Southern Reach."

Kaylin stiffened, then. She was too tired to think, and hadn't been. She started to now. The Hawklord was right. If Moran could fly—and demonstrably, publicly, she could—there was no reason she needed to stay in Kaylin's house. No reason she had to live where the rest of the ground dwellers were forced to live.

"She thought her flying would remove most of the political stress you've been under."

"I highly doubt that." He lifted a hand before more words could follow. "I do not doubt that you both believe that. I find that view entirely too optimistic at this point. Moran can fly. Her duty to the Hawks, her service to the Imperial Halls of Law, has therefore not done irreparable harm to the Aerians, as was first claimed." His expression made clear what he thought of that claim.

"But the assassination attempts, and the coercion of Margot, occurred regardless. They are crimes. If Moran can be pressured—mistakenly believing it is for my sake—into recanting all accusation, the assassination attempts would be removed from our remit. They would become a matter of the Caste Court.

"The events in Elani Street cannot be so remanded. They were perpetuated by a human, not an Aerian."

"Could our prisoner attempt to have the case remanded to the human Caste Court?"

The Hawklord's answering grin was so devoid of warmth or humor Kaylin almost took a step back.

"You're joking, right?"

"I have not said a thing, but were I to do so, I would most assuredly find no humor in it." His wings unfolded slightly, but his eyes remained blue. "Have you ever seen her fly like that?"

Kaylin had watched flying Aerians all her life, and had seen precisely none who could fly the way Moran had been flying.

"Very well. I will not caution you. Moran seems to have done well living with you; if she wishes to continue—"

"She's not going back to the Southern Reach." Kaylin folded her arms. Severn recognized her mutinous glare, but said nothing, content to let the Hawklord shoulder the brunt of the work.

"That must," the Hawklord said gently, "be her choice, surely?"

"Yes. But she likes living with us."

"She is *praevolo*," the Hawklord replied.

"So what? She's a person, not a symbol. And she wasn't happy living in the Reaches."

"Ah. No. No, she was not. Dismissed."

"We need to find out who made the motion to have the case against Margot's attacker remanded to the human Caste Court." Kaylin's steps echoed heavily down the Tower stairs; Severn's, in theory heavier, did not.

"It's political."

"Obviously. But we need to follow the money here. And you know as well as I do that remand means 'dismiss entirely.' There's not going to be a lot of justice."

"Margot is human. If Margot refused to endorse a remand, the request would have gone nowhere."

"Exactly. We're going to have a chat with Margot. What? It's our beat today anyway."

Margot was not in her store. She was not one of nature's early risers, but the meeting with the Hawklord, the subsequent meeting with Marcus and the less-than-gentle aside from Clint, who had abandoned his post at the door to make it, had taken enough time from their daily schedule that Margot should have had more than enough time to put out her shingle.

Her doors were locked.

In and of itself, this wasn't unusual; if Margot was popular—and she was—she had her share of angry former customers, some of whom wanted more than simple words with her.

But current customers—at least two—were waiting almost forlornly on the doorstep. They gave the Hawks the side-eye, but also gave them room. Margot had not been in yet.

Kaylin generally found Margot a safe target for venting spleen. She was almost certainly bilking the stupid and the hopeful out of their money, and she couldn't stand Kaylin. She practically wore a target saying *Hate Me*.

But this?

"She hasn't been in at all? She's not in lockup because someone theoretically more important is in there with her?" she demanded of a slender elderly man.

"No, Officer."

Severn was speaking to the other man, and when he was done, he met Kaylin's eyes. "She's not at home."

"She lives above the store."

"Yes. And she's not at home."

Kaylin didn't ask him how he knew, because they were pretty much thinking the same thing. Margot had asked that the case be remanded to the human Caste Court; Margot was not at home. The prisoner in the holding cells had asked— or demanded, as it turned out—that his case be remanded to the human Caste Court, as well. They knew where he was.

In theory, he was still alive.

"You want me to what, exactly?" Teela demanded. Evanton's mirror was small, and he disliked its use, but Kaylin had convinced Grethan that it was an emergency.

"I want you to go and talk to the prisoner. And I want you to get me permission to break into Margot's store."

"You've done it without permission before."

"I didn't *break in*," Kaylin pointed out. "The store was open at the time."

"Ah. Surely that's just a trifling detail?"

"Caste Court remand, Teela."

"Fine. What exactly do you want me to say to the prisoner?"

"His guards have been *Barrani*. Without exception. But suddenly he's demanding that his case be tried by the human Caste Court. I want to know who his visitors have been."

Teela's eyes were now very, very blue. "He hasn't had visitors."

"He must have."

"He hasn't."

"How do you know?"

"Because the Barrani contingent has been in charge of his safety; it has been made perfectly clear that if he does not survive his captivity, it will reflect very, very poorly on us."

"You're not in charge of that detail."

"Not technically, no."

"But—"

"I'll talk to the prisoner. Marcus says you can go ahead and investigate."

"You haven't asked him."

"Fine. You want a bristling Leontine filling your mirror, you can have him."

Marcus did say yes, eventually. There was a whole lot of Leontine that happened between his first appearance and his permission, most of which was not repeatable, almost literally.

"This is not the day to be in the office," Kaylin said when the mirror image once again receded and she was staring at her own face. She *did* look hungover. "Let's go."

CHAPTER 21

Kaylin didn't break the window—or the door. Given the day, it wasn't even tempting. Margot's outer doors weren't warded. They were locked the old-fashioned way.

The windows on the side of the building weren't barred; they were magically protected. Ugh. Severn took out his chained weapons and managed to open the window without breaking the glass.

"It's not just spinning the chains that offers protection from magic?" she asked as he worked.

"No. It's more reliable that way, but no." He offered her both of his hands; she stepped into them with her left foot and worked her way into the building, feeling oddly like the criminal she had once been. She then headed to lift the impressive bars that had made the front doors impassable.

Margot had enough money that it wasn't just the windows that were rotten with magic. The interior doors were warded, as well. Some of the clutter of decorative kibble was warded, but not in the way the doors were; Kaylin's skin was tingling, but it hadn't reached the rubbed-raw pain pitch yet.

The small dragon was alert. He muttered to himself while

standing upright on her left shoulder; she wasn't surprised when he lifted one of his wings and smacked it against her eyes.

"You and I are going to have to learn how to communicate," she told him. "You can't smack me every time you want me to do something. Well, okay, you *can*, obviously—but I don't like it."

He snorted, rolling his eyes.

Severn headed up the stairs as Kaylin looked at Margot's accumulation of personal treasures. The obviously expensive ones were up front; they would be. Margot was a peacock. She wanted her customers to know that she was valued, was considered valuable, by powerful—or at least rich—clients, and this was the unsubtle way of making it clear.

And it was also, Kaylin thought, frowning, an easy way into a home that was otherwise surprisingly secure. "I see it," she told the familiar. She was looking directly at a small statue. It appeared to be made of gold, with rubies for eyes, and wings that seemed vaguely demonic. It resembled what Aerians might have been if they'd been born with bat wings.

Kaylin didn't have Barrani or Dragon memory. She had no idea if this was new. But seen through the familiar's translucent wings, gold leaf had been laid across obsidian that moved and roiled even as she watched it. She fished about in her pockets, but came up empty: no gloves.

So she borrowed one of Margot's tablecloths, wrapped it around her hand and lifted the offending statue. "This is Shadow magic."

The familiar squawked.

"It's not attacking me; it's not attempting to take over anything—but this is Shadow magic. I'd bet next month's pay on it."

There was a loud crash from up the stairs; Kaylin wheeled,

the statue still clenched in one cloth-covered hand. She took the steps two at a time, bouncing off the wall in the bend of those stairs to give herself more momentum.

When she reached the landing, she slowed. Severn's back was toward her, and he was armed—he'd pulled both of the blades, but the chain itself was not at all useful for indoor fighting in close quarters. Glass shards were scattered across the carpet runner and the wooden floors to either side, and as Kaylin approached, she saw an almost unrecognizable Margot in the hall.

"She threw something?"

Severn nodded.

Kaylin poked the familiar, whose wing had dropped when she'd taken off up the stairs. Teela would have had her hide if she'd headed upstairs without backup, the way Severn had. The wing rose, and this time, there was no accompanying smack.

There was, however, accompanying cursing, all of it Kaylin's.

Margot didn't speak. She opened her mouth, but no words escaped. Her eyes were round and wide and not at all her normal eyes; her hair was a wild mess of tendrils that seemed to move with a life of their own.

This was not good, but it was in line with what Kaylin expected of Shadow possession. The familiar squawked, dropping its wing; Margot, without his aid, looked normal—for a variant of normal that involved enraged beyond belief.

"Shadow," she told her partner.

Controlled?

She hesitated. *I don't think so.*

Can you get it out of her?

The general answer to that question had always been no. The more specific answer was she'd never tried. Not when someone was as far gone as this. But no—that wasn't true, either. To normal eyes, Margot was not—yet—consumed. The Shadow was in her, and clearly someone, somewhere, was manipulating it.

Kaylin looked at the statue she was carrying in her hand. She set it on the floor. The familiar squawked, his voice rising on the last syllable, such as it was.

"Yes," she told him. "Breathe on it."

The small white clouds had the kind of shimmering opalescence that Shadow did. Kaylin had noticed this before, but had avoided really thinking about what it meant. She considered it now. The familiar's breath had some transformative power—she'd seen what it could do to Shadows with her own eyes. She knew that the immortals considered it very dangerous.

She watched him breathe on gold and rubies.

She watched the pale stream that left his open mouth gain weight and color as it made contact with wingtips of gold, and she watched those wingtips melt. There was no heat; as the gold continued to melt, the rug and the floor did not catch fire.

Margot screamed; there were words in it. Kaylin registered them as a protest, but ignored them; even if she had wanted to pull the familiar back, it was too late. Margot rushed at Severn, and Severn, realizing that she intended to impale herself on his blades, moved; he let her momentum carry her, and gave her a little shove; she spilled onto the floor, twitching, shouting and struggling.

Severn caught her arms, pinning her in place with one hand and one knee. "She's still in there," he said.

Kaylin nodded. "I think they meant to kill her with our help."

The gold congealed in an uneven circle that looked more like a spill than anything else. Somewhere in that mess were rubies. Neither were important. There was a small nexus of Shadow that looked, to Kaylin's covered eyes, like a hole, a rip in the fabric of reality.

The small dragon circled it, breathing steadily until it suddenly snapped shut.

Margot slumped instantly, unconscious.

"Can we alter the report so that you didn't head up here without backup?"

"We could if you were a better liar." Severn reached out to touch Margot's throat; Kaylin caught his hand, pulling it back.

"Let me."

Margot was alive. Her pulse was steady, her breath even. She looked like she'd fallen out of bed and had avoided the many mirrors she owned, but she appeared to be healthy, if sleeping.

The small dragon was, once again, slumped across Kaylin's shoulders, but he was muttering like an annoyed bird. Severn made use of Margot's mirror to report to the Halls of Law; Kaylin could hear Leontine cursing from the other room.

"Teela's coming."

"Why?"

"Because Bellusdeo insisted."

"Wait—Bellusdeo's coming?"

"Shadow."

Kaylin indulged in some very Leontine cursing herself. "But who's staying with Moran?"

"Given her aerial maneuvers this morning? Probably every Aerian in the Halls. I think the Dragon bodyguard might be superfluous at this point."

"It was Aerians who were responsible for the other assassination attempts," Kaylin quite reasonably pointed out.

"That was then. This is now."

Bellusdeo was orange-eyed, but had not ditched clothing for the very practical, but very martial, Dragon scales. The lack of scales didn't make a difference to the very martial bit, sadly. She was almost breathing fire. "Tell me everything that happened."

Kaylin did. Bellusdeo had come from a world in which Shadow, in the end, had swallowed all life; she had seen Shadow in its many forms, had seen it used, had almost fallen to it herself. She knew more about Shadow than anyone who wasn't part of Ravellon.

This, however, confused her.

Teela lounged against one wall; Tain kept an eye on the door. "Did the prisoner have much to say?" Kaylin asked. And then, when no answer followed, "Is the prisoner still alive?"

"The prisoner is still alive," Teela replied, brooding. She glared at Tain, who, in fairness, hadn't even opened his mouth.

Mandoran entered the room. "Don't give me that look," he told Kaylin without bothering to see what her expression actually was. "If the Dragon can be here, so can I."

"The Dragon has experience with Shadow and its incursions."

"Honestly, it's a small wonder to me that your sergeant hasn't removed your throat by this point," Bellusdeo muttered.

"He doesn't hold me responsible for Dragons," Kaylin replied. "He probably doesn't hold me responsible for Mandoran, either—he's Teela's fault." She did turn to Mandoran. "Why are you making that face?"

"Which face?"

"The something-is-wrong-here face."

"Teela's shouting in my ear." And glaring at the side of his face. "Have you ever tried to concentrate on something when she's shouting in your ear?"

"She doesn't shout in my ear. Often."

"So that's a no." He turned to the familiar. "Do you see this?"

The familiar squawked.

"Yeah. Me, too."

But Bellusdeo turned to the familiar, as well. Kaylin wished he was perched on someone else's shoulder. "Where?" she demanded. The familiar sighed and launched himself off Kaylin's shoulder, where he fluttered pointedly above the circle of melted gold on the floor.

"That was the statue," Kaylin offered.

Bellusdeo whispered a word and Kaylin's skin developed instant goose bumps in protest. To Kaylin's surprise, the Dragon turned to Mandoran. "Here?" she asked him, without any other identifying information that would make the question make sense.

Mandoran, however, frowned. "I think so. There's a bit of haze about two feet above the floor. You said he breathed on the Shadow?"

"Yes," Kaylin replied, although technically she hadn't said it while Mandoran was in the room.

"And he breathed on the statue?"

She nodded again.

Teela was pinching the bridge of her nose, as if a headache had taken up residence and she had no hope of evicting it.

"What happened with the prisoner?"

"One of the Barrani Hawks was paid to pass a message on."

"Paid by who?"

Her smile was grim. "Not someone human."

"How ugly is this going to get?"

"Well, that depends."

"On what?"

"We have an appointment in less than an hour. Go home and get changed."

Kaylin wilted. "An appointment where?"

"At the High Halls."

"But—"

"It's the safest neutral ground we currently have. Trust me." The High Halls was not neutral ground for Teela.

"Who are we meeting?"

"Evarrim."

Evarrim was an Arcanist of long standing. Kaylin disliked him, which was a step up from the very visceral loathing she had felt on their first acquaintance. He was a Barrani High Lord, he was old, and he was power hungry; he disdained the merely mortal as ignorant ephemerals. And he wanted the power of the marks of the Chosen.

But she had watched him fight to save the same people she had fought to save—the Consort, for one—and she had seen him surrender some part of his power, and in one or two cases, put his own life at risk. She couldn't like him. She didn't trust him. But she knew there was more to him than the disdain he had always showed her.

She told herself this with as much force as she could muster while she dressed for the High Halls. She didn't understand *why* she couldn't wear her tabard and her working clothing, but she accepted Teela's grim command. She just wasn't happy about it.

Severn was also required to change, which he couldn't do at her house; he headed back to his apartment, leaving Kaylin with Bellusdeo and Mandoran. Bellusdeo had no intention of going to the High Halls, and there'd been some argument about the designated "neutral" venue, but Teela was having none of it.

Mandoran, on the other hand, wanted to go.

And Teela was having none of that, either.

"Don't argue with her," Kaylin murmured. "Not when she's in this mood. It'll just make her angry and it won't change anything."

"And not changing anything is making me angry."

"No," Teela snapped, "it's making you petulant."

Tain had absented himself from the argument, and came to stand beside Kaylin. She glanced at Teela's partner, and he shrugged. "They're siblings for all intents and purposes— and only a fool gets between siblings while they're arguing. What will he do?"

"Mandoran? He'll sulk, but he'll accept it."

"I heard that," Mandoran said to Kaylin.

"If the Dragon accepts it, I don't see that you accepting it is any more humiliating."

"They're *my* people, not hers," he snapped.

"Yes, and some of them are the people who sentenced you—sentenced *us*—to the green," Teela interjected. Her eyes were blue and her voice was ice.

"Aren't most of them dead yet?"

Teela said, "You've spent far too much time recently with the mortals. We are going. You are staying. There's enough instability in the present situation that I will go Leontine if anything *else* breaks. Understood?"

Mandoran's brows rose. After a brief pause, he surprised Kaylin; he grinned. "I think I'd like to see that."

"You really, really wouldn't—not at this distance," Kaylin told him. Tain relaxed slightly, and Kaylin took that as a good sign. She'd known Teela for over a third of her life, but she didn't know Teela the way Tain did, and she'd always found Teela's temper unpredictable.

Severn appeared at the front door dressed for Court.

Kaylin had one dress that was appropriate, and had no luck arguing her way out of wearing it; she did, however, get a jacket from Bellusdeo that more or less covered the exposed skin. It was too large, but it was vastly better than nothing, in Kaylin's opinion. Helen didn't entirely share that opinion, but Kaylin put her foot down. If she couldn't wear the jacket, she was going in her patrolling clothing, and that was final.

"It's not like I haven't met Evarrim before," she told Helen. "And I wasn't wearing a fancy dress for any of those meetings."

"No. But I believe you did have appropriate clothing when you visited the High Halls."

"Yes. And it got destroyed, and the quartermaster hated my guts out for months afterwards. We're only barely speaking now, and I am *never* requisitioning clothing from him again."

"Then you will have to spend some of your pay on appropriate clothing. The Emperor has indicated that he will visit again."

Some of her pay was not the same as all of her pay, and all of her pay was pretty much what would be required. Kaylin didn't bother to say this out loud; Helen could hear what she was thinking.

Since she had to be dress inspected before leaving, she made Teela promise that they would hire a carriage. Contending with stupid clothing was bad enough; she was certain nothing would survive Teela's driving. Teela sourly pointed out that Kaylin had demonstrably survived her driving on previous occasions, but agreed.

"Why Evarrim?"

"He is the least untrustworthy Arcanist we could speak with on short notice."

"And on longer notice?"

"Short is relative. I believe I could find another if we had between three and five years."

Tain's brows rose, and Teela gave him a look. "You can't mean—"

"No, clearly I can't. Leave it alone."

Unlike Mandoran, Tain did.

"What do you expect him to tell us?"

"I don't know. The Aerian Caste Court—or at least the dar Carafel flight—clearly has fingers in the upper echelons of many of the Caste Courts. The remand to the human Caste Court must have been a barter decision. I'm fine with that. But the *request* was not delivered by humans. It was delivered by a Barrani Hawk. The Barrani Hawk in question was not, by the by, breaking any laws. He, however, was given the message to carry—"

"By someone Barrani."

"Indeed."

"Someone with power."

"Yes, Kaylin. A Lord of the High Court."

"But that wouldn't be Evarrim."

"No, fortunately for us, it was not."

"So we're going to the High Halls for two reasons."

"If it comes to that, yes. But the meeting with Evarrim is necessary at this point. An Aerian Arcanist was mentioned, and that statue—it screams Arcanum, to me. I could, of course, be wrong." Before Kaylin could speak, she added, "Yes, I know. Any 'bad' magic screams Arcanum to you. It's the one way in which the Hawk training lacks anything remotely resembling either objectivity or subtlety."

"If you look at the objective record where magic is concerned, the Arcanum is often at the heart of the worst of the problems."

"Perhaps in the last decade. That was not always the case, however. The immortals—in particular, the Dragons—did not practice sorcery in packs; they did not require either companions or cooperation."

"Fine. But this case is occurring in *this* decade."

"Kitling, you will have to find a way to take criticism of the Hawks less personally. It really isn't about you. If you want personal criticism, however, we can talk about your clothing."

"Thanks, Teela."

Kaylin was, in theory, *Lord* Kaylin. She had inadvertently taken—and passed—the Test of Name that the Tower of test offered Barrani would-be lords. The fact that she didn't *have* a Name at the time was a bit of a sore point for the Barrani who had not yet taken that test. It was probably a sore point for the Barrani who had, as well. The fact that a mere mortal had taken the test sat particularly poorly with Annarion, who had been forbidden to make the attempt himself. She had some sympathy with his frustration, and had attempted to be logical about it.

"I didn't have a Name the way Barrani do. Whatever was being tested, it wasn't me, precisely."

He had taken exactly zero comfort from the words, and Kaylin had stopped trying. But as she placed her right foot on the grand, wide stairs that led into the tranquility and perfection of the High Halls, she wondered why anyone would voluntarily subject themselves to this.

Teela, dressed in forest green, her hair caught and held by combs of diamonds and platinum, looked entirely at home. The Hawk was nowhere in sight; to look at her, she was a Lord of both power and significance. She wore rings. She made Kaylin wear the one ring that the Barrani Lords would recognize. Usually, the ring was kept in a box under her bed. In Kaylin's childhood, wearing something obviously valuable had been an invitation for throat slitting and theft. She understood that this was no longer true, but old habits died hard. Best not to stick out. Best not to be noticed.

She couldn't help being noticed here; she was mortal. She wasn't the only mortal—Severn was beside her—but it didn't matter. There was nowhere she could walk in this getup that wouldn't draw or demand attention, but in the High Halls, it wasn't the clothing that attracted the stares. It was the mortality.

Mortals were only barely considered people by some of the old-school hardliners. Were it not for the fact that the Eternal Emperor considered them people, Kaylin doubted most of the Barrani would; at best, they'd be pets. It annoyed her, but annoyance ran a distant second place to survival. She kept her annoyance to herself.

She forced herself to consider the elements of her silent presentation: her posture, the way her arms hung at her side, the tilt of her head, her chin, the speed of her movements. Elegance, apparently, involved an absence of urgency. Diarmat's Dragon voice was ringing in her ears, and she almost missed him. She certainly missed Bellusdeo.

Had Bellusdeo chosen to accompany them, no one would have given Kaylin or Severn a second glance, or possibly even a first one. She blinked when a man she did not recognize bowed before Teela. Teela's eyes had shaded from green to a green blue the moment the carriage had pulled to a stop, but that was normal for the High Halls.

"Lord Teela, Lord Kaylin, Lord Severn. The Lady bids you welcome."

Kaylin relaxed, but only marginally. She had offended the Lady on a previous occasion, and had since managed— barely—to work her way back into the Consort's good graces. She was afraid to spend time with her, though. She didn't want to end up at the bottom of the ladder again.

"If you have a moment in your otherwise busy schedule, she would be gratified for your company."

Kaylin wilted.

She is not angry with you, a familiar voice said. Kaylin could—and often did—forget about Ynpharion from time to time, in part because she now could. She knew his Name, his True Name. She couldn't figure out how to forget that she knew it.

But he had also offered his Name to the Consort, and in the end, the Consort's power, the Consort's certainty, the Consort's lack of fear, had stabilized her internal relationship with the only person who had not given her knowledge of his Name willingly.

Does she really want to see us? Or is this some sort of game? I'm not sure I like the look of that man.

You dislike the look of any man who is not a Hawk, Ynpharion shot back. By man, he meant Barrani. *I am not, however, saying that this is unwise. You do not understand how to be cautious when you are among the powerful. This is, in part, a game; the Lord attempts to curry favor with the Consort by carrying a message, as if he were a lesser servant. But she does wish to speak with you.*

With me, or with Teela?

With both.

We're here to speak with Evarrim.

Yes. And it should come as no surprise to you that, as the Lady is aware of this, she has made certain that your paths will overlap.

Evarrim is with her.

She could feel Ynpharion's smile. *Yes, Lord Kaylin. He is.*

He's supposed to be meeting Teela. Nowish.

He is indeed. But he must balance the demands of the Lady with the demands of Lord Teela. Who do you think has precedence?

Fine. I'll tell Teela.

She didn't have the opportunity. Teela seemed to understand—without the necessity of actual information—what was happening, or what had happened; she reacted with elegance and what seemed sincere pleasure at the request. Her eyes remained a martial green, but did not slide into blue; if she wasn't happy, she wasn't angry or worried, either. Or rather, wasn't more angry or more worried.

"How long did you live here?" Kaylin asked quietly.

"I have had an official residence in the High Halls for centuries. It was not until I chose to join the Hawks on a whim that I adopted a domicile closer to the Halls of Law." Her smile was pleasant. Her tone said *shut up*.

Kaylin shut up. She noted that Severn felt no need to make conversation; he neither shrunk from attention nor demanded it. He seemed, in fact, to be at home in the High Halls, and Kaylin almost resented it.

This amused him; she could feel it. She resented that, as well.

The High Halls are a part of your job right now. They're not otherwise part of your life. If the Barrani disapprove of you because you're mortal, what of it? The only people you have to worry about are the High Lord and the Consort, and they clearly favor you. It annoys some of the Lords of the Court, he added. *They feel it's entirely too modern. They are only willing to hold their figurative noses because they don't want to annoy the two most powerful people in the Court.*

Yes, but—

When you leave here, you're going home. Barrani ancestors weren't capable of destroying your home, or you, while you were in it. To harm you right now, the Barrani would have to go through Teela—and I wouldn't give an hour's pay for their chances. You are in control here.

She didn't feel like she was in control at all. But maybe, just maybe, no one did.

The Consort was waiting in the courtyard in which the Court gathered when called to do so by the High Lord. The Court itself was scattered throughout the interior grounds so artfully maintained in the heart of the High Halls; the Consort was on her throne. It was obviously a deliberate choice. She was the only person seated; to her left, Ynpharion had the position of honor. This surprised Kaylin, and her surprise annoyed Ynpharion. None of his annoyance showed, however.

Unlike your surprise.

She offered the Consort a perfect bow. The Consort didn't actually make her hold it for more than a few seconds, and when Kaylin rose, the Consort rose, as well. She then crossed the distance between them and enfolded Kaylin in a hug. She left her arm around Kaylin's shoulders as she turned to the rest of the Barrani milling in the open space. "I am not certain that all present are familiar with Lord Kaylin," she said, with very mild emphasis on the last two words. "I believe you have made Lord Evarrim's acquaintance."

Evarrim bowed. Kaylin had come to understand that he was not a terribly politic man, although he was political. His expression was clear, readable, and annoyed. "Lord Kaylin."

He then turned and bowed to Severn and Teela in turn. They offered him the same courtesy. All of this took time.

Manners, apparently, always did.

"My apologies," Teela said to the Consort. "Had I realized that Lord Evarrim was occupied by matters of greater import, I would not have attempted to meet with him."

"Lord Evarrim has been extremely helpful to me in the past month," the Consort replied. "He has barely had a chance to attend to his own work, and he has uttered no word of complaint."

That was a patent untruth, in Kaylin's opinion. Evarrim's grimace acknowledged that opinion, but he held his peace. He was, she thought, a little like Mandoran: his opinions, even given no voice, were kind of obvious. In that, he wasn't like Teela.

"I am aware, however, that his knowledge and experience are without parallel." She glanced at Teela. Teela's eyes were a shade bluer, as if the Consort's words had been a warning, or possibly even a threat.

"I do not wish to be at the beck and call of the Emperor," Evarrim said. His eyes were entirely blue, the martial shade. Teela winced—possibly for him—and the Consort spared him a pointed glance, but left the words out.

"It is not," Kaylin surprised them all by saying, "exclusively an Imperial concern." She spoke in very precise High Barrani. Severn nodded, but said nothing. Nor did he move. He was capable of standing still for a very long time; Kaylin could manage At Attention without fidgeting, but it had taken years.

"No?" Evarrim asked—of Kaylin.

"You are aware of the reason for the existence of the fiefs and their Towers."

He looked mildly insulted, but nodded anyway.

"This matter may pertain to those defenses—or a breach in those defenses."

Evarrim proved to be Barrani. He *relaxed*. Kaylin was never going to understand him. "Very well. An'Teela implied that this meeting was of import, but failed to give any information when she...requested...my expertise."

"Conveyance of the information is of Imperial concern, regrettably."

Both Teela and the Consort looked mildly surprised.

"Of course it is." Evarrim's reply was sour, but he was definitely interested.

"How much of your studies over the past few centuries have involved—directly or indirectly—the Aerians?" She watched him like, well, a Hawk.

"That is an interesting question," he replied; she now had the whole of his attention. She felt ambivalent about that, given the Arcanum. "And it might surprise you to know that you are not the first person in the past handful of months who has asked it of me."

She almost said, *What do you want in return for telling me who?* But it was harder to construct a sentence like that in High Barrani. High Barrani wasn't invented to be direct; every sentence required a few byways, as if the speakers needed many, many ways to get out of what they were trying to say if it didn't end up being the right thing.

She hated the feeling of being watched and measured, and she was being watched and measured by at least two of the Barrani present: Teela and the Consort. Neither had decided that they needed to give her a hand or come to her rescue.

"It does not surprise me," Kaylin said, voice about as flat as she felt.

Evarrim raised a brow.

"Perhaps it will surprise you to know that the *Illumen prae-volo* is a Hawk, in service to the Imperial Law," Kaylin said.

"It did, indeed, engender surprise when the information first came to me. In general, the *praevolo* is accorded a position and place of respect and power." Neither of which, he heavily implied, the Hawks could give her. "The information, however, was incomplete, and perhaps inaccurate."

"Oh?"

"I was told that the *praevolo* could not fly. Perhaps, if you understand what a *praveolo* is, you will understand my reaction. If she could not fly, she could not be what was claimed of her. And she could not, in theory, fly."

"Why was this relevant?" Kaylin asked, forcing High Barrani to do actual heavy lifting.

"Your sergeant has had very little support from her own kind because she could not fly. Apparently, this supposition was incorrect. It is relevant," he continued, "because the Aerian Caste Court has its feathers everywhere. They made demands of the Emperor—"

Kaylin winced. Evarrim nodded, acknowledging it.

"And they made *requests* for the support of every Caste Court involved in the governance of the Empire."

"Indeed, they have," the Consort inserted. "They were polite and respectful, inasmuch as demands can be."

"They were, I am certain, meant to be requests," Evarrim said. "The flights are not known for their understanding of the social customs of other races."

Neither, Kaylin thought, were the Barrani. She thought about Moran. Thought about Margot. Thought about Margot's vision, which was very oracular in its opacity.

The one that stuck out at this very moment—like a large hangman's noose—was the Dragon. Because Shadow was involved, one way or the other, and there was only one Dragon who lived in, and who seemed in some fashion to control, Shadow. The outcaste.

"Did the Aerians in question mention that they purchased the services of a sometime-Oracle?"

Evarrim tensed. "They did not."

"In which case they didn't mention the contents of that Oracle. I know oracular vision is not in any way reliable, and it can't be used in a court of Law—at least not an Imperial Court. But the Barrani do, on occasion, seek out the services of the Oracular Halls."

"We are usually rebuffed," was the stiff reply.

"And if you thought Oracles were garbage, you'd never have the opportunity to be rebuffed," Kaylin said, descending into Elantran, where she firmly intended to stay. "The Aerians—the ones involved in *multiple* assassination attempts—wanted an Oracle. Which implies heavily that they're planning to do something they're not entirely certain will work out well for them.

"The contents of that vision weren't passed immediately on to whoever tried to get it."

"But they were passed on to the Hawks?"

"As it happens, yes." Kaylin folded her arms, shifting her stance as she met and held Evarrim's narrowed gaze. "The seer in question isn't actually a resident of the Oracular Halls, and she didn't particularly want to cooperate with the customer who brought the request in. But the odd thing was, she did. She was compelled to cooperate; she lost control of her body."

Evarrim said nothing. The Barrani were, and could be, subject to such a loss of control, which was the particular peril of allowing one's True Name to be known. Humans, however, had no True Names. Control, if it was exerted, had to be exerted in an entirely different way.

"You haven't heard of this."

"No. But no information that travels in the political ether is complete. Ever. You are implying that you are aware of the mechanism used."

"Yes."

"And?"

Ynpharion said, *The Lady wishes me to advise you that caution is a virtue.* He winced when Kaylin winced.

We're here to get information about *the damn mechanism.*

If you will permit me, was his stiff reply. *I stay as far from your thoughts as possible, and your domicile thankfully makes it* impossible *to approach without direct permission. I am not entirely aware of the events that have occurred, and the Lady wishes to know.*

She asked?

Yes, in fact. She is unwilling to have me struggle to gain information you do not wish to share, but she feels that she is now at a disadvantage. Please *control your facial expressions.*

Kaylin had one moment of satisfaction in that long day. Ynpharion's eyes went almost blue black instantly when she let him in, and when he shared whatever it was he chose to offer the Consort, so did hers. She felt faintly smug, and then faintly guilty. Now was not the time to be petty.

The Consort then turned to Evarrim. "I believe," she said, "that the time for certain negotiations or games has now passed."

CHAPTER 22

Evarrim frowned, his gaze moving from Kaylin to the Consort and back. The Consort didn't blink. Kaylin probably did, but that was now irrelevant. He could toy with Kaylin to his heart's content, could condescend to her and treat her like an ignorant street rat. He would never treat the Consort that way.

He bowed. To the Consort, of course.

"The Oracle's vision," Kaylin said, "involved a Dragon, ringed by Aerians, flying above Ravellon." Among other things. She chose which other things to reveal by continuing. "It also involved the current *praevolo*, or at least a person I assume is the current *praevolo*."

"In the vision—" Evarrim's eyes were now the same shade of almost black that the other Barrani eyes—with the exception of Teela, to whom this was semi-old news—had become "—was the *praevolo* at the side of this figurative Dragon?"

"No. She was, in theory, standing alone."

"Against the Dragon?" he pressed.

"It wasn't my vision. I don't think the Oracle in question implied combat on her part, but it definitely implied martial forces on the Dragon's."

"What color was the Dragon?"

"She didn't say. She couldn't say. It was too dark. This caused predictable annoyance on the part of the man who was forcing her to have this partial vision."

"I can well understand why."

"The method by which she was controlled involved Shadow."

Evarrim stiffened. "Do you have proof of that?"

"Yes, actually. It isn't the only time Shadow has been used—and in both cases, it was used to control someone. The man who came to force the seer to have her vision contained Shadow that did not appear to have significant control over *his* actions. He used the power he'd been granted with no awareness at all that the driving force behind it was Shadow."

"Impossible."

"Is it?" the Consort asked, voice cool. "We are, none of us, servants of the Imperial Laws, but we are assured that those who do serve are well trained. Perhaps you suggest that Lord Kaylin was misinformed?"

It was not the time for petty, Kaylin reminded herself. "I wasn't informed. I observed. Shadow was forced out of him, and when he realized what it was, he panicked. He didn't intend to die, and he realized that he was no safer than his victim in that regard. He volunteered to aid us. Until today. Today, he demanded the protection of the human Caste Court, and a remand for his possible sentencing."

Evarrim said nothing.

"The request, however, that he make that demand? It came from one of the Barrani Hawks. They're guarding him against 'accidental' in-cell suicide."

"And you believe I had some hand in that request?"

It hadn't really occurred to Kaylin until he asked the

pointed, chilly question. Kaylin knew that the composition of racial Caste Courts varied—often greatly—by race and racial customs. She'd assumed that the Caste Court of the Barrani was, to all intents and purposes, the High Lord and his Court.

And Evarrim *was* a member of that Court.

"We didn't come here today to question you about your role in the Caste Court," she replied, picking her words with care, but resolutely clinging to Elantran. "We came to ask you questions about your acquaintance with both the Arcanum and the Aerian Arcanist."

"Which Aerian?"

"The Arcanist."

"There are currently two."

"Fine. With the Aerian Arcanists, plural. If, however, you would like to volunteer information about the role of the Barrani Caste Court in this entire mess, we'd be grateful."

"Human gratitude is ephemeral."

And Barrani gratitude was almost nonexistent, in Kaylin's opinion.

"Mortal gratitude persists in comparison to the length of mortal lives," the Consort said gently. "To expect otherwise is to fail to understand mortality."

Kaylin exhaled. "We want two things."

"Oh, do continue."

"We want to meet the Aerian Arcanists."

"And?"

"We want the Barrani Caste Court to stop interfering in matters that are none of its damn business." Ynpharion coughed. Teela exhaled. Kaylin inhaled, held her breath and turned to face the Consort. "Apologies, Lady," she said, voice curt. "I spent the night with the midwives, and I'm hideously short of sleep." It wasn't a very gracious apology, but it was an explanation.

An explanation that possibly only the Consort would accept with any grace. But she was the mother of her race, in a way that a mortal couldn't be to their own. "I see." Her eyes were no longer the dark blue that all the rest of the Barrani eyes were. "I cannot, of course, compel Lord Evarrim to make the introduction you demand. I am not, and have never been, a part of the Arcanum. Even were it my calling, it would have been forbidden.

"I can, however, find out what the Caste Court barter is or was. If we aid the human Caste Court in some fashion, it will of course be to our theoretical advantage." Her tone implied heavily that she could see no advantage the human Caste Court could possibly offer. She glanced at Evarrim.

Evarrim was a peculiar shade of white. He bowed to the Consort, and held that bow for much longer than necessary. When he rose, his expression was composed, almost neutral; his eyes were all midnight, but at this point, the surprise would have been green, not indigo.

"I am not at all certain the Arcanists in question will agree to a meeting."

Kaylin said nothing.

"At the moment, both of those Arcanists are residents of the Southern Reach. They have quarters in the Arcanum, but those quarters were not designed with Aerians in mind; for obvious reasons, they find them uncomfortable. If the Arcanists agree to meet with you, you may be required to visit the Southern Reach."

"Fine."

"As you no doubt suspect, Lord Kaylin, one of the two is

involved in an unusual branch of magical study. It is considered somewhat esoteric."

"And forbidden?"

"We are not children, to be forbidden our natural curiosity. Our responsibilities are to our own studies, and their relative safety. We do not police other members of the Arcanum. I believe that would be considered *your* job."

"Arcane bomb, did I forget to mention?"

He stiffened.

"Arcane bomb," she continued, "with a very, very small magical footprint, an unfamiliar-to-me sigil. The bulk of the splash effect appears to have been Shadow."

Kaylin had seen corpses in rigor less stiff than Evarrim.

"And this...Shadow, was it unusual in any way?"

"Funny you should ask that. It appeared to be inert. If I had no experience at all fighting Shadow, I would say that it was simply an alternate form of magical power. It did not distort or transform anything it touched; it seemed devoid of any purpose of its own."

The Consort shifted position slightly, a polite demand for attention, which she instantly received.

"Lord Evarrim," she said in a winter voice, "you will offer Lord Kaylin all necessary aid."

Necessary was generally a weasel word, in Kaylin's experience. Clearly her experiences with the Consort hadn't been broad enough in the past. Evarrim bowed instantly, and the bow he chose—if Kaylin was remembering her lessons correctly—was one offered a superior of far greater rank.

When he rose, he was pale; his eyes were indigo, his posture stiff. But something about his demeanor had shifted between the start of the bow and the end of it.

"You're aware of what this Aerian has been studying," Kaylin said, voice flat.

"I am aware that he has received a large bursary from the Aerian Caste Court; it could be entirely unrelated."

"It's unrelated." Kaylin had shifted her positioning on her feet, as if she expected a brawl to start at any moment; she locked her arms to make certain she wasn't the one who started it.

"Is it? You are certain?"

"Almost certain." There was no way that the study of Shadow would or could receive a bursary from the Caste Court. It was a visible, obvious act of treason that cut across Exemption Laws. Private funding, maybe. But if the caste-lords knew that Shadow was involved, Kaylin doubted they'd front the money in a way that was obvious to a Barrani Arcanist.

"Well, it *is* your duty to police, not mine."

"When did the funding arrive?"

"I am not privy to all financial details."

"Was it this decade?"

"Ah. The rumors of the influx are older than a decade." He paused. "You feel this has something to do with the *praevolo*? The *praevolo* has been an interesting side study for a small handful of our members."

"Why?"

"The power appears to be passed on, whole, with some bloodline markers. I believe there was a great deal of embarrassment at the birth of the current *praevolo*, however. She was not legitimate, and this matters for mortals.

"The actual power of the *praevolo* is not well understood. Where the Aerians were or are religious, it is assumed to be a grant, a gift, a decision made by gods." His tone made clear that he thought the religious were idiots. "Where the Aerians are not religious, it is assumed to be something other. The other, of course, has consequence. Some study was done—discreetly—on the regalia of the *praevolo*. It was determined that the bracelet was key, but it could not be studied with any great efficacy unless one also had access to the *praevolo*.

"You are aware of the effect the bracelet has on one who is not *praevolo*?"

"Not specifically. I know it kills them. Or at least I've been told it kills them." Kaylin tightened the arms she'd folded, as if she was holding her temper.

"Indeed. Was more information forthcoming?"

"No. The Aerian Hawks aren't Arcanists or scholars. They just know what they've been told. They don't know the details, but the details are irrelevant to our lives and our jobs. We don't—we *didn't*—need them."

"And now they have become strangely relevant."

"Yes—because *Barrani ancestors* got pissy and tried to destroy the High Halls we were defending. If it weren't for that, none of this would have happened."

"None of this, Private Neya?"

Kaylin bit back every intemperate response she wanted to make. Ynpharion's disgust was tempered by the barest hint of approval, mostly of the *about damn time* variety, although that wasn't how it was worded. "Do you know the effect the bracelet has on an Aerian who doesn't have the wings?"

"Yes, as a matter of fact, I do." His smile was almost pure malice. Or maybe she was being unfair. Evarrim wasn't above being petty, but clearly neither was Kaylin. She struggled to keep this in mind.

"Are they devoured by Shadow?"

"A curious question. Why do you ask it?"

"Is that a yes or a no?"

"It is, Private Neya, both a yes and a no. They are not devoured by it; they are often, however, claimed by it."

"The Shadows we've seen used have no will of their own to make such claims."

"No. It is my belief—and I offer it as a sign of my good faith in the discretion of the Hawks—that where the infusion of Shadow is small, it is very like fire or air: summon it, and it has no notable will. You might light candles or torches, and the effort would be similar to the nonmagical attempts to do the same. The fire does not fight you, except in the act of summoning; you must have an understanding of what you call."

Since this had been the question that Kaylin had been trying very hard not to ask of the people who might have some knowledge, she fell silent for a long beat. "And if you summon a lot of it?"

"It is my belief—and again, this has not been tested—that it is very like fire. The summoner must have, and must retain, control. In the case of the immortal, it is a small Test of Name, each time. But in the case of the mortals, it is an act of pure will."

"Do you think there's any possibility that the bracelet itself is somehow a repository for contained Shadow?"

"That would be the question, yes. It is considered the primary source of legitimacy for the *praevolo*. I believe that your sergeant has donned it?" Kaylin failed to answer, which was a yes, and Evarrim understood it as such. "She has not, I assume, been consumed by it."

"No."

"She is rumored to have been gravely injured in the actions surrounding the defense of the High Halls."

Kaylin nodded.

"She is also rumored to have flown, very recently, in spite of those injuries." His smile was slender.

"You're in contact with the Arcanist."

"Yes, Kaylin, I am. We are not friends—that is far too much a stretch of the word—but I have, oddly enough, been tasked by the High Lord with minor surveillance of certain branches of mortal study. The Barrani have their reasons for disdaining research into the nature of, and the utility of, Shadow. As a Lord of the High Court, you must know what those reasons are."

Kaylin nodded.

"I have seen no evidence, however, that the research that was being conducted was more dangerous, or more insidiously dangerous, than prior research into different disciplines."

"What happened to those who put the bracelet on?"

"They died." At a small inhalation from the Consort, Evarrim surrendered his side of the game. "The Shadow that inhabited them did not seem to have will in the way fire does when it burns. It had a similar effect: it destroyed them, reducing them to the pools with which you are familiar. But it did not, in that act of destruction, appear to consider taking them over or remaking them in a different image."

"Our Shadow does."

"Yes."

"Which implies something."

"Yes. Our Shadow—the Shadow beneath the High Halls, the Shadow that attempts, on a daily basis, to escape Ravellon, will transform anything it inhabits, turning it into a tool that follows only the will of Shadow. But this Shadow did not."

"You saw this personally?"

"I am unwilling to incriminate myself further, given Imperial Law."

"Suicide isn't illegal," Kaylin replied, but she felt the slow clench of the pit of her stomach. "I assume there were volunteers."

"Yes, actually. Those who believed they were strong enough to deserve the power of *praevolo*, without the wings, were given permission to don it. Permission, not commands. You may choose to disbelieve me if that is more comfortable."

"It really isn't."

He shook his head, and Kaylin saw a reflection of her *I will never understand Barrani* expression written clearly across his face. She tried, for a moment, to think as Evarrim did—or as she believed he did. "What were they promised?"

"That, I cannot tell you. It is possible they were offered power, or the possibility of power."

"Do you have any of their names?"

"No. I am certain the Arcanist does."

"Do you have the Arcanist's name?"

"May I remind you that membership in the Arcanum is not illegal?"

She shrugged. It was a fief shrug. "What is the name of the Aerian Arcanist?"

"Aguila. Aguila dar Carafel."

Teela's eyes were already about as blue as they could get; they didn't get any lighter. The same could be said for the Consort. Evarrim, however, was happier, for a Barrani value of the word *happy*. Severn's eyes changed shape rather than color.

He was not very happy to hear the name.

You knew. It wasn't a question; it was almost an accusation.

No. I didn't. But I've done some research in the past week into the Aerian Caste Court and the members that comprise it.

Let me guess. Aguila's one of them.

Yes. He is not the castelord, however.

And the castelord is?

His father. Fauconne.

"We'd like to speak with Aguila."

"Of course you would." Evarrim turned to the Consort and bowed. "With your permission, I will leave to make the arrangements."

The Consort's nod was regal, even stiff. Evarrim departed. The Consort did not, however, excuse the rest of her informal guests. She rose instead. "Come. I find this chair confining at the best of times—and clearly, this is not the best of times. Kaylin, attend me. I wish to know everything about this case you are allowed to impart."

"Everything?"

"Everything."

Severn had some disagreement about what Kaylin was allowed to impart, and to her surprise, he made this known, lifting a hand or speaking where it was necessary. The Consort didn't seem to find this offensive; she accepted his corrections without comment and without changing eye color.

"Think what you will of Lord Evarrim," she said, as she led the way to the fountain at the far end of the internal forest. "But he has saved my life many, many times. He has put his own life in danger in each of those cases; in two, I was concerned that he would not survive.

"He does not care for mortality—but, Kaylin, most of my kin don't. He finds it somehow offensive that you bear the marks of the Chosen. At first, he thought it was due to your natural deviousness."

"He thought I cheated?"

"Yes. He has come to understand, however, that that particular type of devious is not in you. I believe he feels some kinship in this one regard with Aguila."

"Aguila doesn't feel that Moran should have the wings of the *praevolo*."

"Yes."

"Is he trying to figure out a way to somehow transfer them?"

"That is what I took from Evarrim's elliptical answers, yes."

"That's impossible!"

"Is it?"

Kaylin thought of Lillias then, and froze in place. Lillias had no wings. They had not been chopped off or crippled; Clint said they had been removed. And if the Caste Court had that in their power, why couldn't they remove Moran's wings and give them to someone else?

Except someone had said—Evanton? Clint? Lillias?—that Moran could not be made outcaste. Not the way the rest of the Aerians could. Kaylin considered this in a different light, and came to a conclusion. The *praevolo* could not lose his or her wings.

"I wish Evarrim were still here."

"I am almost shocked, Lord Kaylin."

"I'm worse than shocked," Teela said, in Elantran. "Next time, give me enough warning that I can sit down first."

"Very funny. I'm thinking about the process of making an Aerian outcaste."

"I really do need to take a seat."

"I'm being serious."

"I know. I was wondering when and if you would get to this part."

"You could have said something."

"I could have," Teela agreed, stretching like the cat she sometimes reminded Kaylin of. "You're not stupid. You would have gotten there eventually. And I was thinking about Caste Courts and politics, just not the Aerian version."

"Lillias has no wings. I would bet you every cent I've ever earned that that's literal: she has no wings. No hint of ever having had wings."

The Consort's expression was one of pity.

"If they can remove the wings of any Aerian—any *other* Aerian—the idea of transferring the wings themselves doesn't seem as stupid."

"Is it reversible?" the Consort asked.

"I have no idea. I'm not sure who to ask. I'm only sure that it's important, relevant, and magical." Ugh.

"The expression you're making is priceless. None of my kin—not even the very young—would do so in public."

"And by 'in public,' she means where any other living person could see it," Teela helpfully added.

"Mandoran does."

"Another reason never to let him leave home."

Kaylin was already red, and turned to offer the Consort her apologies. The Consort's eyes, however, were almost green.

"I think I can probably get more answers from the Arkon."

"And that discomfits you?"

"I get answers only after I've been told I'm ignorant, lazy or rude. Or some combination of the three. He's consistently arrogant and condescending."

"But you like him, and you do not care for Evarrim."

"Yes. And I'm not sure what the difference is, when I think about it—but I really hate being told I'm stupid."

"Ignorance and stupidity are not the same. Remember that. Ignorance can always be alleviated."

CHAPTER 23

"You're worried about more than just the Arkon calling you stupid."

Kaylin nodded at Teela's verbal prodding. She had used the mirror in the High Halls to make an appointment—such as it was—with the Arkon; she had mirrored Helen, and Bellusdeo had amicably agreed to join her there. Like Mandoran, she didn't trust the mirror network, and didn't generally ask for possibly dangerous details when speaking through it.

And then Kaylin had said excruciatingly formal goodbyes, which had taken fifteen minutes. The only bright spot of the day was the fact that she hadn't been summoned to attend the High Lord and his Court in person.

The city streets looked a lot grubbier in comparison, but that just made them feel more like home. "It's the outcaste. The outcaste Dragon."

"You think Margot's vision pertained to the outcaste?"

"I can't see how it doesn't. He was flying over Ravellon. Bellusdeo has history with the outcaste. It's not a happy history. But she met him on a different world. He was part of Ravellon by that point—and Ravellon, in theory, existed on all worlds."

"You're worried about the Dragon."

Kaylin was. "Bellusdeo lost almost everything. She still feels the loss, the lack of home, her lack of place here. She's strong," Kaylin added quickly, feeling vaguely disloyal. "But—she's a Dragon."

"And Dragons are very, very good at bearing long grudges."

Kaylin nodded. "I don't know what the outcaste wants. I've never really understood it."

"You don't know what most other people want," Teela pointed out. She paused to kick a loose stone; she wasn't any more comfortable than Kaylin was. "You assume they want what you want. You assume they hate what you hate, even when experience has taught you otherwise."

"I assume," Kaylin said with emphasis, "that if I understand what someone wants, I can either help them or get in their way. And I'm pretty damn sure that whatever the outcaste wants is the opposite of what *I* want."

"You're not."

"Not?"

"Not certain. Why?"

Kaylin exhaled heavily. "When we saved Bellusdeo, he was in the air. And I heard his roar. It didn't sound angry— I've heard enough angry Dragon to last a lifetime, and I recognize it. It sounded almost—" She shook her head.

"Almost what?"

"Almost heartbroken, if you want the truth." She had never said this out loud before. She wasn't even certain why she was saying it now. "Bellusdeo wants him dead. And Bellusdeo heard Margot's Records entry. She's certain that he's involved somehow. Look, I know you think I'm reckless a lot of the time. But I'm not reckless enough to go charging into Ravellon to confront a giant black Dragon. I wouldn't charge into the High Halls to confront a random Barrani Lord, either."

"Bellusdeo is not a fool."

"No."

"That sounded like a yes."

"It really didn't. She's not a fool. But…it's personal, for her. And I know I don't do well when things become personal for me. I can't figure out what the Aerians want, but I'm almost certain that what they want must have started with the damn Dragon. And that's a twofold problem."

"Is it?"

"Dragons aren't exactly invisible when they take to the skies. They can mostly pass for mortal if you don't know anything about Dragons—but there are always telltale signs if you do. If the Dragon came to the Reaches, he did it one of two ways: he flew—invisibly—or he walked. I'm leaning toward the walking, myself.

"He had to have some way to set up an appointment. I honestly can't imagine that the Aerian Arcanist would have gone to the fiefs searching for the Dragon. I can't actually imagine…" She cursed. "The Arcanist didn't have to meet with the Dragon initially. I can guarantee that he didn't go through Tiamaris. I can't guarantee that he didn't contact a different fieflord. But he'd still be visible, and an Aerian flying into the fiefs might attract some notice. Unless he flew at night."

"Or unless he walked?"

"Walking would draw less attention if he walked in the dead of night, yes—but Aerians have great, honking wings."

"Assuming they do exist, how long would it take to find those witnesses?"

Too damn long.

"Let's go with the hypothesis that the Aerian Arcanist somehow visited the fiefs," Teela continued. "The ferals and most of the Shadows wouldn't be the threat they once were to you—Aerians can fly. Ferals can leap a great distance, but they can't follow or attack from the ground."

Kaylin nodded. "I just don't understand what they want."

"And you can't follow the money."

"Not if I don't understand the coin, no. You have any suggestions?"

"Yes, oddly enough."

"Let's hear them—I assume you're not going to accompany me into the Arkon's library."

"I have never been comfortable standing in the middle of a Dragon's hoard, for reasons which will perhaps be obvious if you pause to reflect." When Kaylin failed to answer, Teela said, "Tain and I are going home. Or rather, we're going to your home. We'll wait there."

"But—"

"Mandoran is in a snit."

"Did he get stuck in another wall?"

"Something like that. He's not speaking to Annarion. Forcefully and loudly not speaking."

Great. Just what they all needed. "I suppose Nightshade is there, as well."

"Now that you mention it, yes."

The Arkon's condescension was looking better with each step she took toward the palace.

Bellusdeo met Kaylin at the library's closed and forbidding doors. Bellusdeo's was therefore the hand that pressed the door wards that caused those doors to roll open. Kaylin could have hugged her.

"Your appointment in the High Halls?"

"No one swore at anyone else, no weapons were drawn, and no blows were exchanged."

"That bad?" the Dragon asked in sympathetic Elantran.

Kaylin grimaced. The familiar, mostly forgotten in the excitement of the rest of the day, lifted his head. He squawked, but it was a sleepy sound. "I don't suppose you want to go home and keep Mandoran and Annarion from doing something they'll regret?"

His answering squawk was longer.

Bellusdeo winced. "Teela told you?"

"She said Mandoran was in a snit, and also that Nightshade was visiting."

"'Snit' is not how I would have described it."

"How would you describe it?"

"Later," the Arkon said. "She would describe it later, when it doesn't waste my time." He glared at Kaylin, but offered Bellusdeo a very exact bow.

Bellusdeo laughed at Kaylin's expression.

Kaylin, Severn and Bellusdeo followed the Arkon; generally he preferred to have private meetings in the rooms that didn't house any of his vast collection. This time, however, he took a left turn instead of a right. They didn't end up facing a wall while he magically summoned an arch or a door; they ended up in a room. The significant feature of this room was the many glass cases that made it seem much smaller; in those cases were a variety of smaller objects, with the single exception of a suit of armor that had clearly seen actual battle. Or earthquakes.

But one object drew her eye almost instantly. It was a feather, a long, pale flight feather.

"Yes," the Arkon said, before she could ask. "It is, as you no doubt suspect, Aerian."

She didn't ask him what it was doing in the collection.

"I am informed that you met with an Arcanist today."

"In the High Halls, yes."

"The meeting was no doubt related to the current difficulties facing your sergeant."

"Why don't I just tell you the contents of the meeting? I'll skip the excruciatingly boring etiquette bits, so it should only take ten minutes."

It took longer. If the Arkon was willing to dispense with the excruciating politics of manners, he had questions, and interrupted frequently to ask them.

"And so you've come to me."

Kaylin nodded.

"You've been staring at the feather for some time."

"It seems out of place in this room, given the rest of its contents."

"Does it?"

"Lannagaros."

The Arkon glanced at Bellusdeo.

"She is not insulting either your curating or your collection; she is mortal and fails to understand the choices you have made. You might explain them," she added mildly. "I myself find the composition of this area of your collection somewhat odd."

Bellusdeo, of course, could with safety. The Arkon frowned at her, but didn't glare. "It is, as you must imagine, an Aerian feather."

"They took an Aerian feather to Margot's."

"Did they?"

Kaylin nodded. "But it wasn't a flight feather. It wasn't this large. Did this belong to a *praevolo*?"

"Yes."

"How did you get your hands on it?"

"As it happens, we traded. An Aerian family of some lesser renown is in possession of a Dragon scale."

"You wanted this for a reason."

The Arkon nodded. "I have noted that you have the current *praevolo* living under the same roof as Bellusdeo. I have therefore returned to some of my earlier studies, in the hope that they will prove irrelevant."

"Meaning they're bad."

"Meaning that there are some inherent difficulties that present themselves, yes." He glanced at Bellusdeo. "Ask your questions, Private, and let me return to my studies."

"What do you know about the Aerian process of making someone outcaste?"

"Very little."

"Compared to me?"

"I know very little of nothing when compared to you. I will," he added as Bellusdeo opened her mouth, "attempt to feel less insulted for the duration of this discussion. I know, as you have learned, that the Aerian wings are removed. They are not chopped off, as one would the thumbs of a thief; they are removed."

"How?"

"That is, and was, the question. I found it fascinating, but I find the cultural phenomenon of assigning outcaste status to be fascinating in general."

"Even where Dragons are concerned?"

"No. I understand the Dragon concept. It is not, as you must feel it is, like the Barrani custom; it is not political in that way. Dragons have, historically, been much more direct: they fight. The stronger destroys the weaker. The flights rise and fall on the basis of the strength and power of their leaders.

"We may swear eternal and immortal enmity, and we may throw our entire focus into the destruction of those enemies—but we do not doubt that they are Dragons. We do not make our enemies outcaste simply because we can. That is the Barrani way. The human way. It is not the way of our kind. We destroy what we feel we must, and for our own reasons—but we understand, at the same time, that our most dangerous enemies are…us."

"But the outcaste—"

"Yes. It was determined that the outcaste was no longer kin. He was no longer Dragon. It is fundamentally different." The Arkon bowed his head for a moment, almost as if in prayer. When he exhaled, there was smoke in his breath; to Kaylin, it had the scent of ash.

"You are aware of the Barrani Test of Name, the Barrani Tower of that test."

Kaylin nodded. "There's no such test for Dragons."

"No. And yes. Our existence as Dragons is our test. When we are born, however, we take one form. We are either Dragon or human. As children, we cannot easily switch between the two; half of our existence, half of our life, is empty. Waiting. We feel its absence, but cannot alleviate it. The whole of our childhood is training to do just that.

"As the Barrani do, we require True Names. It is my belief that our names are more complicated than Barrani names, but in essence, they serve the same function. The Barrani have the Consort. The Dragons do not. When we speak of Dragons in the Empire, we speak of adults. In our own tongue, the children are not Dragons.

"Barrani children will become Barrani adults, if they survive. Human children will become human adults. Likewise the Aerians, the Leontines, the Tha'alani. That is not true, however, of the Dragons. Our children will not inevitably become adults—Dragons. Many fail to mature."

"What happens to them?"

"For the most part, they die."

"You *kill them*?"

"No, Kaylin. Not unless it is necessary. But they are not counted as Dragonkin."

"The outcaste was a Dragon."

The Arkon's breath once again came out in a mist that smelled of ash. "He was considered a Dragon, yes. He could walk as man and fly as Dragon."

"But you said he's not a Dragon."

"Lannagaros." Bellusdeo placed a hand on the Arkon's shoulder. "This is not necessary."

He seemed to draw strength from her hand, although his eyes were now upon Kaylin. "Until we have our Names, we cannot conquer the duality of our existence. We are not one thing or another, in either form; we are always both. It is why we can breathe fire when we stand on two legs.

"The Draconic form or the human form do not come easily or naturally—but even at birth, we retain an echo of the knowledge of either, depending on our gender. To become one or the other is an act of both will and faith."

"And the outcaste could."

Silence. Kaylin waited for the Arkon to break it. She had never seen him so somber.

"Yes." He bowed his head again. She thought he had finished. But he raised it as Bellusdeo let her hand fall from his shoulder. "Yes, he could. What we did not know—what we could not know at the time—was that he had *also* failed.

"You have noticed that I have taken an interest in your friends, Mandoran and Annarion."

"This is relevant because?" Kaylin asked, although she thought she understood.

"They are not Barrani in most senses of the word. They are other. In a like fashion, the outcaste was other. He could walk as a man; he could fly—and fight—as a Dragon. But that was not all he could do. He understood, far before we did, that he was not a duality.

"Some hatchlings cannot cohere. They cannot wed the concept of the two forms into an indivisible whole. They are not attached to their first form, as the majority of the failures are; they are not attached to their second form. They are not wed to the concept of *form* as a single cohesive attribute.

"You understand why Mandoran and Annarion are of specific interest."

She did. She didn't like what it said, but she did. Annarion could, when he fought, lose his physical shape; the battle defined it, not Annarion himself. Mandoran had gotten himself stuck in a wall, because he was trying to walk through it. "They're not a threat."

"They *are* a threat," he countered, although his tone suggested that he would not immediately demand they be destroyed.

"They don't *want* to have the trouble they're having. They spent centuries trapped in a space in which form was a cage. They had to spend those centuries learning how to ditch that form in order to have any freedom at all."

"I am cognizant of that. And they are, regardless, not a

Draconic problem. In their entirety, and unless they threaten the Empire, they are a Barrani problem."

Bellusdeo said nothing, but in her way, said it loudly enough that the Arkon looked warily in her direction. She then spoke. "You spend too much time thinking about things that are not, as you put it, your problem."

The Arkon predictably ignored this. "To Draconic eyes, the outcaste appeared Draconic. He could move fluidly between his forms; he was therefore considered adult. His martial prowess was almost uncanny, and his resistance to the magic of the Barrani, second to none. It is not a wonder to me that any irregularities would be ignored." The Arkon exhaled. "He was my friend. He was my friend, and I would have followed him into any skies, no matter what storm they contained."

"And he was greatly altered by the war?"

"No, Bellusdeo. That is a polite fiction. He was not altered by it. If he was altered at all, it was in Ravellon. He was drawn to it, just as young Tiamaris was drawn to it."

"Tiamaris is a Dragon," Kaylin said, voice flat and a little on the hard side.

"Yes. No questions surround Tiamaris; he is young. The Shadows that fascinated him did not touch or alter him. He did not perceive them as *power*, per se; he perceived them as a natural disaster. One that had will. He was not born to war, as we were; he was born in its aftermath. There were no great flights to which he might aspire. To Tiamaris, Shadow is the enemy; it is the battlefield. He studied, and he learned, to prove himself. And he has taken the Tower in Tiamaris to stand sentinel against the incursions that would otherwise destroy us."

"You do not need to tell me the dangers of Shadow," Bellusdeo said.

"And the dangers of the outcaste?" the Arkon asked. Given Bellusdeo's expression, Kaylin wouldn't have dared.

"Or that." Her answer was chilly; her eyes were orange. Before the Arkon could answer, she raised her inner eye membranes, which slightly muted her eye color.

"Did you not hear him, on the day you emerged from the fiefs?"

Bellusdeo didn't answer.

"He did not want your destruction. I do not believe he wants it now. I do not know what he found in Ravellon—or perhaps what found him there—but if he is driven, if he is no longer truly Dragon, some base part of that remains."

"He almost destroyed me."

"It is the way of our kind, when our wishes are thwarted. The Emperor is the shining counterexample. But I do not believe that destruction was his intent. You are female."

If Kaylin had had a direct link to the Arkon she would have been screaming down it, about now. Then again, raised eye membranes and orange eyes were probably enough of a signal. She considered leaving the discussion, the room and, with luck, the library, before the two Dragons started speaking in their native tongue.

That would certainly distract them, Severn said.

"I believe he hoped—he intended—to share his new kingdom with you. I believe that he wished to have a clutch, and children of his own."

"He destroyed my sisters," Bellusdeo continued, her lips a thin line, her knuckles white.

"They are part of you, now. Perhaps he understood what you must become—I am more learned than he, but I would have made different assumptions. And I would, regardless, never have attempted to force a choice on you; I had enough experience with you in your youth to know how well that would have worked."

Some of the tension left Bellusdeo's expression, then. "Do you still think you can save your friend?"

"No. He is outcaste, and he is dangerous beyond belief. It would help me greatly to believe that there is nothing of my friend left in the outcaste. I cannot, sadly. And so I think he did not fully emerge as an adult by our standards; he was, in the interior of his thoughts, outcaste, always. He was everything I was not—everything most of us were not.

"But he was like mortal kin to the Emperor. It is a blow from which the flight has never fully recovered, and his death will not change that. And I wonder if he might not have become consumed by Ravellon if we had approached him as the private and her friends approach Mandoran and Annarion. He did not, in the end, belong with or to us; perhaps what he desired was a place that would truly be home to one such as he."

Kaylin frowned; it was the thoughtful frown. "If all of this is true, why does he take the form of a large black Dragon? If I understand what you've said, he should be able to take different forms. I mean, if he's *not* a Dragon, if he's found a place in which he can mostly be himself, why does he still choose the form of a Dragon?"

"I cannot answer that question," the Arkon replied. "And it pains me, Kaylin."

She was silent for a beat, an acknowledgment of the awkward nature of this kind of pain. But she was here for a reason.

"What does the outcaste have to offer the Aerians?"

"You believe Margot's vision to be substantially true?"

"She's an *Oracle*. You can't expect reliability out of Oracles."

"Exactly. But you expect, somehow, that there is reliability in this vision?"

Ugh. "I think the outcaste is somehow involved with the Aerians, yes. Possibly only one Aerian Arcanist—but if that's the case, the Aerian Arcanist is causing Caste Court problems for the current *praevolo*."

"And?"

"We're going to meet him. I mean, *I'm* going to meet him. With a Barrani or two for company."

"And a Dragon," Bellusdeo added.

"I don't think—"

"*And a Dragon*, Kaylin."

She decided against arguing with Bellusdeo in her current mood. "…And a Dragon."

"What do you intend to discuss?"

Kaylin exhaled. "I don't know. I have a growing suspicion that the bastard thinks he can somehow remove Moran's wings and affix them to someone else."

"The *praevolo* cannot be made outcaste."

"Do we *know* that for fact? Or is that just another 'truth' that's been passed down through the generations?"

The Arkon's smile seemed genuine. "We know nothing, of course, for fact. We sift through known truths in an attempt to see what underpins them. I assume, however, that there *is* some truth in the fact. Were there no truth—or were there no perceived truth—it would not be necessary to have your sergeant assassinated."

"But they tried. So they thought it was necessary to kill her—to release the *praevolo* power, somehow. If they thought they could just remove her wings and give them to someone else—"

Silence.

"Kaylin?" Bellusdeo asked.

"Well, I know this is going to sound stupid, but—if they did assassinate her, if she did die, where would the body go?"

The ensuing silence was texturally different.

"We know—we have definitive proof—that wings can be removed. Is there anything to say that those wings have to be removed from a living body?"

CHAPTER 24

There was a lot of silence on the way home. The Arkon didn't have an answer to Kaylin's question; he suggested that the Aerians might. He couldn't tell her *how* the wings were removed, and was willing—with obvious and great reluctance—to accept her statement that they were.

But he had done some study on the single flight feather in his possession. It was, he said, immune to most things. The obvious ones—water, air—had not been extensively tested, but fire had.

And Shadow.

Kaylin didn't ask how he'd tested the latter. She understood the Arkon's concern with Shadow—in a strange way, it mirrored Bellusdeo's. It was not as personal, on the surface, but that was probably because the Arkon was old enough that experience tempered pain or anger. But he spoke with authority when he spoke of testing, and Kaylin accepted it, with questions.

He then asked, politely and without edge, if he might speak at length with Moran dar Carafel. Kaylin said, "I'll ask."

He accepted that, without demanding that she succeed,

and then pretty much ushered them out of the library, making certain they exited the doors before he returned to his research.

"He wants to see the bracelet," Bellusdeo said, when they were quit of the palace.

Kaylin nodded; that was her guess, as well.

"You have a very grim turn of thought, by the way. I almost admire it."

"What I don't understand," Kaylin said, "is why they waited."

"Why they waited?"

"Until she was injured."

"You can't guess?"

At Bellusdeo's tone, Kaylin frowned. "Politics?"

"Almost certainly. Ever since Moran donned the robes and the bracelet, she's been treated entirely differently in the Halls. You must have noticed it."

Thinking of Clint on one knee for an extended duration, Kaylin nodded.

"People can be both political and religious at the same time. Since Moran chose to wear the bracelet, have there been any assassination attempts?"

"Not that we know of, no."

"It's political. The Caste Court is, in my opinion, divided. I'm beginning to think that the people who wanted the augury—the Oracle, as you call it—weren't necessarily the people who were trying to get Moran's wings, either figuratively or literally. Or, rather, they were willing to do things up to a point.

"But when Moran flew, everything changed. The wings *are* injured. In your opinion, they shouldn't be able to carry her—but they did. They can. So. Before she flew, there was uneasiness. I'd say there's a split in the Caste Court now.

Moran is *praevolo*. People with ambition can delude themselves; they can talk themselves into believing anything. The fact that Moran didn't fly when injured would be proof to them that she was a fraud.

"Now, that can't be argued. And if she's not a fraud…"

"It's an actual crime to some of them?"

"That's my take. I'm not Aerian," she added. "But I did rule over a bunch of ambitious, fractious, frequently selfish people in my time. I would say that there are some who are old-school—I like that term, by the way—and they're afraid of what the more ambitious among their kin are planning."

"Well, that makes two of us. It's nice to know that conniving, backstabbing political jerks have *some* sense."

"Well?" Kaylin asked, arms folded, back against the nearest stretch of blank wall. She was bracketed by paintings; Moran had been in the dining room when Teela, Kaylin and Bellusdeo had returned from the High Halls. Teela had chosen to stay; Tain had headed home. He wasn't, he said, up to listening to the children squabble.

The children, as he called them, were not squabbling now; the entire house seemed blanketed in thick silence. It was not the happy, peaceful kind.

Mandoran was at the table. To his left, to Kaylin's surprise, was Maggaron; they appeared to be speaking. Moran was perched on her stool, her back stiff, her eyes the wrong color; they had lightened when Kaylin entered the room.

They'd darkened when Kaylin asked the only question she wanted answered at the moment. "Can a dead person be made outcaste by the Aerian Court?"

Moran didn't answer. Kaylin prompted her again, and she maintained her silence. It was a rigid, stiff-winged silence, with a lot of blue in the eyes.

422   *Michelle Sagara*

"What would the point be?" Mandoran demanded. He looked as if he hadn't slept for weeks. Barrani didn't, in theory, need sleep; they did need rest or repose or something similar. Kaylin had never entirely been clear on what. "Making a dead person outcaste has to serve some purpose."

"Outcaste means something different to the Aerians," Kaylin replied, silently willing Mandoran to either shut up or leave.

"What does it mean to the Aerians?"

"Mandoran. Trying to have an *important* conversation, here."

"I am joining it. I am tired of thinking about Barrani politics, the Barrani Court and Barrani bloody family. It is *very* loud in my head at the moment, and I'd appreciate any attempt to distract me."

This seemed to amuse Moran. It didn't amuse Kaylin. Because she was unamused, she wasn't diplomatic. "The Aerians don't kill their outcastes. They remove their wings. *Remove.* They don't cut them off. They take them away."

Mandoran frowned. "What do you mean, take them away?"

"I mean the wings cease to exist. The person who had them is still alive, but the wings, and their ability to fly, are gone."

"But they don't kill them."

"The don't have to—"

"They used to remove the wings of the outcaste," Moran said, "and then throw them off the peak of the Aerie."

Kaylin almost blanched. Teela and Mandoran seemed entirely unmoved.

"They don't do that anymore. The person is cast out of the Southern Reach, but they are set down on the ground, where they are doomed to remain." She rose and headed to the door, but paused midway between door and table, as if she had forgotten what she'd intended to do. "Why are you asking?"

"Because we've been thinking that assassinating you would free up the power of the *praevolo*. You were born in obscurity, and that's offended someone in power. You're dar Carafel, but in name only, and frankly, you hate the name and don't use it.

"But what if that's not what they intend? The *praevolo* can't be made outcaste."

"You're certain of that?" Moran asked, lifting a brow and using her sergeant voice.

"Yes, sir." Kaylin grimaced. "Yes."

"Why?"

"Because Clint believes it. I think *all* the Aerians in the Halls believe it. You've gone from being a pariah to being the local hero, by the way."

"Do. Not. Start."

Kaylin had some sympathy with this. She *hated* it when the Barrani Hawks called her Lord Kaylin in the office. But it wasn't the same thing, and they both knew it.

"Do you have any idea how the whole wing removal thing works?"

Moran was silent.

"I'm not asking for the fun of it. It is not fun for either of us."

"You're asking for a reason."

"Yes."

"And that?"

"Big, ugly outcaste black Dragon who calls Ravellon his home."

Moran's eyes shaded to what Kaylin thought of as Barrani blue. So did Mandoran's. Bellusdeo's eyes were the orange they generally became when the outcaste Dragon was mentioned at all.

"What does the outcaste Dragon have to do with outcaste Aerians?"

"What if the outcaste Dragon could offer the outcaste Aerians their wings back? What if he could offer the ruling Aerians the power of the *praevolo*, without the inconvenience of having to worry about who that *praevolo* actually is?" She drew a deeper, longer breath. "Moran, what if the power of flight, and the power of the *praevolo*, were somehow related to Shadow and its magic?"

Moran said a long, long nothing. Kaylin thought she would leave—she was making eyes at the door as if seriously considering that option. But in the end, she exhaled heavily and said, "I owe you at least this much."

"You don't," Kaylin countered. "You don't owe me anything."

"You've given me shelter, Kaylin; you've given me a place in which I can feel at home, even if it's not my home. That's a rare gift, at least for someone like me."

"I didn't do that, though. Helen did."

Helen coughed. She was not currently in the dining room, but of course her voice was. She was aware of anything that occurred within her walls.

"You've never seen someone declared outcaste." It wasn't a question.

"No. You have?"

"Once. Only once. It is not a private ceremony. Many cultures approve of, and even encourage, public executions."

"They believe," Teela said, taking a seat, but turning it around so the back faced the table, "that execution serves as a deterrent. If the death—the punishment—is publicly seen, the reasoning goes, people will assume that they'll face the same fate if they commit the same crime. It doesn't work that way, in my experience."

"No?"

"People see the condemned as stupid. They believe that they would never be in that position because they are not stupid. And my apologies, Moran. I did not mean to interrupt."

"Interruptions—*most* interruptions—are gratefully accepted. I admit that Annarion shouting at his brother wears a bit on the nerves; there's almost nowhere you can go in this house that drowns it out."

"If it helps," Mandoran said, "Nightshade is shouting, too. His voice doesn't carry the same way if you're far enough from it."

"Because he is only speaking on one level," Helen told him.

Mandoran joined Teela, moving from his chair into one closer to the Barrani Hawk. He leaned into her left shoulder as if his spine had momentarily deserted him. Teela rolled her eyes, but didn't move.

"There is ceremony involved in the...excision of wings."

"Ceremony? Like—religious ceremony?"

"Very like, yes. In theory, the gods are not invoked."

"In theory."

"In practice, however, there is very little difference. Up until the moment the wings dissolve, the supplicant, the criminal, has hope that the sentence will be stayed. In theory, the removal requires permission."

"From who?"

Moran shook her head. She started to answer twice, but barely made it through the first syllable of the first word.

"They ask," Helen said, coming to Moran's rescue, "the spirit of the *praevolo*."

* * *

For one long moment, silence reigned. Moran did not, however, deny Helen's words—and once those words were out there, Kaylin understood why Moran hadn't been able to give them voice.

"And the living *praevolo* gets no say?"

"Maybe in the past. I've been the living *praevolo* since birth, and no one—no one—has asked my permission." The words were bitter, terrible, desolate. "I would never have allowed them to take Lillias's wings. She saved my life. Her crime—if I understand the politics at all—was *saving my life*. I'm not a god. I'm not the Avatar of a god. I'm a sergeant. I'm a Hawk."

Kaylin heard the guilt, the anger, even the self-loathing in Moran's voice. "You think somehow if you were a better *praevolo*, if you'd played their game, Lillias wouldn't have lost her wings."

Moran didn't answer.

"You were *a child*. Lillias lost her wings because she wouldn't allow you to be killed. There is nothing you could have done to prevent what happened."

"And now?" Moran asked, bitterness seeping into her expression, which hardened and aged her face.

"Right now, I'd like to concentrate on my question. Could the wings be removed from a corpse?"

"I don't know."

"Are there stories of it being done?"

"Two or three."

"When the wings are removed, what happens to them?"

"When I said dissolve, I meant it. The wings fade. They disintegrate, starting from the flight feathers and moving in. It isn't—I'm told—a painful process. It doesn't physically hurt."

Kaylin disagreed with this, but did it silently. "It's considered civilized? That's why they don't throw them off cliffs anymore?"

"Yes. I'm sorry."

Civilized people could be incredibly cruel. Kaylin thought of the Barrani and their High Court. "Civilized," she said, in a tone that was anything but, "would be leaving their wings alone."

"Being outcaste isn't a trivial matter—and before you attempt to bite my head off, I understand that the power can sometimes be abused. I could hardly fail to understand that; Lillias lost her wings because I'm still alive. But in *theory*, only traitors to our race are cast out from it."

"So the wings are *gone*?"

"Yes."

"They're not removed—they disappear?"

"Yes."

Kaylin deflated.

"Why are you asking this?"

She glanced at Teela, who shrugged, leaving it in Kaylin's hands.

"...We were wondering—"

"The private was wondering," Teela corrected her.

"Fine. *I* was wondering if the wings that were removed could be transferred."

"Not apparently. The wings don't survive."

It was Teela who asked, "Are you certain?"

Moran started to answer, and stopped. "...No, actually. I know what I saw—but I've been a Hawk for years; appearances are often deceptive. I'm not certain. It's *believed* that the wings are destroyed—the destruction being symbolic."

"Which brings us back to the original question. Sort of."

"And that?"

"By what? What's the mechanism for the removal of wings?"

"The *praevolo*."

"You didn't remove her wings."

"No. But the guidance of the *Illumen praevolo* is very like a deity, to the Aerians. The loss of the wings is deemed the judgment of the power that *also* bestows wings like mine on an Aerian."

"This is going to get confusing."

"Welcome to my life."

"Aren't you on a leave of absence?" Clint asked pointedly. He'd lowered his weapon to bar her entrance. This was going to cause him problems because the person behind her was Moran.

"A leave of absence was *requested*," Kaylin replied. "I happen to think it's unnecessary."

Tanner whistled. "Wasn't the leave 'requested' by the Hawklord?"

"Does it matter? It wasn't an order."

"You're braver than you look."

"Or more stupid," Clint added. He glanced at Moran, and the weapon rose. His expression changed. So did Moran's; hers instantly soured.

"If you call me *praevolo* in the Halls, I will break your arms."

Tanner snickered. "He's not technically in the Halls at the moment, Sergeant."

Moran had chosen to fly to work. Bellusdeo was therefore sporting Dragon-scale armor. Teela and Tain had pulled up the rear on the ground, and the guards weren't generally stupid enough to block the Barrani without heavy-duty orders from above. The Barrani idea of a passing resentment lasted longer than entire mortal lives, and they really resented obvious disrespect. They'd learned to live with most of it, but it wore on their nerves.

Teela—the only Barrani Hawk who was also a Lord of the High Court—was actually better about it than the rest. Tain only took exception to disrespect offered his partner, all other disrespect being beneath notice or contempt.

Clint let them in. Kaylin let them pass her. Only when she was certain Moran was beyond the range of hearing her— the Barrani would still catch it all, as would the Dragon— did she speak. "I need to talk to you."

Clint met her gaze, his eyes a momentarily weary blue. "You just can't keep your nose out of things, can you?"

"Not these things."

"If it helps at all," Tanner said, "it's one of her most endearing traits." As if Clint needed the reminder.

"Not finding it endearing at the moment."

"Well, no. It's also frequently highly inconvenient."

"I'm still here, guys."

"Of course you are," Clint replied. "It's been that kind of a day."

Clint found a replacement; there were relief guards who gave them breaks for meals, among other things. He headed toward the mess hall, but Kaylin shook her head. "West room?"

"Fine." He was in a bad mood, and made Kaylin touch the door ward. The room was only infrequently in use, and today it was empty. Kaylin entered, waiting until Clint had done the same, and then closed the door.

"Did you know there's an Aerian Arcanist?"

"Yes. I was aware of it."

"We think—we're not certain—that an Arcanist is probably responsible for the earlier assassination attempts."

"And water is wet."

"Work with me a bit here."

"I've already explained why that's a very bad idea for any Aerian."

Kaylin nodded. "I wouldn't have asked you—but in the past couple of days, the attitude toward Moran has shifted markedly among the Aerians in the Halls."

Clint nodded. "She's the *praevolo*."

"She's always been the *praevolo*."

"Yes—but no one can argue with that fact now. She's the *praevolo*. If there are further assassination attempts, they won't come from Aerians." He spoke this as a flat fact. Kaylin wasn't nearly as certain. "She's out of danger now. And the rest of us aren't being pushed by the currents, either. But you've got that look that says this isn't good enough—for you."

"I've got that look," Kaylin countered, "because I don't believe it's over. I don't believe things are settled. This didn't just start when Moran got injured in the battle over the High Halls. It's been going on all her life. You know that they tried to have her killed when she was a child, right?"

Clint stiffened. That was a no. If the stiffness wasn't enough, she could see the color of his eyes. She really hated Barrani blue when it settled in Aerian eyes. On Barrani, it was more natural.

"It didn't just happen once, either."

Clint's jaw muscles were twitching.

"One woman was made outcaste because she saved Moran's life. And don't tell *me* that the power of the *praevolo* is sentient enough to decide that it made a mistake. Lillias was made outcaste because she thwarted the will of the Caste Court. It was political."

"You're certain?"

"Dead certain, Clint."

"Kitling," he said, in a very familiar tone. He almost never used the endearment anymore. "How far is this going to go?"

"I've got an appointment with the Hawklord in an hour. I'll know then." She hesitated. "I think the outcaste Dragon is involved."

Clint's wings rose, stiffening. It was a visceral reaction, and he got it under control again. "Why?"

"The Oracle. I don't know if the Dragon will literally show up—but I do believe he's involved."

"Does the Emperor know?"

"The Emperor knows of the vision, yes." She hesitated again. "I'll be visiting at least one Aerian Arcanist sometime this afternoon."

"When?"

"Whenever I get the mirror call. It's being arranged by a Barrani Arcanist."

"This gets worse and worse. Dragons? Barrani? Arcanists?"

"I didn't start it, Clint."

"Doesn't matter who started it." He ran his left hand through his very short hair. "Where are you meeting him?"

"The Aerie." Before Clint could say anything he'd regret—or, more honestly, that Kaylin would—she lifted a hand. "I'm going with Bellusdeo. She's flying."

"And Moran?"

"I'd like her to stay put."

"Meaning she's going with you."

"Meaning exactly that. There's a possibility the Hawklord will order her to remain in the Halls."

"She won't disobey a direct order."

"Not while she's on duty, no. She'll just demand that the arranged meeting be moved."

"What, exactly, do you want to ask the Arcanist? He's dar Carafel, and he's at the heart of the Caste Court."

"I'd guessed, given events. I want to ask the Arcanist about the power of Shadow—and the power of the *praevolo*."

"You are not suggesting they're the same."

Kaylin chose not to answer the actual question. "I think the Arcanist has actually been using the power of the *praevolo* in a limited fashion. He can't use it now—Moran has the bracelet. People who have power are reluctant to let it go. He's had power. I'm certain he considers that power his, by right of birth. He certainly doesn't consider it the province of an unclaimed, unacknowledged bastard from the Aerian equivalent of the fiefs."

"She has the wings. He doesn't."

"And I'm sure that matters to almost every Aerian alive who knows. I'm also sure it doesn't matter to him."

"Kaylin—"

"I think he's trying to remove Moran's wings somehow. I think he intends to wear them himself."

Clint's eyes were almost black. He couldn't look more dangerous unless he were bristling with weapons.

"Moran said that when an Aerian is made outcaste, their wings dissolve."

Clint's nod was controlled. It had to be. She'd seen him annoyed and irritated in her time with the Hawks. She had never seen him angry. Not like this.

"I'm not sure that's true."

"It is true for the Aerian. The wings dissolve; they are no longer wings. They have no right to the power of flight, and it is taken from them," Clint said.

"Is the bracelet used in this ceremony? Moran was a child the only time she saw it. I'm not sure she paid attention to the particulars; the horror of watching wings dissolve had all her attention."

"The bracelet is used. It is not worn, unless the *praevolo* is present."

Moran had been present. She hadn't been wearing the bracelet. Kaylin said nothing. But she had her answer now. She frowned.

"You're thinking."

"I am. Someone gave the man who took control of Margot the bracelet. The bracelet, a feather, and a collar."

Clint stiffened further, which shouldn't have been possible. "A collar."

"Yes. Is a collar part of the regalia? Moran didn't seem to recognize it."

"If it was taken to the Oracle, it's significant. A collar is worn *by* the traitor during the ceremony. You kept the bracelet. You gave it to Moran. Did you keep the feather and the collar?"

"Technically, no."

"Are they here?"

"In the evidence lockers, probably. The bracelet seemed important."

"You're going to think the collar's important as well, if you're investigating the ceremony of exclusion." He headed toward the door.

"Where are you going?"

"The lockers. The Hawklord is going to want the evidence in hand by the end of your meeting."

The Hawklord was grim, dark-eyed and high-winged. Clint had apparently gone to the evidence lockers and circumvented Hanson; he was in the Tower when the doors opened.

But so was Moran. Since Moran was there, Bellusdeo was also there. She was still wearing scale armor. Severn and Kaylin were the late arrivals, and they interrupted what was only barely a conversation from the sound of raised voices. Those voices stopped abruptly as the doors rolled open and all eyes turned to the newcomers.

"Private. Corporal. Please join us," the Hawklord said, voice heavy with sarcasm.

"We made an appointment, sir."

"Yes. You were the only people considerate enough to do so, given the current political fracas. I have had to put off a mirror meeting with the Caste Court—the Aerian Caste Court. Until I have that meeting, I have had to put off a meeting with the leader of the human Caste Court. And until I have endured both, I am putting off a report to the Eternal Emperor."

No one in the room except Clint and Kaylin seemed worried about either the Caste Courts or the Emperor.

The collar was not like the bracelet. It wasn't obviously valuable in the same way. Kaylin had found it creepy and disgusting, and hadn't bothered to evaluate either reaction. To Kaylin, collar implied one of two things: pet, which was the cheery one, and slave, which was not. And she had seen people in collars before, in her early life in the fiefs.

"Do you know what this is?"

She did, now. "I didn't, at the time. I'm sorry. I don't know a lot about Oracles—"

"You know more than most of the Hawks," the Hawklord pointed out.

"Fine. I *still* don't know a lot about Oracles. The Oracles in the Oracular Halls aren't quite sane. They fall into visions. They're obsessed by them. Until they express that vision somehow—painting, quilting, singing, shrieking—they remain caught in it. I don't recall that we ever brought them things to touch. Maybe it would help—I don't know. I think Sabrai—Master Sabrai," she added, as the Hawklord cleared his throat, "would toss us out on our rear ends if we tried.

"But they didn't go through the Oracular Halls. Master Sabrai would never have given them access to his Oracles. They went to Margot. They *did* think that handling these items would somehow control the flow of vision, or they'd never have sent the items out of the Aerie."

"They want them back," the Hawklord added.

"They can bite me. Us. The Emperor."

He seemed amused by this, and amusement had been very absent in the Tower of late.

"Have they asked?"

"Yes."

"They want the *praevolo* to return what's rightfully hers?"

"They contest the 'rightfully hers' part, but yes."

Clint looked like thunder. Or like thunderclouds.

"And the collar?"

"They want the collar, they want the feather, they want the bracelet. They have evinced a willingness to accept the *praevolo* as part of the condition of the return of these items."

Kaylin uttered a string of inappropriate but heartfelt Leontine.

"The Emperor has refused to even entertain the petition. He has asked for legal advice from Aerians, and the Aerian advisors—not, of course, part of the Caste Court—have made clear that the bracelet belongs to the *praevolo*. Period. The collar and the feather are more contentious—one expert believes that while there *is* a living *praevolo*, the collar belongs entirely to her. One expert believes there is legal standing in the demand of the collar's return. The collar functions when there is no *praevolo*, as it happens.

"The Emperor is considering the ramifications of this legal advice. He has not, therefore, made a decision. The two items in question will remain *in our evidence lockers* until a decision has been reached."

Clint was not a legal advisor. He was a Hawk. But it was absolutely clear that he felt it *all* belonged to the *praevolo*, commands from the Emperor notwithstanding.

"We, uh, have an appointment to meet with an Aerian Arcanist," Kaylin said.

"So I have heard."

One look at both the Hawklord's and Moran's faces made clear what they'd been arguing about. Kaylin understood the Hawklord's concern—she felt it herself. But she hated to be cozened, to be treated like a child, a liability. She was damned if she was going to do it to Moran—who was, coincidentally, a sergeant to her private.

"Lord Grammayre," Bellusdeo said softly, "Moran is *praevolo*. It has meaning to the Aerians. This concerns the use of the power of the *praevolo*—"

"It concerns the *misuse* of that power," Moran corrected her.

"—and it is both natural and possibly necessary that the *praevolo* be present."

The Hawklord's wings rose and stiffened. "There's a risk—"

"Yes. There is *always* a risk. But she is the natural leader, the natural ruler, of the Aeries."

He started to argue. Stopped, glancing at the other Aerian in the room. Clint's entire posture and attitude made clear that, on some level, Bellusdeo's claim was true.

Clint, however, was not the Hawklord. "If anything happens to her—"

"I wouldn't worry much about that. I'll be there."

"And if anything happens to you?"

"At that point, it won't be my problem." Bellusdeo smiled; it was an almost Leontine smile.

Kaylin, however, wilted, because it would be *her* problem. The Emperor would completely lose it. And it didn't matter. Bellusdeo was going. Moran was going. Kaylin privately thought they'd be stuck with Clint as well—but if Moran rejected him, he'd probably stay put.

Moran, however, said, "It is not necessary for the private to accompany us."

And that touched off an entirely different argument—one over which Kaylin had some control.

CHAPTER 25

Kaylin was given permission to go to the Aerie—probably because she intended to go anyway. Bellusdeo pointed out that Evarrim had arranged the meeting between *Lord Kaylin* and the Arcanist; Kaylin was, in the Dragon's opinion, essential.

Moran believed that her position as *praevolo*—a position she had ignored and all but denied for the entirety of her life—made Kaylin's inclusion unnecessary, but the Hawklord surprised Kaylin by agreeing with the Dragon. Clint did not demand to be included at all, which surprised Kaylin.

She was vastly less surprised when they made their way to the carriage courtyard and Bellusdeo transformed. Moran was not riding the Dragon to the Aerie—an Aerie she had not visited since she'd been injured. It was apparently beneath her dignity. Kaylin was, and if Kaylin was, Severn was, as well. Teela and Tain came along—but Bellusdeo could carry the four of them without any apparent effort. She aimed a grimace over Kaylin's shoulder and Kaylin turned to see what had earned it.

Clint was there. He was not alone. He wasn't wearing the Hawks' tabard, either—but none of the dozen or so Aerians who were standing beside and behind him were. His expression was forbidding.

Moran said, curtly, "I don't need an escort."

Clint said nothing just as curtly, which was a neat trick. Clint, however, had always been of the strong-and-silent variety. The oldest of the Aerians present stepped forward and lifted his wings in a kind of salute. "It is not an escort," he said. "It is an honor guard."

"I *really* don't need an honor guard. You're all Hawks. You're all on duty."

"We are on leave," he replied. "And we will provide the escort you are due. We have not been what we should have been in all the years you have worked in the Halls of Law. That is our shame. We have failed you.

"We are done with failure, *praevolo*. We will be the honor guard your position demands. And it is not, perhaps, merely as an honor guard that we will be necessary. You have faced assassination several times. You will not face it alone again."

Moran's expression was pure sergeant: unfriendly, forbidding and ill pleased.

Teela, however, said to her, "The Hawklord did not demand you remain. You threatened to stand down, if I recall. They are not different, in that regard. They are not on active duty at the moment; they have taken a leave to do what they feel needs to be done. They are acknowledging previous failures in the only good way they can: by refusing to continue to fail.

"I am not, of course, *praevolo*. I am not Aerian. But were I, I would accept what they offer."

"And if another attempt—or worse—is planned?"

"I do not think the Arcanist has any inkling that you will attend that meeting in person," Teela replied.

Moran's wings flicked as she surrendered. She did it gracelessly, in Kaylin's opinion; she certainly didn't actively improve the morale. But it was clear she didn't have to. What the Aerian Hawks wanted from her they now had: permission to *do better*. Permission to offer her the honor that had been conspicuously—Kaylin had not realized how conspicuously until very recently—absent.

There was a lightness to their eyes, an odd majesty to the line of their wings, a clarity to their expressions, that she'd rarely seen. And it came to her, watching them, that the last occasion had been during the defense of the High Halls, in which Aerians had died.

She understood Moran's reluctance then. And she understood that the reluctance was wrong. Moran had claimed the robes, the bracelet and the *flight* of the *praevolo*, and maybe there were responsibilities that came with the claim, one of which was to accept that men and women would be willing to fight and die for her—and that some of them probably would. Die.

People didn't flock to the Chosen the way they flocked to the *praevolo*. Kaylin had, in her childhood, daydreamed of receiving the kind of attention Moran was now receiving— and she was reminded, again, that she'd been an idiot. Daydreams weren't reality. Daydreams could never be reality.

Only when she was a child had she believed that the two could become one. She clambered up on the Dragon's back with Severn's aid, frowning.

"Bellusdeo?"

"Yes?" The Dragon's voice shook the ground.

"Have you gotten bigger?"

"I am not sure that is ever a politic question," Teela pointed out.

"Why?"

"Never mind, kitling."

"What? Am I saying something rude?"

"No," Bellusdeo answered. "It's not rude. I wouldn't advise that you ask that of any of the Barrani—or most mortals over a certain age—that you meet. For some reason I do not understand, they frequently take it poorly."

"And you don't."

"No. But for Dragons, size *is* power."

"The outcaste," Teela said in a cooler voice, "is very unlikely to be present."

Bellusdeo did not reply.

A Dragon and a dozen out-of-uniform Aerians rose from the carriage yard into the open skies. Beneath her feet, Kaylin could see the people in the streets below as they looked up, and up again; several pointed. Not all of the people were aware of what was going on above their heads, but that was understandable; when Kaylin wasn't on duty, she sometimes forgot to look at anything higher than her shoes.

"Are we ready for this?" she asked Teela, shouting to be heard.

"I am."

"You're enjoying it."

"I'm not bored."

"Boredom is underrated," Tain told her. "I've only come to realize it in the last year. I could do with another two decades of quiet before I found it boring."

"I don't like the quiet," Teela replied. "I can be quiet when I'm dead."

"Which is going to be sooner rather than later at the rate Kaylin's been going."

This was hugely unfair. This situation had nothing to do with Kaylin. Not directly. *Why is it always my fault?* she asked Severn.

She could feel his amusement, his affection. *It isn't, of course.*

Then why do they always blame me?

It's like the conversation after dinner the night the Emperor visited. You're safe to tease, and it gives them something in common. All of your friends in the office have always teased you.

Caitlin doesn't.

No, but she's more like a substitute mother. Imagine what Teela would be like if she didn't.

Teela as a mother filled Kaylin with instant dread. *You win.* She fell silent as the Aerie came into view.

From the ground, the Southern Reach looked like a lot of fancy cliff side. Up close—and Kaylin had been a visitor on a handful of occasions, most in her early years at the outskirts of the Hawks—it was more complicated. There were caves, and the caves were natural; she wasn't certain how they'd come to exist, but didn't question it. She didn't really question why there was ground beneath her feet when she patrolled, either.

But the caves had been worked, the way rough stone was; some of the working had been magical in nature. She could see the muted colors of faded sigils. The Reach was divided into social tiers by both centrality and height. The more important your flight, the higher up the cliff face you lived, the single exceptions being the outlying caves, which were almost entirely natural.

Those had been Moran's early home.

The rooms that Helen had provided for Moran had been very much like that early home. Kaylin imagined what Clint's reaction to seeing them would be, and snickered. If he now considered Moran *praevolo*, he'd probably find them insulting or inappropriate.

Or maybe not. Maybe he'd understand that it was where Moran felt most at home. She hadn't really had a home for a long time.

To no one's surprise—or at least not to Kaylin's—the Aerian they were to meet had either residential or meeting rooms at the peak of the Southern Reach. At this height, winged guards patrolled the skies; two of them, armed, headed out to intercept Bellusdeo. When they drew close enough, Kaylin could see that their eyes were Barrani blue—and no surprise there, either. Aerians against a Dragon had about as much chance as an untrained human against a Barrani or Leontine.

These guards were trained, however. They flew maneuvers that were tight, they kept a respectful distance, and they stayed in their patrolling formation.

It did take a bit of time to find an appropriate place for Bellusdeo to land. Bellusdeo wasn't fussed, but the Aerian guards were. Kaylin could almost see the argument the golden Dragon was having on the inside of her head, but she came down on the side of *don't cause unnecessary difficulty with the Imperial Court*. It was probably why they were friends. Bellusdeo had as much difficulty with the restrictions of political life as Kaylin did.

The landing space was, to Kaylin's surprise, well accoutred; it was not a level or two down, as she'd expected.

Severn found this amusing. *How many Dragons are likely to pay a personal visit to the Aerie?*

Oh. She could imagine the Emperor's reaction. The Emperor had no difficulty whatsoever with the restrictions of Imperial political life. He'd probably take offense, and in general, offending the Emperor was otherwise known as suicide.

She was less impressed by the obvious magical protections, and the small dragon, so much a part of her that she could—

and did—forget that he was there when he wasn't actively biting her hair, rose up on his haunches. She thought of his scarf-like posture as his bored Barrani posture. When he sat up, it wasn't generally a good sign.

But she didn't need him to sit up to realize that if the Emperor was accorded the respect due his rank and station, he was also accorded the respect due his power. There was so much magic in this giant room that Kaylin was surprised there was any space for anything normal. Like, say, stone.

Moran came in at the same time as Bellusdeo. She landed very, very lightly on her feet, her injured wings spread as if to imply she didn't require ground. With her came the twelve Hawks.

Greeting them were Aerians Kaylin privately dismissed as the equivalent of Palace Guards. They were, to a man, blue-eyed, but their attention was split evenly between the golden Dragon—now human-sized and encased in scale armor—and the *praevolo*. Whatever had happened to change the way the Hawks saw Moran hadn't made it this far up into the rarified atmosphere.

The two groups—Hawks out of uniform and Palace Guards, by any other name—sized each other up with about the same amount of friendliness their grounded counterparts usually displayed.

None.

But there was no attack and no exchange of insults; each group was aware that bad behavior on their part would reflect poorly on the people they served.

Teela hadn't bothered to ditch her tabard; neither had Tain. Severn was in Hawk gear, as was Kaylin. Moran was *praevolo*; Bellusdeo, Dragon.

Into this room walked an Aerian. He had chosen to enter on the ground, which was unusual; Kaylin wasn't sure if it was a good sign or a bad one. He did have wings; they were high and stiff, his eyes, blue.

The small dragon squawked. Loudly.

Bellusdeo, frowning, looked back at the familiar.

The Aerian who had entered the room looked at the familiar as well, his eyes narrowing, his expression betraying actual surprise. His face was about as warm as the stone floors, and about as animated, otherwise.

The small dragon lifted a wing, almost casually, and laid it against Kaylin's face—without smacking her first.

But the Arcanist lifted a hand as well, and Kaylin threw herself to the side and ducked as the air just above her shoulder burst into blue flame.

As the start to a delicate interaction, it wasn't promising. Kaylin had her hand around the familiar before a second bolt of blue fire was launched, not that it was likely to protect the familiar.

For his part, the familiar roared. Although he was not otherwise in the large form he sometimes adopted, his voice suited it; it was like listening to Dragon rage, up close and personal.

Bellusdeo moved, as well.

Teela, however, raised a brow and lifted only a hand. Kaylin's arms, which were already tingling as if slapped, went numb—as if a sharp, impossible pain spike had passed through them.

Severn's weapon chain was already spinning. The Aerie had very, very large rooms and very, very high ceilings—it was the ideal space for its use.

The only person who didn't move a muscle was Moran. She met the gaze of the Aerian who was clearly the Arcanist with folded arms.

"I suggest you contain yourself," she told him, her voice the kind of loud a sergeant's can get—all volume, no screech. "If you accidentally injure Lord Bellusdeo, the Aerie will be worth less than ash to the Eternal Emperor. The room itself is impressive," she added. "But it's not nearly enough to contain an angry Emperor."

"I don't think it's the Emperor he's afraid of," Bellusdeo added. She sounded so subdued, Kaylin was instantly on her guard. Or more on her guard.

The Aerian's eyes had narrowed into blue slits.

"The familiar," Kaylin told him sharply, "is mine. If you try to harm him again, I'll let him breathe on you."

"And you can stop him from doing so?"

She looked at him as if she thought he was an idiot. Mostly because she did. "Yes. He's eaten dinner with the Emperor. The Emperor, incidentally, didn't panic and attempt to reduce him to blue ash."

"That was not the purpose of that spell."

"Don't bother. The particulars don't matter. If you have some issue with his presence in the Aerie, we can meet on the ground. You've clearly spent some time there recently."

The familiar squawked.

"Do not attempt to harm the Chosen or her familiar," Bellusdeo said, letting a rumble enter her voice. "I will consider it a hostile—and illegal—act, and will be forced to respond. In kind."

The second time the familiar lifted his wing, no one moved—not even Kaylin. Severn's weapon chain was readied, and his back was, broadly speaking, pointed toward the wall. In the Aerie, this would make a difference. No one wanted to fight while retreating here—retreat in the wrong direction and, unless you had wings yourself, the resultant fall would kill you.

The Arcanist had thus far failed to introduce himself. He didn't correct this oversight now. His wings rose enough that Kaylin thought he might take flight, a distinct possibility in this cavern. He held his ground.

Kaylin looked at him. She had expected—or even hoped—that she would see Shadow in him or around him; that the familiar's wings would indicate instant villainy. This didn't happen.

She'd assumed that he'd tried to take out the familiar to protect himself. If the familiar were dead or gone, his wings would reveal nothing. She was, or had been, wrong. The Arcanist had no prior experience with the familiar or his abilities—why would he assume that he could somehow show Kaylin something that shouldn't be seen?

Seen through the familiar's wing, the Aerian looked exactly the same as he did when viewed the normal way. And if he had nothing to fear from the familiar, why had he launched that magical attack?

What he said next surprised her. "How can you carry that *thing* on your shoulder?" He'd recovered enough of what Kaylin assumed was his usual poise to convey disgust with a smattering of outrage.

Kaylin didn't dignify the question with a reply. Instead, she looked at the rest of the room, bristling as it was with occupants. The small dragon didn't generally lift a wing to cover her eyes unless he wanted her to see something. Since it clearly wasn't the Arcanist, her gaze moved on.

It came to rest on one of the Aerian guards. The small dragon crooned in her ear. The man looked Aerian, even seen through the translucent mask. His wings were gray, but not black and not speckled; he was almost as tall as Teela, but that wasn't unusual for Aerians. She wasn't certain what had caught her eye, but something had, and as she stared intently at him, his lips curved in a smile. It was faintly mocking.

And she realized what it was, then: his eyes were the orange-gold of cautious Dragons.

To Kaylin's shock, he turned toward the Arcanist and breathed. Fire cut a swathe through the guards that stood between the Arcanist and the Dragon. She didn't even wonder which Dragon he was—there was only one he could be.

But the fire didn't reach the Arcanist; it killed two Aerians, but failed to kill the other four, because it was met, halted, by a similar fire that pushed it back. Bellusdeo had breathed, as well. Her eyes were now bloodred.

Teela had moved into position between the Dragon and the Arcanist; Kaylin's skin almost screamed in protest as the Barrani Hawk used magic. In her role as a Hawk, she almost never did; magic was confined to small, practical and non-threatening things, like lighting a very dark room.

This was not that magic.

"It's not an illusion," Kaylin shouted. Every word that the Arkon had spoken about outcastes returned to her as she looked at the Dragon-eyed Aerian. For one panicked half second, the rest of the Aerian guards were frozen. When they moved, however, they didn't move to defend the Arcanist they were, in theory, protecting. They moved into a defensive position around the outcaste, making it clear who their leader actually was.

The Arcanist shouted something in Aerian—Kaylin barely caught the gist of it. The Aerian Hawks, however, were hearing their mother tongue, harshly and quickly spoken, and they responded to what they heard. They didn't treat the Arcanist's words as commands. Even if they were of a mind to do so—and Kaylin highly doubted any of them were—they had their priorities.

They'd come to the Aerie as honor guards for the *praevolo*, the real one. In a firefight of this nature, it was around that *praevolo* that the Hawks grouped. This left Kaylin and Severn on their own for the brief moment of time it took Bellusdeo to shed all semblance of her human form. When she roared her rage—with fire—it came from the full throat of a very large, very angry gold Dragon.

The outcaste roared back. His eyes were orange now; they were not the bloodred that spoke of an almost killing frenzy. Whatever the Arkon thought the outcaste wanted—or had wanted—from Bellusdeo, what he would get if he dropped his guard here was death. To give Bellusdeo credit, if it were at all possible, it would be a short, brutal one.

Kaylin hesitated for a fraction of a second longer, and then shouted, "Mandoran! Tell Helen to mirror the Emperor *right now.*" She couldn't hear his response because he was at home—but he'd be watching through Teela's eyes. At the moment, Teela's expression gave nothing away. Tain was to her side, a step back; he was armed with the usual Hawk weapon: a stick.

Teela, however, was armed with something a little more substantial.

Oh, hells.

A *lot* more substantial. Kaylin recognized the sword: it was one of the reputed three Dragonslayers.

Nightshade.

You wish me to pass a message to my brother?

Or to Helen directly. You can see him?

I can see, the fieflord replied, *what you face. I will not tell you that discretion is the better part of valor.*

Don't. I lived that life until I was thirteen and I'd sooner die—

horribly—than go back to it. And he was a large part of that early fear.

The stone flooring cracked beneath the feet of the Aerian who was not Aerian. Orange-eyed, his smile no longer looked lazy or condescending. But when he breathed again—and he did—he wasn't aiming at the Arcanist. He wasn't aiming at the *praevolo*, either.

He was aiming at Kaylin.

She stood her ground, not because she was counting on the familiar, but because she was counting on her partner. He'd set the weapon chain into a slow spin, and it had worked its way up to a fast one; it was a wall of chain and blade. She had no doubt that it would stop the fire from reaching her; it had stopped magical fire before.

Fire hit the moving wall and splashed to either side of it. The rock it hit in that splash sizzled. A second breath broke, as well. The third breath wasn't aimed directly at Kaylin; it was aimed toward the ceiling above Kaylin's head. The ceiling was a long way up, but given the way the rock had sizzled, she didn't think it would be any safer than a direct hit.

And then it wasn't a problem, because Bellusdeo leapt. Something as large as a Dragon, when grounded—and if the cavern was large enough for Aerian flight, it was very, very cramped for Dragon wings—should have been ungainly. Awkward. It shouldn't have had the grace and suppleness of movement that Bellusdeo displayed.

She had been, she had said, a warrior queen. Kaylin could see why.

The outcaste snapped his wings to either side; they extended, and then extended again, their span far larger than an Aerian's. They snapped shut on Bellusdeo's jaws, scraping her scales as if their feathers were made of metal or stone.

His guards leapt into the air; they didn't land. Unlike Bellusdeo, the Aerians didn't find the cavern too confining for actual combat. They weren't stupid enough to think they could take on a Dragon.

She reared back, roared, breathed; the outcaste stood in the stream of her fire, his Aerian face upturned as if to meet her gaze. He was still, silent; fire lapped at his wings before sliding off them, just as fire did off Dragon scales. Or Dragon skin.

One of the Aerian guards shouted, *"Praevolo!"*

He wasn't talking to Moran.

CHAPTER 26

That single word made so many things clear. The Aerian guards would not bend knee to Moran; they didn't recognize her as *praevolo*. They believed the outcaste was *praevolo*; to them, Moran was a pretender, a fraud.

The Aerian Hawks maneuvered in the air as they tightened their formation around Moran. They moved, their flight a weave that implied wall. There were drills and flight formations that were characteristic of the Aerian Hawks, and Kaylin recognized them as they fell into place.

The outcaste's Aerian guards were aiming for Moran, and Kaylin was wingless. There was nothing she could do for the Hawks in the air.

The outcaste lifted wings that were far too large for his current body.

And the familiar roared.

It was a Dragon roar, it occurred beside Kaylin's ear, and before she could react, the small creature had propelled himself off her shoulder with enough force to cause a stumble on Kaylin's part. She lifted a hand to grab him—not the world's smartest move on a good day, which this wasn't—and missed.

He headed straight for Bellusdeo, roaring, his minuscule form home to a voice that would have been impressive even from the Emperor.

Bellusdeo drew up short, skidding across the stone floor; her weight gave her a less easily controlled momentum. Given her size, it should have taken her longer to stop. The outcaste's wings closed in a snap of sound and, oddly, light. The light was multicolored and shifting, as if every color it contained was fighting for dominance. But they closed inches from her Draconic face.

When the outcaste spoke, he spoke in pure Dragon; the world shook. The air moved. Bellusdeo reared up, and up again as her wings spread; she answered in kind.

The caverns took their voices, magnified them, sent them bouncing against the walls and the ceiling. And if Kaylin couldn't understand the words, she almost understood the tone of them.

The outcaste was offering Bellusdeo something. Kaylin wasn't entirely certain that the closing of his great wings had been meant to harm her; she thought it might have been meant to restrain her, to hold her in place, while he spoke. The intervention of the familiar meant that there were no restraints; she reared, and her left wing clipped a low-flying Aerian—but not a Hawk. The Aerian in question was thrown against the closest wall, and did not immediately rise again.

She had always understood that Dragons were death, but on a visceral level, Bellusdeo was just…Bellusdeo, to Kaylin. It was jarring, to watch her so casually dispose of a random enemy as if he were a fly. Or a mosquito.

Severn eyed the Aerians; he continued to spin the chain, but shifted the direction of the spinning wall as he made his way to the only other people who were trapped on the ground: Teela and Tain. Teela was eyeing the sky with frank apprehension, which also surprised Kaylin.

It shouldn't have. She gripped a dagger in hands that were locked with tension, and turned away from the Dragons and the Aerians that were in the air. One Aerian wasn't.

The Aerian Arcanist stood behind Teela. He hadn't once attempted to fly. Kaylin had thought, initially, that his choice to walk might be political—the act of a gracious host. Now she wasn't so certain. He was pale, his blue eyes narrowed; he looked, as she approached him, like he'd had way too much to drink and way too little time to sleep it off.

The familiar roared again. Neither Bellusdeo nor the outcaste responded as his voice rebounded off stone walls, stone heights; nor did they respond as he turned, at last, toward the entrance of the Aerie, flapping in place while the shadows of Aerians cut across his small body.

Limned in a kind of white nimbus, two familiar figures joined him: Mandoran and Annarion. They hovered a moment in the air, wingless but weightless, before they caught sight of Kaylin and Severn. They both avoided meeting Teela's gaze, which was pretty much all glare. Or at least that's what Kaylin assumed they were doing. She was wrong, as it happened. They were staring at the outcaste.

And the outcaste turned the attention that had been focused so completely on Bellusdeo toward the two new arrivals. He fell silent, then; utterly silent. His wings stilled. He might have been made of flesh-colored stone, he moved so little.

Mandoran gained instant weight; Annarion lost it. They parted in midair as a focused beam of dark fire erupted across the exact position they had previously occupied. The outcaste's eyes were red, his expression wild as he breathed again; he forgot the Aerians, or perhaps didn't care about their survival.

She understood that he wouldn't care about the Hawks—they were too mortal and slight to damage him without preparation. But the Aerians that had served him, the Aerians that had called him *praevolo*, were caught in the tail of this oddly colored flame, and it devoured them in an instant.

And as it did, the outcaste grew in size.

He had not shed his Aerian form, although his wings were almost Draconic at this point. They still had feathers, but the feathers glimmered as if metallic, as if scales had somehow been warped and transformed in a very specific way.

Kaylin turned toward Teela and the Arcanist who sheltered behind her.

"I told them not to come." The Barrani Hawk didn't shrug; her jaw was set in a very hard line, her eyes were almost indigo. Tain looked pained at their arrival, but not surprised, or rather, not surprised at them. He was worried about Teela.

So was the outcaste, because Teela drew her very big sword. Kaylin could almost hear the sword's name in the scrape of metal leaving sheath; it felt syllabic. The Barrani Hawk, the only one who was a Lord of the High Court, stepped forward, away from the Arcanist; her partner did the same.

Kaylin took her place. There wasn't a lot she could do about Dragons, Dragon outcastes or winged combat; the Hawks weren't generally supplied with ranged weaponry, and even if they were, her ability to draw a bow or aim it was laughable, if one took the weaponsmaster at his word.

Bellusdeo roared.

The outcaste roared—and breathed.

The familiar added his voice to theirs.

Mandoran, damn it, laughed.

And Kaylin turned to the Arcanist. "You can't fly, can you?" she asked.

The Arcanist was stiff, silent, possessed of the natural hauteur that came from a life of power and a lack of privation. It had clearly been dented badly sometime in the recent past.

"I have wings."

"Yes—but they're not doing anything. You can't fly."

A whistle sounded in the air above and behind them; it was high and piercing, which it pretty much needed to be to be heard over the Dragons.

"What," the Aerian demanded of Kaylin, "did you bring here?"

She laughed, although most of what fueled that laughter was tension and outrage. "You're asking that of me? You have a Dragon outcaste who lives in *Ravellon* in your Aerie—in your personal damn guard—and you're asking that of *me*?"

"They'll destroy the landing," he replied. As a reply, it sucked.

"Fine. Bellusdeo won't let us fall."

She wouldn't bet much on his chances. Neither, apparently, would he. He appeared to be making a decision. "No. I cannot fly. My powers have been curtailed, of late."

"Because Moran has the bracelet."

He said nothing, but tensed. The outcaste roared.

And the roar that answered was not, in fact, Bellusdeo's. The great shadow of the Emperor's indigo form intercepted all the natural light that normally poured into the mouth of the cave. Kaylin didn't need to look to see that his eyes—which were the size of her head—were a bloodred.

They were the same color, after all, as Bellusdeo's.

"We must retreat," the Arcanist said. Out and down were much closer than in, at this point—but none of them could fly. "The Emperor is not going to be happy to see your confederate's sword."

"Probably not," Kaylin replied. "But it's not like he doesn't know she owns it. And she's not going to be his big concern at the moment."

No. That was reserved for the outcaste, who at last shed the Aerian form and its resultant wings. He seemed to absorb all darkness, all natural shadow in the cavern, as he shifted into the Draconic form; he was ebony to the Emperor's indigo and Bellusdeo's gold.

The Aerians who had served him froze for a moment—but only a moment. Clearly, he had never gone full Dragon in their sight before. But their faith in him, such as it was, appeared to be unshaken. They obviously believed he was capable of miracles.

They had called him *praevolo*.

He wasn't. That was owned by Moran.

"You can't fly," Kaylin once again said to the Arcanist. "How far can you run?"

The Arcanist wasn't stupid. As the Emperor roared, as the outcaste roared back, he answered in the only practical way possible. He ran. Kaylin wasn't far behind; Severn took and held the rear. The weapon chain could interrupt Dragon fire; when the wall was spinning, there wasn't much in the way of magic that could get through it.

The one great thing about having Dragons and Barrani

as friends? They were far, far less likely to die than Kaylin herself. She could, without guilt, worry about her own survival when the breathing started.

"You are so boring," a familiar voice said as Mandoran stepped into the hall. He raised one brow. "We're going to have problems," he continued, as if he were talking about light afternoon rain.

"More problems than outcaste Dragons?"

"Well, no. But..."

"Mandoran. If you've got something to say, say it now."

"He's more like us."

She almost tripped over her feet.

"I mean, not like us, exactly. But...he's a Dragon the way we're Barrani." He winced. "Sorry. Sedarias is pissed off. Also, she hates it when I think in Elantran. Speak in Elantran," he amended. He winced again. "She says I don't think at all."

Kaylin had only briefly met Sedarias, and was grateful that Sedarias was in the West March and not here. On the other hand, she couldn't imagine the composed, regal and controlled Barrani woman making a hash of things. Or getting stuck in a wall.

"Skip the reasons Sedarias thinks you're an idiot, or we'll be here all day. What is he doing?"

"Annarion is trying to head him off—but he can move the way we move, and, um, he's had more practice at it."

"You did it for centuries."

"Yes—then. But we didn't have to come back. We didn't have to interact with the rest of the world or its many cages. He does, and can. He can do it much more easily than we can."

"Meaning he won't get stuck in walls."

Mandoran grimaced. "Not accidentally, no."

"Why did you say we've got a problem?"

"Because he's clearly been here for a while." This time, Mandoran turned to the Arcanist, who was ash gray. Or maybe gray-green. In either case, the colors didn't suit anyone who wasn't already dead.

Kaylin was not slow. "What are we facing?"

"How well do you fly?"

"Not at all."

"Then you're facing imminent disaster. The whole of the floor here—beneath our feet—is permeable. It exists in a state similar to us."

The Arcanist, however, said, "There was a reason I wished to retreat. If you can shut up for five minutes, you will be in less danger of imminent disaster."

They ran.

"Annarion is informing Bellusdeo of the danger. Bellusdeo will tell the Emperor." Mandoran frowned and added, "Annarion doesn't mind the Dragon we live with. I think he still holds a grudge against the Eternal Emperor. Where's small and squawky?"

"With the rest of the Dragons."

"I think you want him with you." Mandoran had stopped just short of the arch that led to another room. There was no door; in general, the Aeries had few closed doors.

Her skin, and the marks that adorned most of it, didn't react as if magic was present. The Arcanist crossed the threshold before he staggered to a stop. He considered this room safe. And it probably was, if you were the Arcanist.

"Mandoran?"

"The room should be safe for you." His voice was dead

neutral, his expression unusually grim. "I've spent enough of this week trapped in a wall—and that was my own fault. If it's all the same to you, I'm not going to fall to my death if the floors become brittle, porous or nonexistent."

"If Teela is telling you to stay with me, tell her to bite me."

"She says she'd rather slap you, but can't oblige at the moment." He was staring through the arch at the Arcanist, who had unfolded from a stumbling crouch. In this room, he looked like Kaylin expected an Arcanist would: his natural arrogance reasserted itself.

Kaylin turned to the Arcanist. "You sent the man to talk to Margot." It wasn't a question.

The Arcanist nodded. There was a mirror at his back; it was a tall, rectangular mirror whose surface was entirely reflective.

"The mirror has no connection to the outer world," the Arcanist said before she could ask. "It does not connect, in any way, to the mirror lattice."

"Let me guess. It's not secure enough for you."

He nodded again, his expression betraying a flicker of surprise. "I sent the man, as you call him, to talk to Margot, yes."

"And you sent him with the bracelet, the collar, the feather."

"Yes."

"Which you shouldn't have had."

"Not even the pretender could wear that bracelet for long," the Arcanist replied with a thin, sharp smile. "He could wear it, however, and he did, when he quietly made the claim that he was *praevolo*. He claimed to be illegitimate, as Moran dar Carafel is. As proof of that claim, he was tested—but the test was private, and witnessed by only a handful of the Court.

The bracelet did not destroy him, but he was unwilling to wear it for long; he did not wish, he said, to cause a civil war. He did not have the wings; Moran did. It is my belief that the wearing did harm him, but I came to it slowly."

"How long has he been considered *praevolo*?"

The Arcanist took time to reply; he was clearly moving into a political mind-set. "Just under a year."

"You knew he wasn't."

"No, *Private*, I did not." This was said with more vehemence. Kaylin was genuinely surprised. Arcanists weren't generally given to superstitious or religious thought, and in many ways, that's what the *praevolo* seemed to engender.

"Moran had the wings."

Silence.

"She's had the wings from birth."

"We were not immediately aware of her birth." The words sounded as if they had been dragged from him by main force. They were interrupted, twice, by roaring that shook a floor that was theoretically stable.

"And when you became aware of it, you tried to have her killed." She folded her arms. "Who is her father?"

His brows rose; the distasteful question had surprised him, and not in a good way. "Perhaps this is not the time to have this conversation," he pointed out as roaring grew.

Mandoran said, "It's safe, for the moment."

"That was pain."

"Yes. Teela sliced off part of a toe. She survived. Some of her hair didn't."

"What?"

"He breathed on her. It was not the composition of normal Dragon breath. Her sword cut through most of it—but not all."

"And Tain?"

"Tain has pulled back to a safe distance. He hasn't been trained to fight Dragons up close."

"Teela has."

"Yes. She's the only one of us who's had the actual experience. Technically, she and Annarion were trained the same way."

"Is Annarion—"

"Fighting, yes. But not the same way Teela is." At Kaylin's expression, he added, "You remember how he fought the ancestors?"

She nodded slowly.

"The outcaste is like us. He is in the Aerie, he is fighting the Emperor. But he is in a space that overlaps the Aerie, and he is—" Mandoran shook his head. "It's too hard to explain clearly."

"He's phased?"

"That'll do. Annarion is fighting him in an Aerie that overlaps the one you can see."

"And you're just standing here?"

He folded his arms and grinned his unrepentant, not-bored grin. "I'm keeping an eye on you. Teela seems to feel it's necessary, given the role your familiar is playing."

"...My familiar."

"Yes."

"Let me guess. He's no longer small and squawky."

"No longer small, no. But very squawky."

Kaylin.
Definitely no longer small.
There is a danger in the Aerie.
There are a lot of dangers in the Aerie at the moment. Is there one I can do something about?

Silence. *Bellusdeo has been injured.*

This was not a surprise; it wasn't the first time it had happened. One didn't throw oneself in raging fury at a Dragon without injury—even if one were a Dragon.

It is not a normal injury. It is, to her mind, minor; she is too focused on destruction.

What do you mean, not normal?

Shadow, Kaylin. It is subtle; it is not slight. If you cannot heal her quickly...

What is the Shadow doing?

I do not know. But it is the outcaste's power.

Kaylin swore. In Leontine. The Arcanist clearly didn't understand the finer points of Leontine.

Mandoran's lips quirked further. He looked smug.

The Arcanist, however, looked confused—and, if possible, frightened. "What is that creature you carried in with you?"

"My familiar."

"And you are a witch, now, to have a familiar?"

This was not the usual reaction of Arcanists to the concept of a familiar. "A witch?" she asked. "No. Maybe. I'm sorry— I'm not familiar with the word the way you're using it."

"That creature is dangerous. He is as dangerous as the pretender."

Kaylin would have argued if she'd had any ground to stand on. "Fine. But at the moment, he's on my side."

"And what side is that?"

"In the Southern Reach? Moran dar Carafel's side. The *Illumen praevolo.*"

The Arcanist's eyes narrowed as he studied her. "Do you even understand what the *praevolo* is?"

"I understand Sergeant dar Carafel," Kaylin shot back.

"And she's the *praevolo*. What that means to the rest of you doesn't matter."

"It matters," he said, and his voice was unaccountably bitter. "You guessed that I cannot fly. Most of my kin have not drawn the same conclusion. Those who serve as *my* guards know, of course, because they serve *him*."

"Fine. I have to go back."

He stared at her as if she'd lost her mind. "Unless the marks of the Chosen grant you invulnerability—or flight—you will die. You will accomplish nothing else!"

She turned to Severn. "Stay here. Have whatever conversation is necessary. Bellusdeo's been injured."

Severn nodded.

"I'll be back as soon as I can."

Geography had never been Kaylin's strong point, and the run to the Arcanist's so-called safe space had been long and not entirely straightforward. She was saved from panic by Mandoran, who was still lounging against the wall when she ran out of the room.

"Where do you think you're going?"

"Back," was her curt reply. "I'd appreciate it if you could get me to Bellusdeo."

His brows rose in obvious surprise. "You want to *go back*?"

"Yes."

"Teela's going to have a fit."

"I'll deal with Teela's temper. Can you get me back there?"

He nodded and held out a hand. Kaylin stared at it, almost confused. But in the end she took it.

"Hold on," he advised her.

"To what?"

"Me, and anything you don't want to lose."

★ ★ ★

She'd expected Mandoran to lead her back down the series of halls to the open landing area in which they'd first arrived. Mandoran, however, had other ideas. The "hold on" part developed urgency with the first step Mandoran took, because he wasn't precisely stepping *on* anything. She remembered that he had managed to get stuck in a wall—a concept which had been both boggling and hilarious.

It was a lot less funny now.

"You can do this," he whispered. "Severn couldn't. Teela can't. But you can."

"How do you know that?"

"Instinct?" He grinned. "You're the Chosen. You can carry the familiar on your shoulder—and frankly, that would break mine. Or Annarion's."

"He doesn't weigh anything."

"That's what you tell yourself. You can open your eyes."

"I'd really rather not," Kaylin told him. She could feel that he was in motion. That she was in motion, as well. But she couldn't feel anything—anything at all—beneath her feet. "You're sure you know what you're doing?"

"Funny, Teela's screaming that in my other ear. The figurative one."

Kaylin's lips twitched. She opened her eyes a crack. She could see the walls of the Aerie. The halls, the height of the ceilings. They were a lot closer than they had been on the way here. And they were colorful. The heights were illuminated, but not with what she thought of as natural light, that being sunlight; they glowed. She could see a thread of multicolored light above her and beneath her. The beneath part was a long way down.

"You're following the light?"

Mandoran nodded. She glanced at him; his face was set in concentration. She thought about getting stuck in a wall again. She'd thought it was funny because he'd clearly survived it. She was not at all certain that she would, or could. Whatever Mandoran was, she wasn't.

"I'm not sure you're going to be able to get through to the Dragon," he said. "They seem to have the outcaste cornered." The way he said this was bad.

"What do you mean, 'seem'?"

"It's hard to see the way you do," he replied. "It's hard not to see what you can't see. They see the Dragon form— and he has that. But I think they *only* see the Dragon form. He's like us," Mandoran repeated. "Like me and Annarion. The Dragon form *is* there, and it's bloody dangerous—but it's not the only danger here. Not even close."

She heard the outcaste roar.

She knew it was the outcaste, because while some of that roar had the timbre of Dragon rage—or triumph, which was more disturbing—there was *more* to it; she heard it as a chorus of voices. The Dragon was, no surprises there, the loudest of that chorus—but there were other voices blended into it. She could pull Leontine out of it; she could pull something like ancient Barrani. She could hear the screeching battle cry of the Aerians. She could hear something that sounded a lot like her own voice.

And they overlapped; they existed in one space, at one time, in harmony. A command.

She felt the air grow cold. Or maybe that was just her.

"You heard him?"

"Did you understand a word that he was saying?"

"Yes. All of them. We're trying to get the Aerie evacuated."

"Who's *we*?"

"Moran. Moran is *praevolo*, and she's sending the warning out to her people."

She wanted to ask him why they needed to evacuate the Aerie—but she knew. At heart, she knew. The outcaste had summoned the Shadows, and the Shadows—in the distant heart of Ravellon—had heard.

CHAPTER 27

Do you even understand what the praevolo *is?*

Did she?

She understood what she'd heard, but was aware she hadn't heard all of it. Even if she had, she probably couldn't reconcile it with the Moran that she'd known for years. She knew the title had significance for the Aerians. Clint had convinced her of that, not in words, but in actions. The way he treated Moran right now was almost embarrassing for the sergeant.

Kaylin had sympathy. She would have found it excruciating, herself. When you worshipped someone, you placed a burden on them. You expected them to live up to your ideals, expected them to be worthy of your worship. And who could do that?

Not Kaylin. She was uncomfortable when people recognized her marks and called her Chosen, because she knew they had expectations of her, even if she had no idea what they were. She meant something to them—but actually, no. Her *marks* meant something. Her *marks* defined her.

And Moran was defined by her wings.

Kaylin could see her take flight. She shouldn't have been able to see any such thing. There were oddly colored walls between her and the Aerian—but those walls were like windows where Moran, and only Moran, was concerned. Kaylin could see her. She could see her wings.

And her wings were fire, her wings were air, her wings were gold and silver and platinum. They were larger than any natural Aerian wings; they reminded Kaylin, in span, of the wings of the pretender, the outcaste. But only in span. In no other way were they alike.

And she was suddenly certain that the Aerians could see Moran take flight. That they could feel the thrill of it, the joy of it, and the desperate need for it. But Moran didn't tell them to flee, didn't tell them to evacuate their homes.

"I don't think Moran is evacuating the Aerie," she told Mandoran.

"Then what is she doing?"

"…Flying. Now shut up and get me to Bellusdeo."

Getting close to Bellusdeo was almost impossible. Mandoran hadn't exaggerated: the Emperor and the golden Dragon had cornered the outcaste. Gold and indigo surged forward and back against a scaled, black background. The outcaste was enormous. Kaylin had never seen him so large. His wings had grown, and grew again as he raised them; the halls were the color of night.

And she realized that she was seeing him as Mandoran saw him; she wasn't certain why.

"You're with me," he told her. "And it is *really difficult* to keep you here. I need to let you off."

She nodded, and felt stone slam into her feet, as if she'd been dropped from a moderate height. She was already bending into the drop, trying to control it.

Tain appeared almost instantly.

"I need to get to Bellusdeo," she shouted. She had to shout. If he'd been mortal, he wouldn't have heard, regardless.

He looked even more dubious than Mandoran had.

"She's been injured."

"She's given better than she's received."

"She's been injured by Shadow—I think the outcaste is deliberately fighting a delaying action. He wants it to *take effect*."

Tain paled. He didn't ask if she was certain. He didn't have time. The familiar swooped down and landed to one side of her. He had to—he was the size of a Dragon.

She didn't try to mount him. She couldn't reach Bellusdeo on his back. He seemed to understand this; he didn't speak. Nor did he attempt to place a wing over her eyes—at this size, he'd probably break her cheekbones. Instead, he took to the air, and when he'd gained enough height, he reached down for her with very large claws.

She dangled above the floor of the cavern, which now looked like normal rock. The odd glow of light that Mandoran appeared to have followed had vanished. She could no longer see the Barrani; she couldn't see Annarion, either. She half wished large and majestic was his normal small and squawky size.

I cannot be, he replied. *There is too much here to contain.*

He was talking about the darkness that Kaylin could no longer see.

Yes. Mandoran is perceptive. He sees what is there. And he is not entirely wrong: The outcaste Dragon and Teela's chosen kin have similarities. But they are not the same.

"Did he just call Shadow?"

Yes, Kaylin. The Towers will prevent most of those from obeying that call.

Kaylin hesitated.

The familiar frowned. Or rather, she felt as if he had frowned; she couldn't see his face. She couldn't see any of him except for the claws across her shoulders. He was attempting to maneuver himself above the golden Dragon. Kaylin didn't actually give much for her chances if she was dropped onto the Dragon's back without the Dragon's permission.

She could scream her lungs out and not get Bellusdeo's attention at the moment. The golden Dragon was practically berserk. Her wings were high, and she used them to effect against the Aerians who had served as guards to the outcaste. The Hawks stayed well away from her. They'd seen her fight, and they knew she could take care of herself.

But she broke the other Aerians with a wing slam, and Kaylin wasn't going to fare any better if she couldn't get the Dragon's attention. She was afraid now.

She was afraid because, carried as she was by the familiar, her vision had shifted. The shift was subtle, and entirely unlike having a small wing draped over her eyes; she saw the cavern as a cavern, she saw the outcaste as a Dragon; she saw a gold Dragon, an indigo Dragon—and in the distance, she could see two Dragons hovering. There wasn't space for them to join the fight without causing trouble for Bellusdeo and the Emperor, but she could almost *see* their anxiety.

She could see some Aerians. She could no longer see Moran; she assumed that Moran was deeper in the Aerie, and at this point, Moran wasn't her problem.

Bellusdeo was. She could see the wound Bellusdeo had taken. It wasn't, as Mandoran had said, a significant wound. Bellusdeo had taken worse in the fight above the High Halls—and that injury *had* slowed her down. This one? She'd barely notice it, and clearly hadn't.

But Kaylin noticed it. She could see it, not as a wound—

although it did bleed—but as a net, a thing that was spreading slowly, subtly, from the point of entry into the rest of Bellusdeo's body. She had said that the outcaste was fighting a delaying action; it had been a visceral hunch. It was fact now.

Whatever he'd wanted from Bellusdeo all those centuries ago, whatever he'd wanted when Bellusdeo had first appeared as a Dragon above Elantra, he still wanted.

And Kaylin was certain that whatever he wanted for Bellusdeo, she didn't. She needed to touch the golden Dragon *now*. And she needed to survive it. She wasn't at all certain that she could accomplish the first and guarantee the second—but if she died, she couldn't heal the wound.

I can help, the familiar said.

How?

What Mandoran and Annarion do, I can do.

Yes, but I can't—

You are with me, Kaylin. You are part of the world that I touch. Mandoran's clothing does not remain behind when he transitions; Annarion's weapons do not disappear.

She'd never thought about that before.

Your marks are glowing.

I know. She hesitated. She'd felt this before: the tingling, and the weight. *I think I'm about to lose some of them.* Even as she thought it, marks began to lift themselves from her skin; they passed through the cloth that usually hid them from public view without tearing anything.

They did not cohere; they traveled slowly out from Kaylin, their trajectory affected by the movement of the dragon familiar, as if they were simply large, golden landmarks, drifting weightless in the currents of a room that was such a fury of sound there should have been gales.

Kaylin flinched as Bellusdeo's wing rose and swept in a scythe of motion toward the familiar.

Blink, he told Kaylin.

She had, of course, attempted to throw herself out of the way. She hadn't received any training in aerial combat—beyond witnessing it when she could sneak into the Aerie in the Halls—and her survival instincts were honed for ground work. The dragon familiar, however, had both of her shoulders in his figurative hands; throwing herself out of the way had done precisely nothing.

Get ready, he said while she was trying to remember to breathe. The great, slashing arc of Bellusdeo's wing should have sent her flying in the opposite direction—at best. It seemed to pass through her instead, but she felt it anyway.

Yes, I'm sorry. There will be bruising. I do not think anything is broken.

He roared. He roared, and Kaylin vibrated with the sound, the sensation of sound. It was like, and unlike, the usual Dragon roars. The familiar's voice caused the floating runes to vibrate in a way the regular Dragon roars didn't.

"Kaylin!" She turned, or tried, as she heard Mandoran's voice.

The Aerian guards that had survived were now aiming for her.

"Can everyone see me?" she asked the familiar, as she was jerked to the side to avoid becoming a large pincushion for spears.

No.

"But they can?"

Demonstrably. I believe they are aware of what you intend. How much injury are you willing to risk?

"Just get me down to Bellusdeo."

As you wish. There was a pause, a lurch, and something that felt a lot like an uncontrolled drop, as the familiar obeyed. *But remember, Kaylin—there is always a cost.*

She accepted the cost—whatever it was—as she landed. The dragon familiar's claws clung, for one moment longer, to her shoulders as Bellusdeo bucked at the sudden addition of an unfamiliar weight; Kaylin screamed her lungs out just to stop the Dragon from breaking her.

And even in her rage, Bellusdeo somehow heard it. Kaylin wasn't certain how, and didn't question it, because she didn't have time. Her hands descended to the flat, hard surface of golden scales—scales that were a little too warm to be comfortable, but not hot enough to scald or burn.

"Mandoran—"

The black Dragon breathed. His fire was a focused beam, more like a stream of liquid than breath, and it was aimed in its entirety at Private Kaylin Neya. But the familiar had collapsed in on himself; he was small again, and he was perched stiffly on Kaylin's shoulder; the stream of fire split to either side of Kaylin as if she were a rock and it were water.

And that was as much as she had time for. She focused on Bellusdeo's so-called minor injury, cursing the golden Dragon as she did.

I heard that, Bellusdeo said. The healing built a bridge between them; it was like, and unlike, a True Name bond. And it was the single biggest reason why immortals usually refused to be healed.

Sorry.

You are not.

Well, no, I'm not. He goaded you. He tried to enrage you. It was just as much an attack as his fire or anything else about it— and you let him. My drillmaster would have eaten you for lunch if he'd seen you do that.

Oh?

If he could enrage us, we got the worst dressing-down ever. Hawks—and Swords—can't afford to let their anger or their tempers decide the battle. Other people, yes—but we wear the damn tabard. We lose control, and the tabard suffers. The Hawks suffer. Now can you shut the hells up and let me heal you?

Bellusdeo was the only immortal Kaylin knew who would. She didn't like it—none of the immortals did—but a lot of her dislike was measured in the cost to Kaylin, and not the exposure of her own secrets, her own interior life.

I have nothing to hide now—because I have nothing. I am not Emperor. I am not the leader of my flight. I am not the Queen of the mortals. I have—

Maggaron. And me. Now—

There. She'd found the point of entry. And she felt the Shadow as if it were in her literal hands; it was cold enough to freeze. It was sharp enough to cut. And it did both.

The power that had been funneled, slowly and subtly, into the slight wound Bellusdeo had taken became fully focused in an instant. It was no longer attempting to lay down a structure to support itself within the golden Dragon; it was trying to remove Kaylin.

She shut her teeth, hard, to muffle the sounds the pain caused. The Dragons were continuing to roar, continuing to fight—but Bellusdeo had, if gracelessly, allowed the Emperor to take the forefront in their two-pronged attack.

And I resent it.

Kaylin heard the golden Dragon at a great distance. Everything was at a great distance. She could no longer see or hear her familiar. She could no longer see or hear anything. No, she thought, that wasn't entirely true. She could see Shadow. She could see darkness. She could see the glimmer of light that implied that color was dangerous. And she could hear a word, a whisper of a word, as if it were being repeated, out of sync, by a chorus of ragged voices. Ragged, desperate voices.

She remembered, then. She had seen the outcaste before. She had seen his *Name*.

And she couldn't hold it. She couldn't hold enough of it to use it; it was too large. It wasn't really a word; it wasn't a paragraph, or even a page. It was a whole damn book. She might be able to tell someone else what the book was about—but to repeat it, word for word, with intent and will?

Not a chance.

She wondered what happened to those who tried to use the True Name of someone who was, in the end, more powerful than they were.

Nothing good, Ynpharion said, startling in the sudden appearance of his voice. His name, she knew. She could speak it, call it, use it.

You could, he agreed. *You are both stronger and weaker than you think. Do* not *try to speak his name if you cannot contain even the shape of it.*

What'll happen?

You will be his. The name is a bridge, Kaylin. It is a contested bridge. When you have knowledge of the name, you bring an army across it. If you engage the powerful, they come with their own army. There is no guarantee that you will win that fight, and if you lose—the bridge still exists.

She thought the outcaste knew this. He was probably reminding her of his name on purpose. Because she'd be desperate. Or overconfident. And, in truth, she was one of those things. But when faced with Dragons and immortals, she'd never, ever been the other. She had been so far down the bottom of so many hierarchies, the people at the top had probably never been aware of her existence.

That's how she'd survived. And she intended to survive now.

Ynpharion, who had a lot to gain if she died, approved. Then again, he probably considered most of mortality only slightly more important than earthworms.

Less. The Consort, however, considers you necessary to our people.

But you don't agree.

What I think doesn't matter. She has my Name. This was said with pride. *And even if she did not, what she considered a necessity would move me regardless. She is the Lady. She is the mother of our people. And she is concerned.*

You're telling her everything that's happening here?

Yes. She wishes to know. And your control over what you reveal is deplorable. It takes more effort not *to hear you than the inverse. If you intend to contest the outcaste, do not do it with his name. Not yet, and in my opinion—*

Which I haven't asked for.

—not ever.

The part of Kaylin that sometimes said, *Oh, yeah? Take this*, reared its ugly head. She squashed it. Just because Ynpharion was condescending and arrogant didn't mean he was wrong.

She felt Shadow surge beneath her hands; she saw the slender, subtle lines of it withdraw from where they'd spread in Bellusdeo's body. If it had been because of her healing, she would have been happy. It wasn't. They were regrouping, changing the line of defense and offense. All of that line was now Kaylin, but the power itself was still anchored in Bellusdeo's body.

In her blood.

Bellusdeo wasn't particularly happy about this. *Let go of me.*

Kaylin shook her head and willed herself to ignore the increasingly frantic Dragon. If Bellusdeo wanted to, she could shrug—with some force—and shove Kaylin off her back. Short of that, Kaylin wasn't going anywhere until she was done.

This Shadow had no will of its own. It wasn't inert, exactly, but it was a tool; it moved at the will of the outcaste. He could direct it, and defend against the attacks of two Dragons, without apparent effort.

Kaylin's marks were a steady, almost blinding gold. Her skin burned with the heat of the light shed. But they were words. They weren't a net, the way the outcaste's Shadow was. They had the power inherent in True Words. But the nature of True Words wasn't elastic. It wasn't malleable the same way Shadow was.

That was the strength of it: it wasn't malleable *by* Shadow, either. But she felt the tendrils of Shadow as if they were needles; they pierced her skin, bit into her flesh and expanded like grappling hooks. She reminded herself that she wanted this. The more the Shadow focused on her, the less there was in Bellusdeo.

She had no idea what the outcaste had intended for her roommate; she assumed it wasn't good.

"Kaylin, what in the hells are you *doing*?" Mandoran shouted.

The small dragon—and he was small again—squawked just as loudly in her ear. She didn't answer either of them. Shadow had spread up, through the palms of her shaking hands. She could no longer let go of it, even if she wanted to. It had not, however, entirely let go of Bellusdeo.

Kaylin said, "I'm sorry, this is going to hurt." She wasn't certain if Bellusdeo would hear her or not. Focusing through her own pain, she looked at shapes: specifically, the Dragon's and her own. The injured body knew its correct shape, its correct state. But the transformed flesh didn't; Shadow changed the base state. It changed the concept of healthy. What might remain in its wake as its new, best self was not what had existed before the incursion.

This was true of Bellusdeo.

It was also true of Kaylin. Changes were being made in the flesh of her hands, in the length of her fingers, in the color of her skin. They occurred instantly, the way wounds did when your opponent was armed with an edged weapon. The outcaste didn't care what happened to Kaylin.

But this implied that he did care what happened to Bellusdeo; that the changes wrought in her would be subtle and careful and deliberate. What he wanted from Kaylin was her death, which was the opposite of what she wanted. It hadn't always been.

She absorbed his Shadow almost by default, allowing it to enter; she dampened her resistance slightly while she worked to isolate it. She did not want to have to cut off her hands— but she wanted to free Bellusdeo of its taint, and there was really only one way to do that.

She removed a chunk of the Dragon's flesh.

Bellusdeo did not roar, but Kaylin could feel the Dragon shudder beneath her. She could feel her own power struggling to replace what she had removed. The Shadow did not immediately react. The outcaste had yet to notice what she had done. At any other time, she would have found this interesting.

Not now. Now, she wrenched her hands up, and free, of Bellusdeo.

All of the Shadow was now hers. No, that wasn't right: it was in her, but it wasn't *of* her. On the very, very few occasions she had managed to hold the name of fire in her mind for long enough to light a bloody candle—when lighting one the normal way would take minutes at best—the fire had been no part of her. It had responded to her, but it hadn't invaded her.

If Shadow was like fire—or any of the other elements—it was necessary to maintain control. But control in this case was the outcaste's, not her own.

There was, however, one flaw with this. Shadow was unlike fire, or the rest of the elemental powers. To control fire, she had to know its name, and its name was the whole of it, at greater and lesser sizes.

Shadow was not part of Evanton's garden. Shadow was not part of the Keeper's duties or responsibilities. Shadow had no name, no central, single truth at its core upon which all other truths about it were built.

To the familiar, she shouted, "Get me away from Bellusdeo!"

He shifted out of the small form without materially altering his position on her shoulder. What should have broken or crushed that shoulder made no difference at all. He was Dragon-sized, but he did not fill space the way natural Dragons did. And yet he was solid enough to grip her shoulders in his feet, and solid enough to remove her from the complicated chaos of Dragons at war.

She trusted that he wouldn't drop her, and that was as much thought as she could now spare. She had the Shadow within her hands, and within her arms, and it was no longer trying to spread: instead, it had begun its act of transformation. She wasn't certain that she could cut off her own hands. If she *could* manage that, she wasn't certain she could regrow them. She could reattach limbs, if she was on the scene in time—but she had never regrown a missing appendage before.

She cursed the Emperor—silently—and the Hawklord, then. They frowned *heavily* on experimentation with healing powers. They allowed her to use them only under the condition that they not be made aware of them; their cooperation was entirely in the way they turned a blind eye.

None of that was helpful now.

But the marks on her arms were. If the flesh to which they were attached on most days was being transformed in some fashion, these words weren't. They were inert, immovable. The Shadow didn't touch them—but it did try. She felt tendrils break, needlelike, from her forearms to wrap themselves around the runes.

The light of the marks dimmed slowly.

The color of the Shadow didn't change.

She knew the moment the outcaste realized what she'd done because he roared in raw fury. No other sound in the cavern was as solid, as all-encompassing, as his voice; she vibrated with it. He collided with the Emperor in a sudden physical rush; Kaylin heard the clangor of scales colliding with scales, all but indistinguishable from the sound of a sword doing the same.

She could hear only one such sound, and she had a pretty good guess which sword it was.

The Shadow itself continued its strange incursion. It hurt a lot less, which was probably a bad sign overall. The familiar dropped her somewhere near Mandoran, and away from the wings and tails of the Dragons. She looked up to catch a glimpse of the Aerians.

There were no Aerians.

None of the ones that had served the outcaste in his Aerian form. And no Hawks, no Moran. The air was empty.

She turned to Mandoran to demand an explanation and stopped. He was staring at her hands, his expression a mixture of fascination and horror—but mostly horror.

"What are you doing?" he demanded again. "Get rid of that!"

Since she'd been trying to do exactly that, this wasn't helpful. It was annoying, though. And annoyance was better than fear or uncertainty.

"If you'd care to help?" she said, voice loaded with almost lethal sarcasm.

"Eeew."

She almost laughed. Or punched him. She decided against the punching because she wasn't certain what the Shadow would do to Mandoran, and she really did not want Mandoran to be reshaped and redefined by the outcaste who lived at the heart of Ravellon.

But if Mandoran was squeamish—and clearly he was—he wasn't a coward. "Teela," he said in an ominous tone of voice, "was right."

"Oh?"

"You're never boring." He reached out with both hands, flinched, and then grabbed the Shadow that had pooled around Kaylin's hands, seeking further entry. "And Tain might be right as well—and I'll kill you if you ever tell him I said so."

"Bordeom is underrated?"

"Yes. Apparently there *is* too much of a good thing." His eyes were a bright shade of…gray. It was not a Barrani color. Kaylin didn't consider this a good sign, but said nothing. Or tried. "What are you doing?"

"I'm—Helen calls it phasing. Remember how Annarion

fought the ancestor outside of the Barrani Halls? This is like that, but without the swords."

"And where am I?"

Mandoran twitched. His hand moved through the Shadow as if it were a very thin liquid.

"In both places. There, where the Dragons are. Here, where the Shadow is."

"Here," an unfamiliar voice said, "where the *Dragon* is."

Both of them looked in the direction of that voice. A man was standing maybe five yards to Kaylin's left, where the literal tail end of the Emperor had been.

CHAPTER 28

Kaylin could still hear roaring. She had seen Annarion fight the ancestor, and in that space, the only noise was the two not-quite Barrani and their weapons. Here, it was different.

"You are a very annoying mortal," the man continued. His eyes were black, not a regular Dragon color. She wondered what color her own eyes were; she assumed they were brown, because human eyes didn't shift color with mood.

"You're a very annoying Dragon," she replied. Her hands were stiff and rigid as they began to rise. She wasn't lifting them.

Mandoran, however, seemed to understand this.

"I am not, according to Dragons, a Dragon at all." He began to approach them; he moved slowly and deliberately. She looked for Severn. Severn wasn't here. Mandoran was.

"That is harsh," a familiar voice said. Or rather, a familiar's voice. To her left, the familiar materialized. He was not in his Dragon form. Nor was he in his small and portable form. He looked almost human.

No, she thought. He looked almost Aerian. She had seen him this way once before: mortal in form, glowing slightly and winged. Her eyes slid off him, to the outcaste and back, and she thought of the form the outcaste had worn in the real world.

Real world.

If this wasn't real, what was it? It wasn't *known*. It wasn't familiar. She hadn't been trained to handle it. The tabard in which she took so much pride—sometimes to the embarrassment of the rest of the Hawks, who considered the tabard a job—was almost irrelevant.

Almost.

"You were born a Dragon," the familiar said.

"I was. What of it? She was born an infant." He meant Kaylin, of course. "She drew breath on her own, without interference. She required no name, no external blessing, to become what she was meant to become." He spoke with the faintest trace of resentment.

"She bears more words than you yourself house," the familiar replied. He glanced, briefly, at Mandoran, and then more pointedly at Kaylin. She flushed and turned her attention back to her hands, to the Shadow that surrounded them, to the Shadow that had already invaded them and was seeking further entry.

She felt no pain.

No wonder Bellusdeo hadn't noticed the injury.

The familiar's gaze was fixed on the outcaste. "I will ask you, once, to cease what you are attempting."

"And if I do not?"

"I will not ask again." The familiar rose. His wings were spread, but he didn't actually move them; he didn't flex them; he didn't flap them.

Mandoran's hair was beginning to stand on end. In this world, where color was skewed, he still looked pale and nauseated to Kaylin's eye. She looked at her own hands and froze; her skin was translucent. The Shadow wasn't. But this Shadow didn't sprout random eyes or mouths. It had no voice that she could hear. It moved, yes—but it moved the way fire might, if there was nothing to get in its way.

Mandoran hissed. It was an almost catlike sound. He yanked his hands back, and strings of Shadow followed. Without looking up, he said, "Breathe on it."

This confused Kaylin for half a second, until she realized he was speaking to the familiar.

"I am not certain that's wise."

The Shadow strings thickened, becoming both irregular in width and almost mucus-like. Kaylin saw that although the Shadow continued to attempt to snake its way up the inside of her arms, it was also attached in the same way to Mandoran.

"Wise?" Mandoran almost shouted. "Just—do something with it—get it off!"

The outcaste smiled. It was almost, but not quite, gentle. "If you are as you appear to be, it will not harm you." He frowned as he glanced at Kaylin.

"You'll pardon me if I don't take your word for it," Mandoran said.

"My pardon is irrelevant." He was staring at Mandoran now.

Kaylin was staring at the Shadow. Those tendrils that had wrapped themselves around the words on her skin—even the flat ones that should have had no dimensionality—were different. The transformation was subtle, and it had happened slowly. They were becoming transparent, just as Kaylin's skin looked transparent to her eyes.

The outcaste didn't appear to notice.

She could move her hands. She could control her own

movements. Knowing what had happened to Margot, this wasn't a given. As she moved them, she noticed that the Shadow tendrils didn't move with them. This was more disturbing.

Mandoran and the outcaste seemed to be more solid here. Mandoran, who had accidentally gotten himself stuck in a wall. A wall. Mandoran could travel in ways most people who lived in the city couldn't; he was learning how *not* to do that.

"Shadow," the outcaste said, "has much to offer you and your kin."

"My kin are dead."

"That is not what I meant by the word *kin*. This world— her world—is confining. It is a narrow cage. We accepted its boundaries. We tried to remain within them. But it is not natural, to us."

"It would have been," Kaylin interjected, "for Mandoran and his cohort. Without the ceremonies performed at the heart of the green, it would have been."

"Does it matter?" The outcaste looked at Mandoran. "What was done cannot be undone. I perceive you now: you are trying to limit who you are and who you can be in order to live a diminished life. You are trying to adapt to the rules of people who will not—and cannot—adapt to you.

"Do the Barrani even understand what you are?"

"I'm Barrani."

"Is that your decision? Is that your choice? Unlike almost all of the people you know, you have other options."

Kaylin thought of Terrano then. Of the cohort exposed at too early an age to magic they could not reject, Terrano was the only one who had had no desire to come home. He was happy in the outer worlds that people like Kaylin couldn't see and would never be aware of.

"Why," she asked the outcaste, "are you even here?"

He did turn to look at her then.

Kaylin's translucent hands clenched in fists. "One of Mandoran's friends chose not to come back. He could see the name he had once had. He could see that it didn't fit him. He wanted the full range of possible lives he could live. He didn't have a lot of interest in the Barrani or their politics or their wars. He wanted his friends to have the same choice—but he let them make a choice he couldn't make.

"Why are you here at all, if you have all of that? Why didn't you just walk, or fly, away?"

There was silence for one long beat, and then the outcaste roared.

This roar, unlike the attenuated and oddly distant roars of the other Dragons, reverberated. Kaylin shook with it; the ground beneath her feet shook with it.

The familiar, in his winged and almost human form, roared back in response. It was, note for note, the same sound as the outcaste's, as if sound could be mirrored exactly. She felt it the same way.

But the Shadow that loosely bound her to Mandoran responded differently.

The outcaste's eyes rounded; they lost some of the midnight blue that was characteristic of Barrani. No normal Dragon color replaced it. Here, in a world that was very like the real one, but sapped of color and almost transparent, he began to change shape.

Kaylin had watched Dragons shift from their mortal to their Draconic forms. It was interesting in a way that destroyed appetite the first time; it was almost natural to her now. Watching the outcaste reminded her of the first time.

Here, the mechanics of the shift in form were far less fluid, far less natural—if that kind of change could ever feel natural to someone who was stuck in a single body. He did not transition in one flowing movement, flesh becoming small scales, small scales gaining both color and size. The scales did come, but everything about their appearance was jerky; it wasn't so much transition as…building.

But his scales here were black. They were black like dark opals; they were glimmering and iridescent, scattered through with oddly bright colors. Those colors moved from scale to scale, as if the body was landscape or canvas.

"Kaylin," Mandoran whispered.

She turned, mouth half-open, toward him, and froze. Again.

The Shadow whose incursion she had all but halted had spread up through his arms to his shoulders, and across them. To get into Kaylin, the Shadow had to work. To invade Mandoran in a similar way, it clearly didn't.

She reached out to touch him; realized her hands were still webbed with Shadow. It was thinner now; the bulk of it had traveled to Mandoran.

The familiar roared again, and this time, when the outcaste used his Dragon voice, the rest of his body matched it. She assumed. She was staring at Mandoran, at the Shadow.

It had no name. It had no will that was not the outcaste Dragon's will. She had no way of calling it back, no way of diverting its attention; she would have, if it were fire. Fire's name, she knew.

Shadow had no name. No single word to define it.

Annarion appeared by her side, sword in hand; he tried to cut through the strands that bound Kaylin to Mandoran. The familiar roared at him, and his blade stopped an inch above the webbing. Kaylin didn't understand what the familiar said; Annarion clearly did.

He was afraid.

Mandoran was afraid.

It was why she couldn't really think of either of them as Barrani: they were too open, too honest with their emotions and reactions. Teela would have been impassive. Tain would have been the same.

Ynpharion, she shouted.

I am here.

Ask the Consort what I should do—how do I stop this? How do I save him?

Silence. A beat. Two. Kaylin stopped herself from repeating the question at greater volume only with effort. She had no intention of giving in to panic.

Of giving in any more than you already have. Even his condescension was better than silence. *The Consort says she does not understand what, exactly, you face. She does not understand your compatriot. She would like to meet him in future*, he added, in a tone that implied he strongly disapproved, *but for now, she has no advice to give you.*

Kaylin wilted.

She says, however, that in your position, she would plead her case—very quickly—before the praevolo.

What?

Very *quickly.*

The familiar and the outcaste—both in Draconic form, and neither actually Dragons—clashed. Scales sparked, scraped; the air moved as they roared. Kaylin turned to Annarion, who was ashen.

"I can't touch him," she whispered. "And you shouldn't. We need to find Moran."

"Moran? What can she do?"

"I don't know. But she's the *praevolo*, and this is the Aerie. Do you know where she went?"

"I was kind of busy," was his curt reply. "But I'll find her now." He was gone before Kaylin could argue. She was grateful. In the meantime, she gritted her teeth, grabbed the strands of Shadow, and pulled.

Some of the strands were solid enough that she could. They were the strands that had wound themselves around the marks on her arms, slightly dimming their light. They hadn't changed those marks; Kaylin assumed the Shadow hadn't been changed by them, either.

But that, she saw, was wrong. They were more solid. She could—and did—loop them around her own palms. She had control of her hands. Mandoran had lost voluntary control of his. His eyes were wide; he clearly hadn't lost control of his mouth, because he was cursing. In Leontine. Kaylin found this a comfort.

Hands bound by specific lines of Shadow, Kaylin put her weight behind them and pulled.

Mandoran flinched. He didn't scream. He didn't demand to know what she was doing. "Teela's swearing at me."

"If that's all she's doing, you're fine. She swears at everyone." She wound the lines as tightly as she could, and said, "Sorry about this." She pulled again. She could see his face stiffen, his skin pale. And she could see that some—not all—of the Shadow tendrils were retreating.

She wondered if she wanted that. If somehow these strands

of Shadow had been altered or changed enough, maybe she didn't want to leave only the unaltered Shadow to do its work.

This wasn't like healing. She was afraid to touch Mandoran because there was Shadow in and around her hands, and it had clearly done him no good.

"Annarion's found Moran."

"Is that good or bad?"

"Good and bad."

"Just give me the bad part."

"Some of the Caste Court is trying to kill her."

Kaylin cursed. "Give me the good part."

"She's got a Dragon on her side."

The Emperor was with Bellusdeo in the cave. "Which Dragon?"

"How in the hells would I know?"

"What *color* is the damn Dragon?"

"Blue. Oh, no, wait, I was wrong."

"He's not blue?"

"There's more than one."

"How could you miss a *Dragon*?"

"I have other things on my mind at the moment. And before you ask, the other one is also blue."

Blue meant Diarmat, which was bad, and possibly Emmerian, which was neutral. If the Aerians were stupid enough to attack Moran while she was being defended by Dragons, they deserved the death that was coming. Kaylin viscerally felt they deserved it anyway, but that wasn't the Hawk speaking, and she'd learned the hard way to let the internal Hawk make the choices.

"Umm," Mandoran said. It was almost a hiss of sound, without the sibilants. "There might be another problem."

Of course. Of course there was. "The Caste Court isn't normal."

He nodded. "Whatever the pretender did, it's spread. Annarion has gone back for the Arcanist."

"What good will the Arcanist do? This is probably *all his fault*."

"He probably knows exactly what was done. Look—I'm not any happier than you are. But—keep pulling."

She didn't watch the two non-Dragons fighting; she couldn't help but hear it. She did look up, once, when one of them cried out in pain; it was the outcaste. In the thinner color and light of this cave that was a half step removed from the cave everyone else seemed to be occupying, she could see that the outcaste was bleeding.

His blood was not, as she half expected it would be, black; it was red. It was a bright, scarlet red.

And she remembered that Teela had come with a sword. She didn't know the sword's name, and it didn't matter. Teela wasn't here, she was there. But Kaylin was positive that the wound that was bleeding here was also bleeding in the real world. Or in Kaylin's world. This one was also real—but it wasn't hers. It wasn't where she belonged.

It wasn't where Mandoran belonged, either.

"Can you get out of this place?" she demanded.

"I can't move, no."

"I mean—not get out of the Aerie, but get out of where *we* are."

He stared at her as if he couldn't understand her words. She asked again in High Barrani. He still stared.

"Look—am *I* in the big cave with Bellusdeo and the Emperor?"

"Yes."

"I mean, am I there right now?"

"Yes. I don't understand your question."

"Can Teela see me?"

"No—and before you ask, she's a bit busy right now."

"Can anyone but you see me?"

"I can't exactly take a poll."

"I want you to go to where Severn is."

"We're *in the same cave*, Kaylin."

"We're not in the same cave *to me*. I can only see you, the familiar and the outcaste. I saw Annarion—but he didn't stay."

"You told him to find—"

"Moran, yes, I know. I can't see Severn. I can't see Teela or Tain or the Hawks. I'm here—to me—with you, and only you. I want you to try to go to where Teela or Severn are."

"It's the *same place*," he replied, in obvious frustration; the pain probably didn't help. "Just because the others can't see you and we can doesn't mean we're not in the same place!"

She yanked at Shadow, and the tension slowed its spread. Slowed. She was afraid she wouldn't be able to stop it. Behind that fear there were other fears; she knew what would happen if she failed. Or rather, she knew what would happen to Teela, to Annarion. She knew that Helen would be upset.

She wanted her familiar to help her somehow—and that was unfair. He was helping. He was fighting the Dragon. She had no hope of surviving—or winning—against a Dragon.

"Annarion's found Moran," Mandoran said.

"You said that."

"I mean, he's trying to talk to her. It's chaotic up there. One of the Dragons has just tried to reduce him to ash," he added, frowning in something other than pain.

"That would be Diarmat."

"The other Dragon is speaking—shouting—at the first one. Oh. So is Moran. She recognizes Annarion," he added, as if this were necessary. He laughed.

"That's funny?"

"No—what she just told the first Dragon is funny. The first Dragon has just told her that *most* Barrani don't appear in midair without warning."

"That's what he said?"

"No—what he said was longer and politer. And more annoyed."

Definitely Diarmat. It was a bad day when she found anything about Diarmat comforting.

"He isn't trying to toast Annarion. He is trying to toast some of the Aerians—but she's not defending them. Annarion's telling her that you need her help." He winced. "She says she's kind of busy."

"That's how she worded it?"

"Yes. But shorter. She's really angry at the Arcanist."

"What is the Arcanist doing there? He can't fly!"

"I told you—Annarion went to get the Arcanist. He then went to get Moran. The Arcanist just shouted something in Aerian—I don't understand most of it, but the Aerians do. Even Moran." He paused, winced again. "Especially Moran. She's...angry."

"She's always angry."

"No. Not like this. She is really, *really* angry." In spite of the pain or the fear, his eyes were round. He was looking at Moran through Annarion's eyes, and whatever it was he saw robbed him, momentarily, of words.

There was a thunderclap of sound. It was louder than Dragon roars—here, or there. It was louder than any thunder Kaylin had ever heard—but thunder described it best: it was the heart of the storm, and it was suddenly here.

She could not make herself heard in the wake of that sound. She turned to Mandoran, and saw that his jaw had kind of joined his eyes; it was wide open. She shouted to catch his attention, but no sound escaped her mouth. Or maybe it did—her throat felt raw—but none of it reached her own ears. None of it appeared to reach Mandoran's, either.

The light in this quasi-cavern changed. The colors that had appeared faded brightened considerably as a hole opened up above Kaylin's head and sunlight flooded in. Or at least she assumed it was sunlight. But there was no falling rock that implied natural—or unnatural—disaster; there was simply light. It was radiant.

She half expected the Shadow wrapped around her hands to burn. It didn't. But the Shadow around Mandoran's hands began to smoke as if it were on fire. She expected him to relax, but he stiffened until he was completely rigid.

The Dragons had stopped their roaring. She couldn't hear the echo of either the Emperor or Bellusdeo. Even the familiar and the outcaste had fallen silent, as if sound itself was some kind of profanity and they had all entered a very stuffy cathedral.

Kaylin looked up, and up again, craning her neck back. Mandoran did the same, but raised his arms to cover or protect his face as he did. The Shadow within him froze and then began to melt away. This was good; he didn't seem to be aware of it. Whatever he saw was somehow worse than Shadow that intended to devour him from the inside.

Most of the Shadow within her arms melted as well—but not all. In particular, the strands she'd wrapped around her hands to give her some purchase over the ones inside Mandoran remained where she'd wound them.

But she forgot about them as Moran dar Carafel descended, at last, from the sky.

She had known Moran for the entire time she'd known the Hawks. Moran had been in the infirmary before Kaylin had even been the official mascot. She had seen Moran give Marcus a dressing-down—in the infirmary—that had been impressive and awe-inspiring. Marcus caused a visceral fear in most people simply by growling; Moran had put her foot down, claiming control of her space and everyone who was in it.

That had been nothing compared to this.

The Aerie was not the infirmary. The Aerians were not the Hawks. They had a political hierarchy that had, by all accounts, made Moran's early life a living hell. It had almost killed her.

Watching her now, Kaylin knew that this would never happen again. She wasn't certain the Aerie would survive it. She couldn't speak, but had stopped trying. Moran's wings were, end to end, larger than Dragon wings. They were feathered, each feather distinct, concrete, although it hurt to stare at them for long. At the height she occupied, the color of her eyes should have been impossible to discern.

It wasn't.

They were blue.

They were a blue that bled into black, and they matched her expression. Moran was angry. Moran had always been angry.

Chunks of rock fell away from the curve of natural cave walls. Chunks of architecture—obviously less natural—fell as well, shaken free from their moorings. If Kaylin couldn't make herself heard, she could move—and she did. She grabbed Mandoran first; he was still staring, openmouthed, at Moran.

At the *Illumen praevolo* of the Aerians.

At the Aerians who fell from the skies above. They didn't dive. Kaylin watched as their wings—which seemed to be flapping—lost the innate magic that kept them in the air. As if they had gained a density, a weight, that their visible wings could no longer support, they were captured by gravity.

It wasn't clean. Kaylin was almost certain there would be broken limbs and possibly even deaths. But the Hawks who had accompanied Moran remained in the air, flying patrol circles above and beyond her spread wings.

She looked down at the outcaste. She looked down upon the Emperor and Bellusdeo—and Kaylin could now see them both. She could see the Aerians in the distant sky. She could see Diarmat and Emmerian.

She was back in what she thought of as the real world. So was the outcaste—but he'd never really left it. He existed, as Mandoran and Annarion could, in two places simultaneously. Or more.

The outcaste pushed himself off the stone floors of the cavern; the Emperor and Bellusdeo watched him rise. But they were hesitant now. Everything about Moran implied that this was her territory, not their battlefield. They didn't doubt that the *praevolo* was in control of the Aerie.

And they didn't doubt her intent.

The outcaste opened his mouth. He breathed as he spoke—and he did speak. Kaylin didn't understand a word, which would have been fine if he'd been speaking his mother tongue—she didn't expect to understand Dragon. But he spoke almost familiar syllables. He did not speak in rage, but he didn't speak as a supplicant, either.

Moran looked down at him.

He continued to speak, and as he spoke, the mass of his body shifted; he lost the Draconic form. Kaylin wasn't certain she would take the chance, given the proximity of Dragons who had reason to want him dead. None of those Dragons were enfolding themselves into their much more human forms. Given the color of their eyes, it wasn't going to happen anytime soon.

She cringed when she saw his wings. They were as wide as Moran's, as impressive; they were, however, ash gray, and if there were spots across their breadth, they were multicolored and did not seem fixed in place. Moran's wings were pale and speckled, as they'd always been.

Moran's reply, like the outcaste's, drifted just beyond the edge of her comprehension. It was frustrating. It was more frustrating because, across her skin, the marks of the Chosen began to glow. To thrum. There was almost a musicality to the noise they made, or there would have been had it not been so uncomfortable.

She looked at the Shadow that remained in her hands. It seemed both weightless and inert. It had no temperature, and no actual texture, but it was fine, thin, dark.

Kaylin.

She looked up at the sound of her name. She didn't recognize the voice that spoke it.

Private.

It was Moran.

Come here.

Kaylin stared at her. She then looked mutely at her familiar; like the actual Dragons, he was large and scaled. Unlike those Dragons, he was translucent. He understood what Kaylin hadn't dared to ask, and he moved toward her.

"I don't think that's a good idea," Mandoran whispered, proving he could still be heard.

"You think ignoring her is a better one?"

He shrugged, flexing and shaking his hands. "I think we're going to leave." Annarion appeared beside him.

"Is Moran okay with that?"

Mandoran grinned. It was weak, but genuine. "We'll find out, won't we?"

Kaylin. It was Ynpharion.

What now?

The Consort says you must do as the praevolo *asks.*

She's not exactly asking.

He was frustrated. So was she. *The Lady says Moran is calling you for a reason. She is newly born, newly come to herself; she is not what she was. She needs an anchor. The Lady says that that anchor must be you.*

I can't be an anchor—

Or it will be the outcaste.

Over my dead body.

Yes. Over all of their dead bodies, saving only the two who are fleeing. Wisely. An'Teela will not leave, he added, as if this were necessary.

What the hell is an anchor anyway? Kaylin demanded as she began to run toward her familiar.

The Consort says you will not understand the words she might otherwise use. She offers only this one: friend.

She needs a friend?

I am conduit, Kaylin. I do not presume to divine the whole of the Lady's thought. But that is the word she bid me use. She did not think the rest would suffice.

It was enough, though. She clambered up the back of her familiar; he had not shrunk or diminished, as if Moran's appearance had decided his shape. Or perhaps he'd understood what was happening. To Kaylin, the fight was over the moment Moran had punched a hole through the ceiling and forced them all to exist in the same space.

Or it had been. She was afraid, now. The familiar pushed himself off the cracked floor at the same time the outcaste did. Bellusdeo opened her mouth to breathe; a plume of fire left it. The outcaste stood bathed in flame without condescending to notice it. Bellusdeo leapt—or tried. She seemed to struggle with both gravity and weight.

Kaylin had no doubt that her forced inaction was entirely due to the *praevolo*. The golden Dragon was *not* going to be happy with Moran.

And did it matter? It wasn't like Moran was going to be living with them anymore. It wasn't like she could just turn around and come home. This was *her* space. This was her home.

"Can you please, *please* hurry?" she asked the familiar.

I am moving as quickly, he replied, *as I am allowed.*

"Allowed?"

She is defining the space we occupy. She is creating the rules for it, and everyone who remains within its boundaries.

"What are its boundaries?"

He didn't answer. He flew, but his flight was heavy, ungainly; his wings seemed to labor against gravity in a way they never had before.

And above them both, Moran waited.

The outcaste, unencumbered by the attacks of the Dragons who were pretty much honorbound to destroy him, rose as well, and he rose far more gracefully, far more easily, than the familiar did. Kaylin ground her teeth. He looked Aerian now—or rather, he looked like Moran. His wings were as prominent as hers; his voice as clear.

Moran had been angry. She was still angry. But the anger itself had lost some of its heat, some of its dangerous rage. She remained standing in the air as if the wings were mere decorations; she didn't move them because she didn't need to move them. The air was hers, and it held her, carried her. As Kaylin approached, she thought she could hear the faintest trace of the elemental air's voice.

She had always found Moran intimidating; Moran was a sergeant; Moran was the head of the infirmary; Moran had threatened to have Marcus strapped to a bed when he was injured—and Marcus hadn't even tried to tear the Aerian's throat out.

But she hadn't found Moran so intimidating that she hadn't offered, many times, to heal her injured wing. She hadn't found Moran so terrifying that she hadn't pressured her to live with Helen. Moran was a Hawk.

And Hawks, to Kaylin, were family. Having spent years listening to mess hall gossip, Kaylin was aware that "family" involved a lot of conflict, that mothers could be terrifying, that siblings could refuse to speak to each other for months. Or longer. She didn't expect Hawks to be perfect. But she was part of them. They were part of the Halls of Law.

Moran was part of both.

Moran was *praevolo*. Moran had been born *praevolo*. But Kaylin understood the Consort's words as she approached the Hawks' sergeant. Whatever the wings had signified, whatever the bracelet had signified, neither had prepared her for this.

The familiar said she was remaking the space they all occupied. Moran, a handful of hours ago, couldn't even see it. Something had changed—obviously—since their arrival. And that something was…Moran. Kaylin couldn't see the bracelet on Moran's wrist anymore. It wasn't necessary. Nothing, Kaylin thought, would be necessary again. If the Aerian Caste Court was allowed to continue to exist, it would be a Caste Court of one: Moran dar Carafel.

Or Moran something or other. Kaylin wasn't exactly confident about the survival of the dar Carafel flight, either.

The outcaste glanced at Kaylin, at the familiar on whose back she struggled to rise.

"You are not wanted here," he said. He flicked one wing in her direction. It knocked her off the familiar's back.

CHAPTER 29

Kaylin fell.

She could feel gravity assert itself in the absence of her familiar; she could feel the familiar's concern, could see the cloud of his breath as he turned to the outcaste; she could hear the sudden blurred rush of sound and voices as everyone watching reacted at the same time.

But she didn't land. She didn't hit rock. The familiar didn't catch her.

The air did. The air, or something else. She rose, and she rose far more quickly than she had while clinging to the back of the familiar. The familiar, in response, dwindled in size, his shape changing as he once again became the small and squawky conversation piece that was so much a part of her life she could forget he was there until he shouted in her ear.

"You will not fall," the *praevolo* said, "unless I desire it."

"I don't have wings, Moran."

"No, you don't. They are not, however, necessary—not here. Not when you are with me." She spoke Aerian, but it was stiff and formal to Kaylin's ear, and she had to really listen not to lose the words to the syllables. She wondered if there was a High Aerian, like there was High Barrani.

Moran then turned to the outcaste, her expression neutral. "You are supplicant here; you are not lord. Kaylin is of my flight. Harm her, and I will destroy you." She spoke without any doubt at all; it wasn't even a threat. It was a simple statement of fact.

The outcaste nodded in acquiescence.

His calmness annoyed Kaylin. "You told the Aerians you were the *praevolo.*"

Moran glanced at her. The outcaste did not deny it. Kaylin glared at him; he looked down his nose at her, as if she were inconsequential. But his brows rippled, because the marks on Kaylin's skin were beginning to gain dimension.

Moran didn't ask him if this were true. It was, and she knew it. She seemed to know a lot that she hadn't known a few hours ago. Above her, the Hawks flew in formation. They hadn't changed. The air carried them.

"Do you even understand what the *praevolo* is?" he demanded—of Kaylin.

"I know she's *not you*. She's not yours. You wanted the power of the *praevolo* because you saw it as simple power. But that's not what it is."

"Kaylin," Moran said.

Kaylin understood that she was being asked to shut up. But it wasn't an actual command, not yet. "That's not *all* it is."

"You do not understand—"

"Neither do you!"

"Kaylin—"

"For you, it must have been a nameless, central power. Something you could siphon. Something you could divert or adopt or abuse. But that's not what it is. It's not what it was supposed to be."

"And how would you know anything? You are mortal; you are only barely considered of age among your own kind.

You lack knowledge; you obviously lack wisdom. You are not, and will never be, a power, because you cannot understand what power *is*."

"Power is a tool," Kaylin countered. "A sword is a tool. A crossbow is a tool. A crowbar is a tool. It's something we pick up and put down. People aren't meant to be tools. Moran is *praevolo*—whatever you think that means. But she's a *person*. She has a choice. She has will. She has goals of her own. She is not simply a tool you can take and use for your own ends."

"Moran is not you. You are Chosen, but you were not born to *be* Chosen. You are an accident. Some might say you are an act of desperation or folly on the part of the dead. But you are not what she is."

"Neither are you. And only one of us has claimed to be something we're not."

"Private." Unlike the use of her name, the use of her rank pulled her up short. She glanced at Moran, closing her mouth.

"Without my presence," the outcaste said, "without my planning, the *praevolo* would never have emerged. She would have remained trapped in a cage of potential whose door she could not open."

"And you're telling me you did all this to *free* her?" The scorn in the question should have been lethal.

Moran said something brief—in Leontine. Kaylin's face flushed. Moran didn't generally curse, and when she did, she didn't use Leontine. "He is not making that claim. He is, however, strongly implying it." Moran looked down at her feet, or rather at what was beneath them—which was almost everything. "He claimed to be *praevolo*. He could wear the bracelet and it did not consume him."

"He's—"

"Yes, Kaylin. He could wear it; he could not *use* it." She turned to her right, whistled something sharp and brief. To

Kaylin's surprise, the Arcanist—the reason they had come to the Aerie in the first place—flew in from the distant right. He could fly.

He could fly because the *praevolo* desired it. He bowed—to her. He glanced at the outcaste; it was a murderous, enraged glare, but he didn't add words to it. Probably because they weren't necessary.

"Some of my people believed him, because he could. Some believed him because he could do other things—things attributed to the *praevolo* in our long history."

"Such as?"

"He could deprive the people of flight."

"That's the opposite of what the *praevolo* was supposed to do."

"It is the other edge of a sword. What one can give, one can take away. The ceremony of the outcaste is some part of that." She lifted her arm; the bracelet was invisible. Or gone. "I do not understand it all, but I understand enough. When someone is exiled, when they are made outcaste, the power of flight is literally removed from them. That power returns to the *praevolo*. If there is no *praevolo*, the power returns to the bracelet.

"It is a power meant to be used only by the *praevolo*. It is meant to be used only by an Aerian." She gave Kaylin a much more familiar look, the one that meant *now please shut up*. She then focused her attention on the outcaste. "You are not an Aerian."

"I am not a Dragon."

"Define yourself as you please. What you are—or are not—is of concern to me only in this regard. You are not an Aerian. You are not *praevolo*, and cannot be. I do not understand how you used the power of the *praevolo*; it is clear to me that you somehow did, and could."

"You must ask your servant," he replied. The Arcanist flinched.

"I have." Her wings spread, and spread again, the flight feathers ranging in size and shape, their essential color unchanged. "You are not of my kin. You are not of my people."

And the outcaste said, "Perhaps not. But are you?" And his wings spread as well, stretching and extending as he mirrored her posture. He gestured, and wind howled, as if it had been trapped in those wings, and was now being released.

The implication was clear. Moran was as he was: different, other. Moran had always been that. But she'd never been what she was at this moment.

"You fear your power," he continued. "I once feared mine. I do not fear it now. You were created to sustain the Aeries. You were created to sustain the flights. No permission was asked. It was assumed. You were different. You were *blessed*." The tone of the last word implied the opposite of its meaning.

Moran's expression rippled briefly, and Kaylin knew why: that blessing had cost her her childhood and anything that had made it safe. It had almost cost her her life. No permission had been asked, true. No permission had been granted. She had been marked as different from the moment she was born.

The Hawks hadn't loved or revered her for that difference; she had been treated with a kind of wary deference Kaylin had always assumed was due her rank in the Halls, her position in the infirmary. Kaylin had never found her welcoming or kind, but that wasn't her job—her job was to deal with the injured, and to force them, as she could, to get better.

"You are *praevolo*. No one else in any flight in the Aerie could become what you are. You *have* the power now. Will you live as you lived before? Will you be hemmed in by the simple fact of your birth? They welcome you now—but they did not always welcome you. Many would have seen you die."

The outcaste said nothing that Moran wasn't thinking.

But beneath his feet, Kaylin heard the rumble of Dragon. It was Bellusdeo.

The outcaste looked down at her. The gold Dragon seemed to be welded to the ground—and struggling to change this. "You could be so much more than you are," he said to her. "You could have true freedom of the skies. You could be the mother of a race that is not beholden to the dead, to the whims of the flights—even if only one remains.

"You could have *freedom*. What you have now is only a step up from servitude and bondage."

She roared. There were syllables in it.

Moran, however, lifted one hand. "Perhaps, had you come to me and spoken of this *choice* and this *freedom*, my answer would be different. But you—as they did—chose for me. Or against me. You saw the power. Perhaps you understood the mechanics of it in a way that I did not or could not. But what you wanted was what they wanted: control. You did not particularly care if that power came to you through my death. I was of no consequence, no value, to either my flight or those who accepted you.

"But you are right in one regard. I am me. I am a Hawk. I am a sergeant. I am an Aerian. The power that I did not want and did not ask for is nonetheless mine—by design. And by choice. I accept it. I accept what it means.

"Do you understand what wakes the *praevolo*?" she asked.

The skies were simultaneously full of movement and hushed with stillness.

He did not answer. Three beats passed before she made clear that the question was entirely rhetorical. "Danger to the *race*. You were here, as was he," she added, indicating the Arcanist, "before my birth. What you discussed, what you attempted, the plans you made—those were responsible for *me*. For my birth. And for the deaths," she added. "You wanted power.

"Now, you face it." Kaylin heard thunder in her voice.

Lightning followed.

The wings of the outcaste were not wings: they were Shadow. They were a Shadow whose shape, whose form, he obviously controlled. Those wings snapped up, folding as lightning streaked past him. His hair flew in its aftermath; his eyes were the color of light.

Kaylin's arms and legs were glowing, bright; symbols rose to ring her. They encompassed Moran, as well. Moran didn't appear to notice.

The outcaste didn't, either. Kaylin was irrelevant to both of them. The small dragon—and he was small now, and attached to her left shoulder—squawked and lifted his wing.

Kaylin shook her head.

He smacked the bridge of her nose, hard enough her eyes smarted. She blinked back tears and looked through the translucent flap. The outcaste's wings were Shadow—which she'd expected. She expected the rest of him to somehow conform to that. He *wasn't* Aerian. He wasn't mortal.

He wasn't a Dragon, either.

Shadow had a multiplicity of forms, or a lack of form; it shifted in place. It was malleable in some fashion, and that fashion differed from creature to creature. There were one-offs—as they were called in the fiefs—who could have multiple jaws, eyes, legs; they might have horns or wings that didn't provide flight. They looked like bodies that had been randomly chopped up and stitched together, except that they moved and spoke.

Sometimes they spoke intelligibly.

Had the outcaste looked like a one-off, Kaylin wouldn't have been surprised.

He looked instead like a…god. Like an Ancient.

She froze in place, almost afraid to attract his attention; she could see nothing else of significance in the sky, where she floated beside Moran. She could see nothing of significance anywhere else, either.

He was there, and that was all that mattered.

He frowned, his glance sliding momentarily off Moran to meet Kaylin's gaze. She drew breath, but she had no words. She could see his name.

She could see his name and she knew that she was not seeing the whole of it; that she might look at it, study it, for a lifetime and still not see enough of it to attempt to speak it. She knew that even the attempt would end in her death, because the attempt seemed profane.

And she knew that this name was not the one she had seen in the fief of Nightshade. It was not the same shape. It didn't have the same weight. It was, in its entirety, too large. She thought it might be the name of a world, shrouded as it was in Shadow and darkness.

His eyes were words. She had seen them as trapped lightning without the small dragon's wings; she saw them differently now. She almost raised a hand to push the small dragon's wing away, but she had enough of his attention, and she was determined to do nothing at all that would attract more of it.

But his eyes narrowed—or the shape of them changed—as he looked down on her. And he did look down. It wasn't a figurative description. He frowned; she felt instantly ashamed of whatever it was she had done to earn it, too. The rest of her anger at this reaction tried to assert itself and failed.

He held out a hand, the movement jerky; it was both a command and a struggle. *Chosen.*

She started to move. She started to obey, and she struggled to regain control of herself, of her visceral reactions.

Moran slid an arm around her shoulder, and the impulse died. Kaylin reached up and shoved the familiar's wing away from her face, almost dislodging him. Her shoulder, in case of magic and its possible offensive use, was exactly where she wanted him to be—but not if she had to look at the out-caste. Not that way.

This way, he looked Aerian. This way, he looked like an enemy, an arrogant, powerful man. This way, she could fight him, despise him, pity him or hate him, because all of these things seemed relevant.

She didn't know what Moran saw when she looked at the outcaste, but it didn't matter. As soon as Moran placed that arm across Kaylin's shoulder, Kaylin was in Moran's space, and Moran's space was the Aerie and everything that comprised it: the sky, the caves, the *people.*

Flight and its power here were the *praevolo's.*

The *praevolo* did what she'd been born to do: She denied the outcaste flight.

Or she tried.

He dropped five feet, maybe ten, but the grip of gravity faltered. He had called himself *praevolo.* Aerians—some Aerians—had believed him. Since he didn't have the wings, he had to have had something that would convince them of the truth of his claim.

He halted his own downward progress. Looking up at Moran—and he had to look up—he smiled. Kaylin braced herself as he opened his mouth.

He didn't breathe. He spoke.

The marks that now hovered above her skin began to glow. This wasn't unusual. But Kaylin could understand, or could at least recognize, the language the outcaste spoke.

He was reading the words. *Her* words.

The familiar's claws pierced her shoulders. She knew this only because she felt the pain that followed the clean incisions, and turned to glare at him. And froze.

What was seated on her shoulder should have broken it, it was so large. She knew the familiar could change size and shape, she'd seen it often enough. But this shape was not the large, translucent Dragon. Nor was it almost Aerian. It was disturbingly cloud-like. She had seen Shadow coalesce in just this way: it had edges and distinct shapes that seemed to be clashing against each other, as if for dominance, and none of those shapes made sense.

She had never seen it in her familiar before.

The words rose as the outcaste continued to intone them. As if they were somehow his. As if what she had seen through the wing of the familiar was true. And if it was? If he was somehow an Ancient, a thing that spawned whole worlds? These were his words. This was his language. It had been written across more than half her body without her permission.

The words had never been hers. She was Chosen, yes—to carry them, to bear them. She only barely understood their use.

She felt the lull of his voice, the odd rightness of it. These were his words.

But the pain in her shoulder grew sharper and colder, and the thing that now inhabited the left of her body, the right being occupied by Moran, grew darker. There were colors in that deepening haze, and those grew brighter. No, *brighter* was the wrong word. They felt lurid, out of place; they made light disturbing.

She reached up to pull the claws out, but there were no claws. Of course there weren't. There was Shadow, and it threatened to spread the way the other Shadow had.

"Let go of me," she told her familiar, speaking an Elantran so thick it was practically inaudible.

I am yours. She felt the words; she shuddered with them. She couldn't hear them otherwise.

She wanted to deny it, but it had been true since the moment she'd been handed an egg by a justifiably shattered parent. It had been true since he'd hatched. He had tested her, and that had caused pain—but not this pain. Not this fear.

He spoke.

The outcaste spoke.

She realized only slowly that they were saying the same thing. The words flared; they grew larger as they detached themselves.

The outcaste turned from Moran to Kaylin. "Chosen," he said. He repeated the single word, and Kaylin realized that it wasn't what he was saying. It was what she was hearing. True Words.

No, the familiar said. It was denial. It was the heart of denial, the visceral meaning of it. But it was not spoken in rage or fear. It was a word. It was a True Word.

She closed her eyes, and this was a mistake. The words that surrounded her—words that usually took up residence on her skin, as part of it—were still visible. They'd always been visible when she closed her eyes.

But the outcaste was visible in the same way. The familiar's presence was more profoundly wrong. She looked away.

There was no ground beneath her feet, and no Aerian beside her.

No, there *was* an Aerian beside her. Moran, as translucent as the small dragon usually was, remained to her right, her wings luminous, her eyes the color of sunlight on water. The Shadows surrounded her flight feathers, her hands, her arms, but they weren't part of what she was.

She was Aerian.

And she turned to Kaylin, and said, in Aerian, "What's wrong?" In a very familiar, very sergeant-like tone. Kaylin wanted to weep with relief at the sound of it. Things had gone to hell, but Moran was still sergeant to Kaylin's private.

"The outcaste is reading my marks."

"Will reading them give him control over them?"

Would it? That was Kaylin's fear. She knew the marks had power. They gave her the power to heal. They gave her the ability to stand where she was standing now, neither here nor there, but in both places at the same time. The only times she had chosen to use the words deliberately, she had struggled to divine their meaning, because without meaning, she couldn't find the place they were meant to be.

But understanding their meaning hadn't given her *more* power. It had allowed her to use them as she hoped they were meant to be used.

"I don't think so."

Moran gave her a look that was pure sergeant. She returned a look that was visceral private.

"True Words can be True Names. But that is not what your words are."

"You are wrong," the outcaste said. And he spoke in High Barrani. But he continued to intone the words as he did, without pause.

So did the terrifyingly strange familiar. Was this what he

was? Was small and squawky like the heart of Shadow? She fought panic; his Shadow entered her, flowed into her, in a way that the other Shadow couldn't. And why? Because she'd fought it. Because *he'd* fought it, for her. She looked down at her hands and blinked.

They looked gloved, in this space. They looked like pretty lace gloves. She lifted her hands again. Crossing her arms, she placed a hand just above each collarbone.

The pain ebbed.

The familiar continued to chant. He might not have noticed her at all.

"That Name," she told the outcaste, "is not your Name."

His eyes widened; his recitation stumbled.

She had been afraid that speaking the words would give him power over them. She had assumed that the familiar's recitation was supposed to provide balance—as if she were a rope, and this were tug-of-war. But that wasn't the way language worked. True Names, maybe. But not True Words. Not these words.

The familiar continued to speak, and Kaylin swallowed hesitation and fear, containing them. She began to speak the words as well, to echo the familiar's steady, slow reading.

Unlike either the familiar or the outcaste, she couldn't read them and speak at the same time. But it seemed important to her that she speak, that she follow the familiar's lead.

You couldn't own words. You couldn't own language. You might invent one, but to speak it, you shared. You couldn't control what anyone else made of the language; couldn't define how they spoke, when they spoke, or what they spoke about. Only when they were with you did you have that control, because conversation involved two. Or more.

Speaking these words didn't change them. They weren't True Names. They had existed before Kaylin—*long* before

Kaylin—and they would exist after she died. She wasn't the words. The words weren't hers. But the skin they were on? That *was*.

The outcaste could speak. He could recognize the language that even the Arkon struggled with. But it *was* a kind of language. Speaking it didn't change its essential nature, because speaking it couldn't. People spoke words in order to communicate.

"Private."

Or intimidate, or invoke emotion. Often conversations caused more confusion, not less; people used the same words in different ways, and therefore heard them and weighted them in ways the speaker might not have intended.

These were True Words. In theory, such misunderstandings weren't possible. In theory, the words had meanings, and those meanings did not, could not, change. But…if these were True Words, if True Words could be spoken as if they were just another language, like Barrani or Aerian, there'd be no need to have the words attached to her skin, or the skin of any of the Chosen before her.

Regardless, the skin was her damn skin. While the words occupied it, they were as much hers as anyone's. The marks rose as the recitation continued.

One of them was devoured, slowly, by the shadow on her left. The outcaste's voice dipped again, as his eyes widened. They were orange now. They looked truly Draconic.

"What are you allowing him to do? Foolish girl—"

"It's not the only time he's done it," Kaylin snapped back, losing the thread of the familiar's steady voice. "But you know what? He needs permission. He doesn't take what's not offered. He doesn't lie about what he is or what he wants. He doesn't try to give a young Dragon a fake name so he can control her!"

Bellusdeo roared. She couldn't see the gold Dragon, but she could hear her so clearly she lifted her hands to her ears.

The outcaste lost the thread of Kaylin's words, lost the focus on Moran, lost height. It was to Bellusdeo that he looked; he could see what Kaylin couldn't. "Is that what you think?" he roared. Kaylin shouldn't have understood a word of it. She almost wished she couldn't. "Is that what you think I was trying to do?"

Bellusdeo roared again, longer and louder. After a pause, she said, "Sergeant dar Carafel, *let. Me. Fly.*" This last was in Elantran, but spoken with all the depth and fullness of an angry, red-eyed Dragon. "...Please."

"I cannot allow you to continue your fight in the Southern Reach. Enough damage has already been caused that this landing area has become unstable. If you fight here, you might destroy half the cliff face before you're done. If only that. If you wish to fight, you must do so well clear of the Reaches." She paused, and then added, "The outcaste is a matter of the Dragon Caste Court. There is a reason no one interferes in the wars of the Dragons, and I would not interfere now were the cost of inaction not to be paid by my people."

The outcaste continued to look at Bellusdeo. "I did not destroy your sisters."

"The Shadow—"

"I did not destroy them. I freed them. I freed *all* of you. You were one mind. You were nine existences. The walls between each diminished you and what you could be. As long as one of you existed, nine existed. How do you think you were saved? I did not intend to control you. I did not intend to subvert you. Child, I—"

She roared bloody murder. The floors shook. The walls shook.

Moran's lips compressed into a single—and very familiar—line. She flicked her wings. Both the outcaste and the enraged gold Dragon flew out of the Aerie, if by *flight* one meant "were thrown."

"And *you*." Moran turned to Kaylin. "Whatever you're doing, stop it *right now*."

"I'm not—"

"I mean it. I'm getting a headache looking at you, and I have already had enough headache for one damn day. If you don't want to be busted back down to mascot, *cut it the hells out*."

Kaylin blinked.

The world shifted. When she dared a glance at her left shoulder, the familiar—in his small and squawky form—was perched there looking very much like an owl that had caught all the mice. All.

She stared at him. He met her gaze, his opal eyes wide—and small, and contained. In spite of herself, she shuddered. He leaned forward and bit her ear.

One Dragon rose from the floor of the giant cave, and it was clear he had control of his movements.

"Eternal Emperor," Moran said.

"Sergeant dar Carafel."

"I cannot allow the fight to take place here." The respect due an absolute monarch wasn't entirely absent, but it was close.

"No, of course not. Release the members of my court to me, and we will carry the fight to them."

"A word of advice?"

"Very, very cautiously and respectfully offered?"

"Your Majesty." She bent her head; it was as much a bow as she would offer. "He does not intend her death."

"You think he will not harm her?"

"I think he does not *intend* to harm her," was the quiet reply. "But if I understand what I've heard here, he has caused her far more harm without that intention than anything else she has faced. She will kill him if she can."

"Of course. She *is* a Dragon."

"We're going to have to talk," Kaylin told her familiar. "I mean it. We're going to have to have a *long* talk."

He squawked, which was very disheartening.

"You are going to have to have it at home," Moran said firmly.

"But I—"

"You are shaking as if the temperature is cold enough to freeze water. And it's not cold."

"I don't—"

"I mean it. You are going home, or you are going back to the Halls of Law, where you will be strapped to a bed until you recover." She folded her arms.

Kaylin felt, oddly, like weeping. "But, Moran—the flight, the Dragons, the—"

Moran lifted her face to the skies. "Corporal!"

Clint came down.

Kaylin cursed in Leontine under her breath; Aerian hearing was very much like human hearing. Moran, however, was standing beside her, an arm still wrapped around her shoulders. "You know we're not on duty, r-right?"

"You think that's going to make a difference?" Moran grimaced; it was very slight. When Clint was close enough to hear her without the need to raise her voice sergeant-style, she said, "Take Kaylin back to the Halls of Law and deposit her in the infirmary."

Kaylin's jaw dropped. "We don't even *have* an infirmary

anymore!" But the truth was, she was shuddering. She was cold. She was exhausted.

Clint didn't argue. He glanced at Kaylin and shook his head. *"Praevolo—"*

"And if you call me that again today, I'll break your right arm. Don't test me," she added. "I have a meeting with the Caste Court—or as much of it as we can find—and I'm in a foul mood."

CHAPTER 30

Clint was silent for half the flight from the Aerie. Although Moran had told him to take her straight to the infirmary, he stopped, flying to his own home first. There, he borrowed blankets, his wife hovering in a silence weighted with questions. She didn't ask anything out loud, but clearly Kaylin wasn't the only one who intended to have a long and involved conversation later.

She did, however, wrap Kaylin in a blanket designed for Aerians, and her expression was much gentler as she did so. "It's good to see you. You should visit more often."

"I have no doubt—at all—that she will," was Clint's reply. It was very, very neutral in tone, which earned him a glare from his wife. He removed Kaylin as quickly as he possibly could, but his wife was not going to be *rushed*.

"I like her."

Clint raised a brow. His eyes were the Aerian version of gray that implied calm. Kaylin thought of the way Clint had fallen to one knee in front of Moran the last time she'd entered the Halls of Law. There was very little that Moran could command that he wouldn't do. It was a disturbing thought.

Kaylin, for instance, would obey any order the Emperor gave, especially if she was standing in the vicinity of, say, his figurative jaws or his literal breath. But it wasn't because she revered him. It was because he could reduce her to her component parts without blinking an eye.

Kaylin would obey any order Marcus gave her, because that was her *job*. It wasn't her life. At one point, she wouldn't have been able to separate the two—but Clint was a Hawk, and Clint was an Aerian, and Moran had become, in the course of a single significant day, his life.

If Moran—no, if the *praevolo*—gave Clint an order, he would obey it. If Moran told Clint to do something that broke the law, Kaylin wasn't certain it would matter to Clint.

And that, she told herself uneasily, *is not my problem. It's none of my business*. But…they were all Hawks. Their personal lives were part of their work, because their personal lives were part of who they were, and they brought that to work.

In Moran's absence, Clint became more himself. On the other hand, he did deposit her in the temporary infirmary. He didn't strap her to a bed, because the meeting room only had two, and they were narrow emergency cots; he did tell her to sit in one of the many chairs. He then stood by the door.

"She didn't tell you to stay here."

"No."

"I'm not *injured*."

Clint said nothing.

Kaylin cursed. In Aerian. He said more nothing, but folded his arms.

★ ★ ★

Moran came to the infirmary what felt like days later. Clint implied heavily that her whining had made it feel like days for him as well, although it had been a paltry four hours.

Moran was wearing the colorful dress that the *praevolo* wore during ceremonial occasions. She was also wearing the Hawks' tabard. She had been wearing it when she had first arrived at the Aerie.

Moran frowned, but it was a familiar frown. An infirmary frown.

"What," Kaylin asked, "did the outcaste want?"

"Power, I think." She frowned. "The outcaste did approach the Arcanist claiming to be *praevolo*. The Arcanist was justifiably suspicious—but my own wings had not yet become public knowledge. He claimed parentage—illegitimate—of the dar Carafel clan; he chose an Aerian who had died decades in the past as his father. Two Aerians accompanied him; they confirmed that he had lived in the Southern Reach, but not in the higher peaks.

"He did not wish to publicly make that claim, not immediately; he flattered the Arcanist, implying that he had far too much to learn about the duties of the *praevolo*. Instead, he set about proving that he had the abilities expected of him.

"The Arcanist has some influence with the Caste Court. In time, he arranged to have the outcaste take the most dire of our tests: he donned the bracelet. Because he lacked the wings, the ceremony was conducted in privacy, but most of the Caste Court was in attendance. I believe he hoped that the pretender would fail; he had begun to have doubts."

Kaylin already knew that it had not destroyed him. "How convenient for him."

Moran grimaced. "He was thus provisionally believed. But he did not have the wings."

"I don't understand why—if he could make himself look like an Aerian—he didn't. Why couldn't he have your wings?"

Moran shook her head. "I don't know. I told you that I had worn that bracelet once. It was a test. But the bracelet didn't destroy me, either. There had never been two *praevolo* before, and I had the wings. The Caste Court was split.

"But the Arcanist began to question things, and as time passed, he became less certain of the outcaste. He knew that the outcaste was attempting to harness the power of the *praevolo*, but that power was not—and is still not—well understood. Not even by me." Her smile was rueful.

"When I was injured, when I could not fly, it was 'proof' that I was a fraud. The outcaste—and his supporters—pushed heavily for my death. But the Arcanist's worries were gaining traction among the Caste Court, and it was the Arcanist who pushed for the Oracle. It was also the Arcanist who talked the Caste Court into allowing the three items out of the Aerie. It was the outcaste who created the enchanted statue given to Margot, and the outcaste who created the enchantment worn by the human who visited her."

"Did the Arcanist expect that they would end up with you?"

"He hoped, at that point. Or so he says." Her smile was sardonic. "They did end up with me. I did wear the bracelet. And I *flew*. At that point, the outcaste was pressured into taking a more active role. He suspected the Arcanist of treason—there's not another word for it—at this point, and he once again proved that he was *praevolo* by denying the Arcanist flight.

"And then an appointment was made—with the Arcanist, who was always under observation—and we arrived."

"What did the outcaste want?"

"I think he wanted to understand how the *praevolo* harnessed and controlled Shadow." She shook her head. "It doesn't feel like Shadow, to me—but it wouldn't, would it? And according to the Arcanist, he did learn. He learned enough that my control of the Aerie and its skies could not control him. And it makes sense. He lives—according to the Imperial Court—in the heart of Ravellon. He can command the Shadows that move and think and speak, but he cannot use them the way the *praevolo* use their own power." She stopped speaking and stared at a pristine tabletop. "What do you think I should do with the people who believed that the outcaste was the *praevolo*?"

Kaylin shrugged, a fief shrug. "If they'll serve you?"

"At all."

At the moment, Kaylin didn't really care. She tried to see the world from the eyes of the grounded, misled Aerians, and couldn't. Kaylin was certain that the would-be assassins that characterized Moran's first few days with Helen would be found among the Aerians Moran had grounded.

They were just following orders.

Kaylin had once followed orders that were very, very similar. She wanted to believe it was different. She could argue that she had been a child at the time. But she'd followed orders because she was afraid of what would happen—to her—if she failed. She hadn't obeyed Barren because she worshipped him; she hadn't obeyed him because he was almost a deity. She'd obeyed him because he had hurt her, and would hurt her again if she failed.

She wanted these Aerians punished. She wanted them punished for doing what she had done. And why? Because it meant Moran had all the power? That Moran was no longer going to be their victim or their target?

"You're thinking," Moran said.

"Teela says I think very loudly."

"She's right. You do. I've gotten used to Helen explaining what you're thinking," she added.

"You could just ask me."

"I have, once or twice. Helen's answers make more sense."

Kaylin exhaled. "I was thinking about my answer to your question."

"And?"

"I don't trust my own answer. I want you to take their wings. And I hate the idea of it. I want you to throw them out. I want them to suffer for trying to kill you. For killing your mother or your grandmother. For removing Lillias's wings. For treating you so badly when you should have been treated well. I want them to *pay*."

"So…you see my problem."

Kaylin nodded. "I guess that's why I'm not Emperor."

"You're not telling me to do it."

"It's not my decision."

"And if I said I'd leave it in your hands because I owe you so much?"

"I'd say it was a terrible way of showing gratitude."

Moran's smile was looser, more natural. Her wings, however, were still larger than life. "Then I won't. I don't feel that it's a decision I can make. But I don't feel that I have any choice."

"If they choose to leave the Aerie, will they be outcaste?"

"Yes. But…not in the normal way. I don't think so many people have been made outcaste at once in our history. In theory, murderers are still Aerians. In theory, so are thieves and petty criminals. We have our own way of dealing with crime."

"Lillias—"

"Yes. People are people, no matter how lowborn or high-born they are. Some will be exemplary. Some…won't. The same is true of humans, of Leontines, of Barrani. Maybe it's less true of Dragons. Lillias did not deserve what happened to her. In all possible ways, it was a gross miscarriage of justice; it was a gross abuse of power.

"But I can't give back what was taken."

Kaylin's shoulders sagged, because she realized that was what she'd been hoping for. In the midst of Dragons and Arcanists and outcastes and Shadow, she had wanted Lillias to get her wings *back*.

"I can reinstate her name. I can return that to her family. I can tell people the truth, over and over again, until they understand what Lillias sacrificed for my sake. And I will. But I can't give her back her wings."

"Why? If they could be taken—"

"They were destroyed, Kaylin. And the *praevolo* isn't a maker. If you cut off a man's leg, you can't just grow him another one while he waits."

"But…you could give her back flight?"

Moran glanced at Clint. He met her gaze, his own clear. "No."

"But you gave *me*—"

"While she is physically with me in the Southern Reach, she could fly. I could keep you in the air while I touched you; I could stop you from being dashed against the rocks. But her wings are gone, and I have no way of returning them. Being outcaste was not meant to be reversible."

"Could she—could she go home?"

Clint and Moran exchanged another glance, and this time, Clint exhaled. But the look he gave Moran was less tinged with awe; it was normal. For Clint. "Kitling, when someone is made outcaste, they lose their family. They lose their flight. They are a shame, a stain. If Lillias is exonerated, she will no longer be that shame. But her family turned their wings to her. Her family cast her out, just as the flights did."

"But they were *wrong*—"

"Yes. And now they know it. Guilt is not a comfortable home. Lillias has made a life for herself. It is not her old life."

"Can't you at least let Lillias decide that?"

Moran bowed her head. "Yes. But sometimes the burden of decision isn't a kindness."

"Are we going home?" Kaylin asked.

"For tonight, yes. We are going back to Helen."

"You aren't going to stay."

"For tonight I will." Moran's smile was weary. Whatever power or authority she had assumed in the Aeries had deserted her; she looked as tired as Kaylin felt. "But yes, as you suspect, I can no longer make my home with you and Helen." She sounded as if she regretted it.

"Your wing is better," Kaylin said, as they headed toward the door.

Moran flexed it, but said nothing. Neither did Clint.

Helen was waiting for them. Moran had insisted on walking, although flight was faster. Kaylin had recovered enough that she merely looked terrible. She was no longer shaking with cold.

Moran pulled ahead and approached Helen, who stood in the door frame. Helen opened her arms, and the Aerian sergeant walked into them, dropping her forehead into the space made of collarbone and shoulder and neck. Helen held her for a long, silent moment, and then pulled her into the house; Kaylin trailed behind.

"No, dear," Helen said—to Moran, although Moran hadn't spoken. "I don't think there is any reason to retire from the Hawks."

"You don't know the Caste Court."

"Well, no. I am not certain that I want to, either, if we are being honest." Helen was always honest. "Given the actions of the Caste Court, however, I think it is safe to disappoint them."

"Again."

"I do not believe they are disappointed now. It is conjecture, of course, but if I had to choose a word, I would hazard *terrified*."

Moran laughed. "I want a bath." To Kaylin, she added, "You can join me if you want."

Helen's voice remained with them, but the rest of her went off to help Mandoran. Again.

Moran relaxed into the hot water, tilting her head back against a convenient stone ledge.

Helen appeared in the room—without actually opening doors or walking—standing to one side of the outcroppings that had formed around the hot springs' water. She looked at Kaylin's familiar with some concern, and spoke to him.

Kaylin couldn't understand a word of it. Neither could Moran. The familiar could; he lifted his head, opening a single eye as if Helen's questions were both wearying and boring.

Helen's voice grew louder, and the room seemed to lose some of its perpetual sunshine.

Kaylin poked the familiar. "You'd better answer her questions."

Squawk. Followed in turn by even more squawking. Almost all of it beside Kaylin's ear.

Helen looked at Kaylin, and at Moran. "You are certain that's what you saw?" she finally asked the younger Hawk.

This caused some confusion. Helen could read minds, or

hear thoughts, but none of Kaylin's current thoughts seemed to suit the very worried question. "Saw when?"

"When you looked at the outcaste, at the end. You perceived him as...an Ancient?"

"I'm not certain that I saw it accurately. I was somewhere slightly off-kilter and looking through the familiar's wing from wherever I actually was. Mandoran might understand it better."

"Mandoran did not see what you saw. We have discussed what he did see. He is recovering, but he will need to recover here." To the familiar, in a softer voice, she added, "Thank you."

The familiar warbled.

"And me?"

"You are clean," Helen replied.

Kaylin lifted her hands. Shadow still gloved them like dark, fine lace. Or like a different kind of mark.

"I know, dear. I can see. But it is yours now."

This wasn't what Kaylin wanted to hear.

"Yes, I'm sorry. But I do not consider it in any way harmful."

"Is it inert?"

"I am not certain I understand the question. It will not, however, attempt to alter your base physical structure without your guidance."

"Explain Shadow to me."

"I believe I've done that before, to little effect."

"Try again?"

Helen was silent for a long moment—long enough that Kaylin thought she wouldn't reply. But at length, she did. "Without some element of Shadow, there is no mortal life."

"...I don't think that's what you said the last time."

"Mortality *is* change. From your births to your deaths,

you are in a constant state of flux. There is no single *you*; your identity evolves, unravels and is remade. It is a constant process. The Kaylin of five years ago is not you. The Kaylin of ten years from now will not be you. The separate states of you are continuous, contiguous. They are connected. But they are not the same."

"But the Barrani—"

"The Barrani and the Dragons are both similar and dissimilar. Both require Names to live. But it is not true that they require Names to exist. Without Names, however, they do not exist *as* Dragons or as Barrani."

"Mandoran and Annarion—"

"They are edge cases. They are not their Names; their Names are only tenuously a part of who they have become. It is enough—barely—that they can function. The Names are fixed, Kaylin; they are solid. They are unchanging. They are the heart of the immortal."

"But, Helen—the Name of the outcaste—"

Helen fell silent. After a long pause, she said, "That was not a Dragon's name."

Squawk. Squawk.

"Then you must explain it. I will speak with the Tower of Tiamaris," Helen added, almost gently. "I believe Lord Tiamaris has access to some of the other Towers."

"Speak with Nightshade as well, if he's here."

"I will. He will not give me leave," she added with a grim smile, "to speak with *his* Tower, and I have a thing or two I would like to say to his Tower." None of it good, though all of it, in Helen's opinion, clearly long overdue.

"Good. But what exactly are you going to tell them?"

"That Ravellon is waking."

"Pardon? Ravellon is a place, right? You're saying it's sentient?" Kaylin rose from the water. "What do you mean when you say it's waking?"

"I will speak with Tara," Helen said again. "While I have had more exposure to you, Tara has known you for longer. She may be able to explain what seems obvious to me." Helen shook her head. To the familiar, she said, "Explain it. That appears to be your job." And walked out.

The familiar warbled. And flopped.

Bellusdeo returned home four hours after Kaylin and Moran had. It was late. It was very late. The floor shook with the roaring.

"I'm sorry, dear," Helen said, as the sound diminished. "I wasn't expecting poor Bellusdeo to express herself so forcefully."

"Please don't tell me she's angry at the Emperor."

"As it happens, no, she's not. She is *very* angry at the outcaste. Her attempts to kill him failed, and she was not alone. The Emperor has—wisely, in my opinion—informed her that her involvement is too visceral and too personal to be entirely safe, and this has not made her any happier."

"I thought you said she wasn't angry at the Emperor."

"She's not. She is, however, angry at herself, because she knows the Emperor is right."

Which, as Kaylin knew, was vastly worse. She dragged herself out of bed and headed down the stairs.

To her surprise, Teela and Tain were with the golden Dragon. Kaylin stood frozen at the height of the stairs, and finally said, "You went out drinking." Her tone was very flat as she crossed her arms.

"No taverns were burned down in the process," Tain said.

"Not completely," Teela added. She glanced at Bellusdeo.

"You were in the infirmary," Bellusdeo pointed out.

"You didn't even take Maggaron."

"Maggaron is sulking because I went to the Aerie and confronted the outcaste without him. I am sulky enough for a small army, and if we're being honest, he was making me feel guilty."

"He wouldn't—"

"Not on purpose, no. If he were *trying*, I wouldn't care."

"So you called Teela and Tain?"

"As it happens, Teela happened to be in roughly the same spot when things were over. She suggested it."

Teela shrugged. "I did. She looked tense."

Going out drinking with Teela and Tain was like running an obstacle course—with angry people on either side of it.

"You look terrible," Teela added.

"Thanks, Teela. I was sleeping."

Bellusdeo had the grace to flush. She didn't apologize, but Kaylin wasn't expecting one. She fully understood why the Dragon was unhappy, and was fairly certain she would have done the same thing. Mostly because she often had—she just didn't have the innate volume of Dragons.

Looking up the stairs, Bellusdeo straightened her shoulders. "Now," she said, "it's time to face guilt, grovel and apologize." She climbed up three steps, stopped and turned to look back at Kaylin. "I'm sorry."

Kaylin wondered if she were dreaming.

Kaylin expected Moran to return to the Aerie the next day, and was surprised when Moran came home to Helen. She also came home to Helen the following day, and the day after, lingering. The mirror room was...busy. Moran largely ignored it, which caused Helen to purse her lips with mild— but obvious—disapproval.

Mandoran joined them for dinner on the third day, looking pale, exhausted and bored. Annarion joined them as well, looking concerned. He had come, in the past few days, to some state of compromise with his brother. Kaylin didn't ask what it was. If it were dangerous to Annarion, Helen was certain to tell her, because Annarion certainly wouldn't.

"What happened?" Kaylin asked Mandoran.

"You don't want to know."

"Could it be any better than getting stuck in a wall?"

"The wall was *not* my fault."

"And this was?"

"No. This was worse than the wall. I'm once again confined to the house."

Kaylin glanced at Helen, who nodded. She was worried about him. To Kaylin's surprise, Moran was worried, as well. She wondered if that was why Moran had stayed. The Caste Court—which apparently still existed—was vastly more deferential in its communications with Moran than it had ever been. But deferential or not, the *praevolo* didn't want to talk to them.

He said, "I blame you."

"*Me*? This was *my* fault?"

"What the hell were you doing with your hands, anyway?"

"I was *trying* to—"

"Heal me," Bellusdeo rumbled. "Which I'm certain you won't imply was a waste of effort."

Mandoran grimaced. "What are you doing with *that* now?" He was still staring at her hands.

Kaylin shrugged. "Don't know. It's like the marks of the Chosen—it's on my skin. I can't feel it. It's not active."

"Helen. Talk sense into her."

"I have been trying, dear."

Helen hadn't said much—at all—about the Shadow gloves. This probably meant that Mandoran was thinking, and Helen was answering the part of the conversation no one else could hear. She was about to demand that she be included, when a chime sounded.

Moran rose.

"Yes," Helen said. "It's for you." She turned and walked out of the dining room to answer the door. Moran hovered near the table.

"Who is it?" Kaylin asked.

"I believe her name is Lillias," Helen replied. "And she believes Moran is expecting her." To Moran, Helen's disembodied voice said, "Should I show her to the dining room?"

"No! No. If you don't mind, I'd like to speak with her in my rooms."

"Of course I don't mind."

Kaylin rose as Moran left the dining room.

"Maybe they don't want company?" Bellusdeo suggested. Dragon suggestions generally came across as commands.

"I—"

"I'm teasing. You've been fretting about Lillias ever since you first met her. Go on."

Kaylin followed Moran and entered the foyer as Helen opened the door. Lillias stood on the other side of it, looking very uncertain. Looking, Kaylin thought, as uncertain as Kaylin herself would have looked if she'd had to stand at the door of this house while living in her own apartment.

Her apartment had been home. It had been convenient. But it had been what Caitlin called "modest" and what Teela called something vastly less complimentary. Without Evanton's intervention, Lillias would never have come here. She would have walked halfway up the street, realized that it was far too fancy, far too snooty, for someone like her, and retreated. Kaylin, however, was dressed the way she always dressed; she was not fancy and not particularly well turned out, as Teela liked to call it.

"Lillias," she said, channeling her inner Caitlin, and holding out both hands.

Lillias exhaled a few inches of stiff height. "Kaylin."

"Did you see her?"

"Every Aerian in the city saw her. It was difficult to explain to my employer," she added with a wry grimace. "I don't usually drop everything and run out to stand in the middle of the streets."

"Rooftops are probably better, at least in my experience. No wagons or carriages."

"Experience which you do not need to share," Moran told her. She came to stand beside Kaylin and said, to Lillias, "If you let her start talking that way, she won't stop. You will hear all kinds of hair-raising stories about her childhood."

Kaylin released the older woman's hands, and Lillias held them out to Moran, who hesitated briefly before she took them. Moran bowed her head.

Lillias smiled down at her bent head, and then up—at Helen. "You've been taking care of the fledgling," she said—in Aerian.

"I've done what I can. It is very seldom that I have Aerian guests."

"She's grown stronger. You should have seen her when she was a child."

Moran's head didn't rise. It fell. It fell to Lillias's shoulder and rested there.

"What was she like?"

"Lost. Lost, and without kin. It's hard, to be without kin. It's hard to lose the people who love you when almost no one loves you. She was afraid of heights, did she tell you?" she added, to Kaylin. There was an almost maternal fondness in her, and Kaylin realized then that it had always been there—but it had been swamped by anxiety and fear. Lillias had no reason to be afraid for Moran now.

"But she's Aerian."

"Yes. An Aerian fledgling, afraid of heights. She was afraid to fly, and flew very late, for a child. Had she been living in the heart of the Reaches, she would have been forced to fly much earlier. But when she flew—ah, when she finally conquered that fear…" She put her arms around Moran.

Moran said nothing. Kaylin wanted to leave them, to give them privacy, but they were standing in the foyer, in the doorway, and Lillias was looking at Kaylin while she spoke.

"Fledgling," she said, arms around Moran, whose face couldn't be seen, "I am grateful for your offer. You have given meaning to something I doubted had meaning in my darkest hours. You've made my actions heroic, just by existing. But…the action remains the same. I didn't do what I did to become a hero. I did it because you were my charge, and I was responsible for you.

"I did it because you had finally learned to fly. And when you flew—ah, Moran, when you flew—it was the very heart of flight. I had never seen a flight so beautiful. I have learned to live with all of the consequences, because in my heart I know that were I to be thrown into the past, were I to be given the same choice, I wouldn't change it. I couldn't.

"You think that you ruined my life."

Moran said nothing. Lillias's arms tightened.

"It wasn't you, child. It was never you. You think if I had wings, I could fly. I could have a life. But, fledgling, I *have* a life. I won't lie—it was hard. Change is hard. Loss of family is shattering—but you know that just as well as I do. The only thing I worried about was you. I always, always worried. Now, I don't have to.

"But let me pretend. Let me say that if, knowing what I know, I could go back in time. I could change my decision. I could let you die."

Moran stiffened, but didn't pull away.

"I would have wings. I would have flight. I would have family. And I would have had to buy those things with the life of a child. Never mind that you were *praevolo*. You were a *child*. Do you think my life would have been better with wings when I could never, ever respect or trust *myself* again?

"Oh, I could tell myself I had no choice. But that would be a lie. Others might believe it, but I never could. I *had* a choice. And I made it. And if I could never change my decision, this *is* the life I was meant to have. The Aerie is not my home. It hasn't been home for half my life. Even with you there, it couldn't be my home now. The only person who would welcome me is you."

"That's not true," Kaylin began, because Moran didn't speak.

"I found a home with people who accepted me. Is that not what you did, in the end?" She asked the question of Moran.

Moran remained silent. Kaylin joined her.

"But I will visit, if you wish."

Moran said—without lifting her head, "Visit me instead of Evanton. Come flying with me, instead."

Lillias swallowed. After a long pause, she nodded, which Moran couldn't see. "I will. I will, Moran. Come, I think we are blocking the door."

She glanced at Kaylin, who pointed up the grand staircase and mouthed directions.

"I will keep her room as it is," Helen said before Kaylin could speak.

They had both watched the slow progression up the stairs toward Moran's room in silence.

"She will not stay. She is *praevolo*. I believe she was born because there has been some corruption of the Reaches. Think of her as a living Tower, but without the absolute control of her environment that Towers exert. She must be in the Aerie to affect it. And she knows this.

"She knows that she can return here. She knows that this small piece of home will always be waiting for her. It will be here tomorrow. It will be here in decades."

"What if I die? What if the new tenant—"

"Hush, Kaylin. It will take time to find a new tenant. It took time to find you. I will keep Moran's room as it is while she lives."

★ ★ ★ ★ ★

ACKNOWLEDGMENTS

My home team (Thomas, Daniel, Ross) did not strangle me during the writing of this book. My mother probably wanted to, but: sunk costs.

I wrote the entirety of this book on a twelve-inch Mac-Book, which is light enough that I could carry it off to the local Timothy's, get coffee and work. When I walk in the door, the people are already pouring coffee before I get to the counter; I've been pretty consistent. This wasn't actually my idea, but the MacBook was a gift, and in the way of significant gifts, I felt I had to use it fully to the best of my abilities to even begin to justify it >.<.

So: special thanks to Terry, because he was right. Working in a noisy, crowded coffee shop *is* actually much easier than working at home, largely because the noise is not actually my problem. Crying children? Not my responsibility to comfort, because their mothers are right there. Phones ringing? It's not my phone, and answering a stranger's phone is not considered remotely good manners. Arguments? I don't have to referee them. Is the toilet stuck? Not my problem.

The only responsibility I have while there is writing.